WHALES SWIM NAKED

ERIC GETHERS

"Gethers marches along side John Irving: brave storyteller with an inborn skill for joyful narrative detours". -- *Livres Hebdo*

"Why are we drawn to American writers more than others? Because they tell a good story. The great John Irving is not far...." -- *Nice Matin*

"It appears that John Irving has, if not a son, at least a close relative named Eric Gethers who has the same instinct for telling a tale, same capacity to surprise, to lose us in fantasy digressions, and to give us joy and emotion. The story of Henry - moving and delightful with extraordinary, but so, so plausible characters." -- *Le Monde Supplement des Livres*

"With this amusing yet sober book, Gethers re-invents a "thrash" style of writing. Comic and desperate, cruel without being unkind, burlesque and poetic." -- *Rolling Stone*

"A great author is born." -- *Sud Ouest*

"A joyful satire: Exuberant and generous, Eric Gethers embarks us on a delicious journey where stories unfold, one after the other in the manner of Russian dolls." -- *L'est Republicain*

"Novel of philosophic tales, highlighting the fragility of human existence and questioning the thorny premise of happiness." -- *Quinzaine Litteraire*

Text Copyright © Held by Eric Gethers
Published in North America by Running Wild Press. Visit Running Wild Press
at www.runningwildpress.com.
Paperback ISBN 978-1-947041-81-3
eBook ISBN 978-1-947041-79-0

PART I

"The horned owl can see farther than every other bird on our planet. A gray whale can swim longer than any fish or mammal. An arctic tern has been known to fly thousands of miles during migration, all the way from the north to the south pole where Chilly Willy lives.

Now, imagine fields of bluebonnets, dancing back and forth in a cool, gentle breeze, stretching beyond all of those. That's what your mother saw when she stepped off our porch and walked toward the pond on March 21st, the most important day of our lives.

When she reached the fig trees near the water she looked up and found herself staring at a sky Monet might have painted. It was as if he'd created the heavens just for her and it made her feel like everything was right with the world.

Clouds parted and a single beam of light shone down onto your mother's bulging stomach. It was an omen. She knew it as surely as she knew how to breathe and she was filled with the miracle of everything before her.

We'd planned your birth for the first day of Spring because

we wanted it to represent change. Not just seasonal. It was more spiritual than that. We wanted you to enter the world with a sense of wonder, a little adventurer who wasn't afraid of the unknown and would live a life filled with

possibilities instead of possibilities missed.

Your mother felt a sudden trickle of warmth down the inside of her thighs, as if God had turned on a faucet.

It was time to wake me with news that she was ready.

In a few moments we would return to the field where she would crouch down in the bluebonnets, open her legs and squeeze. No hospitals. Not for us. You were a miracle from God and we were going to have you under His God-given sky.

Though doctors swear it was impossible, you smiled at me, Henry, when you came out of the womb, and we had an immediate love and understanding.

If I could have a photograph of the one moment I wanted to remember for the rest of my life, perfect in every way, that would be it."

This was the story my father, Jack, told me about the day I was born till I was five years old. For reasons beyond my control, it began to change.

Horned owls still shamed other birds with their sight and terns traveled implausible distances, but information about gray whales expanded so I knew they were on the verge of extinction. Why? Nobody wanted to enforce the laws that were supposed to protect them. They didn't do anything because, sometimes, it was easier for people to ignore problems than deal with them.

Bluebonnets were nudged by a hot, humid breeze.

The sky my mother saw when she approached the pond was now painted by Rothko, an artist who blended colors till there were no boundaries - no matter how desperately they were needed.

It was drizzling.

The miracle in my mother's life shifted from my upcoming birth to my father's unwavering devotion, standing by her under circumstances ordinary husbands, weaker men, would have

left.

Last, but certainly not least, the trickle down her legs that once announced my God-given arrival became more of a leak.

This was the version till I was nine. After that, everything pretty much went to hell.

The horned owl could still see farther than every other bird, only now it was standing beside my father in town and looking toward Holly Scott's house, all the way over on Travis Street, where she liked to undress in front of the window when her husband wasn't home. An arctic tern still migrated thousands of miles but it was nothing compared to my father's friends at The White Rock Tavern who'd rather walk to the South Pole than spend a Saturday night with their wives. A gray whale could still swim longer than any fish or mammal, but was impaired by obscene weight gains it blamed on imaginary circulatory problems.

Bluebonnets were torn to shreds by the wind.

March 21st was the coldest day of the year.

Water was stagnant, fig trees uprooted, ravaged by worms, fungus and vines that tangled around their trunks and choked the life out of them.

The sky was painted by Turner who died a bitter recluse - a Biblical seascape with rolling waves that reminded my mother of nature's untameable power and filled her with a passion she hadn't felt since her wedding night.

And that was just for starters.

When my mother turned away from the pond head lamps sent shivers of light over the trees lining her driveway, like a beam from a lighthouse. Ten seconds later Lillian's sister, Carolyn, slid out of an old Ford.

If I used anything other than my father's own words, I'd be doing the story a disservice.

"Conservative in manner and dress, Carolyn was partial to dark, loose fitting clothing and wearing her hair in a bun, preferring to blend into a crowd unlike your mother.

When she walked her posture was as regimented as her thinking. It was also a warning. Anyone who got too close would regret it.

All those still applied.

That morning the change was in Lillian. As her sister approached she noticed her breasts for the first time. They were perfect, her nipples taut, tipped up at the correct angle. She also noted the muscles in her calves. They didn't move. Solid like the rest of her. Strong, forceful arms without a hint of masculinity. Broad, powerful shoulders and upper chest. The hard, flat tuck of her stomach. Every step peaked Lillian's curiosity, like some foreign country she'd seen on TV and always wanted to visit.

Rushing to her sister's side Lillian hugged her as hard as she could. As Carolyn felt the protruding belly next to hers, she too thought of change. Wouldn't it be wonderful if Lillian could enjoy the birthing process rather than just endure it? Labor, after all, involved enormous levels of hormones whose increase were supposed to trigger ecstacy not pain. Plus, when a baby enters the birth canal it's not that different than something being inserted.

There was no reason Lillian couldn't have an orgasm.

As soon as Lillian started labor Carolyn kissed and caressed her, never wavering for a second. Two hours later you were born, a product of ecstacy rather than suffering, the intensity and perversity of which will stay with you for the rest of your life."

From the time I was ten, this is what I believed.

* * *

The absolute truth, if there is such a thing, seems closer to this.

It was grey, bitter cold and had been snowing for over a week; its weight toppling tree branches and telephone wires which blocked driveways, caused traffic accidents and blackouts in Dallas and surrounding communities.

My mother was seated at her kitchen table opposite her sister, listening to a radio plugged in next to a sink piled high with three-day-old dishes.

"Stand By Your Man."

Loud and tinny with treble, Tammy Wynette barely got through the first stanza before Lillian's right shoe was airborne. As the radio slid into soapy water with a whir of sparks, Lillian felt shooting pain in her abdomen that doubled her over and caused her mascara to run down both cheeks in a wavy line.

"Are you alright?" asked Carolyn, alarmed by the distress in her older sibling's eyes.

"Do I look fucking all right?"

Pulling her chair back Carolyn crouched down on all fours and crawled under the table like a dog looking for scraps. She examined Lillian where she sat, a cursory inspection that revealed the top of my head peeking out between two sopping thighs.

"Jesus Christ, Lillian! The baby is crowning!"

My mother didn't know what that meant.

She was as unprepared for childbirth as she was for the loss of her virginity, a milestone that took place seven months ago to the day; ten thousand sacrificial heartbeats before I forced my tiny face out for a quick look around.

Birth control wasn't a consideration because Lillian had drunk two Mountain Dews, smoked a joint and downed a cap full of bleach as soon as they were finished. Besides, she didn't think it possible to get pregnant from a first sexual experiment.

Even after this was proven wrong, it never occurred to her to prepare for the day I would change her life irrevocably. She partied all night, drank, smoked and took triple doses of medicine nobody fully understood; pills that could make me grow three heads, restrict blood flow to my lungs and cause aptly-named holes in the heart.

She was more concerned about her hair color, splotches that invaded her normally satin skin and her ever-increasing waistline. Anything about newborns was the concern of parents and in-laws and the rest of their friends who were converging on her apartment, in two months time, to dote over me.

Premature birth wasn't even a concept.

None of these crossed Lillian's mind as Carolyn led her out of the house. The temperature had dropped ten degrees and the ground was hard as cement. Wind reddened their cheeks. Swirling snow prevented them from seeing the car Carolyn filled with gas, that very morning, in case of

emergency.

The Ford failed to show its appreciation.

It wheezed, belched and refused to turn over with the same inflexibility my mother displayed toward pregnancy.

Kicking her door open Carolyn hit the ground running, reaching the road as columns of halogen lights blinded her.

When she could see again, a dented pickup fishtailed around the corner with a deer strapped to its hood.

Thirty seconds later both sisters, their inebriated neighbor,

Mike, and the unfortunate animal were speeding toward Florence Nightingale Memorial Hospital.

With each skid Mike's grip on the wheel grew tighter, draining the blood from his fingers as he struggled to navigate a road that had become more of an obstacle course than the route he knew by heart.

Lillian's pain and complaints also worsened, insisting there was no way she could survive her ordeal. Carolyn tried to distract her by listing the many blessings in her life but Lillian continued quaking as if she were a heart broken child. Trying to help, Mike recounted his own wife's first delivery, likening the birth process to his time in the National Guard. This too failed to console Lillian so he made the mistake of comparing my rapidly approaching birth to pulling a big screen TV out of a man's penis - with remote control.

Grabbing the wheel Lillian yanked it hard to the right. The pickup swerved and slid into a snow bank, winding up half on the shoulder, half on the asphalt. Slightly elevated, the back wheels spun as Lillian jumped out, got on her knees and tried to expel me from her system as if I was a piece of bad shellfish.

Seeing my mother crouched in the slush like people in Tijuana, Mike staggered to the front of the truck and unfastened the buck. Though he was a large, powerful man, dragging it toward Lillian caused him to grimace till he awkwardly wedged it underneath her sweaty, shivering
body.

While she pushed and moaned Mike paced back and forth, swinging his arms, clapping his hands together and stomping his feet so they wouldn't go numb. Whenever he asked Lillian how she was feeling she lost what little patience she had left. Pain, to her, was insufferable. Trying to describe it did nothing but prolong her agony. Frustrated, Mike told how his own children, now grown, never called, wrote or visited. At 11:43 he let his belt out a notch, lit a cigarette and

soberly confessed his kids were nothing but a bunch of selfish cocksuckers. He fed them. He clothed them. He entertained them. He paid for their school. He denied them nothing and how did they show their appreciation? They were selfish. They stole money from him to buy drugs. They lied and acted like they were doing him a favor just by talking to him, as if he never cared or made a difference in their lives.

I slid out at 11:55.

As Carolyn untangled the umbilical cord from around my neck and placed me on Lillian's stomach, I watched my mother look down with an expression that conveyed both reassurance

and unconditional joy at my arrival, albeit eight weeks early. I was too new to know about the capriciousness of a redhaired woman's soul, how it was governed by its own laws and remained half empty no matter how many blessings were poured into it. Truth be told, maternal instincts were as far away from Lillian's heart and mind as my father was from Interstate 30.

If only I'd known then what I know now. I would have realized I was staring up at ignorance and fear. My life might have been different.

I could have been heroic.

I could have gotten up every morning with a warm smile, confident in my abilities. I could have made a name for myself, fearlessly rising to every occasion, conquering anything I was afraid of. I could have been gloriously in love, married and faithful to the same woman all my natural born days. I could have had hundreds of extraordinary moments to look back on instead of lying here, desperately trying to find one that would justify my existence.

But that's not how it happened.

* * *

Lillian couldn't believe Jack wasn't there for my birth, by her side, when she needed him most. Was she destined to be alone for the rest of the week? The month? Her life? If Lillian had the slightest inkling this was going to happen she never would have given him her virginity. It was, after all, her most valuable asset, a last vestige of innocence and only chip in the game of small town ambition.

On the other hand, my father was a real catch. Everybody liked him the moment they met. Part of it was due to his midwest, even tempered manner. He never felt like an outsider. Part was due to his confidence, always sure of himself like some of the rich boys from Highland Park who went to the finest private schools, drove fancy cars, stayed in hotels, never motels and weren't intimidated by anyone. He had their innate sense of privilege, something people who work for a living usually struggle with. Mostly, it was the way he related to people. He listened to what they had to say and never interrupted. When he did speak, Jack had the uncanny ability to make small talk or bypass it completely, sizing you up like those hustlers on ferries to Morocco who learn fifty languages so they can screw you out of a dollar. And though he was sometimes guilty of laughing too easily or forcing a warm, friendly smile, like when you get your picture taken on vacation, whatever Jack said, while not necessarily the truth, was your truth, so you never doubted his sincerity.

His boyish enthusiasm, broodingly handsome face and God-like physique didn't hurt either. The way he combed his hair and rubbed his big blue eyes when Lillian talked about opening a salon. Even the way he smelled. It wasn't a department store fragrance like Canoe or English Leather. It was him. Down deep. Oozing out every pore.

9

There was just one drawback. Lillian paled in comparison. Even if she wore a short skirt and flimsy blouse revealing cleavage, when they entered a room Jack got the attention. It reminded her of a night, years before, when she was in a restaurant in Dallas. Elizabeth Taylor, of all people, walked in. Although she was well past her prime, certainly not the ravishing ingenue, everything stopped. You could hear a pin drop till people rose and applauded. For the first time Lillian understood what it meant to be a star.

Jack had that.

Lillian was willing to overlook her secondary role, however, because underneath all that charm was the gentle soul of an artist. Lillian could tell him her darkest, deepest secrets. Plus, he would never hit her like other boys. She knew it the first time they kissed and she cried herself to sleep because of it. Nevertheless, she should have pulled up her panties that fateful night, walked away

and saved herself for Mister Domoff.

Arnold Domoff, her 12th grade history teacher, had changed her grade from an F to a B after feeling her up in the audio-visual closet. At the peak of sexual cluelessness he also promised to leave his wife if Lillian would "take one for the team."

If she'd been smarter, if she'd played her cards right, she could have had an "A" instead of a baby.

My mother thought about all these things when she looked down at me after I was born.

Despondent, Lillian began to feel the blood rush in her ears and her heart pound faster than she could ever remember. It made her head hurt. She closed her eyes but that didn't help. She concentrated on breathing evenly but that didn't help. She started feeling nauseous. She broke

out in a cold sweat. She wanted to cry. Instead, Lillian

opened her mouth wide, like her legs the night she lost her virginity, and screamed, its decibel level directly proportionate to her lack of good judgement.

Startled, I stopped whining. My mother, in turn, felt a small prick in the nape of her neck, like the pop of a flashbulb or someone breaking a balloon. Everything slowed down. Her eyes rolled back. Her hands slipped. She let go of me, as if I never existed, dropping me onto a cold, stiff

animal badly in need of processing.

The day I came into the world a series of tragic events were set in motion, like a drunk driver, that could not be stopped till lives were ruined and lost.

* * *

Two telegrams for my father sat unopened at Fort Hood, the army base just outside Killeen, Texas where he was stationed. The first congratulated him on my unexpected birth. The second notified him of my mother's death. Neither was delivered because the sergeant on duty couldn't find someone to deliver them to.

Jack had somehow finagled a three-day pass so he could go to a series of appointments with internists in town. Military doctors refused to see him because they felt it was a waste of time. After a dozen examinations they declared him in perfect health and blamed his self-described symptoms, from palpitations to Tourette's Syndrome, on lack of willpower.

"There's nothing wrong with you. It's all in your head."

Jack knew better.

He had enormous trouble focusing on mundane things, getting organized, starting work, completing it and acting impulsively without regards to consequence; all the fundamentals one needs to maintain self-control and self-regulation on a daily basis.

This was the opposite of his father Dwight, by the way, who died before I was born and always complained that the work week was too short.

No one listened to him either.

Dwight dropped dead on his thirty-third birthday, two months after receiving a clean bill of health from the family doctor. Jack likened it to those baseball announcers who interrupt late inning action and say things like "Two more outs and he's got a no-hitter." The next batter always slams a line drive up the middle or hits the ball out of the park, just beyond the center fielder's reach.

It was why Jack, from the time his father's heart betrayed him, vowed to snatch everything from life he possibly could. Succumbing to excess, pushing the envelope beyond reasonable limits allowed him to stand out at a time when he was determined not to fit in - even though that's what he desperately needed. This not only gave Jack pleasure but a sense of unaccustomed power, each transgression a work of art his father would have frowned upon. It also explained Jack's unbridled enthusiasm, on his way back from town, when he bumped into Peggy, the sixteen- year-old niece of General Ethan Parks, his commanding officer.

Not quite blonde and curvy in all the right places, Peggy reinforced the old adage "A long legged girl can do an awful lot without doing anything." Her beauty was particularly striking next to the ruddy faced, unkempt patrons in the bar where Jack first laid eyes on her; both

clients and establishment in the throes of decline. Compared to them she was from another planet. Add an outfit that screamed "up for anything," a sweet face, a voice that was half whimper, half drawl, and she was every soldier's fantasy.

It was easy to see how my father overlooked the fact she was shrouded in sorrow even when she laughed. He noticed her full, welcoming lips instead of the tortured eyes of a woman three times her age. He wasn't even aware of her superior intelligence, although I can't fault him for that either. Peggy was light years away from having her intellect intrude on her allure.

As I grew and matured my father was kind enough to categorize girls like Peggy for me.

"If God Himself appeared in the sky and said you could fuck this woman but would die immediately afterwards you wouldn't think twice. You'd fuck her."

This was why, after three bottles of cheap wine, Jack told Peggy it wouldn't be considered premarital sex if they weren't planning on getting married. Peggy nodded, smiled and explained how condoms could be traced back to 1000 BC. Drawings were found that portrayed ancient Egyptians wearing linen sheaths, although it was uncertain if they were worn for protection or rituals.

They would not surface for three days.

Jack didn't die,...but he did lose six pounds.

My mother's sister, as a result, had to give the eulogy at her funeral. She regretted this almost as much as Lillian's passing because she stuttered whenever she spoke in front of a group, no matter how hard she tried to prevent it.

"This is fu-fu-fucked," Carolyn began.

With nowhere to go but down she continued to stammer. Stumbling over her emotions as well as her feet she lost her balance and struck her chest hard on a statue of Saint Jude. By the time paramedics showed up the blow had disrupted her heart's electrical system, triggering a change from its normal rhythm to a fatal arrhythmia.

Jack returned one week later.

When he arrived at Nightingale Memorial he was greeted

by the nurse on duty. Seated behind a desk crammed with photos of children, miniature wind up toys, votive candles and sediment stained coffee cups, a name tag identified her as Vivienne Holt.

Unlike Jack, who was every woman's fantasy, Vivienne was never in her prime and, therefore, never knew the joys and burdens of being a threat, which was part of her charm.

She was overweight, plain and matronly before her thirteenth birthday.

Kids at school mocked her relentlessly, joking that she'd bought her body on sale at Wal-Mart, discovered it was three sizes too large when she got home and tried it on, but couldn't return it because it was damaged. Though Vivienne assumed the teasing would stop as she aged and matured, it never did. She was always the brunt of ridicule. In time she grew accustomed to the taunts and even accepted some of the mean things that were said, but she never got used to the hurt.

Her mother described her as big boned and encouraged her not to slouch.

Vivienne's smile, on the other hand, transcended all shortcomings. It lit up her entire face and did the same to anyone who noticed, confident she would overcome her disadvantages because of it. It wasn't uncommon for those people to say, usually aloud, "She'd be beautiful if she just

lost forty pounds."

She wouldn't let Jack see me.

Hospital policy isolated any child being treated for a life-threatening condition. In the short time since my mother's demise I had developed pulmonary hypertension, abnormally fast breathing, unstable temperature, seizures and, last but not least, an acute case of dysentery that cut my weight in half.

Conventional wisdom said it would turn out badly.

Even if hospital policy was different Vivienne's conscience

was emphatically clear. It made no sense to inflict additional pain on someone who'd suffered so much loss already. Especially a soldier. In order for my father to move ahead with his life the best hope she could offer was no hope at all.

Though Vivienne believed strongly in the human spirit, man's capacity to rise to the occasion, she also knew the most common cause of premature death in infants was premature birth.

* * *

For the past twenty years Vivienne watched preemies die as routinely as she punched the time clock. Half-formed hearts. Membrane disease. There was even a case where one twin had absorbed the body of the other, suffocating both before they came out of the womb. If they didn't die from genetic disorders they perished from human indulgence. Alcoholism. Drugs. Afflictions of lust.

Vivienne treated them all equally.

She maintained an around-the-clock vigil, checking and rechecking the yards of plastic tubing and electrodes that helped monitor their heart rates, sampled their blood and showed if they'd been deprived of oxygen during labor and delivery.

She wished that death would come swiftly, at first, and put an end to their misery. It wasn't long, however, before she realized this was an abysmal way to think. It was more about sparing her own discomfort before she gave too much of herself and couldn't take it back, like her body.

From that point on she went home every night and studied medical journals and text books about the diseases that were destroying her children.

Their pain became hers.

She began caressing them gently at work. She would rub their backs softly, stroke their tiny chests, drag her fingers over every appendage and muscle, massaging them deeply till they giggled and cooed and fell back to sleep, grateful for a momentary respite from their struggle for

life.

She couldn't figure out why so many parents didn't do the same, preferring to keep their distance. When she realized it was because they blamed themselves, even if their children were born without lungs or brains, she went out of her way to assure them it was beyond their making.

She became as familiar with tragedy and sadness, the futility of life, as she was unfamiliar with happiness and its subsequent rewards.

Vivienne also believed this:

"If false hope was the provenance of each new day, it was the ruin of every disappointing tomorrow."

Unfortunately, she never spoke about things like this. Unlike my father, she was not what you'd call a dazzling conversationalist and rarely offered more information than a subject required. This demure attitude caused most of her coworkers to believe she was evasive and indifferent toward them, which was true, and lacked curiosity, which was not. She was just better with thoughts than words. They gave her the freedom to make mistakes, something impossible in her

professional or social life - such as it was. It's why she remained silent and avoided Jack's eyes when he arrived, acting as if she was afraid. It's also why, when she gained the confidence to speak, she said too much.

She wanted to buy a brown cashmere pullover she'd seen in a local department store. Her favorite sweater, the one she usually wore, had begun to fray around the collar. Though cashmere was more affordable than ever before the sweater was still beyond her means. After a detailed

explanation about the hardy Kashmir goats of Inner Mongolia and why the best cashmere had the longest and whitest fibers, she mustered the courage to tell Jack the truth. She knew this was the right thing to do under the circumstances, but felt a heavy pang in her heart. This wasn't just for Jack who made her surprisingly light headed when she did look into his eyes. It was for the harshness and enigma of life itself.

So, when my father turned to leave, sadness falling down on him like snow flurries the night of my real birth, Vivienne said something she'd regret till the day she died.

"Would you like some coffee?"

My dad removed both hands from his back pockets.

"I could run down to the nurse's station and get you a cup. If you want, I mean."

Raising his head slightly, almost timid, Jack noticed she wasn't wearing a ring on the third finger of her left hand.

"Why don't you tell me more about that sweater?"

* * *

After work Vivienne drove Jack down Jim Bowie Boulevard, the road that led to and intersected her neighborhood, Lone Star Springs. She'd decided to give herself entirely to him,

like a student to a mentor, the moment she felt his sadness and uncertainty. She would ease his pain by passing on the lessons God taught her, demonstrating beyond a shadow of doubt that He sends no cross you cannot bear and life is never lost, irreparable or short of miracles.

"Maximize faith and its infinite possibilities. Minimize tragedy."

She'd preach the same philosophy she used at the hospital. When Jack realized that God had a reason for everything, that He could even create opportunity from the loss of a child, she would lie down beside him. Nothing carnal or perverse like my third birth story. Just a shared respect for life's cruel ironies. If the timing was right,that respect would lead to desire. When it did she'd call in sick so that desire could flourish. Since she'd never taken a day off in fifteen years no one would question her motives.

The thought made her smile.

She wasn't like the other pediatric nurses. Dedicated drinkers all, they'd become accustomed to the tragedy of death and believed that compassion and faith were for the faint-of-heart, the weak and the idle.

Vivienne knew it was always a tragedy.

If she helped my father she was loving and kind.

Though music didn't swell for him yet, when Jack knew this he would gravitate toward her compassion as eagerly as her preemies' parents clung to false hope. His music would come. She had no doubts. He would belong to her and she would belong to him.

At the same time, she had trouble believing she was going to wind up with someone so beautiful. The best, she assumed, was that she'd meet a man as innocuous as herself, more like an old piece of furniture passed down through generations that needed a few repairs and was too cozy to throw out. Functional, yes. Pretty? Not by a long shot.

Of course, comfort was a major plus in her predominantly minus world. It alone would allow her to live the marital life, with all its benefits, that God wanted her to have and her mother, Julie, swore she never would - "because men of any age, size, shape or color were immoral pieces of shit."

Unable to wear bright colors since her husband, Frank, left her for a younger woman who worked at the Post Office, Julie's heart was bathed in sorrow the way my mother's stomach was bathed in light.

Having met when they were still teenagers, Frank was the only man Julie ever dated, let alone slept with. While this gave her a certain moral superiority, allowing her to endure the indignities associated with being dumped, the loss lingered in the back of her mind like a mugger skulking in alleyways. She would have happily relinquished that hurt and returned to her old way of thinking if possible, but she was devoured by rage every time she received mail.

Overwhelmed by an abundance of Christmas catalogues, Julie eventually suffered a massive breakdown and ... I'm getting ahead of myself. Better to stay with something more pertinent.

* * *

I, meanwhile, was more concerned with watching one patient after another, black auras hovering over their heads, wheeled into Intensive Care. As with my mother I couldn't see beneath the surface to understand the gravity of the situation. Theirs or mine. Thankfully, I did know this. Something was beginning to grow and fester inside me. Something bad. I knew I'd suffocate if I stayed inside my mother one minute more, just as I knew I would perish if I didn't leave that puke-colored room with its stale, dense air of discontent.

Like Lillian before me I opened my mouth wide and screamed at the top of my lungs.

Vivienne would have understood.

Nothing had gone according to plan.

Instead of relying on her God-given talent to listen and sympathize when someone spoke about themselves, she monopolized conversation with nervous talk about her addiction to travel shows. This was more than ordinary anxiety. The moment she and Jack stepped into her house Vivienne was assaulted by her mother's convictions.

Trysts such as this were crimes against humanity, not unlike the Holocaust.

She wasn't aware of my father's nervous primping, studying his reflection in a window across the room while she raved about safaris in Kenya. She didn't notice his twitches when she described the Palio horse race in Sienna. Only when she saw the hard-on mushrooming through his pants did she realize it was time to rise above her upbringing. Flipping her hair back Vivienne unfastened the top two buttons of her blouse and smiled, like a young girl asking a boy for a dance.

"Go slow" she said.

Ten minutes later his erection and her hopes were long gone.

Jack didn't mind Vivienne's small talk during sex. He told her so politely because he really was the sensitive young man my mother imagined him to be. There was just a better time to learn about rodents escaping from giant ant hills in western Australia.

He got up to shower the moment he came.

Vivienne went to the freezer and retrieved a quart of strawberry ice cream, food that had provided physical and mental comfort whenever her mother became critical of the men in her world - food God created for times like this when life didn't go the way it was supposed to.

Unlike my father she rushed back to bed because she also wanted to savor the long forgotten fragrance of sex, no matter how brief and mechanical. A man's scent on her pillow excited her and reminded her when she was young and cherished dozens of other misguided expectations.

As water cascaded down her mother's comeuppance in the

adjacent room, as she lay there adjusting soiled sheets around her like a protective seal, Vivienne's mind battled the panic that rose inside her.

Years at the hospital had taught her one thing above all else. Devotion and reverence weren't only about faith. They were the end result of a simple process, having something over and over till you learned to appreciate every nuance, every trait you weren't capable of seeing on preliminary encounters.

Repetition was a patient's Christianity.

Perseverance was Vivienne's best quality.

Her smile returned.

She would replenish Jack's spirit as easily as she refilled his cup with coffee.

* * *

The following morning Vivienne made her way past a dozen bassinets, each holding babies; enough twisted tubes running in and out of their veins they resembled subway maps. Ignoring a blue button that said "Congratulations, it's a boy," she leaned inside my bed expecting the worst. Instead, she found a spirited, sobbing child lusting for life. Lifting me into her arms she instinctively clasped me to her wildly beating heart, as if we were connected by blood

instead of tragedy.

I stopped crying.

This time it had nothing to do with screams or poor judgement. As I looked into Vivienne's eyes the reassurance and unconditional joy were not only there, they were genuine.

Vivienne charged into the waiting room two minutes later, holding me in front of her like a bride's bouquet. My miraculous recovery validated her belief in the human spirit. That it could triumph over medicine's steadfast reliance on technology, diagnosis and prescribed treatment was a bonus. In the back of her mind she also knew my resilience would elicit feelings in their purest, unadulterated form, pushing Jack further in her direction.

Her only problem, when she looked from one side of the room to the other, was that my father had disappeared.

She had no way of knowing he was being driven toward Fort Hood, the only post in the United States capable of stationing and training two Armored Divisions. Both of Jack's hands were restrained behind his back by handcuffs, digging into his wrists and making them bleed.

While Vivienne marveled at my premature miracle, two broad-shouldered MP's entered the hospital, identified Jack from an enlistment photo and arrested him.

His commanding officer's niece, Peggy, had shared my father's philosophy about premarital sex with her father, a methodist minister. The good reverend called Ethan who immediately issued a warrant for Jack's arrest.

While the MP's and their prisoner sped toward the heavily guarded gates of Fort Hood, Vivienne drove down Clyde Barrow Avenue, lined with Maples whose leaves were

preparing to change - as she felt her life was about to do.

After failing to find my father she'd calmly walked down the hall, squeezed into a freight elevator filled with medical supplies, crossed the first floor lobby, entered the garage through a side door that was supposed to be locked, slid into her car and made the only decision possible after decades of pediatric sorrow.

She would keep me.

Vivienne phoned the hospital the moment we got home. She said she was ill and too sick to return. As predicted, nobody cared.

She never took her eyes off me the rest of the night,

studying me from as many different angles as possible. Up close. Far away. She climbed on the sofa. She laid on her back. She held me above her head. She cradled me in her lap. She even curled up beside me as if we were an old

married couple. No matter how carefully she examined me, with each position she found something new to admire.

When it was dark, my features were barely visible but she continued inspecting my normal face, two normal hands, two normal feet and normal colored skin - as if I were a

treasured piece of art that touched her in a place she didn't think could be reached by anyone else but God.

She also knew I would never be normal.

I was smaller and weaker than most infants and would remain that way as I grew to adulthood. I'd probably be picked on by other boys at school, as she had been, and shunned by girls who looked down at me, literally and figuratively. So, Vivienne made a pact with God that night.

She would do his bidding forever, anything He asked, if He watched over and protected me.

For the first time she would see a child triumph over infancy.

The pain in my neck subsided during those hours. Even at my tender age I knew Vivienne was responsible. I couldn't speak a single word, of course, but as I drifted in and out of sleep I thanked her with my eyes. My father's eyes. The sparkling eyes of a man who could charm anyone out of anything they might be reluctant to give.

* * *

If a photograph of my birth represented the crowning achievement in my father's life, a picture of Lone Star Springs was a shrine to everything the mid-west held dear; God, family and Texas - not necessarily in that order.

Each day was like a lazy, Sunday afternoon.

Every street was named after an historical Texas icon. It was the developer's way of making potential buyers take pride in their subdivision as if they were becoming a part of history, something eternal, instead of simply moving into an homogenized, middle-class neighborhood. Not only did this make the community greater than any individual home owner, it was a stroke of marketing genius. A spacious, unpretentious house on Davy Crockett Lane sold twice as fast at twice the price as the same house on Porcupine Court.

Every home was situated on a one acre plot, made of blonde brick and ranch style, although model homes sometimes added a second story or supplementary land. Sidewalks were the same width. Mailboxes were identical and wedged into expansive lawns, a metal American flag raised to denote delivery. Even the fire retardant, cedar shake roofs shared the same contours. As a result, there was no class distinction between east Lone Star Springs and west Lone Star

Springs the way there was in Majestic Meadows, twenty miles north and closer to Dallas. The peace of mind this created was like radio waves. You didn't notice or think about it, but it was always there to reassure you.

When you moved in you were greeted by cheerful, smiling men wearing string ties and women in short skirts and patent-leather boots, the same outfits they wore to the opera. They

brought baskets filled with seasonal flowers from their gardens, locally made preserves, Reader's Digest condensed books and bottles of Texas wine.

You could live anywhere in the United States and wouldn't find neighbors as thoughtful as these good folks. Most of this was due to the fact they rarely concerned themselves with anything beyond the community's boundaries. Nobody watched the news or read newspapers because the media threatened their basic heartland values which centered around the same gifts the welcoming committee delivered to newcomers. Anything else was hubris and could destroy them faster than the outsiders they feared.

Houses may have been modern, but the moment you stepped out your door you were back in a simpler time.

Women, even if they had occasion to be sad, found reasons to be happy. They might go to bed with a heavy heart, but after dreaming of peanut butter and jelly sandwiches, PTA's and children's play dates they woke up with a smile - because that was the best the world had to offer.

They missed their husbands while they were at work and greeted them as if they'd been away on long trips when they returned.

Men appreciated their wives just as much. New outfits. Perfectly styled hair. Hot meals. Nothing went unnoticed. They opened doors for them, be it car or house, and said "ladies first." Their wives were always grateful, never annoyed as they might be today because it would be

considered sexist.

Every boy became a football star, every girl a beauty queen. Children remembered people's birthdays, wrote thank you notes without being told, had lustrous white teeth, played tag, skipped wherever they went and giggled till tears filled their eyes and it was difficult to see. There was no teenage pregnancy, no divorce and no illicit love affairs - that people were privy to at any rate. Cars were American made and nobody used passports or anti-depressants.

The actual town of Lone Star, two short blocks, housed a hardware store that gave away fresh popcorn and had a Post Office and an ATM in the back behind the gadgets department.

Next door was a Chevron station with a shiny blue gas pump and a mechanic who washed your windshield and checked your oil without being asked. Beyond that was my father's branch

office, a single room that resembled a travel agency, the local realtor and Bee's cafe, run by Bee herself. She baked all pies on the premises, setting them out to cool on windowsills as she did in her own home, and kids begged for them the moment they came back from school which was within walking distance.

Since there were no walls or barriers, it wasn't uncommon to see deer nose out of surrounding woods, strolling down the road as if they didn't have a care in the world. Depending on the time of day they'd pass fox, possum, rabbits and the occasional pheasant. Never coyotes. They were well fed and all pets in the community were domesticated and stayed mostly indoors.

Surrounding land was untouched by industrial and commercial development. There was no nearby Wal-Mart. No Outlets. No major highways, busses or trains. People came only if they had to. Whether business or pleasure they never stayed long. They couldn't. There were no hotels or

entertainment and Bee's closed at four.

If you wanted more you had to drive to Majestic Meadows.

A few years before Vivienne moved in, residents had the opportunity to add a 7-11 convenience store but voted it down. It was an invitation to crime and just a matter of time before their streets were infected by drug dealers, vindictive teenagers with vulgar tattoos and hustlers playing

Three Card Monte.

At the time I doubt it would have made much difference since most people rarely left their homes. This had nothing to do with isolation. They were happiest when surrounded by their children, pictures of their children, pictures of their grandchildren and Pat Robertson, the good pastor revered for his unflagging dedication to non-profit Christian organizations, his own among them. If they did go out it was for work, church, vacations and, eventually, their funerals. Convenience was a distant fifth.

Hidden by a clump of oaks, Vivienne's house sat back from the road about twenty yards. From all three bedrooms she had a view of the pond across the street. It could also be seen from a porch with hooks in the ceiling for a swing that was never attached. Rooms were small but had character. Stone walls doubled as headboards which gave the rooms a wintry feel although winters were mild. No two windows were alike. No two doors. This had little to do with haste

or slovenly work. Foundations of Texas homes never settled, shifting as often as southern politicians' morality. It's why there were so few basements and presidents south of the

Mason Dixon line.

The house had sat empty for five long years.

The original owner was an abortion doctor. When neighbors found out they lined up on his lawn at 7:00 A.M., picketed and shouted obscenities till he left for work. One Friday morning, after someone's grandmother threw a brick through his living room window, he packed his lunch, drove off and never returned.

Although realtors brought dozens of clients to look nobody moved in - as if the house was haunted by prenatal misconduct. Vivienne didn't care. Whether an infant's life was cut short by genetic malfunction or a vacuum tube made little difference.

The house needed her.

The only other controversy arose when residents banded together and wrote a letter demanding the local television station take Captain Kangaroo off the air. By making food and puppets appear and disappear at will he was teaching children to rely on him instead of Jesus for miracles and that meant only one thing.

Captain Kangaroo was the Anti-Christ.

* * *

Vivienne was sanding the front door when she received a call from my father's court-appointed lawyer. She was initially shocked by the charges against Jack, but the more she thought about them the more she remembered a conversation with her mother the night her father moved out.

"Men, especially married ones, relate to women the same way foxes who break into hen houses relate to chickens. Once they've tasted blood there's nothing you can do to keep them away."

Jack's actions were deplorable but understandable. The fact that he was facing ten years in prison was genetically unfair.

The drive to Fort Hood, for me, seemed endless. For Vivienne it was just one more hurdle in the race against her mother's dour prophecies.

When my father saw me for the first time Vivienne knew she'd made the right decision. The eyes that were usually quick to mislead became straight forward and clear. She reached for his hand instinctively. Instead of grasping it and holding tight, accepting comfort, Jack patted it as if

she were a small child or stray dog he was trying to keep at bay.

At first sullen, the more Jack explained the more he embellished and justified. Only when he eliminated the smallest trace of blame did he suggest Vivienne find Peggy and persuade her to recant her accusations.

It was a little before noon when Vivienne parked in front of the minister's house and stepped into shadows, looking like every eager salesman who'd come before as she climbed the porch steps.

Peggy was exactly as Vivienne imagined, the bottom of the virtuous food chain, but that perception changed the moment she saw her bedroom.

No posters of rock musicians or movie stars one expects from a sixteen year old. Nothing frivolous at all. Just a small, nondescript area cluttered with books, open and dog-eared. Fiction primarily. Piled high on the floor. Stacked against walls. Overflowing in closets and shelves. Arranged in the order they were read. Nancy Drew and Cam Jansen mysteries. "101 Dalmations." "A Wrinkle In Time." Everything by Mark Twain. All of Jack London. "Pride And

Prejudice." "Jane Eyre." Most covers were hanging by a thread or had fallen off after repeated readings, pages crammed with personal observations written in margins with pencil, never pen.

Peggy spoke about her books the way Vivienne talked about travel shows.

Vivienne couldn't imagine anyone reading that much. She had tried reading "Pride And Prejudice" when she was growing up, but never got past the first chapter. She had too many

responsibilities and had to account for every minute because life was not supposed to be complacent or light hearted. Her mother made sure of that.

"Idle minds lead to promiscuous hands."

Peggy went on to explain that these were only a fraction of the books she'd devoured over the years. The rest were in boxes in the attic, also in stacks and piles. There was no reason for Vivienne to be envious, not when there were ten times as many books Peggy hadn't read, ones she should have since she hoped to be a writer someday. If that was going to happen, if she was going to share her beliefs and experiences with the world, she had to learn from those whose beliefs and experiences were greater than her own.

Like Willa Cather or Edith Wharton.

Unused to confiding in someone, the moment Peggy realized she was being vulnerable she stopped, lit another cigarette and looked away, as Vivienne did the day she met my father. This had nothing to do with avoidance. It gave Peggy a few moments to regroup and imagine Vivienne as a child, nine at the most. This prevented her from feeling threatened because it allowed her to see Vivienne when her heart and mind were free of complications. If Peggy focused on a person's innate goodness instead of the damage in adults, she might be able to figure out why they did the hurtful things they did when they were grown.

Unlike with Jack, Vivienne held her ground. This was more than due diligence. Now that she'd met Peggy she relished the opportunity to be charitable, having gone so long without it herself.

She also realized something else.

The nervous small talk she desperately needed the night she brought Jack home was no longer necessary.

"I wanted to kill you," she said, as if asking for a glass of iced tea, "but now I don't."

Instead of being horrified, Vivienne's honesty touched Peggy. Though secrets were her only protection, her means of keeping shame at bay, she desperately needed to regurgitate not hide them.

"If I tell you personal shit you'll go tell your boyfriend and everyone else."

Vivienne shook her head.

"That's what adults do," Peggy insisted.

Vivienne shook her head again.

Closing her eyes, Peggy leaned back against a stack of Russian novels and ground her teeth.

"It is against human nature to keep a fucking secret."

Floodgates opened after one more denial.

Knowing Peggy's passion for reading, her father, the good minister, bought her a book about Joan of Arc for her tenth birthday. He explained how Joan's life was inspirational. It demonstrated the enormous power God could bestow if you had a pure, virginal heart. While virginity was an erotic and sensual experience in its own right, it was much more than the sublimation of sexuality through denial. It was the essential first step toward a transcending,

spiritual union with Christ. More significantly, the story showed how God punished women when that purity was corrupted.

Then the minister stuck his tongue down her throat.

When he removed it he apologized, admitted he was glad he'd done it and told Peggy three words that would haunt her for the rest of her life.

"Do not tell."

Every Sunday for the next year, as they approached the altar to take the holy sacraments of Communion, Peggy sang "Joan Of Arc," by Leonard Cohen, to her mother in a whisper.

"The world is full of evil fucking people doing evil fucking things that nobody wants to fucking see."

After church, as Peggy stood next to her mother while the faithful descended cathedral steps, gushing about her father's sermon, Peggy repeated those words.

Her mother, who had excellent hearing inherited from her own mother's side of the family and often preached the impor-tance of communication, especially at bake sales, was even better at avoidance.

She simply turned and walked away.

During these confrontations Peggy often felt so light headed she had to sit down where she was, even if that meant in the middle of the street. It wasn't like she was sick. It wasn't panic. She just had the overwhelming feeling that, if she didn't grab hold of something, she would leave her

body and never return. Since this was not a concept she believed in or even thought of before, she decided to pay attention and hold tight.

This was when she started touching things, outlining them with her fingers as if she was blind. It grounded her and, while traffic honked around her, confirmed what she was feeling was real not imaginary.

Over the ensuing years, after every excruciating late night visit, her father would take his right hand and place it on Peggy's forehead. Her chest. Then her left arm. Then her right, enacting the sign of the cross. When this was done, he would bow his head and say:

"Pray for us my sweet girl. We will put our fate in the hands of the Lord."

Since the Lord wasn't exactly helping Peggy while this was going on, she wasn't eager to put her fate, or anything else for that matter, in His slimy hands. She had to do something, however, because she felt like she was losing her mind and couldn't go on another day. One afternoon after

class she went to speak with the school counsellor instead of taking the bus home. In tears she explained about Joan of Arc, inspiration, the pure virginal heart, denial and punishment.

The counsellor listened attentively to every word, nodding and taking notes if appropriate.

Then he stuck his tongue down her throat.

When Peggy protested, he berated her for avoiding intimacy and told her "not to tell."

She never sought help again.

The minister's face frightened Peggy almost as much as his actions. Normally porcelain white, it became bright red when he drank, so there was always the stench of whiskey on his breath. His brow, high, rounded and grooved with lines like scars, had a series of thick veins that ran diagonally, blood coursing through them in direct proportion to his predatory desires. His chin was pointed, as was his nose, hairs protruding and quivering like undersea coral. His teeth were the color of old magazines. Thick glasses magnified tiny black eyes, like a rodent's, that never

blinked or wavered as they swept over her hungrily, taking in her body the way they did when raised toward the heavens during one of his sermons.

And he always licked the corners of his lips.

Peggy's cigarette-stained fingers tapped one Pall Mall after another from their pack as she described her agonizing depressions, self-hatred, alcohol abuse and the dozens of times she sat with the barrel of her father's gun wedged deep in her throat, praying for the courage to pull the trigger.

Unlike Jack she grasped Vivienne's hand and never let go, her grip strong, her fingers cold. She even showed Vivienne the suicide note she carried at all times in case she gained courage.

"I win," it said.

It was at that precise moment Vivienne noticed two things:

1. Most of Peggy's nails were bitten down to the quick, her cuticles encrusted with blood.

2. The lock on her door had been removed.

A bond was born out of tragedy that would have been impossible during happier times, both Vivienne and Peggy finding the one thing that had always eluded them.

A confidant.

Before we could leave, Peggy grabbed the phone, dialed her

uncle and begged him to listen to what her new-found friend had to say.

One hour later, Vivienne held me on her lap as she sat across from Ethan in his office at Fort Hood.

Vivienne refused to make excuses for my father but insisted the time he spent with Peggy was more about alcohol than illicit.

Mostly she spoke about Peggy.

"The more you see what's wrong in the world, the more you have to do something about it."

When there was nothing left to say Uncle Ethan thanked Vivienne for coming and walked us to the door. He assured her he would take everything under consideration but reminded her that matters like this were delicate and time-consuming.

He didn't believe a word.

Rummaging through her purse Vivienne removed a piece of paper Peggy had given her before we left.

"What's this?" asked Ethan.

"Peggy's insides," was all she could think of.

As she turned and fled, Ethan raised the paper to eye level, holding it at an angle to catch the light.

"If only I had another life.
Somewhere far away
with a different name,
a hideous face,
and twisted limbs
that made men turn their heads
in horror.
Even God won't be able to find me
although He'll try.
He'll go from house to house,
breaking in late at night
like a thief,

34

emptying closets and drawers
looking for one more sacrifice.
My capitulation.
There's a sweetness,
a childhood
I will never know.
And when I die a gentle,
loving girl no more,
as I take my last sip
of beloved Vodka
with a splash of orange juice,
I won't know a single person
who cared enough
to take the time
to look inside me,
see my soul
and ask
"How are you?"

Unaccustomed to the passion and nakedness of poetry, Ethan laid the paper down in front of him and opened the desk drawer where he kept personal items. Medals and ribbons. A news letter from the veteran's administration about retirement. Several folded maps and an autographed copy of "Thanks For The Memories." Reaching past all these into the far right corner, he withdrew his government issued Colt .45 and checked the clip.

* * *

It usually took Ethan thirty minutes to drive from the base to his brother's house. This day it took twenty. When the minister answered the bell he was surprised to see the expression on his older sibling's face, more so when he wedged his foot between the door and its frame and handed him Peggy's poem.

"What's this?" asked the minister, scanning the page.

Ethan calmly described the accusations against him.

Feigning shock the minister flung the door open and yelled. "Judith!"

Gesturing for his brother to enter, the minister led him into the living room where Judith, his loving wife of twenty years, was already waiting. The moment Ethan was seated the minister positioned himself across from him, slightly elevated because of a step up, and began pacing the way he did in front of the pulpit.

"Sometimes children are born cursed!"

He spoke in a booming, evangelical voice that was smooth, reasonable and superior, protecting himself against a sexual appetite he knew to be indefensible.

"From the time Peggy was little she was rebellious, and spiteful. You know that better than anyone, Ethan. Nothing made her happy. Not music. Not toys. Not even faith. She was disdainful of any advice I gave her and told one lie after another to escape the horrendous situations she kept getting herself into. Fortunately, both myself and Judith care deeply, unlike so many other parents in similar situations."

He gestured, with an approving nod, toward his faithful companion who smiled as she calmly offered Ethan a plate of mixed nuts - although a faltering voice betrayed her.

"Peggy's so lucky. We live in this wonderful house and have such a beautiful life."

The minister resumed his oration as Ethan set the plate down on a table in front of him.

"We never gave up on her. Not once. Through thick and thin she is our daughter and, more important, a child of God."

Like my father, he was on a roll.

"We've always been confident she would eventually see the light. I've witnessed it with members of my congregation. Wendell Tyler's son, for example. You know the boy. A brawler. Even you thought he'd wind up in the electric chair. You told me so on numerous occasions."

He stopped moving to make eye contact.

"He's now a respected corporate lawyer."

He started pacing again.

"Then there's Jim Duarte's daughter. She was presented with seven other young women at the Lone Star Debutante Ball. She was president of Chi Omega sorority. She caught the bouquet at Melinda's wedding, which is still one of the nicest affairs I've ever been to, and she shot heroin as routinely as some people exercise."

He stopped again.

"She's attending art school in New York and learning how to make stained glass."

A tear formed in his right eye.

"Peggy is just going through a phase. That it's consumed most of her life is more of a test than an indication. Good Christian families recognize that."

His lips began to quiver.

"At the same time, I can't believe Peggy would fabricate a story like the one told to you. This goes far beyond her usual lies.

THIS IS BLASPHEMY!"

During the rest of the conversation the minister's wife kept a respectful distance, her expression pleasant the way it was in the greeting line at her wedding. This was due to her belief that a wife's value, along with remaining silent, laid in being polite, innocuous and accommodating. She hustled in and out, topping off drinks and replenishing bowls with potato chips, nuts and dip. When food wasn't an issue she sat on the sofa with her back straight and ankles crossed primly, wriggling a gold angel pinned to her lapel in hopes of diffusing the evil things that were being said. She never spoke directly to Ethan or returned his stare. When the minister looked at her, however, she chimed in without hesitation, her energy level rising so quickly she was breathless by the end of her thought and appeared as if she might collapse.

Whatever suspicions Ethan entertained quickly flickered away. He was so convinced of his brother's innocence he decided to confront Peggy. He wanted her to know exactly how much damage she almost caused.

"Peggy!"

As he started for her bedroom, the minister failed to suppress a shudder, broke down and confessed.

He attributed his actions, at first, to a moral lapse in competence, not unlike cheating on an exam. He was a good man, a better husband and an excellent provider.

"I forgive people each week for every cardinal and venial sin. Why? Because humans are full of contradictions. We have ideals about the proper way to live. We want to do the right things but sometimes we fail. Falling from grace is not only the center of our universe it's what, invariably, teaches us right from wrong. Just because I'm a minister doesn't preclude me from errors in judgement. I'm a man of God, sure, but I'm also flesh and blood."

When Ethan showed no sign of forgiveness the minister changed tact, blaming Peggy's seductive behavior and dress for luring him into her bedroom night after night.

"She made herself available to me."

Much to his relief, Ethan assured him everything would work out. Placing a consoling hand on his brother's shoulder he used his other hand to reach into his briefcase and remove the Colt. Peggy entered the room as he fired four times with the same zest that earned him a commission during the Korean War. Once in the head. Once in the heart. Twice in the groin. The minister's wife started screaming, a shriek, neighbors later testified, that could be heard all the way over on Jim Bowie Street, three blocks away. As Ethan calmly dialed 911 to report his actions, as the minister's wife ran back and forth, knocking over tables and lamps in her haste, Peggy crossed to the minister's lifeless body and whispered a vengeful but poetically just phrase in his ear.

"Do not tell."

Time and delicacy were no longer considerations.

* * *

Three days later Vivienne and I were huddled beside Peggy at her father's funeral. While a pastor read the eulogy I studied everyone around me. They were strangers but their expressions were familiar, comparable to those wheeled into Intensive Care. Emptiness. Defeat. Sadness. Regret. I recognized life's frailties better than most. I was just too young to categorize them.

As I observed, Peggy fought off waves of anger and revulsion, feelings to which she was obviously entitled. Her father, according to the pastor, was a pillar of the community. He was adored by everyone who knew him and was a righteous man to a fault, his life an inexhaustible fight against lust and greed, an amazing feat in today's morally bankrupt society.

Her mother kept up a patter of her own.

"Your father has nothing to worry about now. He's lucky. I'm the one who has to deal with all the problems left behind."

"Momma."

Her voice was throaty and hoarse. "I wish I could climb in there with him. I need the break more than he does." Gesturing

39

at the other mourners her mouth turned down into a half moon. "Someone with my upbringing isn't supposed to pay the rent."

"Momma."

"From the day I arrived I've given too much to this town and too much to you and it's time I looked after myself. I don't even have a warm winter coat. Haven Lewis over there has two and she cheats at Hearts. I don't know how, but anyone who wins as much as she does has to be doing something wrong."

"Momma."

"You don't care if I'm warm." She gestured again. "None of them do. They say they're my friends but they're only nice to me because I'm the minister's wife. Now that he's gone I'll need something and no one will lift a finger."

Unable to bear another word Peggy straightened her posture and asked a question she'd been wanting to ask most of her young life.

"Didn't you wonder where Daddy was going in the middle of the night?"

Raising both hands in front of her like a Crucifix against Dracula, the minister's wife tried to shield herself. "I'm never going to be cold again."

"Did you really think I couldn't hear you sneaking down the God damned stairs so you wouldn't have to deal with what he was doing?"

This time the minister's wife raised just one, stern index finger. "I'll turn around and leave if you use the Lord's name in vain."

"God damn! God damn! God fuckitty fuck fuck shit piss damn!"

Glaring at her daughter with all the hatred denial can foster, her response was as cold as it was unrepentant. "I never heard a swear word in my life till you were grown. Not one. My parents wouldn't allow it like your daddy did. They wouldn't put up with filth because they knew that anyone who said things like that was damned for eternity."

"Fuck, shit, piss."

"This is your fault. All of it."

Peggy tried to speak but her mother dissolved into tears before she could get the words out.

While those around her offered support, Peggy reached into her pocket, removed a pint of Wild Turkey and took a swig, savoring the whiskey as it slid down her throat. Holding the bottle up to the light to see how much was left she made her way to a Porto-potty used by construction

workers repairing adjacent head stones, disappearing with a wobble. When she reappeared she moved directly to her father's open grave, tossed the now empty bottle on top of his elaborately carved casket and exposed her breasts.

"Daddy thought I had great tits."

Grabbing her heart, the minister's wife took an awkward step backwards. "What in God's name..."

Peggy raised her skirt. "Personally, I think my legs are better. My ass could use a little improvement but I'm working on it. Don't you worry."

Spinning around, Peggy revealed a bare bottom with toilet paper stuck to it.

"Closed For Repairs" was written across the center.

Some of the mourners shouted obscenities. Some stepped menacingly in her direction. Most just leered, enjoying the spectacle.

Peggy couldn't care less. For the first time in as long as she could remember, life wasn't about things done to her.

Jack was released with a dishonorable discharge two weeks later. He moved in with Vivienne that same afternoon and surprised her with a brown cashmere pullover and a marriage proposal before dinner. As she struggled to fit her oversized head through the sweater's normal sized opening, as material snagged on an earring making it impossible for her to see, Jack shifted his attention to me.

"I know you can't understand this son, but no one's ever stood by me the way Vivienne has. She's one of a kind. It's something I'll remember the rest of my life. I'll never do anything to destroy her faith in me because she's a saint and should be worshipped."

Jack's music had come.

* * *

My father loved magic almost as much as Vivienne loved him. When he was a kid he used to hitchhike into Dallas every time a show came to town. Illusionists were his favorite and, over the years, he had the privilege of seeing some of the best. Tigers appeared and vanished with the wave of a wand. Busses levitated with no apparent means of support. Jack was even invited on stage once, with other members of the audience, to examine a woman who'd been strapped to a gurney and sawed into thirds, her guts cascading onto the floor like Niagara Falls. While some

turned and fled and others fainted, Jack merely picked up a handful of entrails, put them in his pocket and smiled.

His favorite act featured the son of a man who did the identical show back when vaudeville was king. Although the performance changed over the years out of necessity, the idea remained the same. Wearing a bulky, full-length overcoat, the son stood center stage and asked members of the audience to name something. Tickets to the 1963 World Series, for example. He'd then reach inside his coat and pull out a pair. This included anything from a turkey leg to a copy of

"Gone With The Wind." It was amazing and no one could

figure out how he did it. Occasionally, the man came up empty. When this happened he usually made a joke and moved quickly to the next request.

Even though my father knew it was all slight of hand, tricks that owed their success to ingenuity and countless hours of practice, to him it really was magic. There was no

other way to describe a process that depended solely on imagination.

He used the overcoat to make a point.

A man, especially a salesman, had to have an explanation for every possible situation at his fingertips. If he did, he would never be caught unawares.

I use the coat to describe how my memory works.

I make a request. Most of the time my brain complies, but sometimes it leaves me high and dry, shifting quickly and unpredictably from one thought to the next as if they were unrelated. This is particularly upsetting because I have always been methodical. My memory was a source of great pride, an impregnable fortress where valuables were categorized and locked safely away.

I never dreamed someone could break in and steal from me.

This is also disturbing because a life depends on its details and there are no small ones. One loose screw on a NASA rocket and we've all seen what happens.

Unfortunately, as I look back, I've discovered my own loose connection, trivial though it may seem.

If you remember, my mother's younger sister, Carolyn, tripped and fell during Lillian's funeral. The impact short-circuited her heart. I still have a copy of the coroner's report in my desk. That's not the problem. The problem is, there's a chance the statue she landed on wasn't Saint Jude. It had long been removed, replaced by a slide show praising Saint Martin of Tours. No one seemed to know when this change had been made, why, or where the original statue was

taken. Not even the priests.

Evidence is conflicting.

POSITIVE: In the church's archives were a dozen ancient newspaper clippings. It used to be common practice, if Saint Jude helped you, to publish a notice of thanks in the local paper. These usually appeared in the personals or classified ads. It was done to enhance the Saint's name and give faith to those who read the notices, so they too could find the help they needed. The typical wording was usually concise and said something like "Thank you, St. Jude, for your

intercession in response to my prayers."

Each one of the clippings represented a prayer that was written by someone in the congregation and thereby answered.

NEGATIVE: St. Jude is traditionally depicted carrying the image of Jesus in his hand or close to his chest; connoting the legend of the Image of Edessa. He's also shown in icons, more often than not, with a flame around his head. This represents his presence at Pentecost, when he received the Holy Spirit with the other apostles. Occasionally he's represented holding an axe or halberd, as he was brought to death by one of those weapons. In some instances he may even be shown with a scroll, a book, the Epistle of Jude, or holding a carpenter's rule.

None of these were present in an old mural behind where the statue once stood, a space that would have depicted Jude and Jude alone.

POSITIVE: Seventeen copies of the following prayer were discovered under the seat of a nearby confessional.

"O most holy apostle, St. Jude, faithful servant and friend of Jesus -- People honor and invoke you universally, as the patron of hopeless cases, of things almost despaired of. Pray for me, for

I am so helpless and alone. Please help to bring me visible and speedy assistance. Come to my

assistance in this great need that I may receive the consolation and help of Heaven in all my necessities, tribulations, and sufferings, particularly (state your request) and that I may praise God with you always. I promise, O blessed St. Jude, to be ever mindful of this great favor, to always honor you as my special and powerful patron, and to gratefully encourage devotion to you by publishing this request. Amen."

NEGATIVE: Down through the ages, many Christians confused Saint Jude, also known as Thaddaeus, with Judas Iscariot, the betrayer of Jesus. As a result, prayers were often avoided on his behalf, which is why he's often called the "Forgotten Saint."

I must consider everything.

If I'm going to have the revelation I so desperately need, it must be closer to foregone conclusion than hunch.

* * *

True to his word my father worshipped the ground Vivienne walked on. Even though his days were long and often involved drives that stretched all the way to Kansas, when he came through the door after work there was never a hair out of place, his clothes were wrinkle free and he always had a bouquet of fresh flowers in hand. Depending on the season he dressed in a light or dark suit, blue shirt to bring out his eyes, striped tie, shoes with a military shine and something red, his favorite color. He'd hand the flowers to Vivienne, pull the brim of his hat down to his eyes, wink at me and say, "Your mother is a saint. I hope you're doing everything she tells you, son, because saints need all the help they can get these days."

Then he'd sweep her into his arms, lean her back till her head touched the linoleum and kiss her passionately.

"Baby, you're the greatest" was what he always said, the same way they did on a TV show Jack watched with his dad when he was my age.

When Vivienne was upright she scolded him for being crude in front of me, but even I, at five, could see it was said without conviction. The moment he knew she wasn't cross Jack would reach behind my ear and make a silver dollar appear, something he insisted I save for posterity.

"Someday, son, you'll be lucky and find a woman just like your mom. You'll need lots of cash so you can show your appreciation."

This wasn't just bravado.

As soon as Vivienne came home from the hospital she'd work her fingers to the bone preparing gastronomical tours- deforce. It was your basic mid-western meat and potatoes, but she did it with style. Her desserts, on the other hand, were extraordinary in any part of the country.

While she once stayed up late scanning medical journals for cures to save her preemies, she now thumbed through cookbooks searching for desserts to make Jack happy. She never cared about eating what she prepared. Perfection was her goal. So, while she experimented she walked down the road and gave whatever she'd baked to the neighbors. It was the neighborly thing to do. At first they couldn't believe their good fortune. It was like a gift from God. After a short while they turned on her, however, like the townspeople in Frankenstein, blaming Vivienne for their exorbitant weight gains and husbands' subsequent roving eyes.

"God damn you, Vivienne" was the usual response when she showed up with a torte or pudding at arm's length. Of course, they never refused. They'd reach out, grab whatever she brought and slam the door in her face to show their contempt.

Vivienne's only revenge, although she wouldn't have called it that, was the direct correlation between Lone Star's increase in heart disease and her love for my father.

Every night after the perfect dessert Jack would entertain us with marvelous anecdotes, as all good salesmen have, about his travels.

A modern day Aesop.

In the small town of Gooseneck, a traditionally tough place to sell dating back to the depression, Jack came up with a sure-fire scheme to make a buck. Inspired by the

buttons they pinned on the bassinets at Florence Nightin-gale Memorial hospital, he pasted bogus birth announcements on every top of the line Hoover he was hawking. Pink for girls. Blue for boys. Upon his arrival he drove straight to the county courthouse and looked up recent marriage licenses. List in hand he went door to door, played dumb and asked each woman if they'd planned on getting married. When they said yes he couldn't believe their good fortune. He wasn't just peddling vacuums. He was selling miracles. Attested to by the pink and blue announcements, each vacuum had somehow been inhabited by the spirit of Saint Mary Frances of the Five Wounds of Jesus, savior of childless women.

Jack would reach into his pocket and remove an old leather pouch, shipped to him personally by a priest in Naples, Italy, which contained a vertebra and a lock of hair from the Saint herself. He would carefully touch their bellies with it, smile and tell them he was summoned to

Gooseneck for their sake, not his own, and "The Saint is waiting for you."

He sold forty-two vacuums in three days.

A teenager in Onyx, Arkansas promised to buy a dozen

sets of encyclopedias if Jack helped him with his chores. After receiving cash for half the purchase Jack happily agreed and wound up painting thousands of ping pong balls red. When they were done they drove to a field and hung them on marijuana plants. The reason was simple. If DEA helicopters flew overhead looking for contraband they resembled tomatoes.

There was even one about a Chinese restaurant in Tulsa that bought depressing sayings from my Dad to put in fortune cookies. Because the economy was in the dumps, Jack convinced them that people didn't want to read how promising life was after being fired or losing their home to the bank. They'd much rather hear the hard, cold truth.

"If you think this year was bad, wait till you see what's coming?"

I feel obliged at this point to say that most salesmen, as a rule, are full of shit. They're entertaining and can charm the pants off you, literally in some cases, but you shouldn't put stock in things they say.

That's what elevated my father from the rest.

He had principles.

Granted, he would use any gimmick he could to make a sale, but he never pressured people or sold anything unless he believed it would improve their lives; as committed to doing the right thing as he was to his own expediency.

Nine months after those women bought the vacuums, eighty percent gave birth.

The boy with the tomato plants used his profits to pay tuition at Harvard.

The Chinese restaurant tripled its business because their offbeat fortunes became a novelty and, when all was said and done, allowed people who were down on their luck to laugh at themselves in spite of their situation.

If something my father sold was deficient or didn't perform as advertised, he bought it back and took the loss himself.

When he finished his stories he'd reach across the table, grasp Vivienne's hand and tell one last tale, a different type that made his face redden and his hands ball into fists.

During his travels, whether he was in a big city or small town, most every married man he met was fooling around the moment his wife's back was turned. Jack understood the indiscretions of youth better than most. They were a natural part of the maturation process and certainly not immoral. But, these men were neither young nor indiscriminate and the only process they were part of was being served divorce papers. He felt sorry for them and wished they could be as

happy as he. If they were, infidelity would be nothing more than a seldom used word in one of the leather-bound dictionaries he sold at a discount.

After that he would look Vivienne straight in the eyes and smile.

"You're not cheating on me are you, honey?"

Her cheeks would flush and she'd playfully punch him in the arm, sometimes as hard as she could. If she'd had a drink or two she'd summon the courage to ask him the same question. His response was always the same.

"Not in your lifetime, my saint."

* * *

Sometimes Jack didn't come home for a week, needing to travel more than a thousand miles to make a sale. When this happened Vivienne baked enough for an entire regiment. Although the neighbors' wives were in an uproar when he returned it was like Christmas morning for us. Jack would walk through the door with an armful of presents, deposit them on the table, sweep Vivienne into his arms and - well, you know the rest.

Whatever Vivienne wanted after a trip like this was fine with him, be it a movie or a new car, although he knew she would never ask anything for herself.

I got equal attention.

Most important, Jack always apologized for his absence. Whether he was in Kansas or Oklahoma didn't matter. He was there for me if I needed him. I was his son and that meant more than anything else in the world. Business especially. He proved this by teaching me skills his own father never had time to teach him. He taught me how to fish. He taught me how to ride a two-wheeler, assuring me it was just a matter of time till I could go like the wind. Depending on

the season we went sledding down the empty hill across the street or into the city to see the State Fair, magicians and Dallas Cowboys. Afterwards we'd go to my favorite restaurant, an old-style pharmacy that made butterscotch milk shakes in metal containers that put a smile on your face

whether you were an adulterer or not.

Sometimes he took me to hang out with his friends at the White Rock Tavern, a local bar he frequented at least three nights a week. They clung to his every word the way I did, what you do when you're near someone destined to have a street named after him like Davy Crockett. What I didn't understand in those days was what my father gained by being around people I considered clueless; men who lived in trailer parks, wore ironed Wrangler jeans, tooled boots with embossed

pictures of Texas and secured seat belts around six packs of malt liquor before their children.

Occasionally he'd take me to work. Without fail the secretaries giggled and said "I just love your dad" the moment we arrived.

On each of their desks was a pen-and-ink drawing my father had sketched of them. The blonde was lying on a four poster bed, smoking a cigarette while a three-headed monster, seated beside her, guzzled a keg of beer. The brunette wore a mini-skirt revealing perfectly proportioned legs that seemed to stretch for miles, men bowing at her feet.

Each was more like a photograph than a drawing. Details were that precise. They weren't erotic or cheap shots either, the way caricatures often are. They simply caught the spirit of the person they represented - although there was also something unsettling I could never put my finger on. Years later, after too many beers to count, my father told me why. He always tried to capture the one secret his subjects didn't want anybody else to know.

Since Jack had never demonstrated these talents at home, this was how I discovered he could draw.

His boss made a point of greeting me personally when I came to visit. He'd bound out of his office, put his arm around my shoulders and gesture at sales charts that hung over a half-dozen filing cabinets, listing items sold by his employees. Encyclopedias. Cooking utensils. Vacuums.

Orders were stapled underneath each category with the names of the person who'd placed them.

Jack topped every one.

"See that young man," his boss would say. "Salesmen like your Dad are what makes America great."

My chest swelled with pride.

I loved my father more than anything else in my world during those days, feelings you can only have before they're tempered by life's disappointments. Before anger. Before rebellion. Before heartbreak. Before betrayals, shame, self- doubt and misery. Before the realization that most of these struggles will last the rest of your life.

I just opened my heart and embraced the joy.

I never imagined Jack was once a child like me. I never imagined him having a life before me, let alone one filled with insecurities, fears or needs, especially ones that had gone unfulfilled. I never even thought about questioning what he told me. He was my Dad and I wanted to be just like him.

No. That's not entirely true.

I wanted to be him. I copied the way he dressed. The way he walked. The way he spoke. He had what they called a widow's peak, where your hair recedes slightly on either side into a V. On my seventh birthday I snuck into the bathroom before he got up, found his razor and shaved my hairline so it resembled his. My Dad laughed when he saw me at breakfast but he didn't make fun. Not then. Not ever. He was flattered and assured me my own peak would develop when I was ready. Till then, I would have to be content parting my hair on the right the way he did.

His character. His kindness. His integrity. They were all qualities I hoped to embody someday. Till then I was more than happy to live in his shadow because he was my loyal and imposing protector. If I was in a plane crash, even if everyone else perished, I knew I'd survive because he would never let anything bad happen to me.

His love made me immortal.

* * *

Most mornings I ate breakfast in the kitchen till I heard the bedroom door slam upstairs. It was always followed by rapid footsteps, whistling, "When The Saints Come Marching In," and my father, dressed to the nines.

He'd wink at me and say "Hiya, son. Don't have time to

chat right now. Got an appointment that could make us a bundle. Look after your mother. Shot gun's in the closet."

Crossing to the door he'd pluck his jacket off the coat rack and leave the house with a spring in his step. It wasn't long before I heard the garage door open and his car start. The engine ran smooth as silk, all pistons in sync and sounding brand spanking new. Even the air conditioning

hummed. I could hear it as he backed down the driveway.

This particular morning, my mother went to a parent/teacher conference. There was no school because of it and I was left to my own devices. Though I had explicit instructions not to leave the house, the moment Vivienne left I ran outside, jumped on my bike and pedaled toward town as fast as nine year old legs would allow.

Because I was disobeying a direct order it felt like one of Vivienne's travel shows to forbidden places in the darkest corners of the world. Danger lurked around each bend. Every street was an alley in Mongolia. Every neighbor a thief.

"Stay out of the shadows. That's where they get you. You're pulled in and never heard from again."

At least that's what the announcer had said.

By the time I arrived at Jack's office I'd fought off a band of marauding Bedouins, almost been trampled by rabid Bactrian camels and made it through the most dangerous parts of the Medina with nothing more than my cunning and speed.

Jack's car wasn't parked in front the way it usually was. When I went inside I discovered his boss was gone, the blonde too, both having come down with the flu. The other secretary said my father was in the field and wouldn't be back till late afternoon. As usual she giggled when she

spoke his name as if he was a celebrity.

Disappointed I thanked her, turned and headed back to the desert. Halfway there I caught a glimpse of my father's car parked in front of a home identical to ours. Cigarette drooping out of his mouth, he was leaning against the passenger door and combing his hair in the side view mirror. The blonde from the office walked out of the house after a moment. Giving him a peck on the cheek she grabbed his hand and led him inside.

I let my horse fall on the ground, crossed to the front door and knocked twice. Receiving no reply I made my way around to the side and peeked in a window.

It was the first time I'd seen a naked woman.

The blonde was playfully bouncing on the same four poster bed in the drawing while my father carefully removed his shirt, pants and socks, draping them over the back of a wooden chair before stashing his billfold and loose change inside his shoes.

I ran back to my bike, jumped on and pedaled off.

Looking over my shoulder I saw the curtains were still partially drawn so I knew I'd escaped undetected.

When my Dad walked through the door later that night not a hair was out of place, his clothes were wrinkle free and he was loaded with fresh flowers. He gave them to Vivienne, winked at me and said, "Your mother is a saint. I hope you're doing every-thing she tells you, son, because saints need all the help they can get these days."

Sweeping her into his arms he leaned her back and kissed her passionately. As always she scolded him for being crude. As always he made a coin appear behind my ear.

"Someday, son, you'll be lucky and find a woman just like your mom."

My throat began to constrict, each word tightening the umbilical cord around my neck, my very being under attack. When we finished dessert, instead of multiple yarns Jack told just one.

He was late for an appointment that afternoon so he was speeding down a side street. About fifty feet ahead of him a woman in a station wagon started to make a left turn but stopped abruptly. There was no way he could avoid her. There wasn't time or room. Next thing he knew he was looking down on the road from a great height and rising as high as any spirit. It sounded bizarre but he swore it was true. As he rose he could see both cars smashed together with him on

the other side of the wreck lying on the ground in a fetal position. Because he wasn't wearing his seat belt he'd been catapulted through the windshield like the guys we'd seen shot out of canons at the circus. He kept rising and the street kept getting smaller and smaller. Without warning he was back in his car, driving on the sidewalk and knocking over a couple of trash cans as he squeezed through an opening a dog would have had trouble getting through. It was only a few blocks before he reached his destination and seemed okay till he stepped out. His legs started wobbling as if he'd been drinking with his buddies. All he could think about was how lucky he was, not only to be alive, but because he had everything a man could ever want waiting for him at home; a wife and son who loved him as much as he loved them. Losing your life was a tragedy but people lost their lives every day. Real suffering came from loss of family. That was

worse than death.

Moved to tears, Vivienne leaned across the table and kissed him gently.

I wanted to tear him apart. I wanted to punch him in the face till his skull caved in like one of Vivienne's preemies. Then I'd climb onto the roof and shout that he was a cheat and a liar.

I didn't.

Even then I recognized a no-win situation when I saw it. No matter what he'd done, the moment I accused him I would be the one who destroyed their marriage. He would deny it, of course. What other choice did he have? Even if Vivienne believed me she'd wind up resenting me as much as I resented him.

Nothing was ever mentioned, but when my father and I looked at each other from then on there was always something left unsaid. I knew he was the three-headed monster and he knew I could ride like the wind.

* * *

We stopped being father and son, at least in the traditional sense, after that day in the desert. We didn't go fishing. We didn't go sledding. We didn't see ball games, magicians or the State Fair. Instead, Jack started taking me to Majestic Meadows on Saturday nights. He'd buy a six pack and we'd sit on the curb watching a procession of high school girls promenade around the square like sheep taunting predators.

What my dad called quality time together.

He would comment on each one's looks and availability, grading them from one to ten depending on a combination of legs, ass, chest, skin and attitude, cheekiness being a
priority.

If we were inadvertently in their way Jack would rise, step aside and gallantly gesture for them to pass.

"Beauty before age," was what he always said.

I assumed this was just good manners but I quickly learned differently. It was so he could watch them walk from behind. As their hips swished back and forth, skirts dancing up their thighs, he would analyze it for me and describe every sway. A flowing, pendulum type of motion was irresistible and drew raves. Forced and choppy was still desirable but practice was needed.

This was more than frivolous observation.

Researchers in Belgium had asked sixteen female students

to complete questionnaires about their sexual behavior. The women were divided into two groups, those who had vaginal orgasms and those who didn't.

They were then videotaped walking in public.

When sexologists reviewed the footage they correctly picked those who could orgasm vaginally ninety percent of the time. Their findings revealed that women with a natural, fluid gait, associated with stride length and rotation of the spine, were more apt to be vaginally orgasmic and, therefore, sexually voracious.

It was like insider trading.

As we sat there that first night Jack asked if I ever thought about what I wanted to do with my life. I told him I had. I'd planned on becoming a cowboy, an astronaut, an English soccer player or a salesman, leaning toward the latter. He was flattered but asked me to hold off on any final decision till we had a chance to talk at length. It was difficult for me to have a realistic perspective of life at nine, while I still thought the world was honorable and people didn't want to do me harm. I needed to rely on someone close, someone I could trust like him, who wanted nothing but the best for me and had only good intentions. Since he never made what he considered real money and didn't foresee any windfalls, advice was the sole inheritance he

could give me; insights that would stop me from floundering throughout my life.

His bequest, as it turned out, was spread over the next eight years, but his primary message never wavered - as straight forward and educational as any lesson I learned in school.

"Sex with the right woman was the greatest pleasure a man could experience. More important, sex with the wrong woman was just as good."

If the reason I was on this earth was primarily about money

and success, when the time came I didn't have either, and it happened to everyone, I'd be lost.

The girls who passed were divided into three categories:

1. Those who didn't need to alter their appearance because they were perfect.

2. Those who didn't try hard enough because they were lazy.

3. Those who tried too hard because they were flawed.

While perfection seemed to be the logical first choice, it was the third that was preferable. Fully aware of their bottom feeder status, these women were anxious to please and would do anything to make a man happy. Even if they were downright ugly, it didn't matter. I'd be nuts to turn down an opportunity like that and I could always find an interesting body part to distract me. A broken nose. The crook of an arm. A chipped tooth that resembled stalactites in one of Vivienne's travelogues.

All three categories had two subdivisions:

1. Girls and women.

2. Crazy and non crazy

Women had children. Girls did not.

Unencumbered seemed to be the natural choice. Once again, all wasn't as it appeared. Women with children were preferred, even if they were still teenagers, because they weren't afraid to get down and dirty. If they could deal with labor and afterbirth they knew there was no reason for shame and enjoyed pretty much anything you could throw at them.

"Girls" were still mortified by acts considered unconventional. Anything involving pudding, for example, and needed to get drunk. Depending on their capacity, this could be expensive. On the other hand, girls hadn't learned to hide what was in their heads yet. You could see it all in their face and it was refreshing. If they stayed like that it would be near impossible to choose between them and women. Sadly, it was a short window of opportunity. Everything changed the moment they realized there were no happy endings. This usually occurred after some guy convinced them it would be fun to stick his smelly dick down their throat because it "tastes like chicken."

Thoughts of marriage and happiness were never the same after that and love was more like being trapped in a burning building than the dreams childhood were made of. Instincts still told them to stay and preserve their innocence, but they knew they would die or be maimed for life if they didn't run as fast as they could.

Crazy women were preferable to non crazy, although "only in the beginning." This condition, unfortunately, wasn't as easily identifiable as children. In most cases I wouldn't have a clue they were insane till it was too late. My father never elaborated, but urged me to seek out musicians,

actresses, psychoanalysts and chess groupies.

This all led to one simple truth.

Life didn't make sense.

It didn't matter if I was single, married, divorced, gay, oversexed, chaste, good, bad, brave, cowardly, adored, hated, rich, homeless, lit my farts, knew the Lord's prayer, was an amputee, my wife was murdered or my child stillborn. Even if I did everything to benefit mankind from the day I came out of the womb, if I gave all my money to charity and invented a cure for cancer, it didn't mean shit. They might seem like milestones at the time, signifying a future that reeked of possibility and people would remember me by, but I was little more than a blip on the radar when I was pushing up daisies.

Eventually, life squashed everybody. The only thing I could count on was that I had no control over it, wouldn't survive its disappointments and it would squash me too.

It's not how Jack envisioned life when he was my age, with

a young boy's heart and mind. He freely admitted that. It's certainly not how he would have drawn it. But, it was real, especially when compared to all the unreal reasons people came up with to justify their own pointless existence.

Fortunately, even though what I did with life wasn't important, it didn't mean I had to sit back, mark my time and live without distinction.

What that meant was simple.

I should never pass up an opportunity to sleep with a woman who wanted to sleep with me. If I did, for any reason including war and famine, I would kick myself when I looked back and realized what I'd missed.

My Dad couldn't remember what he'd eaten for breakfast, but he could describe the eye color, hair style, complexion, weight within half a pound, height, cup size, cleanliness, stretch marks, ankles, knees, nail polish, jewelry, perfume, inclinations, hesitancies, left or right-handed, skirt length and tan line, be it natural or salon based, of every girl he let get away.

It didn't matter that I was not yet an adolescent, terrified of watching a girl walk from any angle and never dreamed of using the word love and batteries in the same sentence. Learning life's lessons at a young age would save me years of grief and frustration. I'd be able to focus on a single goal that would allow me to enjoy life before I too was squashed.

To illustrate this point he told me about an interview he'd heard on the radio with a world famous classical violinist. A Grammy award winner. I don't remember exactly what he won for. That wasn't the important part anyway. The important part was, during the interview the musician was asked if winning the Grammy was the highlight of his life.

Without hesitation he said no. It was wonderful and it was an honor. The highlight of his life, however, was when he lived with two playmates in Malibu, California. If he was tired, they did each other.

I wished I was older during these preliminary talks. I would have understood them better. Whenever my father saw the confusion in my eyes, as he did after telling me that story, he put women into a more familiar framework, something he was good at. I should think of them as Christmas presents. When I first see them they're all wrapped up prettily with ribbons and bows. I get excited even though I can't tell what's inside. I don't know if I'm going to find something I've been dreaming about, like a puppy, or something practical, like socks. Until I open them I appreciate them solely for what they are, thoughtful and precious. If it turns out to be socks there's no reason to be disappointed. When it's cold and they're the only thing keeping my feet warm I'll be grateful. If it turns out to be a puppy, as overjoyed as I might feel, I had to remember one thing. Over time there was a good chance I'd get tired of playing with it, feeding it and cleaning up its shit.

This was all subject to change, of course, if it involved three-inch heels, fishnet stockings or uniforms of any kind.

* * *

There would be problems.

On a minor level, I needed to learn to envision what every woman looked like without shoes. High heels were deceptive and not always indicative of a woman's true stature. Ideally, they'd parade around barefoot in front of me before I made a selection.

On a major level, while I grew and matured I'd encounter people who pretended the world did make sense.

They were threatened by someone who enjoyed life to its fullest. Who enjoyed life at all. They were usually solid, church-going home owners who had 2.2 children they couldn't live without and felt that finding your special someone was the sole barometer of a respectable existence. Single people were incomplete and needed to be pitied because they thought of sex as an all-you-can-eat smorgasbord instead of a joyless act of procreation.

Too much gratification was amoral and cause for suffering, their real Holy Grail.

These self-righteous fanatics also fell into two categories, neither group capable of appreciating the smell, taste, sound or touch of a woman. The first didn't know what it meant to live one day at a time, their next thousand weekends already booked. They were constantly in motion, moving away from aspirations they'd attained or toward ones they hadn't. There was always something more. Something better. Something else.

They even walked fast.

It didn't matter where they were going or if they even knew where they were headed. They were always in a hurry because they were afraid of being late.

The second group knew life had more to offer than obligations and expectations but, somewhere along the way, lost sight of what brought them pleasure and resented anyone who could masturbate away the fear of nuclear war or death of a loved one. They destroyed happy peoples' spirit in the name of virtue, keeping them disgruntled and doubting their values. When this happened I had to remember that a secure man doesn't give a shit about other people's morals. I lived in a free country. As long as I wasn't committing a crime no one's supposed to look over my shoulder and tell me who I can or cannot fuck. Otherwise, I might as well move to China to get laid.

Regardless of my location, no matter who I was with, I had to find an escape route; doors, windows and alleyways all acceptable. If my eyes were weak I had to buy contact lenses.

Never glasses. Glasses impeded peripheral vision and I could be blindsided.

I needed a nice car as well.

Looks and money were important. My father didn't deny that. At the same time, appearance was all about illusion, like magic. It's important to be good at whatever you do but it's just as important to look good while you're doing it. I could get away with a hell of a lot if I pulled up to

the curb in something impressive.

Every morning when Jack went to work he had a chance to score with any girl he saw. He'd screwed half the women in Lone Star Springs. Married and single. He wasn't bragging. He was just being honest and gave most of the credit to General fucking Motors.

"There are only two sure things in this world, Cadillacs and hookers."

"Elvis said that," he told me. "Elvis fucking Presley. If anybody knows about the world, it's him."

Hookers didn't concern me.

* * *

Jack freely admitted there were other things in life besides getting laid. He wasn't ignorant. The problem was, he'd never found anything but sex that allowed him to escape from the ordinary to the extraordinary.

Wait!

There were three sure things.

After Jack and I watched "The Exorcist" one night on TV, he told me that any woman possessed by the devil, who could make her head spin around, rise into the air and puke green vomit like pea soup, was a guaranteed great fuck.

Religion wasn't worth the time and effort it required. It

gave you some peace of mind, sure, and it had some catchy tunes, but it was little more than a distraction for people who couldn't cope with the fact that life was not a prelude to something better.

Education wasn't all it was cracked up to be either. Jack dropped out of high school to join the army and it never made a damned bit of difference. Just because people went to school more didn't mean they knew more.

It didn't teach you how to focus on mundane things, learn restraint or sell a vacuum. The smartest people he knew were educated by life, not in a classroom. In fact, the more you learned in school the more you realized what you didn't have and what you'd never be. Plus, every educated guy Jack knew was boring. I could ask any girl, socks or puppy, and she'd tell me the same thing.

It didn't even matter what profession I chose. Jack had drifted through enough jobs to assure me they were all as useless as education.

Sales included.

The only job a man had to concern himself with was keeping his spirits up. If he didn't, if he was driven to distraction, his family, the whole damned community around him would crumble.

During our drives home from Majestic Meadows my father lapsed into amusing anecdotes, considerably different than the ones at our kitchen table, to liven those spirits.

Aesop on steroids.

My favorite involved his father's dog, a large Husky named Rockefeller. When Jack was a teenager his dad was at work during the afternoon so Jack brought home a German waitress he'd met at the International House of Pancakes, with the biggest tits he'd ever seen. He was so excited he lost track of time till a strange sound snapped him back to reality. Thinking his father had come home and he'd been caught, he raised his head from between the girl's legs and looked around. His dad was nowhere in sight. Instead, Rockefeller was leaning over the foot of the bed, gagging. After the fourth retch he threw up the girl's underpants.

If we had an average evening, the anecdotes were entertaining but cautionary.

When Jack was young, he wanted to become an entertainer. He bought himself a dummy and a book about ventriloquism and taught himself how to throw his voice. He practiced five hours a day. By the time he'd perfected his skills his professional ambitions had waned. As a hobby, however, possibilities were endless. One night, while a girl was going down on him in the back seat of her mother's car, he threw his voice and had his penis recite the pledge of allegiance.

She fainted and had to be rushed to the emergency room. Aware of her deeply religious, moral and conservative upbringing, in spite of her sexual proclivities, when she came to my father convinced her he was only being patriotic.

If we had a disappointing night, stories were more philosophical.

He often longed for the times when he didn't have a realistic perspective of life and what it could do to you.

It wasn't necessarily the innocence of youth he was trying to recapture. It was a longing for the times he mistakenly thought he had control, could learn from lapses of judgement, correct them and move on to a future that was bright, promising and a long ways off. Not around the bend. When your future overlapped your present, it was just a few ticks of the clock before you became the past - and would never fulfill your childhood dreams.

This was how he knew he would die young.

It was also why getting laid was so important.

"The look in a woman's eyes when she likes you, the way she stares into your soul, sees your shattered dreams and fears and finds nothing objectionable, is a moment you will never forget, especially if you're going through tough times and feel like all is lost."

His face was radiant.

"Having someone believe in you, if only for ten minutes, makes it possible for you to believe in yourself."

In the White Rock Tavern or during enlightenment, my father rarely pulled his punches. Unlike his public brawls, these blows landed.

* * *

When we returned home from the square we'd find Vivienne curled up in the overstuffed gingham rocker where she did needlepoint. It faced the television which was always on, a reminder to watch her travel shows in case she lost track of time. I had no idea what they represented to her then, but I did know this. Head leaned back against the chair, she always had a little smile on her lips. And why not? After taking care of everyone else's needs on a daily basis this was the only place that guaranteed her own escape. She didn't just sit there. It was more like she, the chair and the TV merged into one.

The night my father defined the benefits of car ownership Vivienne was flipping through a cook book with photos of France when I wandered in, slow, deliberate steps as if I'd done something wrong.

"Is General fucking Motors in the army or the navy, momma?"

Laying her book down Vivienne stared at me in quiet disbelief for a good ten seconds before starting to giggle, infectious laughter she could not stop.

Encouraged by her response I proudly announced the rest of the night's revelations.

"There are only two sure things in the world."

Whatever laughter slipped out as I finished my thought had nothing to do with amusement. Loosening her hair Vivienne got down on all fours. When her knees touched the ground she told me I needed an adventure. She would fly me any place I wanted to go, anywhere in the world so I could see there was more to it than what Elvis believed. All I had to do was climb onto her back and we'd be gone.

She didn't have to ask twice.

"Okay now. Hold on. These takeoffs can be tricky."

I tightened my grip. "I don't know where I want to go yet," I said.

Looking back at me, Vivienne flashed the same smile she did when she lifted me out of the bassinet in the hospital.

"Someplace with honest home cooking."

Extending both arms at her side she began making airplane sounds.

"Here we go." She swayed to the left. "We're over the house now. Drifting into clouds. It could be a little bumpy. We've had some bad weather lately."

In a matter of seconds we were flying over the Esterel coastline. Marseille. A vineyard in Cotes de Provence. High above towns with cobblestone streets, red roofs, fields of joyful children and serpentine roads that led to enchanted castles.

"Look up at the stars, Henry. Always look up."

Ears pinned back, my hair rose and danced in the imaginary breeze as I floated free as a bird, experiencing the best France had to offer.

It was a welcome relief from the recurring nightmare I'd been having since my father's talks began. Even though I had bad dreams before, aliens from strange planets who tried to suck out my balls with juice-box straws, this was the first time I fell victim to predators from familiar surroundings.

In my dream I was walking up the road to our house after school. Instead of going inside the way I usually did, I turned right at the porch, ducked under a peach tree with a banner stretched across dead leaves that said "Happy Valentines Day," and entered our back yard. The moment I opened the gate I came face to face with everyone who'd ever made me uncomfortable. They were seated on stadium style bleachers cordoned off with orange safety cones and yellow police tape including my math teacher who was convinced I cheated on tests because I always got an A, the principal who knew I went to the nurse's office every time I didn't want to deal with my math teacher's accusations, my father's friends who punched me in the arm till it was black and blue, three heavily perfumed girls from Majestic Meadows. They moved with a swagger and taunted me because my father gave them low grades after watching them walk. Just hearing the grating sound of their voices made my skin crawl. I could see them laughing and grinding their teeth,like coyotes with retainers moving in for a kill, but I couldn't decipher what they were saying. They were speaking loudly too. That wasn't the problem. I don't know how to explain it other than their words were all garbled, like those people who talk real fast or backwards better than most of us speak normally. While the meaning confused me, the emotion behind their words did not.

Something horrible had happened.

I could feel it. I could even see it. Wind was up. Temperature was down. Clouds negated the light. Everyone was there to tell me why but I couldn't understand.

This was particularly disturbing because, although I'm not somebody who believes in dreams, my bad ones were like premonitions. Granted, my balls were never sucked out by aliens, but I did wake up one night in a cold sweat after dreaming our neighbor died. He stopped breathing the second I opened my eyes.

The following morning I awoke draped across my mother's lap, legs dangling off her side like a Lone Star Pieta.

Vivienne began to stir. She was stiff and had to stretch, limb by limb, to get the kinks and the chill of disappointment out of her bones. Before she could say good morning we heard a door slam upstairs followed by footsteps and whistling. Jack appeared after a moment, dressed to kill; white suit, blue shirt, striped tie and shoes with the usual glossy shine. He smiled, winked and said, "Hiya, sport. Don't have time to chat right now. Got an appointment that could make us a bundle. Look after your mother. Shot gun's in the closet."

Crossing to the door he plucked his jacket off the rack and left the house. As soon as she heard him start his car, rev the engine and drive off, Vivienne got back down on all fours and we waited for the wind to start up.

* * *

Every August 6th my father summoned me into the den, a room that became more of his sanctuary than an entertainment center. The moment I entered he'd close the door and draw the curtains, keeping light as dim as his prospects. It was the only time I ever saw his eyes look troubled and cloudy, although his voice remained clear.

"Tomorrow is my birthday, Henry. You know that, of course. What you don't know is, when you wake up in the morning I'll be dead."

The closer he got to his thirty-third birthday, the more he became convinced that life, as he knew it, was about to end. Now that I was a teenager, he was determined to use the few hours he had left to correct anything he'd told me that could be misconstrued, was foolish or just plain wrong, preventing me from making some of the same mistakes.

First and foremost, he didn't want me to worry or feel sad when he was gone. He'd be below ground, sure, but he'd be fine. He knew this because, after my mother died, Mike the child-hating neighbor told him something he'd been mulling over ever since.

My mom left this earth with a smile on her face, one of total repose, as if she knew a secret nobody else did and intended to lord it over them.

Initially this made no sense because, as far as Jack knew, Lillian hated her life, especially the last seven months, with a passion usually reserved for racists and Vegans. This meant only one thing. Something happened in those last few seconds, before she stopped breathing, that changed the way she looked at the world.

After due consideration Jack decided this:

God did exist. He was still a vindictive fuckhead. That hadn't changed. However, He had serious guilt issues which created a moral dilemma resembling a conscience. To alleviate any sense of wrong doing, He took pity on us humans during our last few seconds on Earth, trying to make up for our pathetic lives by divulging all the answers to all the questions to all the mysteries He had failed to reveal when we needed them most. Nothing involving solutions for premature ejaculation. As meaningful as that might be, this was Stonehenge type stuff. Extraterrestrials. The beginning of the universe. Anti matter. Consciousness. Granted, it was akin to a last call while you were rushing to catch a plane, and it was definitely the Readers Digest version, but the print was large and the message easy to decipher.

Assuming we hadn't done anything truly unforgivable to

someone during our lives, this knowledge gave us one true moment of peace, allowing us a smile of total repose before

shuffling off to Buffalo. Of course, it wasn't all altruistic. It was God's way of showing off, proving He was still top dog and could jerk us around at will, free or otherwise.

Even in death.

This made Jack realize that sex needed to involve more than worshipping the female form. With it came great responsibility. During those first few moments a man entered a woman she was as vulnerable as we were delighted. She'd say things, as a result, she wouldn't have under normal

circumstances. It would never be things like she watched too much TV, thought the world would be a better place if everyone tried synchronized swimming or "Mandy" was the greatest song ever written. No. That would be too easy. It was more like she used to give hand jobs in massage parlors and once blew her neighbor's Great Dane. Confessions she never shared with anyone else because, like a wish, once they were told they didn't do her or anyone else any good. My job was to listen and accept what was said. I could never ask questions or offer condolences. If I did, no matter how much I sympathized, she would eventually feel judged and wind up hating me for it.

A simple nod, from time to time, fulfilled whatever communication was necessary.

It was a relatively painless exchange as long as I thought of myself as a journalist who bears witness to crimes against humanity but wouldn't dream of getting involved.

Jack went on to explain that most women he met, like my mother, were lonely, unhappy and involved with men who rarely said anything more romantic than "Turn over" - the main reason he fared so well. Granted, he was like a musical prodigy when it came to mating, displaying talents you're either born with or you're not. It was the temporary relief he provided, however, more than those skills, that made him so attractive. He rescued women from the schools, jobs,

boyfriends, PTA meetings, athletic events, husbands, children, massage parlors and Great Danes they no longer coveted.

I didn't have to fall in love with them. That was beyond the call of duty. But, I did have to love them. It would give them a few moments' peace where they could talk intimately to someone other than salesgirls and believe in happy endings and they would do anything to show their appreciation - like the ugly girls in the square.

Sadly, love did not conquer all and this elevation of spirits was short lived. The woman would start resenting the fact she'd spoken without reservation or censorship, revealing her weakest points. This not only allowed me, but the entire world to see her as she really was, something she herself had probably been avoiding since birth. She would hate me for making her face that reality. It was far easier to turn on me, convinced her trust had been betrayed, her dignity violated. The moment she did she could rebuild her walls, fortifying them with all the emotional cement, mortar and carnage at her disposal, protecting her from the one fact she'd miraculously forgotten.

I was a man, like every other man, driven to misdeeds by an ugly, wrinkled, smelly dick.

This and this alone explained my lack of awareness, communication skills, feelings and intelligence which she, by nature of being a woman, had inherited along with an abundance of insight into the human condition, common sense, sensitivity and an appreciation for anything beautiful.

It was as if women were automatically placed in private schools for the gifted when they reached puberty while men, because of their limitations, were sent off to the jungle where they learned the only skills they were good for - how to make lanyards, wallets, lopsided ash trays and newspaper hats.

This attitude made it extremely difficult for a man to keep his own spirits up which, as I knew, was a necessity.

Although small consolation, being hated by a woman was the ultimate form of flattery. It meant she had put her faith in me, albeit for a short time, and was able to imagine a future she knew to be a pipe dream.

Oddly enough, Jack never mentioned his mother during our talks, although he once told me in a moment of melancholy that whenever he thought of her she was always dressed in red and turned away, her face hidden in shadows, her voice cold and dismissive. To this day I don't know her name, where she was born or much of the life that followed. If I asked about her he'd change the subject, telling me, instead, how important it was to look my best. When a man went for a job interview dressed in a smart suit and tie and another man went in jeans, the best-dressed man would always get hired. I didn't have to spend a fortune either. I could buy a couple of sports jackets, several different colored pants and shirts and I'd have outfits for any occasion.

"Mix and match."

That and Cadillacs were the only things I could count on.

This made me uncomfortable. Not so much what he was saying. While disturbing, I was used to his confessions. It was seeing my father at the mercy of his insecurities that scared me. I'd never seen him at the mercy of anything before except young women in short skirts.

If he'd downed a couple of beers before our talk he'd reminisce about a girl who could swallow an entire salami and the best way to seduce women who worked at The International House Of Pancakes. Sometimes he'd smile, lean back in his chair and ask what my favorite position was. What did I like done to me? What did I hate? Did any of the girls I knew have tattoos? He also wanted to know what the mothers of the prettiest girls looked like and if they wore pleated skirts and angora sweaters to school when they picked up their daughters.

Three beers and he'd lapse deeper into melancholy, wishing he'd spent his formative years doing instead of dreaming.

There's an old saying, "Nobody on their death bed wishes they'd spent more time at the office."

Not my Dad.

If he'd been as dedicated to work as he was to pussy, his life wouldn't have felt so unfinished. He could have left me a real inheritance. I would have been free to enjoy life without the constraints of a daily grind.

Four Budweisers and he'd describe, at great length, how he envisioned himself at ninety.

Five beers and his eyes would flood. He'd slow his speech down to a crawl, enunciating every syllable as if he was just learning how to use his mouth.

The talk was always the same.

"There's an old story about a man who was hit by an automobile. In terrible pain he refused to go to a hospital. Later they discovered why. He didn't wash his feet that day and was ashamed that the people who found him might see the filth. The analogy I make is, you never can tell when you'll be placed in a position where you might have to reveal what's under your clothing. Don't be caught with filth, even in your pockets. People would relate it to your mind and it's tough to live down."

The end of every talk involved a tearful recounting of the day I was conceived.

Carolyn had been thrown out of her parents' home and was staying with Lillian till she got her feet back on the ground. Lillian's house was small, two rooms, an alcove and a kitchen. When Jack came over he and my mom never got to spend time alone because Carolyn was too inexperienced to realize their need for privacy, always busting in on them unannounced. This particular afternoon, while Carolyn watched soap operas, Jack and Lillian snuck into the bathroom. They undressed, lay down on the cold tile floor and started groping one another. To make sure they couldn't be heard, Jack flushed the toilet whenever their passion reached operatic heights.

They stayed in the bathroom almost five hours.

Great sex became known as a four flusher. Three was good. Two or less was better than nothing but rushed.

This was contrary to anything I'd imagined my conception to be. My impression was a lot more poetic. It was something my parents did because they loved each other. The act itself was tender and beautiful and symbolic of that love. It had nothing to do with urinals.

That I was conceived during a four flusher was not a consolation.

When Jack finished his story, he crossed to my side, tussled my hair, pulled me toward him and told me Vivienne was a Saint. Times would change. Circumstances too. That never would.

While good for his soul there was one major drawback to these moribund confessions. He didn't die.

* * *

Every August 7th I'd be downstairs, anticipating the worst while I sat beside Vivienne in the needlepoint chair. We'd hear a door slam, footsteps, whistling and, in due time, a very dapper Jack would appear. He'd smile. He'd wink. He'd say what he always did on his way to work, pluck his jacket off the rack and leave the house as if our conversation was more fantasy than a passing of the guard.

Like my father's eyes, this period is troubling and cloudy. Whether it's my memory or just too painful is uncertain.

One thing I do remember.

Vivienne and I flew a great deal during that time. The Big Dipper would rush by in a blur of light. Flashes of water. Snippets of land. We'd fly till we couldn't keep our eyes open and when we awoke, side by side, we were safe.

With each passing year Jack's physical decline became more apparent, looking like someone who was perpetually jet-lagged instead of the movie stars of his youth. He lost weight. His finely toned muscles went soft as his virtue. His rosy tint became as off-white as the smile on his photo of George Best, his favorite athlete. He admired him because he was flashy, could talk trash and back it up - how he liked to think of himself. A sign over the picture said: "Maradona

good. Pela better. George Best."

Doctors might have identified Jack's problem if he had consulted one, but he shied away from the medical profession as faithfully as I avoided red heads.

I remember the night before his thirty-third birthday the most.

"There's a guy who gets propositioned by women wherever he goes."

This was different than the way his talks usually began and his voice cracked every few sentences, as if he too was on the verge of manhood.

"Let's say it happened a hundred times over the past year. Just to keep it a round number. Because he knew it upset the woman he was married to, even though it went against everything he believed in, he only slept with ten of those women. That means he actually cheated ten percent of the time.

His wife wasn't nearly as attractive. She'd gained so much weight nobody in their right mind would go to bed with her.

Who wants to sleep with a woman the size of a Cadillac and weighs more than most families put together, if you know what I'm saying?"

I didn't.

"She never got a hundred offers. She just got one. And you know what? She cheated with that person. So, she's actually guilty of cheating one hundred percent of the time. Who's worse? That's all I want you to think about when I'm gone. Who the hell is worse between the two, especially if that woman cheated with another God-damned woman?"

Unable to speak I stared straight ahead, allowing a deathly silence into the room. The lull rejuvenated Jack. His eyes began to sparkle and he smiled a triumphant, lopsided grin.

"The best first date a man can have, son, is when you take a girl out to dinner and she tells you not to order anything with garlic and onions."

Even if I wasn't naive beyond my years there was no way I could have foreseen his reasoning.

"They make your sperm taste funny."

Afterwards I went downstairs and found Vivienne in her beloved chair, watching a lion stalk its lunch.

"Is Dad really going to die?" It was the question I'd been repeating every August

seventh for six long years.

"We all die," she said, her face drawn with unhappiness as the lion seized a wildebeest by the jugular.

"Some of us just choose to do it while we're still alive."

Up until the year before, Vivienne happily complied with Jack's every whim. When he was too weak to get out of bed she would sit beside him for hours, content to do whatever was necessary to make his illness bearable.

Abandoning her cook books she went back to her medical journals. Using all the expertise at her disposal she reassured him that, no matter what was wrong, modern medicine was making remarkable strides. Cures were on the horizon.

Jack knew better.

Initially, his pessimism made Vivienne feel strangely blessed, as if she and she alone had the power to save him; a strength rising from deep inside her that could not be denied. They would get through this. The two of them. Together. Unfortunately, Jack's reluctance to fight for his

life eventually wore her down and her fantasies collapsed. Without illusion it was the one thing she found unconscionable after fighting for her preemies on a daily basis. Worse, it made her feel heartless and she hated him more for that than his resignation.

She stopped looking up at the stars, the primary source of light in her life; a glow that could only come from a supportive, joyous sky.

She also stopped seeing the dapper, well-dressed man who trotted down the stairs each morning on his way to work. Instead she focused on the jacket waiting to be plucked off its rack. How the elbows were wearing thin. The collar beginning to fray. The dozens of Cuban cigar burns.

She put on a brave face for the neighbors. She talked about how she and Jack had patched up their differences and rekindled their love, but they could all see she was visibly unhappy. The once plush cashmere sweater that symbolized the beginning of a loving relationship had become an unwitting metaphor for its end, fraying around the collar, ratty, moth-eaten and covered with lint. Worse, she spoke of Jack in the past tense as if he'd been dead for years.

I blame this on Vivienne's conflicting emotions. Till the day she died she couldn't figure out why love seemed like a life saver before you had it and a suicide watch after the fact - wishing for eternal happiness and waking up with MS.

The morning of Jack's thirty-third I listened to the rise and fall of Vivienne's chest as we waited for the sound of his door to open. When none came Vivienne went upstairs and I sat in her chair.

It wasn't long before I heard a door slam but only Vivienne descended the steps. Her forehead was knotted. Her eyes were red and narrow. Her mouth drawn tight.

"Momma?"

Ignoring me for the first time since I was born, Vivienne walked to the hall closet and removed the Browning A-5 shot gun from underneath a pile of linen.

"Are you okay?"

She walked out the front door without a backwards glance, Jack's jacket left behind like a dismembered body on the battlefield. When she reached the Aztec red Cadillac Brougham she slid behind the wheel, adjusted the red cloth and leather seat that smelled of tobacco and cheap perfume, gunned the engine and backed down the driveway. As Vivienne barreled through the stop sign at the first intersection, she began to whistle.

I, meanwhile, stared into Jack's closet; rows of perfectly creased suits, pants and shirts, most handmade, hanging above dozens of Italian shoes that were polished, arranged according to color and cost more than some condominiums. A wooden valet displayed the valuables he carried in those suit pockets. A gold money clip. A solid gold wristwatch made in Switzerland. A few cigars and a silver utensil, to snip the ends, with the initials D.R. On top of a bureau to its right were grooming paraphernalia. Ascending according to size were three Maison Pearson, 100%

boar bristle brushes with tortoise-shell handles. Beside them were Kent combs, also tortoise, a dressing-table comb, a large handled rake comb and one that folded and could fit in his pocket. Out of everything these probably meant the most to him. I bring this up because of what happened next.

Crossing to my father's bed I looked down. He was cold and gray, his forehead calm, his jaw relaxed into the biggest smile I'd seen in as long as I could remember.

One of total repose.

In spite of everything it made me smile too, wondering what mysteries had been revealed to him.

I kissed his forehead gently before doing something I never had the nerve to do during his life. I touched his hair. The widow's peak. I was on the verge of tears for the first time in my life when I was overcome by an impulse I could not control. Running my hand through his hair I messed it up till it looked like the before picture in one of those old Brylcream grooming ads.

"Death, a little dab'll do you."

When I finished I desperately wanted to say a proper good-bye, something that would let him know how much I cared. Though it was impossible to find an appropriate response, I finally settled on the three words I knew meant the world to him.

"Mix and match."

Hunched over the wheel Vivienne drove north, using the same route Jack used every Monday, Wednesday and Friday night. Houses sped by. Traffic became congested, lightened and congested again. She passed the McDonalds where Jack stopped for coffee. She turned left down the alley he used to avoid the busiest intersection. She made the right he used to get back onto the main thoroughfare. When the road opened up and she approached the White Rock Tavern, she pushed the accelerator all the way to the floor. Jumping the curb with a harsh, scraping noise, she braked hard, fish tailed and stopped in the middle of their parking lot next to a giant wagon wheel.

Through darkened windows she caught a glimpse of the bandstand and chairs upended on tables cluttered with empty pitchers of beer. Garlands of party lights hung down above them, none lit because the celebrations, whether birthdays or holidays, had long been forgotten. Walls were inundated with black and white framed photos of couples considered regulars, my dad in at least a dozen, each with a different woman.

When she stepped out Vivienne was holding the shotgun by its barrel. Crossing to the front of the Cadillac she raised the hood, took a step back and wedged the wooden stock into her shoulder.

She fired twice.

Steam shot into the air like Old Faithful. The engine stuttered, missed and quit.

General fucking Motors was dead.

* * *

"We will Galvanize Your Thoughts."

From what I read in the papers, this was pinned over the door to General Ethan Parks anger-management class at the Huntsville prison hospital.

During their first meeting Doctor Mark Coonan, Ethan's counsellor, told the dozen men gathered that anger was an immature, uncivilized response to frustration, threat, violation or loss, representative of primitive behavior. Conversely, staying calm, being cool-headed or turning the

other cheek was a more humane, socially acceptable form of behavior they would have to exhibit if they were ever going to return to society.

Ethan disagreed.

Keeping everything bottled up was unhealthy and, in his experience both on and off the battlefield, led to far more violent actions than simply blowing off a little steam when it was called for. Besides, there were situations where turning the other cheek, avoiding conflict, was the cowardly thing to do.

Anything involving children or family members, for example.

Doctor Coonan listened politely, smiled and promised to discuss it further before the end of class.

* * *

Oppressive summer heat came early and Lone Star Springs was at a standstill the day of my father's funeral. In the time it took Vivienne and me to walk outside and cross to our car we both needed another shower. Relief only came, ironically, when we reached the Memorial Park. It had the most shade and was the sole plot of land in the area that wasn't parched and dry. As Vivienne and I passed a small pond adjacent to Jack's grave, Koi swam up, poked their heads out and begged for food. I could even hear the low rumble of trains headed for Oklahoma, an auditory pleasure my father rarely allowed himself before fading into eternal abstinence.

I stayed close to Vivienne during the service, but my attention strayed to the parade of women, arriving in droves, dressed the same to mourn as they did to tease. There were waitresses, beauticians like my original mother, bank tellers, salesgirls, dental assistants, secretaries, career

counsellors and travel agents - professions no longer important for at least one afternoon. Some were thin. Some fat. Some tall. Some short. A couple were pregnant. One was changing out of a tennis dress into a black knit pullover.

They drove Chevys and Fords.

Only a handful of men were in sight. All wore plain, dark

suits they'd wear to their own funerals and string ties with Lapiz clasps that held it and them together.

Because of the weather most of the women's outfits were drenched and their hair stuck to the sides of their faces. Nothing dampened their spirits, however. Although many were sad, it was more like a bon voyage party on the Queen Mary than a life-ending send off.

Vivienne was clearly unsettled by their presence, looking like she was going to faint. I, on the other hand, found it reassuring. In this world there are few enough people who care about what happens to you, truly care, and are loyal to the very end. Jack was obviously loved. He'd be sorely missed. Was there a greater tribute than a former lover's grief? The answer was an emphatic no. Funerals were a reward, I decided, for people whose life was cut short or had gone awry. They're a reward for everybody, come to think of it. It's one of the few venues where everything takes place according to plan. Nobody's on bad behavior. People don't hide their emotions and care about others. If we all went to funerals every day the world would be a kinder place. I believed that with all my heart and, unlike those around me who were fighting back tears, I struggled to keep the smirk off my face.

Everyone needs to be remembered.

I realize now that Vivienne's discomfort had little to do with Jack's entourage. It was annoying that he'd slept with half the eligible women in town, including a few widows who weren't, but Vivienne had suspected it. It was more a relief than a burden to have those suspicions confirmed.

"Wile E. Coyote has a better chance of changing his habits than your father." She'd said that dozens of times, under her breath, when he ogled every woman they passed, although she tried not to notice and believed it meant nothing.

No, it was the ramifications of his infidelities, not the act itself, that gave her a fluttery, sick feeling.

From a very young age Vivienne approached living as a simple, never-ending process. You're faced with different choices during various stages of your life. In order to decide which is best, you sort through whatever information is available, much like doctors sort through medical records. They select what's relevant. They make a diagnosis. They decide on the appropriate course of action and do it, hoping the end results are in their patients' favor.

Afterwards they move on, like contestants in the quiz shows that came before Vivienne's travel programs. With quiz shows, however, you couldn't progress to the next level, the more difficult questions, till you'd solved the easy ones.

Life had no such safeguards.

You advanced no matter what. Fortunately, the simple questions, the ones that determined your fate, usually occurred early on when a wrong answer was less likely.

With quiz shows this could be credited to their sponsors. In real life Vivienne attributed it to divine intervention.

"If you put your trust in God, if you thanked Him for all the blessings you've received and the ones still to come, you realized there were no coincidences or mistakes. You're exactly where He wants you to be."

This is what bothered Vivienne as she stared into Jack's open grave. Her first, life-altering question came after the talk with her mother when she was six. Her reaction to it, her contempt for her mom's all encompassing fury had determined not only Vivienne's adolescence but her entire adulthood.

All those years she'd fought against everything her mother became, raged against it as her mother raged against male injustice and the Post Office.

Only now did Vivienne realize the abysmal truth.

Philosophically she didn't exist. Everything she'd thought and done had been for naught.

Her mother was right.

"All men, regardless of age, size, shape or color, were immoral pieces of shit."

Worse, God was a devious Asshole and couldn't be trusted.

* * *

As we began the long walk from the grave back to the parking lot some of the mourners reminisced about Jack when he was my age. Enormously talented he was the town's one shining star, a hard working, sensitive boy with a promising future. Since this was a side of my father I'd never known or even considered in my fifteen years, I listened carefully.

They blamed my grandfather, Dwight, for Jack's reversal of fortune.

The product of an impoverished Lithuanian upbringing, Dwight had the deep-set eyes and no-nonsense face of a back room politician. He rarely smiled and even his oldest associates addressed him as Mister, like you do with your parents' friends when you're a kid.

Starting life with humble beginnings, Dwight had nothing but wound up with everything. He got there by championing working-class values and didn't have patience for anyone who failed to share his level of commitment, took short cuts or compromised. This included people who required spiritual assistance to get through the day. Dwight didn't have anything against Gods per se, be they primitive, traditional or modern. In his own mind he was a God-fearing man although

not a churchgoer. It was how people used their Supreme Beings that got under his skin, relying on them to accomplish tasks they should be performing themselves.

Funny anecdotes violated his tenets as well. Life was hard and anything said should reflect the daily suffering necessary to get through it. This meant that sense came before sentiment, dedication before humor and there was no need for pretentiousness or exaggeration.

His dour attitude carried over to fiction, art, theater and music. They were nothing more than the product of imagination, defied analysis and only existed because the deluded cocktail party set, who were more concerned with leisure than labor, wasted money subsidizing them.

This explained Dwight's contempt for Jack who'd decided to become an artist instead of taking over the family tannery which also processed deer into sausage.

Turning his back on a lucrative and established way of making a living was not only foolhardy, it was a reflection on Dwight, as if he'd raised Jack without values; akin to someone reaching inside Dwight's chest and ripping his heart out like in those karate movies.

The day Dwight realized Jack had no intention of heeding his advice he invited a dozen of his most loyal employees to his house for lunch. After dessert Jack went upstairs to fetch Dwight a cigar, as he always did, clipping the end with a silver utensil Dwight kept in the humidor filled with Cohibas, his main indulgence. When Jack returned to the table and handed it to his father, rather than thank him or light his cigar, Dwight made a statement intended to stoke his son's ambition, although it was addressed to everyone.

"It's time to stop dreaming and ask yourself a question, Jack. Where will you be in ten years? Right now you're at the perfect age. Old enough to figure out what you want. Young enough not to care how much work it takes to get there. Anything's possible. But, if you keep living day to day, if you continue dressing as if you were homeless, you'll wind up looking back on a life filled with missed opportunities."

Jack appeared feverish.

"Take all your drawings, put them in a box in the back of some attic and forget about them. Even if you had talent, and that's a big if, it's not special enough so you can count on making a living. Certainly not one you'd be proud of."

"Mister..."

The shop foreman leaned forward in Jack's defense but Dwight shot him a look before he could complete his name. By the time Dwight turned away the man had folded his hands in his lap, brought his knees together and didn't move, as if confined to a wheel chair.

"I am ready to start a normal, productive life like these hard working, sensible men..."

Dwight gestured around him.

"...or I'll never amount to anything."

"Why do you have to embarrass me in front of your friends?" asked Jack.

"I don't have to do anything. You do a damned good job of that yourself."

Jack remained silent while Dwight lit his cigar, puffed deeply and squinted as the smoke curled into his eyes.

"I am nothing," Dwight went on.

Excusing himself, Jack rose and started to leave, both arms dangling awkwardly by his side like a rag doll.

"Say the words, son."

Staring at the floor, Jack walked toward the door with a sense of helplessness he hated more than anything else.

"If you do nothing long enough, one day that's all you'll deserve."

A month later, with a new foreman, Dwight invited the same group back. When dessert was finished he tapped his water glass, rose and spoke with a sense of urgency. He had no intention of letting his son waste another day, listening to him tell everyone he was an artist when wasn't making a living at it. Fantasy would no longer be tolerated. If Dwight continued to sit back and do nothing it was tantamount to consent. This was Jack's last chance to work with him, side by side, and make something of himself. If he refused, he would have to move out immediately.

Raising his nose slightly, like the lion before it charged the wildebeest, Dwight nodded to his new foreman who stood and spoke with a sentiment that was less than heartfelt, as if he was in front of a senate sub-committee.

"A tanned skin is all about potential and unlimited possibilities. Be it deer, elk or bison, they can be made into jackets, vests, shirts, chaps, shoes, gloves, travel bags, purses and furniture. As long as these things are in demand, and they always will be, the tannery will thrive. The same with hunters and deer. Paintings and drawings, on the other hand, are a dead end. They have no possibilities. They don't benefit anyone and serve no function other than taking up wall space."

When he sat back down Jack looked at his Dad.

"Things will work out."

"What if they don't?"

"I can't think like that."

Dwight gave a nervous little laugh.

"There you go embarrassing yourself again."

His voice sounded harsh and condescending, as it always did when he spoke to Jack, but Dwight wasn't really a bad man. His never-ending fight against imagination was based on his desire for Jack to experience the exhilaration that accompanied success. He knew there was no stability or longevity with artistic endeavors. What was good for one person was shit for another. Money, property, elegant suits and expensive Italian shoes, on the other hand, were right there in front of your eyes and could be relied on.

Dwight also knew what it meant to struggle, to be unable to put food on the table and freeze in winter because you couldn't afford heat. His own father, an immigrant desperate to provide for his family, took a job scabbing when they arrived in this country, driving delivery trucks even though union members were yanking drivers out of their cabs. At the end of his first month, on his way to a warehouse with a load of Tupperware, his truck was surrounded by a half dozen men who beat him to death with Louisville Sluggers.

From that day on Dwight discovered only hard work could chase the awful memories away. He vowed never to join a union, keep food past its expiration date or watch another base-ball game and would do everything he could to encourage others to follow suit. In the tannery he paid his men double minimum wage, raised safety levels, provided non-deductible health insurance, stock options, pensions, never missed a Christmas bonus and bailed them out of jail personally after Saturday night brawls in strip clubs and bars.

Every year a trade union tried to infiltrate his business and were voted down with a resounding "fuck you."

As difficult as a life of struggle would be for Jack, it would be twice as difficult for Dwight to watch - knowing full well how difficult it was to rise above poverty once it had you in its clutches.

Assuming Jack wouldn't dare oppose him, Dwight told him to run upstairs and fetch two cigars in celebration. Jack started toward the hall but stopped abruptly, as if he'd walked into a wall. When he turned, his helplessness had disappeared and there was no anger or fear in his heart. For

some unknown reason he was finally able to stand up to his father and this was the moment fate had chosen.

"No matter what's gone on here today, no matter what you think of me, Dad, you're entitled to your opinion. That's the great thing about opinions. You and I can think completely different about something and neither one of us is wrong. I don't even mind being wrong, to tell you the truth, because at least we're talking. That's progress and all I ever wanted from you. The problem is, you want to win."

Dwight howled with laughter this time, as if Jack said the funniest thing he'd ever heard. "Don't be ridiculous, son."

His face glowed with triumph.

"I won years ago."

* * *

When Jack joined the army a few days later, he phoned Dwight often. As soon as Dwight heard his voice he'd ask who was calling and hang up as soon as his son identified himself.

There were fleeting moments when Dwight was proud of Jack for following his heart. The kid had guts. That surprised him. He almost called Jack back dozens of times, usually late at night when he was alone at the factory and uncomfortable with the empty work stations and lack of

activity. At moments like these his love for his son over-ruled his disappointment. He almost invited him to a tannery picnic celebrating ten years of non-union bliss. He almost dropped in, unannounced, on one of Jack's birthdays but became outraged and turned his car around when he passed an art gallery that had gone out of business and was boarded up.

As the years passed Dwight continued to blame himself for failing to instill the proper work ethic in his son and was tormented because of it. He never invited anyone else over for lunch. He never smiled or laughed or did anything but work. He never spoke with Jack again either, not even when he was dying of emphysema and lung cancer caused, Jack later assumed with a trace of childish dread, by the cigars he brought him throughout his adolescence.

* * *

As was tradition, women who came back to Vivienne's to pay their respects brought food. Cold cuts. Casseroles. Store-bought cookies, brownies and prize-winning crumbles.

When they arrived all conversation ceased. The dining table was filled with delicacies they'd never seen before, the culmination of hundreds of fantasy flights across the Atlantic. Poulet Basquaise. Petit sale de Canard le Petit Marguery. Terrine de Lapin aux Noisettes. Gratin Auvergnat. Ravioles a la Creme du Laurier et de la Sauge. Quatre-Quarts aux Poires. Tarte aux Fromage Blanc Ferme D'Alsace. Tarte aux Framboises. Tarte aux Figues. Tarte aux Pruneaux et

saux Amandes and, last but foremost, Flan a le Fraise.

A far cry from the meat and potatoes they were accustomed to, it made Vivienne's guests uncomfortable. She, of course, encouraged everyone to taste what she'd prepared.

"At a time like this it's important to keep your strength up."

She especially urged anyone she thought needed their spirits raised, repeating one word as if it were a mantra.

"Mangez."

It didn't matter that they'd never tasted anything that good. There was nothing on earth, and possibly beyond, that could make these small-town folks sample Vivienne's worldly cuisine - relating to platters as if they were collection plates at Sunday mass.

Only Peggy ate, having stood by Vivienne throughout the memorial service as Vivienne had stood by her years ago.

Innocence and youthful naivete can last a lifetime or vanish like the magician's assistants I used to see with my Dad. In Peggy's case her allure disappeared, rendering her indistinguishable from other patrons in the bar where Jack first laid eyes on her.

At best someone would say "she must have been pretty when she was young," not realizing she still was.

Her skin, so thin and frail, was almost transparent. The once beautiful face now showed only humiliation and pain. Betrayal tugged at her mouth and eyes. Her flowing blonde curls were cut short, uneven and completely white, like the minister's face before he drank. This was not from age. As with Peggy's spirit, it had simply lost its verve.

Her well-curved legs, the one asset still to be admired, were hidden behind a shapeless, free-flowing dress that prevented the briefest glimpse. Even her arms were concealed by layers of material that cinched at the wrist.

It was like visiting the hospice wing at Florence Nightingale.

Years later I found a photograph of Peggy taken that day. At first I thought it was from another era, possibly even a negative since she appeared so washed out. The more I studied it, the more I wondered if she ever yearned for the times she carried her head high. When every step was exalted. When she threw caution to the wind and shouted "fuck you" at life's indignities instead of succumbing and wasting her extraordinary gifts.

This was why she scared me.

As limited as my experience was at fifteen, as little as I understood, I knew Peggy was damaged goods, always would be and something I didn't want to become.

Throughout the afternoon Vivienne was the perfect hostess but she spent most of her time worrying about Peggy's discomfort in social situations. It wasn't helped by the fact that the other guests were as afraid of her as I was, what she was capable of at the very least.

This was the real reason Vivienne had prepared so long and hard and the party had an air of festivity. She wanted to fatten Peggy up, like a Christmas goose, and show her life wasn't lost or irreparable.

Vivienne was also relieved. When she and Jack first married she assumed she would die if anything happened to him. Now, she was grateful she didn't have to.

This explained the unconventional decorations for such a solemn event, pink roses, daisies and lilies surrounded by bright-colored balloons anchored to the feet of every table and chair.

While Vivienne ladled one spoonful after another onto Peggy's plate the two women giggled like teenagers who'd snuck out of their parents' home to toilet paper a neighbor's yard. They were more like a couple than friends, carelessly brushing against one another, touching each other's shoulders or upper arms - fleeting glances that bordered on amorous, as if they'd been separated the way Vivienne and my father were during sales trips. They'd look at each other with a sort of pleased surprise and then, because something struck them as funny, burst out laughing. It wasn't anything they could share because the joke was always private.

To be fair, they complemented each other perfectly. Peggy was all about feelings. Vivienne was all about restraint.

No one acted as if they noticed but everyone did and it made them almost as uncomfortable as the food. They maintained a constant patter in defense, the ungodly heat, new trucks, riding mowers and their beloved Dallas Cowboys.

Through it all Vivienne made sure Peggy ate everything in front of her. She didn't have to like or appreciate it. She just had to swallow. The problem was, Peggy drank more than she digested and she drank fast. Like a man. Having drained her glass for the seventh time she started for the kitchen.

"Where are you going?" asked Vivienne.

"I need another drink."

"You've already had another."

Raising both hands in front of her mouth to feign shock, Peggy made a face.

"Well then, I guess I'm going for the fucking record."

I had one of my first insights into people that day. Some were good at sports. Some were smart and got straight A's in school. Some were computer whizzes. Some were good at drinking.

Peggy grew up feeling like she'd been cheated out of the happiness normal people experienced and could never find anything to take its place - till alcohol. Although she hated its smell on her father's breath when she was younger, it gave her the energy to get through the day when she became an adult. It let her smile and laugh and pretend she was like everyone else, even though she knew it was only make-believe.

When Peggy dreamed, I imagined it was about tables filled with unlimited Boilermakers, Dirty Mothers, Sidecars, Stingers, Gin Fizzes, Lime Rickeys, Long Island Ice Teas, Cuba Libres, Hurricanes, Tequila Sunrises, Slammer Royales, Bloody Marys, Screw Drivers, Mint Juleps, Man O' Wars, Whiskey Sours, Spritzers, Moonwalks, Black Russians, Creamsicles, Rob Roys, Manhattans and Pink Ladies - all made with the finest liquors and ingredients, all waiting happily for her, celebrating the feeling they provided as they slid down her appreciative throat.

Vivienne was constantly pleading with Peggy to get some help but she refused, insisting that sobriety, like happiness, was overrated and subjective. She wasn't going to wake up one morning, throw open the door to thunderous applause and tap dance into a field of blue bonnets singing "My Favorite Things." She would never be like other people. The smiles and laughter were a temporary relief at best, like putting band aids on cancer. Her life was about pain, which had no expiration date or statute of limitations, and would eventually reach a level she could not bear. When that happened she expected to be put out of her misery like a dog with dysplasia.

Peggy's first step toward the kitchen was wobbly so she had to brace herself against a cupboard. As she prepared for the next step a man to her right, offering a helping hand, placed his drink on top of a book Peggy had been reading and left next to the onion dip.

"What the fuck's wrong with you?"

Retrieving his drink, she wiped the bottom of the glass with her sleeve before handing it back.

"You don't just walk up to someone and offer assistance. This isn't the fucking Peace Corps."

She jabbed an accusatory finger in his face.

"Is that how you got the scar on your lip?"

"What scar?" he asked, unconsciously loosening his tie with his free hand.

Peggy hit him with a quick, hard right and his glass went flying. As ice cubes rattled across the floor like dice, Peggy climbed on the table and started to dance.

Some tried coaxing her down. Others pointed and whispered. Most dispersed quickly, this way and that, like the old drawing-room comedies where people run in and out of doors, barely missing each other.

Peggy didn't care.

Like Lillian and me before her, she threw her head back, opened her mouth wide and howled.

"I'm free."

As the adults around her began to fade and change into

giggling children playing Blind Man's Bluff, Peggy started twirling like some of the rides at the State Fair that made her dizzy when she was a kid. The Tilt-A-Whirl. The Whip. Spinning tea cups. Around and around. After a dozen turns she lost her balance and toppled, face first, into the Flan au fraise, striking her head on the hard oak table underneath.

Long after Vivienne had gone to bed I sat in the needle-point chair which always gave me comfort. I didn't move. I hardly breathed. I felt more numb than anything else. As the house creaked and moaned in the wind I stared at Jack's jacket, hanging forlornly on its rack.

Life's disappointments, before you're squashed, were worse than he'd led me to believe.

I may have hated some of the things my father did, he may have been irreverent and unruly, but he was my one guiding light and that light was now extinguished.

I wanted to cry. For him. For me. For all the women out there who'd experienced loss. I wanted to cry but I couldn't, as if I was born without the crying gene. Truth be told, it was a sadness too deep for tears and if I allowed myself to feel what I was thinking I too would have perished.

Jack lied.

I needed him and he wasn't there.

I was mortal again.

A bottomless sorrow forced its way out in a high pitched, whiny voice like a toddler.

"My daddy is dead!"

I could feel my childhood disappearing faster than Peggy's allure.

About that time I heard what I thought were children playing upstairs, although it took only a moment to realize my mistake. It was Vivienne and Peggy laughing as if the party was still going on. Either they'd forgotten to close the door or thought it was too late for me to be awake. As I

listened, hoping for a hint of melancholy, blood rushed to my face and the room started to swim.

Before I knew it I was above the house and rising, flying over towns with cobblestone streets, red roofs, fields with joyful children and fairy-tale castles.

Although my mind was floating free as a bird, my heart was miles away from imagining.

* * *

I awoke the next morning when I heard a door slam and foot-steps. Bolting straight up my heart skipped a beat as I turned toward the stairs. It didn't restart till Peggy appeared on the landing, holding onto the banister to stop her from falling. Wearing Jack's blue, terry cloth robe, she

descended as if each step was her last, clutching a bruise on her forehead and grimacing whenever she heard the clomp of her shoes strike the old wooden risers.

"I know what you're thinking," she said playfully. "How does she manage to look so good so early?"

She barely had enough strength to cross the room, bend down and kiss the crown of my head.

"The illusion of beauty requires the greatest effort of all."

Her hand was trembling as she massaged her temples, stumbled toward the kitchen and nudged the door open with her shoulder. As I watched her shuffle toward the pot of coffee Vivienne brewed before going to bed, I noticed a small trickle of blood trailing behind her like muddy footprints.

"You don't like me much, do you?" She spoke without turning around.

"No" I said. "Not much."

Coffee cup in hand she faced me and I could see she was smiling.

"That's okay. You'll change your mind once you get to know me. That's what I should say. The thing is, it isn't true. I'm a major pain-in-the-ass. To be perfectly honest, I don't like me much either."

Another door slammed.

"Henry."

Vivienne was drawing the curtains in the den when I found her.

"They've actually done studies about light and women's feelings. Did you know that?"

I shook my head.

"If a woman doesn't get enough natural light every day it has a direct effect on her mood. It even has a name. Seasonal Affected Disorder. S.A.D. Isn't that perfect? Peggy knows everything about stuff like that."

She tied the curtains back.

"Women in Sweden, one of the most beautiful countries there is, are unhappier than women right here in Lone Star Springs because they don't get enough light during the winter months."

I wasn't sure what she wanted me to say, like the man Peggy hit, so I said nothing.

"I don't know if boys can get that, but winters are long here too so there's a good possibility. I made an appointment for us with Doctor Miller on the 26th."

Reaching underneath the desk she removed a large rectangular box and handed it to me.

"I want you to use this ultraviolet lamp every night before you go to bed. I pinned the instructions on the refrigerator."

Although she wouldn't admit it, Vivienne had inherited my father's fear of crippling disease. Unlike my Dad, those fears were for me, not herself. Whereas my father expected the worst and was resolved to his fate, Vivienne expected the worst but was determined to prevent it from happening. As a result she made sure I knew the quickest way out of the house in case of emergency. A ladder was outside my window so I could climb down during a fire. An iron cover was secured next to the bathtub in case of tornadoes.

Sitting across from me she leaned forward and pushed a hair behind my ear before resting all her weight on both elbows.

"Do you know the difference between being in love when you're young and being in love when you're older, Henry?"

I didn't. I knew little about love. At any age.

"When you're young, love is all about feeling a way you've never felt before. It puts a smile on your face. It makes you feel warm inside. Pretty. Tender. Safe."

Her eyes began to water.

"When you're older love is about wanting someone else to feel those things 'cause you know you're not capable any more."

Footsteps interrupted anything else she had to say.

"There must be something wrong."

Shovelling a handful of Aspirin into her mouth as if they were candy, Peggy entered and leaned against the door.

"I barely drank two bottles of wine last night. It usually takes three for me to turn a bunch of crying mourners into a lynch mob."

Her legs began to wobble.

"What's today?"

"Thursday."

"The date, I mean."

"September 2nd."

Peggy's face lit up before she turned and limped back into the hall.

"Where are you going?" Vivienne asked the moment she

disappeared.

"It's almost Vietnamese Independence Day. I have to make Bloody Marys."

"Peggy!"

"Everybody says I can't do anything right so no use doing it half-assed. I've got a fucking reputation to protect."

This was followed by a loud crash.

"I didn't fall. I threw myself down."

It was like having a child of our own.

Six months later I walked alongside Vivienne while Peggy carried their suitcases to a waiting cab.

They were going to France for ten days, using money left over from Peggy's inheritance. It was the first time Vivienne had ventured away from home and she was as unsteady as Peggy after her loss to the dining-room table.

On one hand, this was the dream of a lifetime. On the other she was terrified I would come down with twenty-four hour polio while she was away.

Peggy was also anxious.

Although France was a cultured place where literature was king, it was also one of the last European countries to grant women the right to vote and let them hold office. From what she'd read, French men treated women like prostitutes and it never occurred to them that a beautiful woman could have a vagina and a brain at the same time.

It reminded her of one of Vivienne's travel shows about Pakistan.

Pakistani men believed that if their cow died it was a tragedy but if their wife died they could always get another.

Both women eventually relaxed.

Peggy convinced Vivienne it would be good for me to be on my own for a couple of weeks. I would learn to appreciate what she did for me on a daily basis.

Vivienne convinced Peggy that France wasn't that different than being around the men and politics of Texas.

While Peggy loaded their bags into the trunk Vivienne laid her head against my chest, the way a child might, closed her eyes and wrapped her arms around me as if her life depended on never letting go. She'd made a list of emergency numbers and stuck them on the refrigerator next to the

instructions for the ultraviolet lamp. She put photos of the two of us beside that so I wouldn't forget what she looked like. There was a fresh tub of strawberry ice cream in the freezer. She'd even made a list of the best travel shows that were coming up, including a repeat of the Bactrian

camels, her all-time favorite.

"Your father would have lived if he really needed me."

In the cab, Peggy rolled down her window and leaned out.

"We're gonna be late."

"In a minute."

"If we don't get to the airport in time to drink I'll make a fucking scene and you know what a bitch I can be, with a capital B"

Placing both hands on her hips, Vivienne scrunched up her nose like a petulant child.

"I need to talk here."

"I don't give a shit."

"Well, you should."

"Cunt."

It was the word Vivienne hated the most.

"Don't say that!"

"Blow me."

Peggy's eyes sparkled with mischief.

"I'm just practicing being a bitch."

Turning back toward me the lines under Vivienne's mouth deepened.

"Life doesn't always work out the way you thought it would."

She squeezed my arm just like she did when my Dad stayed out all night. Then she gave me a lingering kiss on the cheek, wiping off lipstick with the heel of her palm before making a mad dash to the cab.

The moment the door slammed shut the taxi lurched forward, splattering dirt over my freshly ironed shirt. I didn't care. I was more concerned with Vivienne as she wrote "I'll miss you" on the rear window.

I almost called after her, begging her to stay, but I didn't. It was the happiest I'd seen her in years. I wasn't going to interfere with that. I owed her big from the day I was born. Whatever I did know about love I learned from her. Besides, a brief vacation was the least I could give someone who flew me across the Atlantic three nights a week.

The moment I entered the house, as I started calculating differences in time zones, as it dawned on me Vivienne would be in our special place with someone else, all that changed.

Even though the windows were open there was a strong, musty odor of decay, as if I was the one who'd been away.

A box piled high with some of my father's clothes sat next to the door, waiting for Goodwill. Furniture was strewn haphazardly around the room. Wallpaper was peeling in corners, folded over molding like ribbon. Vivienne's keys and wallet were on the table unguarded - things in travel shows that connote an abrupt and possibly violent departure.

"Cunt," I whispered.

I was overcome by a sudden rush of loneliness and my heart started beating wildly. I took a series of deep breaths through my nose and tried to calm down. When I did, when I realized everything would be all right, I unplugged the TV and wedged it behind the sofa, picture tube down. I removed all the photos off the refrigerator and stuffed them, along with the emergency numbers, inside the tub of strawberry ice cream. I dumped the ultraviolet lamp into the

toilet and wrote on every wall with one of Vivienne's lipsticks.

"IF YOU THINK THIS YEAR WAS BAD, WAIT TILL YOU SEE WHAT'S COMING."

I couldn't help but smile.

Tomorrow was my first day as an adult without supervision.

* * *

I should say here that, even as a child, I was uncomfortable asserting myself, be it verbal or physical. At the time and for many years after I blamed it on everything from embarrassment to cowardice, but I was wrong.

It was the loss of control that terrified me.

I know it sounds crazy, but I thought I would never return to normal or, worse, die if I ever let myself go. Funnily enough, this applied to music as well as violence. I was studying the clarinet for a few years. I could read pretty much anything, be it classical or rock, but I was afraid of jazz. The idea of never playing a song the same way twice, let alone closing my eyes and improvising,

terrified me.

If I felt myself in danger of losing control I started talking to familiar objects. "Thank you shower, you've done an excellent job keeping me clean today. Thank you chair. Comfortable as always." It calmed me down and made me laugh.

I couldn't avoid aggression altogether, of course, and I did display it when problems arose. It was just more internalized.

For example, a healthy sense of direction was not one of my

strong points. If I entered a house one way and exited another it was the same as if I wandered into the Amazon.

I went to the library every day for six months and memorized maps of all the streets, alleys and highways within a fifty mile radius - till I knew each rise, turn and exit.

My automotive abilities were on a par with my directions. I looked in the Yellow Pages, found a salvage yard and talked the owner into giving me carte blanche.

Since every car that came in was a junker he didn't mind if I dismantled them. If anything, I was helping him retrieve the parts that were valuable. Within a year I'd examined more cylinders, valves, pistons and connecting rods than most garages in three lifetimes. I could put together an engine blindfolded.

Much to Vivienne's delight, this attitude carried over to the house; from ceiling fan to microwave. If something went wrong, I dismantled it till I learned what was needed to fix it.

When problems arose as I got older, the same principles applied.

If someone entered my life with the sole purpose of destroying it, I wasn't about to sit there and let it happen.

* * *

Six days after Vivienne left I received a letter with a French post mark. In the ensuing weeks there were dozens more, but this is a good idea of what they were like.

"Dearest Henry,

After five days in Paris I can barely walk. I'd like to blame it on all the sightseeing we've been doing but I'd be lying. It's all the restaurants we've been going to. Honest to God, I think I've eaten my weight in bread during the past forty-eight hours. It's not just me either. People really walk around carrying baguettes. Like in the movies. I wish I could describe how amazing everything tastes but the only thing I can think of is, "How good can a cheese sandwich be?" That doesn't begin to describe it but will have to do till I get home and can come up with something better.

In a bizarre twist of fate we owe our dining experiences to an Arab terrorist who's in jail here awaiting trial. Tension is high and everyone's afraid of reprisals. Since there have already been a couple of bombings I can't say I blame them. Parisians, as a result, are staying home instead of going out the way they normally do. So, the finest restaurants are empty and eager for customers. Talk about a golden opportunity. Peggy thinks I'm crazy but I told her it doesn't make sense, under any circumstances, to stay inside on our first trip to Paris.

Her feelings about sightseeing, funnily enough, are identical. She wants to go everywhere. If you remember I made a list of the most interesting places for us to visit. I bought maps and plotted a daily itinerary. As soon as we arrived Peggy decided she didn't like to plan. She'd rather walk around and go wherever the wind blows. This is easy for her to say since she doesn't pay attention to what streets we're on or the direction we're headed. North could be south. East might as well be west. If it weren't for me we'd run around in circles while she searched for Worcestershire sauce.

When I reminded her that we agreed on everything three weeks before we left she laughed and said "Three weeks? How could I possibly hold her to something that long ago?"

I finally got her to write down the places she wanted to see. Rouen, where Joan of Arc was executed, is first on her list. She also wants to visit the catacombs, Oscar Wilde's grave at Pere Lachaise cemetery, the Trocadero where Anais Nin had an abortion and the house where Marcel Proust's doctor examined Debussy's first wife after she failed to kill herself with a gun shot to the chest. I don't think these will define Paris, at least I hope not, but this is what she's interested in. It certainly is in keeping with how she looks at the world. When I look out our window every morning I see the city I've always dreamed about. The food. The architecture. The landmarks and museums. When Peggy looks she sees the poverty, crime and dilapidated buildings.

If there's an easy way to do something she'll find the hard way and struggle.

Life's an ambush.

But,...back to the important stuff. Last night we went to a restaurant where you usually need reservations four months in advance. From our table we could see Notre Dame cathedral. That's where Joan Of Arc was tried. Peggy likes to brag they were both born January 6th at 5:00 P.M. She was put in command of an entire army when she was seventeen. Joan, not Peggy. Because of her success she was made a nobleman that same year. At seventeen. My God, I was just learning how to drive at that age!

Peggy admires Joan because she stood up to men's injustices.

Anyway, I started off with a scallop appetizer that had white truffles. Peggy had lobster with citrus vinaigrette. Here comes the best part. The appetizers were served on the ground floor of the restaurant. When we were done we had to take an elevator to the top floor to eat the main course. Can you believe that? Two courses. Two floors. And get this, Henry. While we were eating I looked up and they were opening the roof to let the smoke out. It retracted just like those indoor pools in Highland Park.

Peggy paid, of course. She wouldn't let me see how much it cost. She didn't make a fuss but I think it stopped her from breathing for about ten seconds. All I know is we walked back to the hotel instead of taking a cab. On the way I couldn't stop talking about the food. I only shut my trap when I looked up and saw the sky. It's completely different than the one we've got at home. Stars everywhere. Millions of them. The Big Dipper was right overhead, just like when we fly, only it was bigger and brighter than it's ever been. While I was staring Peggy bought a copy of Time magazine. On the cover was a photo of a mother kneeling beside her dying daughter who was struck by debris when a bomb exploded. Peggy said the terrorists put razor blades and nails in the bombs so they'd do more damage. It was horrible and I didn't want to hear about it. Why ruin a wonderful evening? There was nothing we could do anyway. This upset Peggy almost as much as the terrorism. She didn't understand how I could bury my head in the sand and shut out everything going on in the world.

She urged me to find the power within me, the greatness she knew was there that I've been afraid to tap into because I was terrified of being the center of attention or better than someone else. Only then would I discover what I truly believed in, why I was put on this earth and be everything I was intended to be. It made no sense to live in the world unless I was engaged in it and fought every step of the way. All her heroines, and she considered me one of them, were willing to face any odds and risk everything.

It reminded me of my mother, to tell you the truth, the fury in her eyes, when she used to rant about men and the good-old-boy network that kept women down. God forbid you got in her way.

This brings me to a favor I need to ask of you, Henry. Peggy is sick. It's not like a cold or flu, something you can take medicine for. It has to do with the scars running up and down her arms and the back of her legs. I know you've seen them. Unless she finds some inner strength her condition will get worse. I don't think she's going to be able to do that in the short time we're here. So, would you mind if we stayed another few weeks? As my Grandma always said, it'll go by as fast as you can say "Jack Robinson." I know how much good the imaginary trips to France did for us. The real thing should do at least that for Peggy. Of course, I wouldn't dream of staying if it makes you uncomfortable. You can call the hotel and let me know. The number's printed on the top of this stationery. Remember, I love you. That will never change. It's just that Peggy needs me an awful lot right now.

Love,

Momma

PS. Don't forget to use the ultraviolet lamp."

I called and told her to stay. Except for the terrorism and Peggy's problem, which I couldn't figure out, Vivienne sounded more excited about life than when she left.

I also remembered what my father told me on numerous occasions, enough so I knew he meant it.

"Vivienne is a saint and should be worshipped."

If anyone could help Peggy it was Vivienne, patron saint of neighbor-threatening desserts.

* * *

The second letter I received thanked me and attached a poem Peggy had written.

"Live your life so the preacher
won't have to lie
at your funeral.
Don't sit alone
trembling in the dark
on pure white sheets,
staring out the window

mouthing words no one can hear.
"What might have been?"
Don't listen to the cadaver
with the pinched white face
and beady eyes,
whose slit of a mouth
forms a tight wrinkly button
when he asks
"How was school?"
Rebel!
It is not just a word
but a way of life,
a suit of armor
to be worn daily
in defense of freedom.
Silence has been a simple strategy
but defiance is necessary.
Fire alarms must be pulled.
Toilets flooded.
Classes skipped.
Science labs sabotaged.
Pot deeply inhaled.
Downers swallowed
A free woman cannot adhere
to disabling rules and regulations.
If she does
the cost is high."

Months later I found out the hotel rang the room a few
moments after Peggy finished writing.

"I have a call from Texas," was all the operator said before
the minister's wife got on the line.

"If I never see the people in this town again it will be too
soon."

"Momma."

Just like the minister's funeral, it was the only word Peggy could slip in.

"I bought the most beautiful fur coat in Dallas last week and nobody said a word. They're jealous. I can see it in their eyes. Serves them right for not giving a damn."

"Momma."

"Other women my age don't have to put up with things like this."

"Daddy was a lousy fuck!"

This stopped the minister's wife cold.

Somehow, the fact that the minister had abused her but done it poorly gave Peggy a strange sense of power.

"He wasn't nearly as good as this guy from Liverpool I fucked when I was twelve who liked to scream "The British are coming."

Unsure how to respond, the minister's wife allowed herself a moment to gather her thoughts.

"You've always been a vile girl."

"It's my favorite character flaw, momma."

The minister's wife hung up and Peggy made a beeline for the bathroom. Closing the door behind her she began bouncing on tip toes, like a ballerina, stretching till she reached a hanging Tiffany style lamp - shattering it with a swift and unexpected forearm. As broken glass rained down around her she knelt, picked up the largest shard and nonchalantly sliced the inside of each thigh thirteen times.

When she finished she sat, leaned back against the toilet seat, stretched her long legs out in front of her, crossed her feet at the ankles and gasped a muffled sigh of relief. She felt better. No matter how overwhelmed she became, no matter how deep her memories dragged her down, her heart and mind relaxed when she could ventilate and her pain had a means of escape.

As blood pooled at her feet she felt a strange elation and was tempted to laugh, just a little breathless one to remind her she was okay and that life was different now. She was making a new start. She was with a woman she loved. She didn't have to be sad because she was living the ordinary life she'd always dreamed about. She was even staying in the lap of luxury, a four-star hotel that wouldn't let anyone within a hundred yards unless they were announced.

She caught a glimpse of herself in the mirror at that point. Studying her body in the unforgiving light, it was the first time in years she saw herself without illusion. All the scars and muti-lated flesh. Oddly enough this didn't bother her, pain being the one sensation that gave her pleasure. It even made her smile because she reminded herself of a life-sized Tic Tac Toe.

Leaning back a little more she lit a cigarette and exhaled a perfect ring of smoke that hovered, like the ever- present ghost of her father, around the broken fixture.

She could almost hear him breathing down the back of her neck.

Vivienne stayed in France almost a year.

She didn't really miss me.

Jack fucking Robinson.

* * *

Police were summoned after Peggy, covered in blood, strolled naked through the hotel lobby. Her everyday powers of reason suspended, she wished everyone a happy Chinese New Year and encouraged them to celebrate with a glass of champagne. She also introduced herself as The Maid Of Orleans, blessed the officers and tried to enlist them in her fight against the English.

They drove her directly to the Sainte-Anne psychiatric

hospital on the outskirts of the city, a short drive that replaced cafes and bright lights with dimly-lit streets heaped with rubbish and smelling of poverty - the desolation Peggy saw when she looked out of every window.

By the time Vivienne discovered what had happened Peggy was strapped to a gurney and being wheeled toward the high security wing.

En route she passed several patients, wandering aimlessly and staring into space. Only one, Claude Garin, seemed to be aware of his surroundings. Wearing a T-shirt that said "Not Made In Japan" he was sampling a wedge of Camembert while pinning an abstract water color onto a bulletin board crammed with hospital rules and regulations. Twenty-five, Claude was gaunt but surprisingly strong. The bones in your fingers ached for hours if you were unlucky enough to shake his hand, which was why few people did.

A devoted young man whose parents were accidentally run down by a politician's Land Rover, Claude had an unwavering belief in anything that benefitted mankind and wasn't afraid to put his money where his heart lay.

His intentions, unfortunately, were superior to his instincts and people took advantage. One friend convinced him to invest in a machine that was supposed to change sea water into fuel for cars. It got you from point A to point B but rusted your engine in the process. A second friend got him to invest in a new chemical that was safe for spraying crops and 100% biodegradable. It caused birth defects in mice. A third friend persuaded him to sink everything he had left into Magnesium. More pliable and lighter than steel or iron it was supposed to cut construction costs and pollution in half for airplanes. It performed as advertised with one caveat. If the aircraft overheated, magnesium had a lower flash point than traditional metals and exploded. Complicating matters, if you put water on a magnesium fire the blaze accelerated.

To Claude's credit he never lost his love of humanity or disdain for the vulgarities of big business. It's the reason he ran for mayor against Pierre LePlante, the head of a local agribusiness group who believed that everything existed to be purchased and sold.

Pierre's ingenuity was as legendary as his favorite quote.

"Every man, woman and child should be able to walk into a store and write a check for a 747."

He bought a thousand barren acres in the upper Silesia region of Poland, an area where 96 million tons of mining waste had been dumped, poisoning the environment. Under the auspices of the Polish government Pierre developed an inexpensive technique to revegetate the unusable land, reducing the amount of contaminated runoff and dust which was a major health risk. As soon as it was declared safe he reconstructed the original wooden roller coaster from Coney Island, bought London Bridge and shipped it, stone by stone, from Lake Havasu, built a full scale model of the Statue Of Liberty and opened them to tourism. Three months later he sold to the Chinese, tripling his investment.

He commissioned the famed Benetti ship builders, whose boats had won numerous Admiral's Cups, to build him a three hundred foot yacht, its interior modeled after Al Capone's mansion on Star Island in Miami. Although the venture nearly bankrupt Benetti, Pierre made a fortune when he sold the boat, the day of completion, to a mafia boss from Sicily.

When Pierre had a nightmare this was all taken away.

Pierre also enjoyed misquoting Charles de Gaulle.

"How can anyone live in a nation that has two hundred and forty-six different types of cheese?"

He planned to buy out as many small cheese makers as

possible, unify them and change the centuries old method of making Camembert. Using a modern process that called for pasteurization, he would increase production ten-fold but remove bacteria from the end products. This would extend shelf life in supermarkets which, he insisted, was good for everyone. He cited import restrictions imposed by large world markets, especially America, and health concerns about raw milk to back this up.

Claude, on the other hand, knew it would render the different types of Camembert indistinguishable from one another, denying customers the choice, complexity and, above all, soul of the product.

While he could overlook Pierre's other ventures, chalking them up to the price one paid for doing business, this was inexcusable.

The world looked to France as a bastion of taste and flavor. Variety had its drawbacks, sure, but everyone was better off for it.

Claude assumed people knew this and would be outraged. They would see Pierre's plan for what it was, a marketing scam intended to destroy tradition and raise consumption in the name of global homogenization. How else could they feel after eating Bethmale from the Pyrenees or Bleu de Gex from Haut-Jura?

He was wrong.

While Pierre was ridiculed by some for his less than ethical practices, his results commanded respect. His countrymen, accordingly, had no problem forsaking their heritage in their sprint to fame and fortune.

Claude had no choice.

He would assassinate Pierre. The man had to account for his actions and the only way that could happen was if Claude shot him dead. When Claude had Pierre in his sights the gun, which he'd bought from another friend, jammed and backfired, propelling a 9mm bullet through his left shoulder.

The most disturbing element of this attack to those in power was the support Mr. Garin received from extreme right gastronomical organizations.

Anti-commercialism violence skyrocketed. A pro free-market senator was stabbed days before a crucial parliamentary vote on mass production. Another businessman was murdered after he proposed a new technique to make goat cheese available throughout the year instead of during the spring. The technique required the insertion of hormone sponges into goats' asses to jump-start their milk producing cycle.

France was better than that.

As Peggy passed, Claude followed her down the hall, studying her with a critic's eye.

"I can see your soul" he said.

Gesturing toward her forehead, he seemed to be giving benediction.

"How are you?"

* * *

Breathing hard as if she'd been running, Vivienne marched through Sainte-Anne's doors two hours later. Crossing toward the admitting desk she was overcome by the smell of ammonia, Lysol and loss and could hear shouting in the distance, the way someone does, she imagined, if they're being tortured by terrorists.

When she reached the desk she came face to face with the hairy-armed attendant who wheeled Peggy to her room, a nurse and the doctor on call. Their demeanor was cheerful and sympathetic but their expressions were vacant, like faces in documentaries about cults or starving refugees engulfed by flies. Vivienne explained why she was there but none of those expressions changed, reacting more as if she'd been lost and wandered in to ask directions.

The reason was simple.

They couldn't understand most of what she was saying.

Still, the doctor finally spoke.

He rattled off a bunch of psychiatric terms, many in French. Hallucinations. Psychosis. Delusions. Since Vivienne understood French even less than he understood Texan, she drifted off to a simpler time, back in Lone Star Springs when I was four years old. We were listening to a news report about sixty pilot whales who'd died after beaching themselves on the Australian island of Tasmania.

Researchers did autopsies and found brain damage consistent with impacts from military sonar. They also provided evidence of internal bleeding to the inner ear, damage consistent with intense pressure. Although the government refused to accept any responsibility, only one cause made sense.

Acoustic impact.

When the broadcast was over I proudly announced the one truth I understood about these magnificent and tragic creatures.

"Whales swim naked."

Vivienne thought of most people after that as nude and adrift in the middle of the ocean. Lost and unhappy they were all trapped in the undertow of life, sinking deeper with each passing stroke. The strong never gave up and desperately tried to swim for shore, certain death for the

whales, but possible salvation for them. The weak got frightened, became disoriented and drowned, seeing salvation, whether land or sea, as one might when looking through the wrong side of binoculars.

Every time Peggy was headed for land fate intervened, turned her around and sent her sprawling back toward a place that was as bleak as it was forbidden. Vivienne blamed this on "life impact" and no one except Uncle Ethan took responsibility for that either.

As the doctor finished his diagnosis Vivienne realized she'd drifted away for most of it. Not that it mattered. It was mostly in French and she just wanted to see Peggy. When she informed the doctor of this, he suggested she wait in the lounge at the other end of the hall.

Each room Vivienne passed was scrubbed, mopped and had the charm of a CIA safe-house. The dining area was large and smelled of pungent, unidentifiable food. Occupational therapy was half its size with designated areas for painting, sewing and a kitchen for women who needed to brush up on homemaking skills before returning to society. An outdoor patio afforded patients the luxury of fresh air and flowers but was surrounded by a twelve-foot fence, a constant reminder they could not rise above the confines of the hospital or their illness.

Most doors had doctors' names stenciled on them. Some had functions like X-Rays, Physiotherapy and Geriatrics. Some were padlocked. Even though it was late she expected to see patients in those rooms undergoing treatment, but not a soul was in sight.

It reminded her of Highland Park where mansions were as high as the crime rate was low. She never saw anyone there either, even though houses with Baccarat chandeliers, leather-bound first editions nobody read and Steinway pianos nobody played were tastefully lit and arranged as if on display. When Vivienne was a kid she assumed no one was home. As she got older she realized occupancy had nothing to do with it. It was a class distinction. The rich avoided people beneath their stature as they would black mold; a more effective deterrent than any high priced security system.

"I'm looking out and can see you. You're looking in and will never see me, certainly not during nightcaps or garden parties."

She would not be relegated to viewing life from a distance again, especially in Paris. Returning to the admitting desk she demanded to see Peggy.

The doctor merely smiled before speaking slowly in the little English he knew.

"The good news is, other than this, your friend, she seems to be okay."

She hated doctors suddenly, their phony bedside manner, habits of smiling too easily and philosophy of avoiding anything unpleasant. Things weren't okay. Just his annoying voice. He might have calmed a lot of naive people in the past but Vivienne knew better. Slicing oneself with glass was not okay. Nearly bleeding to death naked in a strange hotel lobby was not okay. Thinking you were Joan of Arc was not okay.

Vivienne wanted to scream. She wanted to grab the doctor by the lapels and punch him in the mouth the way Peggy did the night of my father's funeral.

"How'd you get that scar on your lip, doc?"

She'd watch him gush blood all over his sterile Formica floor. Then she'd tell him everything was okay. What would he say after that? How reassuring would his voice be with a broken fucking jaw?

She did nothing.

No matter how incensed, deep down she knew she had to swallow her misgivings. Like it or not, this was better than the truth that meant so much to her.

* * *

Vivienne went out of her way to make sure I was cared for as scrupulously as if she were looking after me herself. The moment I gave my blessings for an extended stay she got in touch with every one of our neighbors and implored their help in my time of need. To her relief they happily agreed. This was due to a couple of reasons.

One, they were Texans. Texans place family above all else. They're a lot like Europeans in that regard. Two, they thought of Vivienne as the devil incarnate, on a par with Captain Kangaroo. Surprisingly, their contempt had little to do with her newly-discovered cuisine or sexual preference. They accepted both as temporary indiscretions, blaming the shock and confusion of losing a husband. What they could not forgive was her abandoning the mid-west, a betrayal that rivaled, if not exceeded, leaving a teenager to his own devices.

I was their last chance for Texas-centric pride.

Lone Star Springs' wives made a daily pilgrimage to my front door, dutifully lugging sympathy along with the same types of food they brought to my father's funeral.

Mrs. Harvey carried enough Hamburger Helper to feed a platoon. Mrs. Kozlowski showed up with armfuls of freshly picked produce. Mrs. Burton and her daughter, Layla, baked corn bread, although they were always arguing about whether to include chili peppers or not. Mrs. Holloway brought frozen delicacies purchased in Dallas. Things like Shepherds' Pie and Trifle, dishes she said were Princess Diana's favorite. Mrs. Clifford made chicken. Mrs. Lewis fried catfish. Mrs. Scott didn't bring anything to eat but stopped by regularly with Arthur, her six-year-old Fila

Brasileiro, a cross between a Bloodhound and a Mastiff. Brindle in color, his head was larger than my upper body.

After Mrs. Scott's husband died she was not only grief-stricken, she felt unsafe, her home more like an abandoned warehouse than a castle; just a roof over her head where she bided her time. Since another romantic involvement was as unthinkable as a good night's sleep, no solution

presented itself till she passed a newsstand, one afternoon, on her way to market. There it was. Plain as the nose on her face. "Bark" magazine. It's motto, "Dog is my copilot," struck a chord and Mrs. Scott realized a pet would make her feel whole again. It did when she was growing up. There was no reason to think it wouldn't now that she was grown.

Ordinarily she would have driven to the pound in Majestic Meadows but, because this was a life-altering decision, she decided to buy a pure bred. Skimming through the magazine she came across a page advertising the most unique puppies she'd ever seen. Underneath their photo was a

caption that said "Brave as a Fila." It was a saying in Brazil, where the breed originated, that paid homage to their courage and eagerness to protect the family. Owning a Fila, as a result, was a huge responsibility. Because of their unwavering devotion they posed a danger to anyone who

approached.

I tell you this because the first time Arthur laid eyes on me he rushed forward with such determination Mrs. Scott froze from fright. As I braced myself for the attack Arthur passed me in a blur, retrieved a stick the size of a small log, laid it at my feet and waited for me to throw it.

Partially in defense I did, as hard and as far as I could. He ran, leapt into the air, caught it in his mouth before it touched the ground and brought it back for another try.

I threw till I couldn't lift my arm.

Arthur never tired.

This all dumbfounded Mrs. Scott because, in the two years she'd had Arthur he related to other humans as little more than potential homicides with no rules of engagement.

Arthur and I became inseparable.

We swam in the pond. We bounded through tall grass and jumped over fallen trees, chasing each other in fields so large, there was no end to them and we could run forever. Since Arthur was bred to hunt jaguars I shouldn't have been able to keep up. The thing was, he never let me out of his sight. If he got more than ten yards ahead he'd stop and wait the same way he did when I threw the stick.

No matter where we were, no matter what we were doing, he was aware of every sound. The front door creaking. The window slamming shut. The TV being turned off. He even knew when I put on my jacket in case I was preparing to leave the house.

Nobody came near me.

At night Arthur ran over after Mrs. Scott went to sleep. She still needed him but, now that she felt safe, she happily put my needs ahead of her own while Vivienne was away, something Vivienne would have done if the situation had been reversed.

As soon as I let Arthur in he followed me upstairs and lay down on the rug next to my bed, although he barely slept. Instead he patrolled, checking possible points of entry at hour-long intervals.

When he was in my room I'd sometimes turn on the light and read him passages from books I thought he'd enjoy - "To Kill A Mockingbird." "The Catcher In The Rye." Sometimes I'd just curl up beside him on the floor, put my arm around his neck and hold him as tight as I could, the way Vivienne held me the day she left for France.

When he was in a different part of the house I could hear whatever he was doing, like a mother who knows her baby rolled over onto his face in his crib.

Unlike Vivienne, Arthur protected me from loneliness as much as physical harm. Unlike Vivienne and my father, he would never abandon me.

* * *

While my good neighbors came to the house on a regular basis, they also invited me to join them in their own homes. At first I declined. While I appreciated their invitations, I preferred familiar surroundings.

If they wouldn't take no for an answer I fell back on a skill I'd developed over the years and used in case of emergencies.

I could vomit at will.

I didn't have to stick my finger down my throat like most kids I knew or guzzle spoonsful of Cod-liver oil. No. All I had to do was think bad thoughts and puke, the opposite of Peter Pan's sure-fire method for flying.

Out came everything but a pair of lacy underpants.

This gave me a chance to relive the meals my father and I liked best. Bacon and eggs on Monday. Peanut butter and banana sandwiches on Tuesday. Frozen TV dinners on Wednesday. Packaged macaroni and cheese on Thursday and burgers Friday. Saturday was more macaroni. Sundays were reserved for Hostess products; Mars Bars, Three Musketeers, Snickers, Mounds and the under-appreciated Almond Joy.

Nevertheless, it wasn't long before I started feeling the same emptiness Mrs. Scott felt after her husband died. At first I attributed it to excessive amounts of sugar. As weeks turned into months, as my vulnerability increased, I couldn't blame eating habits. Even with Arthur protecting me, loneliness took over and threatened my very existence, like a beating you never recover from.

I sat in the needlepoint chair, night after night, trying to keep my spirits up in spite of the daunting message I'd scrawled on all four walls in vitamin-enriched Vagabond Crimson.

"IF YOU THINK THIS YEAR WAS BAD, WAIT TILL YOU SEE WHAT'S COMING."

I weighed the macaroni and packages of cheese in every Kraft box to see if they were uniform. I counted the steps it took to get from our front door to the hardware store, Bee's, my father's old place of employment and the gas station, calculating how many trips it would take to travel a mile. I counted the words in each of Vivienne's letters and arranged them according to size.

No matter what I did I still felt as if my heart was going to burst. When I ran out of things to count I returned the TV to its rightful place, keeping it on the Travel channel twenty-four hours a day. Even when I was just passing through to another part of the house it distracted me long enough to forget my troubles, if only for a few minutes. I put new photos of Vivienne on the refrigerator, many with us together. I made a new list of emergency numbers, adding those in Paris.

Police....................17
Paramedics................15
Fire Department 18
Poison Emergency Center 01 40 05 48 48
Emergency Medical Assistance...01 47 07 77 77
Drug Squad Hot Line ....0 800 14 21 52 (toll free)
Sexually-transmitted diseases..01 40 78 26 00
Doctors (24/24)..........01 47 07 77 77
Dentists (24/24).........01 43 37 51 00
Burns.................. 01 58 41 41 41
Stolen credit cards : 01 68 22 14 94
Visa : 08 92 70 57 05
American Express : 01 47 77 70 00
Diner's Club : 08 10 31 41 59 15

I also included the Missing Persons Bureau in case Peggy wandered off.

I bought a new carton of strawberry ice cream. I scrubbed the walls, removing everything but three words.

"SEE WHAT'S COMING."

Although that didn't help.

What if I was walking to Mrs. Jennings' house for dinner and had a heart attack? Nobody would know. Vivienne would come home and I'd be missing. She'd notify the police but, by the time they found me, my body would be bloated and covered with slugs, eyes hanging out like a Jack In The Box.

I could be on my way to Mrs. Kozlowski's when thick fog set in. A pickup would round the corner with a deer strapped to its hood. The driver couldn't see because of poor visibility. Even if he caught sight of me at the last second, there's a good chance he'd panic and step on the gas instead of his brakes. Next thing I'd know, kaboom, I'm impaled by antlers going seventy miles an hour.

Mrs. Fairweather and Mrs. Burton lived even farther away so I'd be exhausted before I was halfway there. Let's say a prisoner escaped from Huntsville. It happened all the time. I'd hear a whooshing noise above me. I'd get scared. I'd start to run, not realizing it was a police helicopter. They'd shoot first and ask questions later. This was Texas after all. When Vivienne returned from her trip she'd be chastised by the media for neglecting my fitness.

Staying home wasn't any better.

What if I was worrying about what to do, the way I did every night, and a jaguar from one of Vivienne's TV shows escaped from a traveling circus when Arthur wasn't there? I'd be sitting in the needlepoint chair, lost in thought. The jaguar could sneak up behind me without being heard. Next thing I'd know I'm being dragged outside, a human Almond Joy.

Worse, when Vivienne returned she'd find a life she knew nothing about. The gross of rubbers my father gave me the night before he died. The Green Bay Packers promotional brochure signed by all the players. Pieces of ripped up emergency numbers. Drawings, daily schedules, pages and the wall behind my bed crammed with the word she hated most.

"CUNT CUNT

CUNT CUNT CUNT CUNT CUNT CUNT CUNT CUNT CUNT CUNT CUNT CUNT CUNT CUNT CUNT CUNT CUNT CUNT CUNT CUNT CUNT CUNT CUNT CUNT CUNT CUNT CUNT CUNT CUNT CUNT CUNT CUNT CUNT CUNT CUNT CUNT CUNT CUNT

CUNT CUNT CUNT CUNT CUNT CUNT CUNT CUNT CUNT CUNT CUNT CUNT

CUNT CUNT CUNT CUNT CUNT CUNT CUNT
CUNT CUNT CUNT CUNT CUNT
CUNT CUNT CUNT CUNT CUNT CUNT CUNT
CUNT CUNT CUNT CUNT CUNT
CUNT CUNT CUNT CUNT CUNT CUNT CUNT
CUNT CUNT CUNT CUNT CUNT
CUNT CUNT CUNT CUNT CUNT CUNT CUNT
CUNT CUNT CUNT CUNT CUNT
CUNT CUNT CUNT CUNT CUNT CUNT CUNT
CUNT CUNT CUNT CUNT CUNT
CUNT CUNT CUNT CUNT CUNT CUNT CUNT
CUNT CUNT CUNT CUNT CUNT
CUNT CUNT CUNT CUNT CUNT CUNT CUNT
CUNT CUNT CUNT CUNT CUNT
CUNT CUNT CUNT CUNT CUNT CUNT CUNT
CUNT CUNT CUNT CUNT CUNT
CUNT CUNT CUNT CUNT CUNT CUNT CUNT
CUNT CUNT CUNT CUNT CUNT
CUNT CUNT CUNT CUNT CUNT CUNT CUNT
CUNT CUNT CUNT CUNT CUNT
CUNT CUNT CUNT CUNT CUNT CUNT CUNT
CUNT CUNT CUNT CUNT CUNT
CUNT CUNT CUNT CUNT CUNT CUNT CUNT
CUNT CUNT CUNT CUNT CUNT
CUNT CUNT CUNT CUNT CUNT CUNT CUNT
CUNT CUNT CUNT CUNT CUNT
CUNT CUNT CUNT CUNT CUNT CUNT CUNT
CUNT CUNT CUNT CUNT CUNT
CUNT CUNT CUNT CUNT CUNT CUNT CUNT
CUNT CUNT CUNT CUNT CUNT

CUNT CUNT CUNT CUNT CUNT CUNT CUNT
CUNT CUNT CUNT CUNT CUNT
    CUNT CUNT CUNT CUNT CUNT CUNT CUNT
CUNT CUNT CUNT CUNT CUNT
    CUNT CUNT CUNT CUNT CUNT CUNT CUNT
CUNT CUNT CUNT CUNT CUNT
    CUNT CUNT CUNT CUNT CUNT CUNT CUNT
CUNT CUNT CUNT CUNT CUNT
    CUNT CUNT CUNT CUNT CUNT CUNT CUNT
CUNT CUNT CUNT CUNT CUNT
    CUNT CUNT CUNT CUNT CUNT CUNT CUNT
CUNT CUNT CUNT CUNT CUNT
    CUNT CUNT CUNT CUNT CUNT CUNT CUNT
CUNT CUNT CUNT CUNT CUNT!"

Adding insult to injury, when Vivienne desperately needed comforting to help her through these troubling discoveries, she couldn't use the ultra-violet lamp.

I started saying "yes" to dinner invitations.

The moment I returned home, however, much to Arthur's chagrin, I made sure the door was unlocked. If I went to the bathroom and an Anaconda came up through the pipes, sunk its teeth into my rectum and dragged me down into the Lone Star sewers, police wouldn't have to break down the door, costing Vivienne a pretty penny.

It's important to note here that the more at ease I became at neighbors' houses, the more they became victims of their own kindness.

I preferred the Kraus' hospitality to the Horners', so I always found a way to gracefully decline the latter's invitation if there was a scheduling conflict. Mrs. Holloway, who'd vacationed in London, let me drink a glass of Guinness with dinner. The Burnhams did not. It was a no-brainer. The only drawback was that I had to see all Mrs. Holloway's Princess Di collectables before every meal, as if she was bragging about her own child. This included calendars, magazines, commemorative books, dolls, key rings, an Andy Warhol print, a "Devoted Mother plate" and a cassette of Elton John's "Candles In The Wind."

If I couldn't come up with a graceful excuse, I blamed calamitous allergic reactions, from S.A.D. to osteoporosis, on meals I could do without. All I had to do was stare at these women with a guiltless, honest face, smile and lie.

"You can get anything you want by making people trust you."

It was the cornerstone of every sale my father made. The moment he met someone, the very first handshake was like an investment.

"The more a customer invests, the less they're willing to walk away."

Vivienne, of course, was a stickler for telling the truth and nothing but, probably because of my father's inclinations. A person was only as good as their word. A statement was right or it was wrong. There was only one truth and, no matter how many lies you told to circumvent it, it stayed the same with no room for shades of gray.

On a strictly practical level a lie, even a well-crafted one, gets complicated. You lose track of what you said, who you said it to and when.

More important, I couldn't lie to God.

Although I'd always preferred telling the truth, in my defense, I'd inherited something from my father I could not deny. His eyes. They were the first thing people noticed about me. The first thing they were drawn to.

During this difficult time I had to face up to the harsh realities of life and their lesson was as simple and straight forward as the talks with my father in the square.

Lying gets you things.

In a world where few people ever have what they really want, who's to say that's bad? Besides, anyone can be honest. It takes a man with a sense of humor, style and imagination to stretch the validity of a statement. I believed then and still do that a comfortable lie is better than an uncomfortable truth, especially when none of these women gave a damn about the truth as Vivienne knew it. What was gospel one moment was fiction the next, depending on what they needed to feel good about themselves.

Everything was shades of gray.

* * *

I thought about my father often. His presence was uncommonly strong, especially when I passed the White Rock Tavern. Because Jack had been their most loyal and generous customer they restored the car Vivienne murdered, elevating it in the parking lot facing the entrance as a sort of shrine. Although costly, it proved to be a stroke of genius. Whether they were drinking green beer on Saint Patrick's Day, in the middle of a bar-sponsored softball tournament or just

avoiding going home, my dad's friends drank more whenever they looked at the Cadillac, waxing nostalgic for hazy remembrances of lost camaraderie.

This also applied to the women who slept with my father, which was pretty much everybody. They consumed more and loosened whatever morals they had left after looking at Jack's car. It reminded them of better times, usually without their husbands, although it sometimes reminded them of the multiple sets of pots and pans, encyclopedias, vacuum cleaners and office supplies that sat, unopened, on shelves in their closets.

This taught me another lesson my father would have approved of. "Anything can be restored, from friendship to virginity, after half a dozen Budweisers."

I visited Jack's grave dutifully while Vivienne was away. There were times I had to hitchhike because I ran out of gas or had a flat tire, but I went at least twice a week. I'd pluck the weeds and brush the dirt off his tombstone. I'd stand with my head bowed and think about the times we

spent as father and son. Fishing. Ball games. Shakes at the pharmacy. Even with all that, my thoughts started drifting back to one painful memory.

"Cheater."

One shouldn't think of his father in that way, I know, but I couldn't help myself. I missed him desperately when I was little and he went away for long weekends, but I wasn't able to miss him now that he was gone for good. No matter how hard I tried, I couldn't summon tears I could not shed.

It was the only pointless activity I allowed myself.

From then on, I became determined to emulate Vivienne's lifestyle. If I wanted to succeed in life I had to have a sense of purpose and a strategy that would help me reach my objective. Planning to do the right thing. That's what would make me a better man. Not pussy. If I kept my nose to the grindstone, with Arthur by my side, it would also keep vulnerability at bay.

I altered my routine.

I bought a journal so I could lay out and appraise my progress on a daily basis. This allowed me to anticipate, prioritize and not get bogged down with anything trivial.

I divided my day into regimented segments. If one proved too difficult I checked it off and moved on to the next. I'd lose only a fraction of a day instead of the entire twenty-four hours.

School and chores took up most of my time. I did the wash on Mondays. Ironing and mending on Tuesdays. Small maintenance jobs the house constantly required, Wednesdays. Thursdays were for cleaning. Fridays I went to the ATM. I received a check from Vivienne religiously. It wasn't much, but I managed to sock away ten dollars each week. When all was said and done I wanted to give her a present the moment she walked in the door to show my appreciation.

As much as I hated to admit it, Peggy was right.

The experience brought me closer to Vivienne than ever before. By performing the same tasks she did on a regular basis I began to realize how she must have felt and what she was thinking - as if I was suddenly privy to state secrets.

Like my father when he was my age, I was an artist with a blank canvas in front of me. Unlike Jack, my goals were my subjects, resolve my colors.

The only time I panicked was summer. Whereas most kids need a break from their daily routine to keep sane, removing a fourth of my schedule threw my life into turmoil.

On the bright side I learned that "the situation dictates your actions." If I was going to keep my spirits up, decreased obligations meant one and one thing only. I had to find something to replace them.

The perfect solution came, as fate would have it, after watching one of Vivienne's travel shows. It centered around "dead languages" which were similar but markedly different than those classified as "extinct."

A language was extinct when it was replaced by a different one. Native American speech, for example, was supplanted by English, French, Portuguese or Spanish as a result of colonization. Extinction also occurred when a language evolved into a new one - Old English becoming what

we use today. An extinct language that no longer had any speakers was considered dead, although it could remain in use for scientific, legal, or ecclesiastical functions - Avestan, Sanskrit, Biblical Hebrew and Gaulish among them.

After extensive research, I decided my needs were more ecclesiastic than anything else and began studying Gaulish. It would take at least all summer. Plus, I could speak it whenever I visited my father. What better place?

"Moni gnatha gabi / buutton imon" - My girl, take my kiss"

"Geneta imi daga uimpi." - I am a young girl, good and pretty."

They were the only sentences I managed to perfect so I repeated them over and over, knowing my father would appreciate the thought.

Because I never knew when Vivienne would return, this period of time also reinforced the importance of deadlines, timetables and obligations, establishing ground rules I later referred to as "the three p's."

Punctuality, Precision and Performance.

On the downside I made numerous mistakes during those months. Overcoming them, however, reminded me I was moving forward. I gradually saw each blunder for what it was and rectified it, learning a valuable lesson in the process.

The meek do not inherit the Earth. They ruin it by becoming victims, making ill-advised decisions and seeing them through to illogical conclusions.

Arthur backed me up on this.

My attention to detail impressed Mister Davidow to no end, a neighbor I met during this time who influenced me more than anyone else other than my parents.

The Davidows lived up the hill, across the road behind the row of fig trees in front of the pond. Every other Friday Mrs. Davidow invited me and Arthur over for freshly baked pie. Much to Vivienne's delight strawberry was her specialty, but the strawberry season was short. Apple was second. Rhubarb a close third.

After dessert Mister Davidow would take Arthur and me into his study and regale us with stories, the way my father used to, about his own exploits.

When he and Mrs. Davidow first got married she saw how excited he was about aviation. On their honeymoon she drove out to the local airport and bought him an introductory offer so he could start flying. He thought she was crazy. There was no way they could afford it. She didn't care. He was born to fly and wouldn't be happy doing anything else so it was worth every penny. He just needed to start while they had no kids and a little savings in the bank. There was only one condition. He had to promise he would always come back to her at the end of the day.

He had flying. She had him.

He promised.

After two lessons he could take off and land by himself. After a dozen he joined the flying school as an instructor. They gave him 60 minutes in the air for a week's work. No cash. Just flying time.

He didn't drink. He didn't smoke. He didn't do anything but fly. He related to those days the way other neighbors coveted old family photos. As Vivienne spoke of love. As my father mentioned women he'd failed to seduce.

Years later Mister Davidow did some barnstorming. He was a crop duster for awhile and a wing commander during the war. He flew for the Civil Air Patrol. He patrolled borders. He did search-and-rescue missions, counter drug and recon-naissance.

He always came back.

He was also the best commercial pilot United Airlines ever employed, till advances in aviation and sophisticated technology made pilots superfluous and he decided to replace flying with air traffic control.

Amazingly, his feelings of excitement and enthusiasm didn't change. Only his priorities were different. When he was a pilot his daily routine was all about him. His experience. His skills. His pleasure. Now, it was about his passengers.

It was his duty to make sure they always came back. He preferred it that way and likened the job to being a surgeon.

"People's lives are in my hands twenty-four hours a day. Every decision, every move I make involves life or death."

It was the closest I came to flying with Vivienne, only Mister Davidow wasn't pretending.

* * *

Peggy was still under restraints, heavy leather straps binding her chest and thighs, when Vivienne arrived with flowers the following day.

Her first instinct was to rush over and hold her but she knew it wouldn't make a difference. Peggy's eyes were open but as dead to the world as the language I was learning. Even when they shifted it was more reflex than recognition.

The color and character were drained from the rest of her face. Her hair was wet with perspiration and plastered against her forehead, although her lips were parched and chapped. She wore a sickly green hospital gown that was thin, translucent and made her body look more fragile than it was, if possible.

Her bed had collapsible wooden slats, like a crib, to keep her confined, a red tag attached to the post signifying she was a danger to herself. In case of emergency, thick rubber mats were positioned on either side to cushion any fall she might take.

Doctors and nurses hovered around the bed like paparazzi. One took Peggy's temperature. Another drew blood, filling half a dozen vials before breaking the needle and throwing it away. Bruises on the back of Peggy's palm and forearm were like a treasure map, marking the spot where previous needles had been inserted badly. Another doctor studied the psychiatrist's report and asked questions like "What day is it, what's your name and what drugs are you on?" When Peggy failed to respond a nurse jotted something down, withdrew a safety pin from her coat pocket, jabbed Peggy in the heel and calmly asked if the pain was sharp or dull. As with the other questions Peggy said nothing. Vivienne found this unbearable and hated the term "safety pin," another of life's repugnant oxymorons.

As the nurse continued her assault Peggy shut her eyes. It looked as if her body relaxed but that wasn't the case. Life had just left her for the moment, allowing her to drift deeper inside to hide from her demons.

Whatever bond connected her to the world Vivienne knew had been severed. It was not her world any more and she had no reason to be there.

Under normal circumstances Vivienne would have cried but she, like me, could not summon tears. This frightened her and made her feel even more awkward. Not for herself. Never for herself. She was terrified Peggy would notice.

Suddenly, Vivienne couldn't breathe.

There wasn't enough air in the room to support her, let alone an entourage, and the only window was shuttered and blocked by half a dozen iron bars.

She turned to flee into the corridor but the nurse with the safety pin blocked her exit.

"You're lucky" she said, folding her arms defiantly in front of her. "Your friend cut her wrists horizontally. That's more a cry for help than a real suicide attempt. Only when it's vertical,..."

She demonstrated on herself with a forefinger. "...is it time to say goodbye.

* * *

During Ethan's second session in the prison hospital, Doctor Coonan reminded everyone that, if they returned to society, it made no sense not to enjoy all its benefits. Financial well being. Honest, hard work. A loving marriage with adoring children. They couldn't accomplish these unless they changed their ways. He then described several scenarios that led to inappropriate anger, both passive and aggressive, and asked each member of the group to select the one they identified with.

Feelings of powerlessness and resentment were his first example. When a person feels as if they are no longer in control of their lives, that their fate is in the hands of others, they often become angry. He went on to say how people like this often resent those who are making choices and decisions for them. All day long they take orders. They hate their situation but can do nothing till they burst.

Ethan disagreed.

It was normal for your fate to be in the hands of others. This wasn't a bad thing since the people above you in the chain of command, who were responsible for making decisions about your life, were more knowledgeable than you. It was important to follow what they said, without question,

because your survival depended on it. Whether you agreed with their decisions was irrelevant. It wasn't a superiors' job to be liked, just to lead.

Ethan didn't understand why that would cause anger or resentment.

Doctor Coonan listened politely, smiled and promised to discuss it further before the end of class.

* * *

While Peggy slept or doctors performed new batteries of tests, Vivienne waited in the lounge. Windows were shuttered and barred in every room. Furniture was pushed back against the walls, the way you make space to dance at your parent's house when they're not home. Unlike your parent's house it was nailed to the floor, as if doctors expected it to lurch forward and attack anyone within striking range.

The decrepit and non-violent rolled in and out like low tide, sat, rocked or paced. Some wore pajamas. Some T-shirts and jeans. Some dressed as if they were on their way to the office and had dropped by for a quick cup of coffee.

Hospital staff came in to use the snack machines or watch TV. Every now and then a doctor entered and spoke to visitors in the same tone Vivienne used with her preemies. These consultations, as a result, made her extremely uncomfortable so she distracted herself by running errands, picking up food from the cafeteria and delivering messages for those in need.

When doctors were elsewhere Vivienne sat and read French magazines she couldn't understand or spoke with people who failed to grasp the nuances of what she was saying. Not that it mattered. In a world where life was reduced to eating, waiting, tolerance and intolerance, clarity was as immaterial as my father's vows. It wouldn't have made a difference if Vivienne screamed fire, rape or venereal disease. Be it in English, French, Polish or Martian, the translation was always the same.

"WHAT THE FUCK AM I DOING HERE?! WHY IS THIS HAPPENING TO ME?! SOMEBODY HELP! I'M SCARED TO FUCKING DEATH?!" HELP! HELP! GET ME OUT!"

Vivienne didn't leave.

It was like when we went to see the reptiles at the zoo. We were scared. We were repulsed. But, we had to watch if one of the snakes was eating a mouse. No matter how many times we looked away we always turned back, till there was nothing left but the end of a wriggling tail.

Although the hospital's primary goal was to cure whoever walked through their doors, personnel were terrified of thoughts like this, of any possible complications that originated outside their walls. It's why they all possessed unflagging inner resources and a sadistic supply of good cheer, the opposite of France's prevailing pessimism.

"Each day I look at all the people who blame everyone else for their problems. Each day I choose to be someone else."

"For every unfair event in life I try to find a fair, good and exciting counter-event."

If any of them let in the bad, genuinely acknowledged the horrors that had infiltrated their lives, they couldn't go on living. Like Vivienne's preemies they would keel over and never see it coming. Their only other option was to go as crazy as the people they supervised and they couldn't let that happen.

Vivienne's fellow visitors, on the other hand, confronted their horrors. They had no choice. Cramped in a room that was sweltering in summer and freezing in winter there was no common

etiquette, accepted code of behavior or boundaries. People who wouldn't ordinarily have spoken to one another became instant friends and confidants.

At first this made Vivienne as uncomfortable as the doctors' smiling faces. A relationship with one person was difficult enough. Now, she was barraged by an entire group that talked about their lives from the time they were five, blurted out their innermost secrets and expected her to do the same.

For once she was grateful for her dysfunctional upbringing

and diminished communication skills. It rendered her immune to this type of vulnerability.

By the end of the first week she'd told them everything about Peggy, Jack, her mother and me as if the waiting room was a confessional.

The overwhelming feelings of shame she experienced after sleeping with Peggy, for example. If only she'd had the strength to say "no."

Vivienne had also been uncomfortable with Peggy's neediness and embarrassed by her outrageous behavior. She often felt she would be better off without her and prayed she would find someone else. The man of her dreams. A man. Any man.

Four times she avoided Peggy when she was sick.

On five occasions she hoped that something bad would happen to Peggy, simplifying her own life by eliminating any difficult decisions.

There was even a fleeting moment, after one of Peggy's outbursts, where Vivienne felt like no one could put up with her and she deserved what she got.

"Synthetic Intimacies" is what she called her confessions when she returned to Lone Star Springs, and no one was immune.

Some of her stories were entertaining. Some were cautionary. Some were from the heart. There were so many I get confused when I try to remember them, like with my father, although one does stand out.

Vivienne fell asleep in her chair. Exactly how long and what took place during that time is unclear, but when she awoke she discovered a man's heavy wool coat draped around her. Nobody claimed it till visiting hours were over. Since it was a particularly cold afternoon he wanted to make sure she didn't catch a chill. Instead of being grateful Vivienne despised him for it. What if she'd died? No one would have known. He would have let her sit there, dead, because he wanted to be so damned polite and she'd be rotting away.

It smacked of God.

No screwing around this time. He wasn't going to waste energy on locusts, pestilence or His sentimental favorite, first born. No. This time He was serious.

This time it was manners.

Vivienne was positive He was looking down with a scowl thinking, "I've given you enough happiness during this lifetime. You've blown it. Fuck you. You're not getting any more."

It was such a debilitating thought she closed her eyes and wished she were dead. When she realized there were few advantages, that it wouldn't be that different than her present existence, she changed her mind and tried something she hadn't done in a very long while.

Hands joined in the traditional supplicant position, she prayed that life, which could obviously fall apart at a moment's notice, would right itself just as quickly.

Nothing happened.

This meant only one thing. God was still a devious Shit-Head and she hated Him more than ever.

* * *

The next time I spoke with Mister Davidow he was visibly unnerved. It was the fifth anniversary of the crash of United flight 516, a giant twin-engine 767 on its way from Dallas/Fort Worth airport, where he was based, to Los Angeles with three hundred passengers.

There were no survivors.

The flight had taken off early in the morning. It climbed to 27,000 feet and flew for nearly ten minutes before making a nose dive into Lake Ray Hubbard, thirty miles east. The initial investigation focused on reports that the crew had been in constant contact with controllers on the ground. They didn't accuse anyone of negligence or wrong-doing but it was implied, singling out controllers who'd been forced to work fourteen hours in a single shift, a gross violation of federal air regulations governing fatigue.

Three men had to put in extra hours because the controllers scheduled to work the late shift called in sick. Due to short-staffing no one was available and the decision was made to extend controllers from the afternoon until morning.

Mister Davidow was one of them.

What the report failed to mention was that the pilots of flight 516 had stopped all radio contact long before they dropped off Dallas radar. During past flights there were rumors of these same pilots nodding off but nothing was ever official.

As soon as the government started their investigation it became clear it was more of a witch-hunt than a truth seeking mission. The problem was not so much the magnitude of the disaster but the inexplicable fall from the sky on a quiet day during an uncritical stage of flight.

This made no sense to Mister Davidow because the 767, an aircraft that flies across the Atlantic more than any other plane, is surprisingly responsive and steering it is much easier than people imagine.

Its mechanics are elementary.

It has superior visibility through large windshields and a cockpit that may look complicated but has eighty-two percent fewer parts than most other planes. It can be flown by the standard two-person crew but is manageable for one person alone. If it's not on auto pilot, which is usually the case, it can be flown by hand. If those hands are removed from the controls, the plane would continue on, although it may wander a bit. That isn't a problem because it would return to steady flight with the slightest adjustment. Even if the engines were shut off completely, the plane would become a well-behaved glider.

The biggest problem flying an airplane like this is tedium.

While not idiot proof if circumstances were out of the ordinary, engine failure or unexpected wind-shear during takeoff or landing, things can happen.

None of these existed on that fateful day.

Mister Davidow went on to explain that he works with high-performance equipment. It can analyze aircraft movement, communicate with pilots, manage traffic and prevent collisions. He was trained to handle emergency landings, diversion for medical reasons, poor weather conditions and all other unscheduled events. There was only one thing he could not control. It was the bane of every controller's existence. He fought with the FAA about it every time there

was an accident because it was as difficult to disprove as it was to prove. That meant lawsuits and plenty of them.

Pilot error.

* * *

In the beginning, after visiting hours were over, Vivienne went directly to her hotel. She ordered room service, ate in silence, stared out the window searching for reason and went to bed the moment she started feeling self- righteous or self-pity.

As days turned into weeks, weeks into seasons, she altered that routine. She began going to a cafe off the Champs-Elysees that smelled of lemon peels and Gin and catered to expatriates who preferred Jack Daniels to just about anything else, welcome relief from the hospital's cloying good cheer.

Most were deathly afraid of being alone, boredom, because it was the ultimate enemy of a good time, and driven by the need to socialize with others like themselves. In so doing they could recreate the culture they were most comfortable with and avoid the French experience, including

food, museums, music and language, in its entirety.

August was their favorite month.

No one was ever drunk nor were they sober. A handful were rich and spent their money guardedly. Most barely got by and spent their money recklessly, but always had enough for coffee and cigarettes and were greeted, in English, by the owner of the cafe with the same warm enthusiasm as the affluent.

Some thought Paris was nothing but a bunch of dirty old buildings. Some hated it because it smelled like Venice. Some were upset because they couldn't find a decent slice of pastrami.

They were experts on real estate markets, Jews who controlled the banking system, although none were anti-semitic, and what constituted the perfect Martini. They said things like "If you need diamonds I can get them for you whole-sale;" "I'm too old to kill again;" and "I could never live anywhere else but Beverly Hills because of my Tuesday night Mahjong group." When you were fed up and couldn't stand to hear another word, they'd tell you how much your friendship meant and describe your life perfectly, from the day you were born, after reading your palm or tea leaves - information they might have gathered from gossip.

One woman told Vivienne she'd refused to stop smoking unless her husband bought her a diamond. When he died she was distraught. Not because of the obvious loss. She'd given up smoking, her one true love, for ten long years and could never get that back.

When Vivienne first set foot inside the cafe she felt out of place, the way she did when neighbors slammed doors in her face after grabbing a pudding. The more uncomfortable, the more she substituted Ricard for coffee. The more she drank, the more she socialized. The more she spoke, the more at ease she became. The more at ease, the more outgoing. The more outgoing, the more people discovered her talent for making anyone she talked to feel like family; her ability to befriend, without threat, both men and women.

They all began confiding in her.

As with my father's anecdotes, I remember two more than others.

Howard, a pink-faced American from Southern California who lived with his parents till he was thirty, worked at Disneyland Paris since its inception. He roamed Fantasyland dressed as Goofy and was an integral part of light parades and photographs.

He saw families from all over the world. It was the highlight of their year, possibly their lives, but when they arrived the children were out of control and the parents argued about money, lack of facilities and shade. This was more than unfulfilled expectations. They believed that being

part of the Disney magic would allow them to forget, if only for a weekend, their dismal existence.

They never did.

Howard had been on Lithium as long as he could remember and blamed Uncle Walt for his mood swings. He stopped taking his medication and fucked Tinkerbell, one Sunday afternoon, on Captain Hook's pirate ship ten minutes before the park was closing. Unfortunately, it was watched enthusiastically by Boy Scout troop #75 who'd traveled all the way from Montana for an International Jamboree.

Howard was let go unceremoniously.

On Bastille Day he begged Vivienne, in the Goofy voice, to suck his cock in the unisex bathroom.

Ambrose, from Sussex, was anything but Goofy. Well mannered to a fault, he was proud of the fact that he sacrificed passion to maintain an orderly, quiet existence. It didn't matter what was being discussed, be it war or child abuse, Ambrose's response was restrained and impartial. The

only time he became outraged was when Howard asked a British couple what they were eating because it looked appetizing.

It was the ultimate invasion of privacy.

After a few months Vivienne had trouble breathing, the way she did in Peggy's hospital room. It didn't matter that there were dozens of windows or that they were usually wide open. There wasn't enough air to support her and Ambrose.

She wanted to shove his rolled umbrella up his ass. The only thing that stopped her was the belief that Ambrose wouldn't react or change expression, preferring to light a cigarette while inquiring about the length of the handle.

She changed routine again, forsaking the cafe for a twelfth-century church set back on a narrow, cobblestone street she wandered down after one too many Ricard's.

She'd enter and go directly to the holy water, splash her face as if she was taking a bath, cross herself and stare at the stained glass behind the pulpit till her eyes hurt. She'd wander around the cathedral after that, right to left, never left to right, and study the saints in front of their well-preserved frescoes, pausing at whoever touched her the most; usually Saint Catherine or Saint Margaret. The reason wasn't always clear. It was more of a feeling.

She'd light candles and stare into the flames. As her lungs filled with holy spirit she prayed. Methodical, as always, she did so in chronological order. Her mother. Her father. Her brothers. Me. Peggy. She asked for the things we didn't have and wished we did, including sanity. Never

things for herself.

As the months dragged on, when she didn't receive any

revelations or salvation, she felt cheated and fantasized about shoving a handful of memorial candles up the priest's ass. When she seriously considered tracking down Jim Duarte's daughter to make it into a colorful piece of stained glass, she calmly pushed a grieving couple aside, stole a chalice from the altar and changed routine again.

She spent all her free time at the catacombs, Oscar Wilde's grave at Pere Lachaise, the Trocadero where Anais Nin had an abortion and, though it was a long walk from the hotel, the house where Marcel Proust's doctor examined Debussy's first wife after she failed to kill herself with a gun shot to the chest.

* * *

The mental hospital lounge doubled as an entertainment center. Every other Sunday it was used for Bingo. Thursdays were reserved for local talent, from inventors to majorettes. Musicians went through the motions on Tuesdays, guitarists and fourth-rate singers crooning standards like "Feelings" and "Oh My Papa." Specialty acts, clowns, comedians, jugglers and magicians highlighted most Saturday nights.

They all came to polish their craft and make enough to pay their rent which was habitually overdue.

Occasionally a patient died during a performance and nobody knew till they were found, the following day, with the same tormented expression they displayed while listening to "Joshua Fought The Battle Of Jericho."

One Saturday night Vivienne asked "Le Grand Francois" if he could make her disappear. She couldn't take it any more. Le Grand Francois looked like he was just sentenced to the guillotine. He had no sense of humor, in French or English, and didn't realize she was joking. He was actually afraid of her, as if her despair was a disease that could rub off. When Vivienne saw the fear in his eyes she amended her request, pleading with him to make the French musician who sang "New York, New York" phonetically disappear instead.

He didn't understand that either.

As attendants started setting up risers for the madrigal singers, Le Grand Francois snuck out the side door. Moving to the farthest edge of the terrace he leaned against the wall, lit a cigarette and stepped in dog shit. Unlike Americans who would have cursed a blue streak, Le Grand Francois actually smiled. Stepping in animal droppings, left foot first, was considered good luck in France. This supported Vivienne's recent observation that there was more dog shit in Paris than all The United States combined. It also made her realize how much of an outsider she was and

that she'd never understand France, the culture or the people, unless she spoke the language. Even then she would be reduced to talking about the lack of rain, the rising price of petrol, the benefits of organic products and France's tradition of playing concussive, physical rugby, although their star had dimmed internationally over the past few years; subjects on a par with the ungodly heat, new trucks, riding mowers and the fucking Dallas Cowboys.

It made Vivienne appreciate Peggy all the more because she never minced words. Their relationship wasn't "raindrops on roses, cream-colored ponies and wild geese that fly," but it was more than Vivienne expected. Peggy was honest, funny, brave and possibly the smartest person Vivienne had ever known. God help anyone who mistook her irreverent directnessfor simplicity. Even when she was drunk her ideas were fascinating, influenced by the thousands of books she'd read to protect her from her own scenario.

As time went on these same books began to peak Vivienne's curiosity. While she sat and waited she started reading Jane

Austen, Colette, Germaine Greer, Lillian Hellman, Juliet Mitchell, Anais Nin and Ayn Rand, confronting issues she habitually avoided; women's struggles and rights.

She also started reading Le Monde, a French newspaper she found beside Peggy's bed every morning, although she required a dictionary for most expressions.

Seeing her interest in the French culture the other visitors began bringing her books, many bound in leather, by French philosophers they held in high esteem. Writers like Abelard, Descarte, Pascal, Rousseau, Sartre and Voltaire.

This information would have been wasted back in Lone Star Springs where anything Vivienne read, saw or heard more controversial than flower arrangements failed to make a dent. But, the more Vivienne's consciousness expanded, the more her new life took over. She spent countless hours contemplating her untapped power. Even if she used it for only a day she could say she was everything she was intended to be. Like Peggy wanted. While she tried to figure out what it was, she also worried that it had passed her by entirely after so many years of neglect.

She was so afraid for so long.

This was significant for three reasons. One, after putting hundreds of people ahead of herself over the years, after saving so many lives, she'd earned the right to save her own. Two, identifying and maximizing her power was the best way she could think of to apologize to Peggy for not being in the hotel room when she needed her most. Three, it was also a way of apologizing to the world for keeping its ugliness at arms length - for failing to realize that when

something horrible was done to one woman, it was done to all of them.

* * *

After Arthur and I demolished three healthy servings of rhubarb pie, Mister Davidow continued his saga.

Because of flight 516 he went to his supervisors and proposed a survey, to be implemented by the National Aeronautics and Space Administration, that could affect the safety of American aviation. It required extensive interviews with pilots, air traffic controllers, mechanics and flight attendants. It included questions about miscues, how often they saw risky incidents like near mid-air collisions and runway incursions. It was a pioneering effort because NASA would be reaching out to airline personnel instead of waiting for personnel to come to them. The added benefit of anonymity would yield insights into problems they wouldn't ordinarily be privy to.

From its inception everyone involved was enthusiastic and knew the idea was sound.

Theoretically it would be extremely beneficial.

Realistically it didn't stand a chance.

NASA lost interest in the study before any useful conclusions could be drawn. They were bogged down by numerous space projects and had an already tight budget reduced. That was no excuse, however, to terminate the study before they interviewed three quarters of their targeted witnesses, the controllers, the mechanics and the attendants.

There was no mention of problems with pilots asleep on the flight deck, complaints about fatigue or difficulty communicating with air traffic controllers, and obviously no indication of how often they occurred or whether they were getting worse.

With air corridors growing more and more congested, Mister Davidow had hoped the survey would turn up problems inherent to air travel that could not only be fixed but put air travelers' minds at ease.

It didn't.

Frustrated, this was the first time Mister Davidow confided

in me, information that airline personnel would never tell because they needed air travel to remain as innocuous as Vivienne's self-image.

When there's a problem, the airlines say things like this:

"In twenty-six of the twenty-nine airplanes destroyed in accidents, ninety percent of the passengers have survived. In a 1995 crash outside Baltimore, Maryland, a wreck so violent the plane broke into multiple sections, two hundred and sixty-six of the two hundred and seventy passengers and crew members pulled through, including a three-year-old girl who was securely belted in as instructed by the flight attendant.

Flight attendants have reasons when they tell you to keep your seat belt fastened. People have been injured bouncing off the ceiling when a plane suddenly dropped a few hundred feet in severe turbulence. For anyone buckled in during an incident like this there is no danger."

The airlines never say things like this:

The human body is anywhere from fifty-five to seventy-eight percent water depending on its size. Not dissimilar to a water balloon. If you drop that balloon from the smallest height, it bursts when it strikes the ground. It's the same with cells in your body when there's a sudden impact. In a plane crash, for example. They explode and you turn to mush.

Depending on the speed the plane is traveling when that impact occurs, the greater the mush. At slower speeds, if you're wearing a seat belt with a shoulder harness, you may survive but will probably have severe bruising where the strap held you in place. If you don't have a shoulder harness, and no commercial aircraft does, your ten-pound head will continue moving forward while the seat belt holds the rest of you in place. If you're luckier than you've ever been in your life, an unlikely variable, your head will bounce off whatever's in front of you, be it instrument panel or seat. More commonly, your head will continue on, ripping away from your body and leaving a bloody stump.

This is the real reason flight attendants tell you, with a cheerful smile, to lean forward and place your head in your lap during an emergency.

They don't want it rolling down the aisle.

Of course, it's all a moot point. There's a ninety percent chance you will be torn in half by the lap belt.

Ground crews assigned to wreckage hate this because it complicates their job and makes positive identification impossible when sorting through piles of dismembered torsos, arms, legs, hearts and lungs, all beginning to rot and stink.

This is why so many controllers live a hard life. They work hard. They drink hard. They play hard. They even have a hard motto:

"God rested on the seventh day. Air traffic controllers never do. They take double shifts."

Now that I think about it, I disagree with Mister Davidow about one and one thing only. Controllers aren't like doctors. Not when all is said and done. Except for theday off, they're much closer to Gods.

* * *

While Vivienne was learning about French tradition from Le Grand Francois, Peggy was receiving an education of her own. The night she was admitted Claude snuck into her room and leaned over her bed with the look of an older sibling mentoring a newborn.

"Your soul starts at the top of your head, moves down through your neck to your chest and then to the stomach."

Peggy said nothing, although her eyes darted back and forth

when he rested his hand on her stomach and began outlining it with his fingernails.

"It's all white and pure like mine. We are the same person."

Claude shook the wooden slats at the sides of her bed.

"I don't see many souls like yours, certainly not here in the house of black souls.

He shook the bars again, grunting like those Russian tennis players who try to maximize power with every stroke.

"In spite of everything that goes on in the world, people have this fantasy it's a safe and wonderful place. It's not. It rears up and bites you when you least expect it."

He took a quick breath and tried to calm himself. His judgement clouded when he lost control and only a fool lets anger get the best of him. He knew that better than most. So, removing a deck of playing cards from his pants pocket he shuffled them quickly, fanned and held them out in front of her.

"Pick a card."

When Peggy failed to do as instructed Claude removed one from the middle and held it up, facing away from her.

The queen of hearts.

"People who have as much in common as we do, Peggy, people who are made for each other, can read each other's minds. Whenever you think of this card it will represent our unbreakable bond. I know you agree because you're American and Americans stand up for what's right."

Unlike his former self-important and condescending attitude toward Americans, this was said with enormous respect.

Most of Claude's life he thought of France and the United States at odds with one another over everything from politics to matters of the heart.

Politically, the differences were obvious.

The French were sophisticated and had a rich history to

fall back on. Americans lacked worldliness and were like cowboys in the old west.

Romantically, the French were liberal and open minded. Americans were puritans, moralizers and hypocrites.

More significant, Americans did not know the difference between a fine Camembert and a Big Mac.

Recently, this changed.

The U.S. had spawned a thriving cheese-making tradition that looked a lot like the France of old. American artisan cheese manufacturers were becoming the new standard for gourmets all over the world, including France, accomplished with a reckless audacity the French outwardly despised but secretly admired.

In essence, they'd become French.

If Claude was to live honestly he had to admit this and trump his cynicism. Reaching into his back pocket he slid out a copy of "Le Monde" and read underlined sections.

Genetic engineering. Mass production. Cheap imports.

Lowering the paper he shook his head in disgust and pointed toward the window.

"People out there don't see these things for what they really are, Peggy. The corporate world presents them as something good that will improve their lives but they never do."

His voice began to waver.

"In five years half the French population will have no memory of what real cheese tastes like."

Reaching under his shirt he slid out a brightly painted water color of a tree and laid it at her feet.

"France is losing its whiteness."

Even though Peggy never responded, Claude returned night after night. It was her soul more than her silence that captivated him. Her pureness of spirit represented everything that was right in the world. She was delicate and fresh and as unfettered by life as most people were burdened -

Norman Rockwell to their Hieronymus Bosch. She never interrupted or questioned anything Claude said because she and she alone understood Claude's beliefs. At the same time, he knew she could hear every word and would speak up if she had a problem. American women were brash and outspoken and told you what was in their hearts. There was no reason to think Peggy was different. Accordingly, he attached great significance to her smallest facial tic. Each was a story unto itself. A confession. A pledge. Agreement.

She was the great love of Claude's life.

Every visit was the same.

Claude would sneak into her room, remove the queen of hearts from his pocket and ask her to identify it. When she failed to speak he replaced the card with a newspaper and read the headlines, extolling ordinary people who had the courage to stand up for what they believed in, usually resulting in their violent and untimely deaths.

Sometimes he paced back and forth. Sometimes he threw the paper down in frustration. Sometimes he performed a mind-boggling feat of strength to entertain her. He'd take an ordinary hammer, one with a wooden handle, and squeeze the bottom till the metal top flipped off from the force he was exerting.

"Only the truth will set you free" was what he always said afterwards.

Leaning over Peggy he'd take her lifeless hand in his and stroke it gently.

"Sometimes you have to die for your convictions."

Peggy said nothing, as always, which Claude took as a sign of approval.

"What are you willing to die for, Peggy? You can't live the

good life till you have the courage to know why you'd end it."

* * *

It was a Monday like every other, so doctors shuttled in and out of Peggy's room, adjusting catheters and tubes while posing familiar questions. They'd stopped asking about drugs since they knew what she was taking; intravenous doses of Ativan and Haldol strong enough to kill an elephant.

As was customary one of the nurses pricked Peggy's foot with a needle and asked if she felt anything. Though Peggy hadn't responded to other questions, this time she sprang straight up as if someone had substituted adrenalin for her precious tranquilizers.

"Do that again, honey, and I'll shove that fucking pin so far up your ass you'll have to go back to medical school to learn how to find it."

Peggy's condition improved from then on.

She began to move and walk and eat. Her altered appearance suggested she was getting happier as well as stronger. Her hair had grown, the small tufts that stuck out every which way, like a cactus, were now combed and slicked back. She began using makeup and wearing clothes that showed off her figure. She even displayed a sense of humor when speaking with her doctors, though they rarely understood.

"Next time I'm going to be Davy-fucking-Crockett instead of Joan of Arc. He had better hats."

It was as if she'd been in a coma and suddenly woke up, with no memory of time passed, and was ready to pick up where she left off.

The doctors were so encouraged they decided to let her out for a day. There were rules, of course. She was not allowed to have alcohol or tobacco. She wasn't allowed to drive. She had to be back in the hospital by closing and needed to be under adult supervision at all times. None of

these were a problem since Vivienne would be her chaperone.

For the first time in ten months Vivienne would venture out into a world where, if she yelled "help," people would respond.

For the first time in ten months, Peggy would be free.

The day before her release staff members discovered random acts of delinquency around the hospital. All the hammers had been stolen from maintenance, their heads removed and strewn haphazardly on dining room tables. Water colors hanging on bulletin boards were shredded and left in the occupational therapy area. Someone had even urinated on the kitchen counters where women prepared for their return to society.

On the morning of Peggy's scheduled departure her alarm rang at 5:45. She'd been up for hours combing out the front of her hair the way Vivienne liked it. She'd chosen Vivienne's favorite dress and applied Vivienne's preferred lipstick.

It felt like a holiday.

Vivienne was there to collect her at nine sharp.

When Peggy walked out of her room Vivienne couldn't help noticing a glow and lightness that hadn't been there for almost a year. After a quick hug she pecked Vivienne gently on both cheeks.

"Whoever invented chlorpromazine should get the Nobel fucking prize."

It was the only thing she said before turning and heading for the exit. En route she passed Claude who was unfastening a water color covering a health regulations ordinance.

"I never thought I'd have to say goodbye to myself."

She smiled but said nothing.

"I must be doing something wrong."

While Claude had seen her every night for the past ten months, this was the first time Peggy was aware of him.

As the two women walked out of the hospital Vivienne suggested they keep their travel time to a minimum. In a place where so many things could go wrong it was best to focus on points of interest close at hand. She'd discovered that, in 1897, a man drove a four-horse-power car from Paris to Trouville and broke the existing speed record. He topped an unthinkable twenty-three miles per hour. Vivienne thought it would be fun to retrace his journey.

Peggy looked at her as if she was the one who'd been institutionalized.

It was May 30th, the anniversary of Joan of Arc's last breath. She wanted to make a special trip to Rouen, the town where Joan was burned. It was a little out of the way but the opportunity to finally close the door on this chapter of her life far outweighed the drudgery of a long drive.

Vivienne protested.

Peggy didn't flinch.

Although Peggy was declared mentally unfit, she held the power in their relationship. I thought this strange because Vivienne always told me that relationships of any kind worked best when the people involved were equals. Equal commitment. Equal intelligence. Equal participation. The problem was, from the time she was young, Vivienne was what my father called "a giver" - someone who sacrificed by putting others' needs ahead of their own. Like a parent, only by choice.

This was understandable since Vivienne's mother, Julie, her lone role model, lived a life that was nothing but sacrifice

Julie's only joy came from cooking.

Whenever she was haunted by her husband's abandonment and unable to sleep, she'd get out of bed, go downstairs, collect ingredients and bake the cookies her husband begged her for at least twice a week. Her secret was four teaspoons of fresh orange juice, something she never told her ex or any other living soul.

During their marriage she associated the smell of orange juice with family and love. Since she was denied that luxury, the scent reminded her that no other woman, young or old, especially if they worked at the Post Office, knew how to make those fucking cookies.

While she baked her shoulders dropped. Her face relaxed. Her jaw loosened. Breathing slowed and centered in her abdomen. It allowed her to forget, for an hour at least, she'd been given the old heave-ho.

When the cookies were done, cooled and perfect, she ground them up in the disposal, climbed back upstairs and slept soundly till morning.

After watching this ritual night after night, Vivienne realized it was where she was needed most, vowing to dedicate the rest of her life making Julie and others like her comfortable.

She'd nurse them all.

If this decision had been made by anyone else it would have involved jealousy, self-loathing and desperation. After the life she'd led, however, Vivienne firmly believed there were those born to lead and those born to lend support. Taking care of someone who'd already carved their niche allowed her to over-come her own insecurities and bask in self- approval, even though she inexplicably burst into tears whenever she saw someone triumph in their chosen field; like winning the hundred meter dash at the Olympics.

Deep down inside, she also clung to the belief that people stopped taunting you if you were fulfilling their needs.

* * *

The closer Arthur and I became the more he left Mrs. Scott unattended. After I was too exhausted to play he'd follow me inside and bark till I locked the front door behind us. When it was time for bed we went upstairs and he lay down on the rug. This routine never changed. His patrolling, however, became more obsessive. He started checking entry points every forty-five minutes. Then thirty. Then fifteen.

The only thing Arthur couldn't protect me from were my nightmares. As soon as I leaned back on my pillow and shut my eyes, I was turning right at the porch again and entering our back yard. No matter how hard I tried to avoid them, everyone was always there. The teacher. The principal. The annoying girls, laughing and taunting. Worse, my dreams became more irrational and unsettling.

My math teacher had positioned herself beneath the banner that now wished me more than a Happy Valentines Day.

"THERE IS NO CHARGE FOR FLESHING AND SALTING."

The principal was on a podium reading from the Old Testament.

"Be careful while skinning. Don't cut part way into the hide. Try pulling out instead of straight down. Use your knife sparingly. Peel the animal."

To his left was a garbage can filled with a half dozen deer heads, complaining that hunters let their hides dry out without adequate salt.

I even started understanding what the girls were saying, although it made less sense than when their words were garbled.

"Dude, St. Jude was born into a Jewish family in Paneas, a town in Galilee later rebuilt by the Romans and renamed Caesarea Philippi. In all probability he spoke both Greek and

Aramaic, like almost all of his contemporaries in that area, and was a farmer by trade."

Breaking into giggles, her friend chimed in as if she were talking about the latest fashion.

"Fucking A. Saint Jude preached the Gospel in Judea, Samaria, Idumaea, Syria, Mesopotamia and Libya, and is believed to have been the first to bring Christianity to Armenia where he suffered martyrdom and was eventually venerated as the patron saint of the Armenian Apostolic

Church."

The last girl jumped up and down, squealed with joy and high-fived everyone.

"This is some heavy shit. Devotion to Saint Jude began again in earnest in the 1800s, starting in Italy and Spain, spreading to South America, and finally to the U.S."

Not to be outdone the deer heads shouted from inside their pail.

"It began around Chicago, owing to the influence of the Claretians in the 1920s, and spread all the way to Texas. Novena prayers to St. Jude helped people deal with the pressures caused by the Great Depression." It finally hit me. Texas? Could this, somehow, be the proof I'd been searching for, verification that the statue that killed my mother's sister was, indeed, Saint Jude? I

walked toward the girls for the first time instead of backing away. Before I could speak all three burst into flames, their heads ripping away from their bodies leaving bloody stumps.

As they rolled past a sign that said "Treat your hides like meat or they'll spoil" they spoke in unison.

"God may have rested on the seventh day,..."

The flames grew higher, heat intensified and the heads blew me a kiss.

"...but we will never leave your side."

They all bounced into the pail and started arguing with the deer about which standard leather color was best, saddle, palomino, black or cream.

I bolted straight up out of my troubled sleep.

Eyes wide, sweating profusely, I remembered that Joan of Arc's father had a dream when she was younger foretelling everything that happened. He saw her dressed for battle. He saw her capturing Orleans. He saw her burned at the stake. He knew what would happen as surely as I knew my neighbor would die.

* * *

The youngest of four, the only girl, Vivienne was the one child that wasn't planned. As such she grew up last in the family pecking order, something that rendered her humorless and, like Dwight, without a sense of the absurd. These feelings weren't helped by the fact that her father only wanted boys and her brothers were considered geniuses. There was no official recognition from clubs like Mensa but people were always talking about their exorbitant IQs. No one, not even her parents, revealed the actual scores to Vivienne. The last thing they wanted was to add to her feelings of inferiority.

One winter night, after everyone had gone to bed, Vivienne discovered an old baby book in her mother's sewing basket. In it were notes about each child with comparisons at different ages. Next to her brother, Thomas, the eldest and most decisive, was a brief description of his progress.

When he was three it said the following: "Showing an amazing command of the English language. Using words like 'cope'." Running her finger down the page Vivienne came to her description at the same age. "Vivienne's making enormous strides. Today she said 'See birdie'."

Resigned to a life of embarrassing incompetence, she never expected much or opened the book again.

Her brothers' intelligence, sadly, proved to be a curse not a blessing. Believing they'd seen everything there was to see in Texas by the time their voices began to change, each rebelled against the staid predictability of the suburbs for more challenging pursuits - and paid the price.

After completing his junior year at Baylor University, Thomas joined a summer expedition going to Columbia to study its ecosystem. They hiked through the Rainforest and canoed down the Amazon and Orinoco River basins. While eleven other students collected fauna, Thomas traversed a slow-moving part of the river. When he reached shore he had the good fortune and considerable bad luck to witness something few people have seen, a cluster of anacondas in a breeding ball - twelve males coiled around one female.

Although the trip leader insisted anaconda attacks on humans had never been documented in that part of the world, by the time she responded to Thomas's cries he was partially digested.

Rather than attend college, Vivienne's next oldest brother, Roger, went to work for an elephant orphanage in Nairobi, a preserve dedicated to rehabilitating young elephants who'd experienced trauma in their lives; from the horror of watching their parents slaughtered for ivory to physical abuse at the hands of poachers. If gone unchecked these memories stayed with them forever because elephants really don't forget. They have nightmares and wake up screaming the same way I did. Though many zoologists maintain that a healthy, happy elephant is one whose life is free from human interference, the preserve taught them how to trust again.

Roger was one of a half dozen employees who helped them get over that hump. He fed them milk, all important for growth.

He slept with them and never left their side for the first two years. The elephants in his care followed him wherever he went because, for all intents and purposes, he was family. He even taught them games like soccer so they could form new social bonds before being reintroduced into the wild.

In his fifth year, during one such game, a usually sure-footed elephant lost its balance on the slick grass, stumbled and fell on Roger who had no warning while standing on the side-lines and, therefore, no time to escape.

Unable to rise, the beast cried out but it was impossible for the other employees to help. Since the animal was thrashing every which way they couldn't get close.

The rest of Roger's elephants rushed to his aid, raising the fallen pachyderm using their combined weight and strength, but by the time they succeeded every bone in Roger's body was crushed, including his skull. While he lay there other elephants came over and touched him with their trunks, some applying clay to stem the flow of blood.

Years later, after they'd been reintroduced into the wild, they still returned, bringing their own children to touch the spot where Roger had fallen.

Kevin, the youngest of the three brothers, enlisted in the air force after a recruiter spoke at his school and promised it was the best way to see the world. For once this proved true. There wasn't a country Kevin yearned for he didn't visit.

During these years he was recognized and rewarded for his dedication and fearlessness, serving as a paratrooper in special forces. Stationed in Germany after five thousand jumps he trained soldiers from all walks of life. On his five-thousandth-and-first jump Kevin was demonstrating what to do in case your primary chute failed to open. Waiting till he was less than a mile above the earth he deployed his secondary chute without a hitch, floating casually toward the targeted area until he was blown off course by a sudden gust of wind, toward a sign that said the following:

"We obey the law to stay in business, but we obey the laws of physics to stay alive."

The simple medical description of Kevin's death found in armed forces files failed to describe the horror of his fate. Death by "multiple amputations" sanitized a grisly accident witnessed by both those in the sky and on the ground, watching helplessly as Kevin landed above a wind tunnel and was drawn into the nacelle's slow-spinning machinery. His chute, tangling on the revolving main shaft, dragged him to his death.

This, more than a roving eye, was the reason Vivienne's father left their happy home. He couldn't cope with losing a son, let alone three, and was unable to receive comfort from his wife who, like he, was immobilized by grief.

His behavior grew stranger every day.

He had eaten the family Cockatiel and begun telling neighbors we were all reincarnated and should be labeled "pre-owned" when he met Emily, who worked at the Lone Star Post Office and delivered the notices informing him of his children's demise. When she offered solace, both mental and physical, Frank accepted with open arms.

From a very young age Vivienne too had the wanderlust of a nomad, but the closest she came to rebellion was a fleeting thought of becoming a Lutheran, something she rejected because she wasn't sure they had Lent and couldn't imagine a religion without sacrifice.

This was why she cherished her travel shows. They reminded her of her brothers' spirit and kept their memories alive. They also reinforced the benefits of a slow, predictable existence compared to none at all.

Unfortunately, a life of acquiescence did not guarantee that Vivienne's formative years were rewarding. Her heart ached constantly because it was handed over so readily. She was always picking up people who needed protection, permission or submission to feel good about themselves. My father was the perfect example, although far from perfect.

Vivienne's feelings were invariably stronger, her intelligence higher, her participation greater than fifty percent.

Except with Peggy.

Vivienne relished her supporting role and wished she could do more, not less. A simple chore like washing Peggy's hair and pinning it up was as rewarding as eating in the finest restaurant. She also respected Peggy enormously. There was her poetry, of course, that elevated her above the commonplace, but it was secondary to her spirit. In spite of all the damage inflicted, down deep Peggy was still as innocent as when she was young, as if she'd made the transition to adulthood in a couple of days, skipping years of devastation.

Not everything was innocent, of course.

Whenever Vivienne looked at Peggy she had the overwhelming urge to rip her clothes off, ravish her and lick every inch. What she was feeling in the waiting room, while true in theory, was nothing more than avid self-protection stronger than even Arthur could provide. What she said to me about love, on the other hand, was the only lie she ever told.

Being in love, the ability to give and have it returned, was the greatest gift a person could receive at any age, especially when it came after you'd given up and never expected to see it again, like someone who went off to war and stopped calling. It kept you hopeful. It kept you young. It allowed you to look out any window and see the good, not the bad. It really was "raindrops on roses, cream-colored ponies and wild geese that fly with the moon on their

    wings."

As difficult as it was for her to admit, it made Vivienne

happy and she felt like crying for joy, the way my real mother did after kissing my father for the very first time.

* * *

When Vivienne and Peggy arrived in Rouen, church bells rang throughout the city. For Peggy, who'd gotten used to hearing traffic outside her window, it was more than a welcome relief. Their resounding reminder of peace, every quarter hour, was inspirational.

One other thing became quickly apparent. Although Joan of Arc had been dead since 1431, her memorabilia would live forever. In any given square you could purchase a plastic Jeanne d'Arc sword, Jeanne d'Arc armor, Jeanne d'Arc peasant clothing, men's and women's identical except for size, Jeanne d'Arc banners, historical maps, coats of arms and pepper mills. You were also welcome to view a Jeanne d'Arc documentary in the local theater, attend a Jeanne d'Arc lecture, purchase one of a hundred biographies, drink at the Jeanne d'Arc bar, sleep at the Jeanne d'Arc Inn or get a medieval haircut.

Beyond all that Vivienne was surprised to find an exuberant, scrupulously maintained city with enough culture to quench the thirst of the most ardent tourist.

Peggy didn't care and insisted they take the Jeanne d'Arc tour.

In the center of the old part of town, on the right bank of the Seine, stood Joan's church, the Cathedral of Notre-Dame, a Gothic masterpiece that had been the focus of many a Monet painting.

This was their first stop.

Massive and beautiful, it more than held its own with its namesake in Paris. Vivienne, quite frankly, was tired of all churches, breathtaking or otherwise, because of Who and what they represented. Peggy, on the other hand, embraced every relic and piece of art on display, delighted that they were described in detail in English on brass plaques hung along the walls.

While others looked on with interest, Peggy dragged her fingers over anything she was allowed to touch, desperate to feel their history.

She ran her hand over the elaborately articulated central doorway on the west front. She ran it up and down the "Tree of Jesse" in the tympanum. When they left the church and continued down the Jeanne d'Arc trail, Peggy touched the richly sculptured Portail des Libraires, honoring

the shops Joan once frequented. She touched the tomb of Cardinals Georges I and II of Amboise, archbishops of Rouen when Joan was executed. She touched a representation of the Death and Assumption of the Virgin, symbolic of Joan's life. She touched the HÃ'tel Dieu where Joan once stayed and Flaubert was later born. On rue Jeanne d'Arc she touched La Tour Jeanne d'Arc where Joan was imprisoned before her execution. She touched the remains of a castle built by Philippe Auguste where Joan was tortured and in the Palais de Justice she touched the crypt where Joan's heart was supposedly preserved.

Peggy explained that, according to legend, Joan's heart remained full of blood and could not be burnt despite all the oils, sulfur and charcoal heaped upon it. This was a sign that she was a virgin when she died.

Virgin hearts did not burn.

Last but not least she touched the spot in Place du Vieux Marche where Joan was executed.

If Peggy was prohibited from touching with her hands she ran her eyes over every surface, crack and crevice.

When the tour was over they passed a square with a

concert in progress. The bandstand was raised above the street a good three feet. Wooden with metal supports, it was as withered as the musicians themselves, ranging in age from post adolescence to those, slightly bent, who needed

assistance reaching their seats. Each was a proud member of the local police force, which is why the gendarme station was directly behind them. They all wore uniforms but there was no homogeneity like Lone Star lawns. Some were buttoned all the way up. Some were open at the collar. Some were unbuttoned and their T-shirts exposed.

Thirty-four in total and not a stringed instrument among them. Saxophones. French horns. Tubas. Trombones. Trumpets. Cornets and bugles.

Leaping into the air for the smallest crescendo, the conductor worked from memory instead of a score and the music exploded the moment he raised his baton, played with so much emotion the elderly musicians sat straighter than ever.

Even Vivienne could not restrain herself, allowing Peggy and everyone else to see her soul.

When the concert was finished an old woman seated in front of Vivienne turned and summed up the experience with six simple words.

"It was a gift from God."

As musicians packed to leave, Peggy rolled over and exposed a vulnerable underbelly. One of her doctors was close friends with the owner of a nearby restaurant that received three stars from Michelin. Customers were kept to a minimum and reservations were required a year in advance.

Knowing Vivienne's preoccupation with food Peggy had the good doctor get them in.

"A restaurant receiving no stars from Michelin is still honored and grateful to be included in their guide. One star signals a very good restaurant in its category. Two stars indicates excellent cooking, meriting a detour from any trip. Three stars means exceptional cuisine, worth a special journey unto itself."

* * *

Even Mrs. Davidow's cooking failed to calm her husband's nerves the next time he sat down for a heart-to-heart with me and Arthur.

Two airborne planes had come within a half-mile of colliding at DFW Airport. It brought back all his worst memories of flight 516 and made him feel helpless, like my father with Dwight, the one emotion a controller can not permit.

Delta Flight 923 was arriving when the pilot decided to abort his landing and execute a "go-around," a routine procedure used during heavy congestion. In this case nothing was routine. It caused the flight to intersect with the path of Comair Flight 720, a regional jet that was taking off on another runway.

The FAA moved quickly to change takeoff and landing procedures on perpendicular runways, the kind involved in the incident, a change designed to ensure that aircraft on one runway clear out of the path of the other runway before the second flight comes down.

The FAA also issued a warning against Delta but it was meaningless.

The reason for this, according to Mister Davidow, was simple. FAA officials were more concerned with airline profit margins than safety because they had a cozy relationship with the companies involved, often changing inspectors' findings or soft pedaling enforcement.

Case in point, the pilot had failed three pilot tests known as "check-rides" since joining Delta and had been suspected of fatigue on several occasions.

When Mister Davidow presented these facts to the FAA, citing possible pilot error, he was told that failure on a check-ride wasn't necessarily a reason for someone not to fly. It depended on what kind of failure it was. Any speculation about the pilot being impaired by fatigue was nothing more than conjecture.

Mister Davidow wanted to go over their heads but, in the past, anyone considered a whistle-blower had been disgraced, demoted or let go, destroying their credibility.

This was why Mister Davidow proposed his legislation in the first place. Anonymity was the only way problems could be broached and resolved. Otherwise people got scared and protected their backs.

It's why Congress rarely held hearings on matters such as this.

It's why controllers never testified.

* * *

Two surprises awaited Vivienne when they arrived at the restaurant. A bulldog wearing a blue beret was seated at the adjacent table, both he and his master enjoying everything set in front of them. The second was far more compelling. Peggy had arranged for their dinner to consist only of the Chef's specialties. This included the three best bottles of wine in their cellar which the owner was instructed to uncork two hours before the meal.

He selected a 1961 Romanee-Conti, a "59" La Tache and a "75" Petrus.

Although Peggy wasn't allowed to drink, she knew alcohol of that quality trumped any restrictions Vivienne would ordinarily adhere to.

Appetizers included Anchoiade Chez Gilbert, Tartines de

Pistou et Poisson Fume la Boutarde, and Saucisson Chaud Pommes a L'Huile. They were followed by Petoncles au Four la Tupina, Canard aux Olives Chez Allard and Lapin Monsieur Henny. For dessert, Mon Gateau au Chocolat and Creme Brulee.

For most of the meal Peggy was surprisingly docile, playing with the food on her plate and seemingly afraid to speak unless spoken to, as if Vivienne was her parent. By the time they reached the gateau, however, all three wine bottles were empty.

Leaning across the table Peggy gently kissed Vivienne's forehead, nose and chin. Unused to public displays Vivienne didn't know how to respond. Granted, there was rarely a moment when the two were together and some part of their bodies didn't touch, but this was far more than a wayward glance or the brush of a hand. Vivienne considered it vain and childish and was better done in private. Not that it mattered. Peggy was determined, especially after watching the bulldog devour a wedge of Camembert.

"You know what sucks about pets?"

Vivienne shook her head.

"They're always there for you. No matter what you do, even if you treat them like shit, they're all excited when you come home, waiting with their fucking tongues hanging out."

Peggy grabbed the back of Vivienne's neck, pulled her head forward and kissed her hard.

"All you have to do is feed 'em and show 'em some affection. They'll never fucking leave because they're not capable of seeing the bigger picture."

She started to say something else but her voice paused for stifled tears.

Vivienne took over.

"And the fuckers always know when you're afraid."

Scrunching up her nose, Peggy made a face like a little girl before speaking in a slightly drunken voice.

"Don't be a bitch. I'm the bitchy one in this relationship. You're the one who's supportive and patient and has a compulsion to make everything right."

"Lucky me."

"You're still being a bitch," said Peggy, before slipping the dog the rest of her cake. Standing straight up she tried to say words that were impossible for her, a simple phrase that was never used in her own home because it was like pissing on an electrified fence. You knew better. If you were stupid enough to do it you got what you deserved. So, instead of "I love you," Peggy settled for what seemed like a lesser goodbye, although it was so much more.

"Mangez," she said, pointing at Vivienne's plate.

Then she was running.

By the time Peggy hit the night she was moving at a speed she hadn't attained since childhood. It was barely a minute before she entered Place du Vieux Marche. Crossing to the exact spot where Joan of Arc was burned she felt an unexpected elation. Falling to her knees she clasped her hands in prayer.

"Our Father, which art in Heaven,..."

That's when she saw it, a dove swoop down from the rooftops and circle directly above her. She felt the same urge to laugh she had that night in Paris. This laugh wasn't intended to remind her that life was different and she was okay. This laugh was supposed to remind her that it was better to die young than be ravaged by memories, like cancer, that devoured you from the inside and rendered you defenseless.

Discarding her dress for a more natural state she reached down and retrieved a razor blade she kept hidden in the soul of her shoe. Placing it in the palm of her right hand she squeezed her fingers shut before running the blade heavily across her left wrist, vertically, severing the radial artery. The little slits remained dry for a second, as if deciding what to do, before red lines appeared and washed together like a Texas flash flood.

As blood spilled onto old cobblestones Peggy experienced the strangest sensation. She wasn't just relieved. She was positively joyful. She couldn't explain it but there was something inherently wondrous in this moment.

When Vivienne reached the square Peggy was smiling a smile she'd never seen before, one of total repose. As others began arriving and saw, with horror, the pool of blood at Peggy's feet, Vivienne saw the softness and innocence return to her face, pain in her forehead and around both eyes dissolving in the overhead light.

Peggy asked for a cross as Vivienne rushed to her side. Having given up her faith Vivienne had none. Luckily, an Italian tourist did, handing Peggy a rosary she'd bought at the Vatican and carried in her purse in case of emergency.

The moment the cross was secure Peggy forgave her mother and father and asked Vivienne to pray for her.

Later, several eyewitnesses recalled Peggy repeating the name of Jesus and invoking the aid of the saints of Paradise.

Vivienne heard none of this.

She could feel Peggy's life spurting out of her while her eyes fluttered and shut, painful memories leaving faster than her own blood.

Peggy also felt a surge of gratitude race through her veins, an appreciation for the end of her struggles and the love she was about to forsake. Reaching for her dress she withdrew a note from the pocket, pressed it into Vivienne's palm and thought something that was so unlike her she wasn't sure where it came from.

You. I would die for you.

Even more surprising was what she said. She didn't know where it came from either, although it made her feel warm inside.

"Queen of hearts."

She burst out laughing, building quickly till her body was writhing and shaking as if she was possessed. It wasn't spiteful or broken-hearted laughter. It was the laugh of a free woman. Unable to restrain herself Vivienne started laughing too, holding her sides and gasping for air. They laughed harder than they did at my father's wake. They laughed till their voices seemed to merge into one. They laughed till Peggy went limp and she left her body, the way she'd always imagined, with a triumphant gurgle, the peaceful journey of a childhood long overdue.

When they'd first met, Peggy described her favorite play to Vivienne. It traced the life of a man named Littlechap whose metaphorical rise to success was offset by the troubles and pain in his private life. It followed him through school, love, marriage, business, politics and, when all was said and done, death. At any given point Littlechap could stop whatever was happening by shouting: "Stop the world, I want to get off." Action froze and he would step out of the scene to address the audience, successfully avoiding events trying to destroy him.

The night my father died everything froze.

Air stopped circulating. Light became opaque and thick, like before a tornado. There was no sound because none could describe my loss.

If a picture is worth a thousand words, watching a loved one die is greater than all the words in all the languages in all the world.

I didn't think my life would ever return to normal. Other people reassured me it would, citing their own misfortunes. They said things like "At the end of the day," "keep your nose to the grindstone" and "time heals all wounds." As far as I was concerned these were nothing more

than cliches created by people who were afraid to get down on all fours and grovel with their pain. Nevertheless, I started sleeping through the night. I went back to school. I watched travel shows. Time really did heal and everything returned to normal.

Only it didn't.

Whatever I'd known or felt or accomplished up till that point didn't apply any more. It was all new, like the day I was born, no matter which version I believed.

This, I imagine, was how Vivienne felt when she read Peggy's note.

"You win," it said.

Underneath was a poem but she wasn't able to read more than a segment. Everything inside her knotted up, causing gut-wrenching convulsions that shook every finger. As her eyes blurred with shock the owner of the restaurant came running.

Even through tears Vivienne could see the enormous concern on his face. Whatever she thought about the French culture when she first arrived, it now included the likes of Abelard, Descarte, Pascal, Rousseau, Sartre and Voltaire. She didn't necessarily agree with their philosophies but there was no questioning their regard for the human condition.

In this case the restaurant owner's angst had little to do with nominalist views about universals, mathematics, mystic understanding, a common good, free will or positive social action. His concerns were far more plebeian, something that would have shown Peggy, and even Claude, that cheese and truth don't always set you free.

In Peggy's haste to put an end to her troubled existence, she'd forgotten to pay the bill.

PART II

In spite of all the rich food, by the time Vivienne returned to Lone Star Springs she'd lost over forty pounds, most of her excess weight. Although this left her thinner than she'd been since childhood, early predictions about her slimmed down beauty proved erroneous. Vivienne had one of those faces that was only pretty when it had a little extra flesh on it. Take that away and her bone structure was awkward, she looked anemic and her nose, which no one noticed when she was heavy, became her most prominent feature.

Whenever Vivienne looked in a mirror she was reminded of the Punch and Judy puppets she'd seen in Les Tuileries. While this was charming and entertaining in Paris' most picturesque garden, back home in Lone Star Springs, in real life, it was the ultimate genetic practical joke.

Her daily routine became little more than bitter recollection. This kept her chained to misery and prevented her from moving forward, constantly looking over her shoulder for the elephants and anacondas to crush or digest her.

Her first Sunday back she read an article in the Lone Star

Chronicle about a woman who'd lost her husband and three of her four children when their car was broad-sided by a train headed for Oklahoma. Every night, said the widow, she thanked God for sparing her son. Vivienne ran out the door, drove to her house and yelled at her the moment she stepped outside. How could she be so stupid? God didn't save anyone. He slaughtered her family the way he'd butchered millions before them. If she had to be grateful, thank the Son-Of-A-Bitch for making one of His patented mistakes. He'd obviously tried to get them all.

The only nurturing person I'd ever known was sinking below life's surface, caught in an undertow of grief that dragged her further and further from shore.

Some of this was due to unforeseen debt, owing the Rouen restaurant a small fortune for Peggy's farewell dinner. Although management absolved her from the food they could not reciprocate with the wine. Even in France certain items are irreplaceable. Under the auspices of the American Embassy a payment plan was worked out before Vivienne was allowed to leave the country.

That was the least of it, of course. Vivienne's real problems centered around her struggles with regret and guilt that brought her to her knees.

Vivienne decided God was right after all. She had no right being happy. Her one saving grace, ironically, turned out to be the same as mine.

Arthur.

She'd basically ignored him till one night while she was baking cookies. Arthur was lying on the linoleum floor across from her, chewing a bone I'd given him the day before. It was making such a racket Vivienne stopped sifting flour, threw up her arms in frustration and screamed.

"That noise is driving me crazy!"

Without the slightest hesitation Arthur picked up the bone in his mouth, walked over to the welcome mat, lay back down and resumed chewing where it wouldn't make a sound. One minute later Vivienne was cradling his chin with one hand and petting him with the other, stroking his back as if trying to smooth out the wrinkles in his coat; thanking him in the same tone Lone Star housewives used when they plied me with food. If she told Arthur to sit he sat. If she said lie down he was on his belly before she finished her sentence. These were simple commands, granted, but she realized his intelligence went far beyond that. Arthur was smarter than all my father's friends combined, although that wasn't anything to brag about.

From that day on she related to him more as a man in a giant dog suit than an animal.

What she admired most about him, it turned out, was something I hadn't considered. He always lived in the present and didn't waste time dwelling on regrets, guilts or things he should have done. He did whatever came up and enjoyed himself while he was doing it, even if it was just

chewing a bone.

What Arthur admired most about Vivienne was that she needed guarding more than anyone he'd ever met. I truly believe he could hear her open her eyes in the middle of the night because, the moment she did, he was by her side.

Her distress was also unsettling because, like my dreams, it was not something Arthur could protect her from.

Most nights we'd lie awake and listen to her, across the hall, pacing and muttering snippets of Peggy's poems.

"She prayed

years ago.

Got down on her knees.

She looked toward the heavens

and pledged her soul.

But nothing got better,
her troubles remained.
Jesus was just another man
who let her down."
It always ended the same.

In contrast to the bloodcurdling declaration of liberty Peggy had made that night on our dining room table, Vivienne gave a feeble cry that was more a plea for redemption, like a prolonged Hail Mary.

"God forgive me. God forgive me. God forgive me."

He might have been absent from her daily activities, but the Son-Of-A-Bitch never went away; one, huge, omnipresent birth mark.

While we listened to her, Vivienne listened to Him breaking into our house, like a thief, emptying closets and drawers looking for her heart. To this day I think He was the Prick who stole my memories.

Long after her pleas died down Arthur and I would sneak into her room and stand next to her bed. It was easier for us to go see her when she was asleep. I wasn't nervous and didn't have to hide my fears. If she was awake she wouldn't have tolerated sympathy, something she would have misunderstood as pity.

Occasionally I fluffed the pillow under her head.

Mostly I just stared, the way I looked at the phone when I wanted my father to call when he was away on a trip, willing it to ring.

She must have felt it because, sometimes, her eyes would start to flitter. When they did, Arthur and I rushed out of the room, afraid she'd wake up and see us guarding her against her demons.

When I was back in my own bed I often thought about going downstairs, removing the Browning from the closet and waiting for God to break in. The moment He stepped onto my turf, robed in all His ostentatious majesty, I'd jump out.

"How'd you get that scar on your lip, Big Shot?"

I'd take Him off at the knees. If He'd planned an escape route, if He had the strength to crawl back outside onto the lawn, I'd have Arthur drag Him back in so we could finish Him off, claim self-defense and avoid the wrath His family was so famous for.

He would not rise again!

Sometimes I just stared at water stains on the ceiling till they resembled countries. Mongolia. Brazil. China. Places that looked interesting in Vivienne's travel shows.

Still other times I wondered if Vivienne ever snuck into my room while I was sleeping and guarded me, like Arthur, against my demons. If she did, I decided she was doing a really shitty job.

* * *

Two days after I told Mister Davidow about Vivienne's troubles he took me fishing. We went on long bike rides. Depending on the season he started taking me into the city to see the State Fair, Dallas Cowboys and to the pharmacy for shakes. When he could he took me to work with him. Some of the secretaries assumed I was his son and, to be honest, I did nothing to correct them.

The subject of controllers versus pilots came up often and always centered around one basic question. How can the two work together effectively? The pilots say it's impossible because controllers like bossing them around. While there are numerous factors that might explain why they feel this way, according to Mister Davidow, none of them were valid. Controllers don't boss pilots around. They simply issue instructions because it's part of their job. It's not personal and they're certainly not fucking them over. The only time it gets personal is when a pilot doesn't comply with a controller's instructions and it affects passenger safety.

As a former pilot Mister Davidow came up with a possible solution. Since air traffic controllers are required to spend a specified number of hours in the air familiarizing themselves with basic flying skills, cockpits and procedures, pilots should be required to spend an equal amount of time studying what goes on in the towers to learn the complexities of being a controller. That knowledge, learned from the realities of aviation, not from books, would lead to understanding and provide helpful suggestions to benefit everyone concerned.

On this particular Friday those suggestions were reinforced a hundredfold.

A Delta flight from San Francisco to Dallas/Forth Worth overshot the airport by a hundred miles. Mister Davidow and the other controllers lost radio contact with the Airbus 320 when it was flying at 37,000 feet and there was no communication for more than an hour. Concern escalated as the pilot neared the airport without making any effort to descend. Mister Davidow contacted two other Delta planes, asking them to try to reach the flight through its last known

frequency. One of those succeeded, prompting the pilot to contact DFW.

When Mister Davidow spoke with him his answers were so vague he feared the plane might have been hijacked and ordered the pilot to make a series of unnecessary maneuvers to convince him he was in control of the flight. During this time the National Guard was notified and fighter jets were poised in case of an emergency.

The pilot eventually stated that he was in a heated discussion with crew members over airline policy and they lost situational awareness.

FAA investigators said the agency is examining all possible explanations for the incident, including allegations that the pilots had fallen asleep. They made clear, however, that instances of this sort were rare, even though these same two pilots had been involved in a similar incident the previous year, traveling twenty-six miles beyond their destination before contacting controllers. They'd been suspected of taking Chantix, an anti-smoking drug prohibited by the FAA because it's linked to drowsiness, confusion and heart trouble.

They were never charged.

Mister Davidow said that no pilot could become distracted enough to forget to land an airplane carrying 144 passengers. There are too many safety checks built into the aviation system that would have prevented or corrected the situation. If nothing else, brightly lit cockpit displays would have warned the pilots it was time to land. So, the only plausible explanation was that they'd fallen asleep somewhere along their route.

As always, Mister Davidow filed a written report listing the facts as he understood them, but he knew they would fall on deaf ears.

Now, he also knew this.

Nothing short of a disaster like flight 512 would change FAA minds, stop them from protecting the airlines and force them to take action.

Hundreds would have to die in order for thousands to live.

* * *

During Ethan's third session at the prison hospital, Doctor Coonan told the group it was challenging and often scary to change behavior, especially when that behavior involved violence. He gave an example of a boy who grew up in an abusive home. His father beat him to within an inch of his life and he hated him for it. But, when that same boy grew into a man and had children of his own, he beat them as brutally as his father had beaten him. Why? It was the only

behavior he knew.

With therapy the man was able to take back control of his emotions, eliminate his shame, raise his self-esteem and reject the conditioning that caused inappropriate outbursts of anger, saving his children from a similar fate. It would have been impossible to do on one's own, so asking for help was the first step.

Ethan disagreed.

Anger wasn't always inappropriate, didn't have to be avoided and, in many cases, was actually a good thing; extremely useful for getting out of difficult situations. You could go back to the beginning of time and that was what the world was all about. An eye for an eye. It was justice on the battlefield and it applied even more off it. If somebody knocks you down, you knock them down, whether it's your father or not.

Doctor Coonan listened politely, smiled and said he would discuss it further before the end of class, but couldn't make any promises because they still had to cover the symptoms of passive aggression, which included illness and avoidance of intimacy as coping mechanisms.

* * *

After a couple of months God began worming His way back into Vivienne's consciousness, although He was unbelievably sneaky about it. While Vivienne was out and about she discovered that if she prayed to the Parking God, within seconds a space would appear. This also applied to the Traffic God, congestion parting like the Red Sea. Last but not least, the Wherewithal God allowed her to accomplish everything she set her mind to on a daily basis, even when she was overloaded and thought it impossible. This eventually led to her realization that God was an all-or- nothing Deity, not just one for small favors near shopping malls.

She forgave Him.

She realized that He and He alone, with all His ineffable goodness, was the power she'd so desperately been searching for to bring the world into focus. This allowed her, once again, to concentrate on His never-ending love instead of His treaso-nous, scum bag assaults.

She drove back to see the woman she read about in the Lone Star Chronicle. This time, when she stepped onto her porch, Vivienne handed her a Bible she bought in the church gift shop, its pages trimmed in gold leaf. It was for her son so he could thank God, every single day, for watching over him.

She even bought a bumper sticker for her car that said "God, don't leave home without Him."

She also realized there was a correlation between turning her back on Him and Peggy's suicide. If she'd honored her agreement and kept her faith, as she'd promised the day she brought me home, Peggy would be alive.

Although I didn't realize it at the time, this had a direct bearing on how she related to me for the rest of her life.

Peggy's death was my fault.

I might as well have swiped the blade across her wrists, like a credit card, myself.

Vivienne's years at the hospital also taught her this:

Grief and sorrow easily turned into self pity. You could never forget that the person you were grieving for had a much greater loss than you. You needed to be grateful for the good things you had, the good things you'd done and the awful things you'd been spared from doing.

As with my birth mother, God closed a door but opened a window. Peggy perished so others could learn from her misfortune.

She'd finally made it to shore.

Vivienne's philosophical void, which had plagued her since Jack's death, was replaced by a new sense of purpose. Though it was difficult to go from an inert person who waited for things to happen, like a counter puncher looking for an opening, to one who initiated responses, like a salesman, Vivienne did just that.

She quit the hospital and started doing the one thing Peggy would have approved of. She shared her beliefs and experiences with the world.

Like Willa Cather or Edith Wharton.

"Virgin Hearts Do Not Die," her first book, dealt with Peggy's poetry, its primary themes and relevance to society.

"Intellect, somehow, has become known as a masculine trait as opposed to the inherent warmth, caring and nurturing qualities of a woman. It's why the world has traditionally placed decisive matters in the hands of men. This couldn't be more wrong. Men make decisions for power. Women, concerned with relationships, base their decisions on ethics, kindness, openness and interdependence."

Though this is freely discussed and debated today, at the time Vivienne was an innovator; a strong, true voice of the feminist movement.

The book's success more than paid for the wine and the additional books that slowly started taking over our house. Open and dog-eared. Piled high in stacks. Overflowing in closets and on shelves.

Ironically, the passion behind Vivienne's writing overshadowed the woman she so desperately wanted to canonize. Peggy became an inspirational figure to millions, but it was Vivienne who became famous and adored.

To Vivienne's credit she never had delusions of grandeur, developed a swelled head or lost focus. If "Virgin Hearts" was the first step to establishing Peggy's legacy, her controversial second book, "With A Capital B," won Olympic gold.

Reviewers got it right for a change.

"This book will delight, infuriate or illuminate. Probably all three."

It dealt with Peggy's abuse, courage and tragic end. Unlike the first book it had a pronounced pedagogical approach that blended a mixture of mysticism and ecclesiastics, emphasizing Vivienne's belief that Peggy, Jeanne d'Arc and the women's movement were interrelated.

Unlike the first book, writing consumed all of Vivienne's time, effort and, for the most part, tolerance.

She often worked through the night. When I said I rarely saw her she told me to buy glasses. When I asked her to sit down and explain the book, she patted me on the head and said I wasn't smart enough to cope.

I went from pediatric trophy to unwelcome distraction in the blink of an eye. Worse, Vivienne stopped spending time with Arthur, his distress as visible as Vivienne's new decisiveness.

* * *

While Vivienne was writing "With A Capital B," in contrast to her usual, mostly somber attire, she started wearing nothing but glistening white, white pants, white blouse, white shoes and her hair pulled back and fastened with a white scarf - a tribute to Peggy's innocent spirt.

I could still hear her pacing and muttering, although she

occasionally substituted the introduction to her book for Peggy's poetry. She must have changed it a hundred times, tiny increments that no one would notice, but this particular night I remember as if it were yesterday.

"In everybody's life there's one moment that smacks you in the head, spins you around and changes your world forever. It doesn't matter whether you like it or not. It doesn't even matter if you understand it. It happens and you'd better be prepared.

For Joan of Arc that moment came when she began hearing the voices of Saint Catherine and Saint Margaret, chosen by God to empower her with the strength to go to war against the English."

Sadly, my protective zeal was long gone so I screamed as loud as I possibly could.

"Nobody gives a rat's ass about Saint Catherine or Saint Margaret. This isn't the God-damned middle ages."

Bursting into my room Vivienne crossed to the foot of my bed, folded her arms defiantly in front of her and told me the following bedtime stories.

"Saint Catherine came from an honorable, well-to-do family and received a first-rate education, unheard of for girls at that time. She was such an outstanding young woman her father arranged a marriage between her and the Emperor. Unfortunately, it didn't work out the way he'd imagined. Catherine refused because she was already married and committed to the baby Jesus. As one might expect, the Emperor did not take this well. He had Catherine thrown into prison, starved, beaten, covered with scorpions and chained to a spiked wheel."

Although I had no way of knowing it then, when I eventually looked it up online, I discovered this was the origin of fireworks, known as the Catherine Wheel, which are common around here, in Lone Star Springs, every July 4th.

"Before Catherine could be tortured the wheel broke, but she wasn't saved. It upset the Emperor even more and he ordered her decapitated.

When they cut off her head she bled holy milk, its pasty whiteness splattering on the Emperor's clothes and spotting the floor. Since milk like that could only come from virgin breasts, angels flew her body to Sinai where it releases perfume to this very day.

Because of her drastic weight loss when she was imprisoned, she became the patron saint of anorexics."

The saga about Saint Margaret was equally disturbing.

"Saint Margaret, like Catherine, refused a forced marriage when she was fifteen. She too claimed she was the virgin bride of Christ and couldn't marry anyone else. She too was thrown in prison, savagely beaten and tortured. While in her cell she was also attacked and swallowed by the Devil who'd assumed the form of a huge dragon. Since Margaret's dedication to Christ never wavered, the dragon spit her out as indigestible. He then changed into a handsome young he-man, not unlike your father. If he couldn't devour her one way, he'd try another. Before he could make his move Margaret tackled him, threw him to the ground and said: "Proud demon, lie prostrate beneath a woman's foot." This proved to be more upsetting than her refusal to marry. As with Catherine, they cut off her head. Whether she was a virgin or not is still up for grabs. But, because of her episode with the dragon, she became the patron saint of women in childbirth."

I couldn't sleep for weeks.

* * *

Three years later, on Vietnamese Independence Day, Vivienne threw a party at our local church sponsored by her publisher.

Since she'd recently been catapulted into the public eye and was on a short list of prestigious authors, people came from all over. High society. Politicians. Industry leaders. Five generations of Harvard valedictorians. American Legion officials. Artists. Musicians. There were even a few housewives from East Hampton, Long Island, controlling stock holders in their husbands' businesses, desperate to set up private liaisons between Vivienne and their daughters, each an aspiring writer, needing nothing more than the opportunity to prove
themselves.

All appreciated the citronella candles and related to the event as if it were the second coming.

After speaking with a half dozen folk singers, Vivienne discovered a common thread. Thematically there was a feeling of isolation, their lyrics filled with sadness and suffering rather than happiness and love. The only time they wrote about the joys of life was when they felt lost. They considered these daily struggles a positive influence, something to be learned from and risen above, similar to Vivienne's philosophy about the human spirit. They also felt that a good life was possible, for others at least, if their songs defined what was lacking.

Surprisingly, many of them had drawn inspiration from poetry. Early music, they explained, was derived from it. Many of Emily Dickinson's poems were identical to ballads of her day and, more often than not, written in the alternating eight-and-six-syllable lines of the hymnal. Shakespeare's sonnets were all singable. Yates was fascinated by the refrain.

Vivienne explained how Peggy revered poetry, especially verse written by those who were misunderstood and in pain. "A Ballad of Suicide" by Chesterton. "A Farewell to False Love" by Sir Walter Raleigh. "And Like a Dying Lady" by Shelley. "Darkness" by Byron. "Death" by Yeats.

The list was as endless as it was depressing and I was

thrilled when Mister Davidow arrived. Mrs. Davidow couldn't attend because she belonged to a women's club that met in Dallas every Friday afternoon, for the past fifteen years, to do charity work. She wasn't one to turn her back on that under any circumstances.

Mister Davidow was visibly unnerved.

A Continental flight from Austin with four hundred passengers had been caught up in gusting winds as it tried to land. The left wing grazed the runway for a moment, but the pilot was able to stabilize the aircraft and take off again in what an airline spokesman called "An absolutely professional maneuver." The plane landed safely a short time afterward on its second attempt in spite of damage to the hydraulic system.

"It was a dicey situation," said the spokesman. "Thank God for the composure and skill of our pilots. They avoided a potential catastrophe of epic proportions."

That was the public version.

Mister Davidow was tracking the flight by radar for twenty-five minutes before it was supposed to land and was unable to contact the cockpit.

The plane was on autopilot.

The FAA was investigating.

As I stood there watching the pain this dedicated, hard working man was in, Vivienne shifted her attention and joined our conversation.

Of the four hundred passengers she wanted to know how many were men. Mister Davidow didn't have the exact figure, but sixty percent was the statistical average for a flight originating in the same state. That meant there were two hundred and forty. Give or take. Vivienne promptly declared that ten percent were divorced, another statistical average, which meant that two hundred and sixteen were married.

In a recent survey she'd taken, seventy-five percent of men

questioned said they'd cheated on their wives and would do it again if the opportunity arose. That meant one hundred and eighty men on the plane were adulterers. In a companion survey, ninety-five percent of wives whose husbands had cheated were completely in the dark. They felt secure in their relationships and were positive their spouses were as devoted as they were loving, as Vivienne once felt about my

father. If those Continental pilots knew this, Vivienne wondered if they still would have saved their plane. Would they be willing to "take one for the team," like my mother with Mister Domoff, if they'd known they could leave the world a better place for one hundred and eighty good women?

"Fighting infidelity, one crash at a time."

It was the last thing she said before turning and rejoining the musicians.

Mister Davidow, having abhorred what Vivienne said, fell into a dejected silence, but it reminded him of his own dilemma, a disaster being the one solution to passenger safety.

It was the moment he decided to become an integral part of my future.

During the months that followed, Peggy's poems were set to music. Vivienne ran into opposition, initially, by insisting that every song rely heavily on brass. Producers quickly changed their minds, however, when its uniqueness caught on with fans and reviewers alike.

"Sylvia Plath with oom pahs."

It was interesting to watch Vivienne during this time. Not only did she protect Peggy's legacy with Arthur-like diligence, she assumed a characteristic she despised in the French doctors at the asylum: their cloying, upbeat optimism.

It was a state of mind, I now understand, she created for her own protection. It was also a world Arthur and I rarely had access to. On occasion, after three bottles of wine, she'd talk about her mother. Sometimes she'd mention her father. She even spoke of Jack. When she did I failed to notice the tears that formed on her lower lids and threatened to spill onto the rest of her life. I can't imagine overlooking this. In my defense, my mind was not fully developed and, though probing, naive and unobservant.

If I threatened to break through and enter her world during these talks her posture grew tight and she'd begin twitching, as if my umbilical cord was reaching out, like a noose, and restricting her air supply. She never raised her voice in anger. No cathartic speeches or explanations. She

simply pursed her lips and looked at me with the same blank expression she had when my father insisted he was dying.

"Henry."

It was a warning that told me not to go any further or there'd be consequences. For a long time I convinced myself it was a temporary condition. The night I realized it was permanent, Arthur and I snuck into her room while she slept, staring at her the way we used to. I didn't want to protect her. I wanted to punch her the same way I wanted to hit my Dad years ago, a good hard right to the jaw. It made me smile to think about her expression when she woke up and saw me towering over her, hands balled into fists, my blood stained knuckles scraped to the bone.

I didn't punch her.

I may have been conflicted but I was still grateful for all she'd done and I didn't love her any less. Besides, I knew that annoying her would prove far more rewarding.

* * *

Up till then I never dreamed of doing anything to upset Vivienne. It didn't make sense, was disrespectful and clearly against my best interests.

This was different.

This was war.

While Vivienne baked or cleaned rooms that were already spotless, I'd walk in and out with Arthur, maintaining a constant patter.

"Thank you for escorting me into the kitchen, Arthur. I can't tell you how much I appreciate it. It's so nice to have company. I'm not used to it, you know, which is why I walk from room to room swatting flies who, at least, want something to do with me."

If Vivienne stopped what she was doing to face me I stared her straight in the eyes and asked a question I pondered every night between Brazil and Australia.

"If God told you you could bring Peggy back but everyone else would die because of it, including me, would you do it?"

She refused to answer.

Sometimes I'd sneak into the living room and start watching old movies a few minutes before her travel shows began, ones that emphasized love, loss or both. If she tried to change the station I'd throw a fit till she retreated to the sanctity of her bedroom or felt obliged to watch. If there were no films scheduled I'd switch to soccer, something Vivienne despised more than my grandfather loathed imagination.

Sometimes I'd tear the last few pages out of books she was reading, depriving her of a gratifying ending. I'd replace them with short messages. "To Be Continued." "Out To Lunch." "Not In Service." This was particularly effective with the Old Testament.

Sometimes I'd barge in while she was writing and ask prying questions. "What was it like to be inside an asylum?

What was it like to be insane? Was it similar to one of my nightmares only you're awake? Did Peggy know she was insane?"

Sometimes I went for the gut instead of the heart.

"Do crazy people know what love is? If they do, are they capable of love? If they are, can you count on it?"

Sometimes I attacked her soul.

"If there's a God, if you go back to the primordial sludge, why would He create a being that was only one cell, let alone one that depended on reproduction to continue? Why wouldn't He create a fully formed organism who would live forever and couldn't die?"

If she tried to dispute anything I responded in the language I'd grown so fond of.

"Moni gnatha gabi / buutton imon."

While this did wonders for me at the cemetery, it did nothing to quell Vivienne's outrage under her own roof.

She started answering in French.

Unlike my beloved Gaulish, her language was romantic and available on cassette. Ironically, the more she learned the more she realized what the French were saying about her when she sat in the Paris hospital. Pigs. Every one of them. Disgusting swine. Her ensuing attacks on me, as a result, were calculated and relentless, assaulting me in the most sadistic way she knew.

With manners.

"J'ai beaucoup de plaisir a vous revoir, vous savez."

"Et moi donc. Vous n'avez pas change."

"Que c'est drole!"

She adjusted her speech to my level of understanding. She spoke slowly and clearly. She avoided idiomatic expressions.

The more desperate I became the more she smiled, ruffled my hair and sang "Mister In Between," off key but in perfect French.

Desperate to retaliate I snuck into her bedroom one after-noon, while she was out running errands, and replaced key phrases on her cassettes with the loudest, most offensive belches I could muster.

"Etes-vous ouverts le...BURP!"

"Bonjour, je voudrais reserver une table pour...BURP!"

"Quel age avez...BURP!"

There were thousands.

When Vivienne got home and discovered what I'd done, Godly forgiveness did not come naturally. She came looking for me with the same balled up fists I threatened her with while she slept.

She never found me because I'd discovered a hiding place in my room. I would wedge a forefinger underneath a small crack in the top of my desk, lift it up and slip into the hollow part underneath. It was a fifth the size of an airline bathroom but I could see through a corner where the wood had separated, like those paintings in horror movies where the eyes move and the person being observed doesn't have a clue.

When she gave up and returned to her own room she taunted me, blaring records by Charles Aznevour, Edith Piaf and Jacques Brel.

Although sitting in the dark was a new experience, I was comfortable with it immediately. It deadened my pain the way alcohol numbed Peggy and made me feel secure. To this day I've never experienced anything as freeing or safe. It soothed me the way Vivienne did when I was born, caressing me gently, rubbing my back, dragging its ebony fingers over every appendage and muscle. If I held my hand in front of my face and couldn't see it, all was right with the world.

I also realized there were two types of darkness:

1. The type that overwhelmed me and made me feel unsure of myself, like in my nightmares.

2. The dark that fortified and made me feel as if I was the center of the universe, like the love Vivienne felt for Peggy, my father and me when I was an infant.

I did my homework inside the desk that night, calculating problems in my head, and stayed there till the following morning. I assumed Vivienne would calm down, but I'd grossly underestimated the damage I'd done, her resolve and resourcefulness.

From that day on she locked her bedroom door while she was working and before she went to bed.

I wish I could say I acted like an adult and rose to the occasion but I didn't. I shouted. I sulked. Once I even pounded on her closed door and crossed an inexcusable boundary.

"Peggy was right. You are a cunt."

Turning, I fled to the safety of my desk. I waited for her to run after me but she didn't. No musical assault either. When I awoke the next morning I thought all would be forgiven but when I climbed out of the desk and walked into the hall Vivienne had painted a thick red line across the floor, dividing the house in two. Anything on my side, she explained, would be in English. Everything on hers, which included the kitchen, was in French. I was free to come and go as I pleased, but if I crossed onto her side and violated this decree, there would be dire consequences.

She started smoking Gauloises.

She sold our dryer and set up a clothesline on pulleys between the house and a towering oak, insisting that fabrics smelled better when exposed to fresh air.

She built a fence around the garden, its sole entrance through a painted iron gate, colored glass in its upper half.

Everything French became more important than anything Henry and it made me feel humiliated and small. If I questioned what she was doing, let alone her motives, her response was always the same.

"In French, 'wisdom' is feminine."

Adding insult to injury, she stopped helping me select my clothes before I went out. Nothing I wore came close to being color coordinated ever again.

I spent more and more time inside my desk, staring through the crack as Vivienne's legs passed by at different times of the day and night. When I wasn't doing homework in my head I clocked how long it took her to walk up the stairs, come into my room, look for me and leave. Time varied according to her anxiety level.

In spite of the desk's narcotic effect, my own anxieties, my dark side, occasionally took over.

I was a crocodile lying in wait for some unsuspecting American writer, preparing to drag her under the surface till her last poetic words failed her. I was an eagle soaring above the clouds, scanning the landscape for a feminist I could swoop down on, pick up with my talons and rip open. While she screamed for equality I would sing in my best bird voice.

"You've got to accentuate the positive
Eliminate the negative
Latch on to the affirmative
Don't mess with Mister In-Between."

I lived in two different worlds. One filled with French and light. The other bleak, treacherous and French-free.

I avoided Vivienne because it seemed as if her cultural desertion mattered less if I deserted her more.

Arthur, on the other hand, never stopped checking on her. His instincts allowed him to see things I could not.

France was Vivienne's desk.

Its memory wasn't enough. In order to go on living she had

to immerse herself completely, as if France were a vital organ that needed saving.

She even started answering the phone in French, whether the person on the other end spoke it or not. As she became more successful, publishers hired translators to make their calls. Vivienne appeared to take it with a grain of salt but I could see she was delighted.

During this time Vivienne began gaining back the weight she'd lost. Like few other aspects in her life it got out of control. Two hundred pounds. Two twenty-five. Two-fifty. The ground seemed to buckle when she walked, like with those giants in cartoons, and her sweat reminded me of beads of fat in fast-food chicken restaurants; meat grilling on racks in display windows to lure potential customers.

Every morning she got up and weighed herself. If she gained a pound she made the sign of the cross before gesturing up to the sky, directly at God, the way we watched soccer players do after scoring a goal.

* * *

I was nineteen and had just finished my first year of junior college when Mister Davidow found a way to help me.

Five thousand air-traffic controllers went on strike after negotiations with the federal government to raise their pay and shorten their workweek proved fruitless. As with President Reagan the controllers complained of difficult working conditions and a lack of recognition for the pressures they faced. Across the country seven thousand flights were cancelled. The President called the strike illegal and threatened to fire any controller who did not return to work within forty-eight hours. The head of the Professional Air-Traffic Controllers Association was found in contempt by a federal judge and ordered to pay $5,000 a day in fines. On June 8th the president carried out his threat and fired the controllers who had not returned. In addition, he declared a lifetime ban on their rehiring.

Mister Davidow agreed with his colleagues but felt it unconscionable to leave the air ways vulnerable and in disarray. No matter what the reason, the United States was the global standard bearer when it came to rules for safety and regulatory compliance. He was not going to jeopardize that. Knowing my propensity for order as well as my interest in flying, he used the opening to shove both my feet in the door.

I quit school without a second thought.

During my training and most of the first year, Mister Davidow recorded everything I did from the moment I arrived at work till the time I went home. I resented it enormously. It wasn't fair and I felt condescended to. I put in my hours and left when my work was done. Not a minute before. I didn't waste time socializing around the water cooler, betting on sports or discussing politics like the other controllers. Plus, my record keeping was as meticulous as Mister Davidow himself.

Eventually, I realized just how wrong a person could be. It was all for my protection and had nothing to do with doubt or ability. Because every choice I made could have dire consequences, those decisions had to hold up if they were called into question.

A definitive history was my only defense.

"The battle in the air can only be won on the ground."

In the case of flight 516, a pilot's decision caused 300 people to lose their lives. Husbands. Wives. Kids. Pets and grandchildren.

Was Mister Davidow responsible in any way, shape or form?

The answers were in the details.

During this time the White Rock Tavern was sold to a

Haitian family who didn't know my father and couldn't understand why a perfectly good Cadillac was nothing more than a conversation piece and taking up space designed for paying customers. They fixed the car, souped it up and cruised around town. Loyal patrons became outraged and stopped coming, taking their business to The Red Lion Inn five miles down the road.

White Rock closed six months later.

The Haitians thought the car had a "hex" and abandoned it where it once was deified. It suffered like everything else. One day the tires disappeared. Two weeks later the seats were gone. The doors. The dashboard. The engine. Eventually there was nothing left but the body that once made it unique.

This was pretty much what happened to Vivienne. Her decline took ten years longer but was no less destructive. By 2000, all her parts had been stolen too. Spleen. Breasts. Kidney. Heart. Especially the heart that made her who she was.

I'd spent the day with Arthur, running, jumping and swimming. When we came home, tired and out of breath, we found Vivienne sprawled on the floor next to her desk, pen gripped tightly between her thumb and forefinger. Her breathing was rough and urgent. Her face had turned blue. I felt her chest to see if she was alive. Then her neck. Then her wrist. She finally opened her eyes, saw me and slurred the following:

"See Birdie."

The ambulance arrived two hours later. By the time we reached the hospital Vivienne had gone into a coma.

For the next three months I helped the nurses change her bed. I shampooed her hair. I blow-dried it. I rubbed her down with alcohol if she developed a fever. I fed her ice chips. I even read her Peggy's poems. Although she couldn't speak, when she managed to look into my eyes I felt like she knew what I was

doing and approved. It was the closest she'd come to appreciating me in a long, long while.

After another month of unresponsive behavior her doctor
took me aside, smiled and said:

"We need the bed. It's time to increase her morphine drip."

I refused, of course, taking Vivienne home for whatever
amount of life she had left.

Every night Arthur and I stood next to her bed and listened
to her breathe, more and more labored, abetted by the same
tubes and machinery her preemies had filtering through them.
Once again we were standing guard, only this time it was
against an adversary far more damaging than

regrets. Three times we made her eyes flitter and open.

The first she stared up at me and said:

"When you're older, it isn't that you're not capable of loving
any more. You are. It's love that's incapable."

The second she pointed to the far corner of the room. "Am I
crazy or is that George Best standing over there?"

I assured her she was sane. But, if she remembered, Best
had died, at fifty-nine, after years of alcohol abuse.

"Not a good sign" was all she said before traveling back to
her own private world.

The third she just stared and I got the distinct impression
she was looking through me, longingly into the next world.
When she appeared to come back, when we made eye contact,
I used the moment to repeat a question I desperately needed an
answer to.

"If God had told you you could bring Peggy back but
everyone else would die because of it, including me, would you
have done it?"

Lifting her head slightly, a miracle in itself, she took a deep
breath and smiled. "I wanted to kill you, but now I don't."

Like the babies she spent most of her life coveting, Vivienne died prematurely. If her heart hadn't gotten her, a toxic goiter would have.

This is what Vivienne's mother should have warned her about. Not men. Men weren't the problem. Life was. Men were just part of its scheme to squash you sooner.

Everyone has a mother and they all die, even if she's a substitute. The thing is, I honestly believed Vivienne would live forever. It was a shock and her not being there was a lot different than when she left for Paris. It made me feel old. It made me feel like a kid again too, afraid after one of my nightmares, only now there was no one to fly me to safety.

I sat on her bed for weeks, saying nothing, waiting for her to return. Every time I walked into the house and saw her chair I thought she'd be sitting there doing needlepoint or watching TV. Whenever I climbed the stairs, walked past her room and peeked inside I expected her to be making notes, writing feverishly or speaking French to some unsuspecting caller.

I continued doing the same routines. Trash pickup on Mondays. Recycling Wednesday. TV rituals as well. I couldn't watch enough travel shows and felt I'd committed a sin if I missed her favorite.

Normal things like that are quickly lost and forgotten.

I started reading her books, in their prescribed order, that had taken over our house. I even removed the top of my desk, leaving it off so light could penetrate and she could see me when she returned.

I didn't want to stop mourning because there was no one else to grieve the way I did. Only I knew what it was like to be raised by her. Only I knew how she loved and cared for me. Only I knew what she had sacrificed. Only I knew the tenacity that gave her life purpose before she was squashed.

And her voice.

The moment I stopped remembering it, the moment it got

muddled with the rest of my memories, not only would it be gone forever, in the grand scheme of things she really would be little more than a blip on the radar. If that happened it was only a matter of time before I felt the sterility of a seldom-used kitchen, the emptiness of the sweater my father gave her and a floor as cold as the deer the day I was born.

Right before Vivienne died she looked me in the eyes, reached up and gently touched my face, outlining every inch. Back then I thought it was her way of remembering me. In retrospect, after all the bizarre things that happened to her, I think she just wanted to make sure I was real.

When she was assured I was, she closed her eyes for the very last time with a smile of total repose.

* * *

The FAA is investigating a near-collision between an American Airlines jet from Dallas to Chicago and an Air Ontario commuter flight from Austin to DFW.

According to the FAA, the close call Wednesday evening was caused by on-board computers that are designed to prevent midair collisions. In this case officials said it put two aircraft on a collision course and took human intervention, a sudden call of "traffic" from the control center, to avert a tragedy.

The planes were flying at 23,000 feet about thirty miles southwest of Dallas. Officials said the planes came as close as they did, within three hundred feet of vertical separation and less than a mile horizontally, because the on-board computer systems told one plane to climb and the other to descend.

FAA Spokesman Mike Healy said the investigation would include a thorough examination of why these systems malfunctioned the way they did.

The controller who saved the day told the Dallas Morning

News the planes were so close the targets on the radar scopes merged into one.

That controller was Mister Davidow.

When he told government officials it was a clear case of pilot error, they prohibited him from talking to the media and declared the investigation "in house."

A committee has promised to hold a hearing, although no firm date had been set.

* * *

Men who'd worked at the cemetery for thirty years told me it was more crowded than ever before, mourners standing shoulder to shoulder or sideways to accommodate the overflow.

I scanned the faces of those gathered and saw the habitual sorrow and regret, people who couldn't bring themselves to say goodbye or, worse, needed to but never got the chance - all except one woman standing directly in front of the casket. Unlike the rest there was no doom and

gloom. Flushed around both cheeks she was fighting to repress a smirk. I could tell by the way her lips were pursed. The same as mine during Jack's funeral. Since I wasn't able to see her full on from where I was standing, I began inching in her direction, zigzagging as if I were a big cat stalking prey on one of Vivienne's travel shows.

Halfway there three mourners began singing one of Peggy's poems that had been made into a traditional blues song.

"How do I describe
the morning after
when every morning is?
Even the simplest words
escape me
so I have to wonder

Is it me?
Or maybe it's that language
cannot accommodate what
cannot be portrayed."

Although their singing was awkward at best, as a wave of emotion spread through the crowd, their confidence grew and their voices soared.

I couldn't have cared less.

The moment I got my first real glimpse of the woman, I was overwhelmed by an attraction I'd never experienced before.

Even now it still weakens my knees.

I'd observed hundreds of women with my father who were breathtaking from the side but suffered full on. Their nose was a little crooked and not aligned with their mouth. One eye was smaller than the other. The right shoulder was significantly lower than the left.

Not this one.

Like Vivienne's desserts, she'd crossed over that fine line between good and flawless. As a result, she was used to being admired. You could tell from the way she stood. She also had an air of mystery about her, something that drove me wild since there was absolutely nothing mysterious about me.

She had mischievous green eyes. A brooding mouth. Blonde hair that seemed to have a life of its own as it blew in the wind. Even the freckles on the bridge of her nose were symmetrical.

She was the girl you waited your whole life to meet and never did.

Intimidated, I tried to keep my distance but she saw me out of the corner of one perfect eye, released the smile she'd been struggling to suppress and raced over to introduce herself.

I should add here that she moved with a natural grace different than the girls my father analyzed in the square; who practiced in front of a mirror to emphasize every mid-western sway.

"Hi. I'm Hope. I was your mother's biggest fan."

"Hope." Of course. I should have known.

She gestured at the hordes of women gathered for the occasion.

"We all were."

Stepping back her eyes glazed over and she joined the others in perfect unison.

"If it's me, I cannot be afraid
to describe the scars
or try to sweep them
under the rug.
They need to be seen.
To be recognized.
To be dealt with.
Somehow, some way, I must
tell the world."

Granted, I was no aficionado, but as her voice built to a crescendo it was so pure, so angelic, it had a quality I'd only heard before in lullabies.

"I hope you don't mind."

I shook my head. It was all I could do since my voice had disappeared along with my courage.

"I look at all these people," she went on, "not a stranger in the crowd. Your mother's life touched so many. Her thoughts changed the way women think. Her emotions changed how we feel. She'll be sorely missed. If there's a greater tribute to anyone than that I don't know what it is."

I remembered Vivienne's thoughts the day she met my father.

"God had a reason for everything. He could even create opportunity from the loss of a child."

Surely, losing a mother was equally traumatic, and my second at that.

* * *

She wouldn't allow me near her on our first couple of dates.

Then again, neither would Arthur.

Whenever we got close he barked. I didn't give it much thought till our third date - which was a record in itself. She was sitting beside me on the sofa while I leafed through an album filled with photos of Vivienne over the years. In order to see better she moved closer and our knees touched.

Arthur, who was lying down across the room, jumped up, rushed over and planted himself on the other side of the coffee table. His pupils shrunk to half their usual size and he barked once, a sound that resonated throughout the house like an earth quake.

Hope moved away.

Arthur's pupils returned to normal.

Walking around the table he placed his front paws on the sofa, stood up and licked her face before going back to his sentry position in front of the window.

I loved it.

Arthur was protecting me the way I'd always imagined. Hope, on the other hand, convinced she was going to spend her last few moments on Earth as human kibble, didn't find it nearly as inspiring.

On the fourth date I kissed her while Arthur's back was turned. Although more of a brotherly kiss, Hope blushed and stiffened, as if she were in that car about to be hit by the train headed for Oklahoma. At the time I associated it with inno-cence, assuming her soul was a reflection of her

impeccable beauty. I was positive because, if I stared

directly into her eyes with the slightest intimacy, she would look down.

Shoes, somehow, cut short her discomfort.

On the other hand, she listened carefully whenever I spoke about anything important to me. She never snuck looks at her watch like other girls I'd dated or said she had to race home to her sick Pekingese, ending our evening before it was time.

While I was never one to rush into anything, especially relationships, I asked her to marry me the following night and she burst into tears.

Reaching into my back pocket I removed a handkerchief and handed it to her, which made her cry even harder.

I was old fashioned.

That's what she called me. Men she knew never would have offered her something to dry her eyes because they wouldn't carry a handkerchief to begin with.

She said she would think about it, turned, ran past a snarling Arthur and out the door.

I called her repeatedly over the next few weeks but she never answered. I sent her letters but they came back unopened, the phrase "return to sender" stamped beneath her address.

I felt like an idiot.

Why did I believe someone like her would be interested in someone like me? I'd never been handsome or charming like my dad. Girls named Hope were attracted to men like him, not ones who weren't special and never would be.

I'd fallen prey to everything my grandfather despised, forsaking a workable, practical reality for fantasy.

Life was hard and sense did come before sentiment.

Since I knew nothing about Hope's past, I also realized something else. Clearly, she was a musician, an actress, a psychoanalyst or the dreaded chess groupie.

Till one rainy night.

Just before eleven there was a knock at my door. When I opened it there she was. Her face was puffy from crying and she looked ill.

"You want me, don't you, Henry?"

I was surprised by her frankness but answered at once.

"God, yes."

"Well then," she said, "Do something about it."

I should add here that the first time we had sex, even after her uninhibited invitation, was conventional and safe. Nothing wild or illicit. Unlike kids today who meet, hook up and go on their way without knowing each other's name, it was an act we both respected. We never used terms like "fucking," "doing it," or the old fashioned "roll in the hay."

We made love with the lightest of touches as if we might break.

I wish I'd paid more attention to how, when we undressed, she did so mechanically, insisted the lights were off and kept her back to me. Once again, I assumed it was innocence. I also wish I'd paid attention to the fact that Arthur planted himself beside the bed, the way he stood near the coffee table, and barked at her every thrust.

He didn't attack.

He was simply warning her.

I had no idea he was also warning me.

When she did stop she dangled an arm over the side of the bed and petted him on the head like he was a tom tom or some other percussion instrument. Nothing tender or soft. Three pats and out.

Arthur didn't have time to climb on the bed and lick her because, next thing he knew, I was dragging him outside by the collar and shutting the door behind me.

Hope and I were married by a judge in the Majestic

Meadows court house the following week and went on a honeymoon that would have made Romeo and Juliet blush.

Nothing was left unsaid.

She encouraged me to share all my dreams and fears. There was no reason to be polite or worry about disclosing something unsettling. If we trusted each other enough not to hold back, we'd eliminate ninety percent of the reasons relationships failed. When I eventually told her my darkest secrets, she not only sympathized, she had many of the same feelings - although I realize now she revealed little about herself.

Nothing was left undone.

Unlike our first sexual encounter, convention was thrown out with the bath water. I couldn't possibly do justice to the most exciting physical experience of my life, but I will say this.

She was the strongest woman I'd ever known.

We made love on the lawn behind our room. On the kitchen counter. On tables. Straddling chairs. Inside an open hearth fireplace. Sitting. Standing. Even pressed against a shelf in the linen closet.

On our drive home my wife closed her eyes, kissed me gently and burst into tears again. It was more relief than anything else, she explained, because she felt an unbreakable bond between us, like we were lovers in a past life. Though she didn't necessarily believe in that, too many strange

things had happened for her to discount it. It was important we didn't waste time in case fate intervened and we were separated again.

She also uttered something no one's ever said before. Certainly not to me.

"I pray I die first, darling, because if you do I wouldn't be able to face another day. I would have no future without you."

I'd never been part of a sentiment that powerful.

During your life, every once and a while, you meet

someone in a profession and you know you couldn't be in better hands. There's not the slightest doubt you're going to receive the best treatment for any problem you might have. It happened with a doctor Vivienne went to. He shook her hand the day they met. He looked in her eyes and told her to see a thyroid specialist.

It turned out she had thyroid cancer.

It happened another time with a contractor, of all people, who my father once worked for. The son-of-a-bitch could build a house better and in half the time than anyone I've ever known. He was honest and decent and resented contractors who overcharged and were a blight on his profession. When he finished a job in five months instead of six, he sliced 16.66667 percent off monies owed.

Now there's my wife.

Her expertise was love.

* * *

From the moment Hope and I returned from our honeymoon, she treated me with the devotion of a pilgrim at a shrine.

"Whatever you want, dear husband. Your happiness is my only desire."

She told me this every day.

Although she swore I was old fashioned, it was she who was more from Vivienne's generation, thriving in a nurturing role.

If I moved a piece of furniture there wasn't a hint of dirt underneath. Pictures were balanced. Silver was polished.

She cleaned the gutters.

She beat the rugs.

She planed the front door, stopping it from squeaking for the first time since the house was built. After I told her about my father's annual farewells she made lace curtains for the den so there would always be light. When we had a problem with the downstairs bathroom she bought a book, figured out what was wrong, got the parts, crawled under the house and replaced two faulty pipes.

She kept immaculate records, took care of all legal documents, paid our bills, did the taxes and tuned my car.

She also got up every morning at five to make me lunch before driving me to the train station to catch the seven o'clock shuttle. Everything was prepared from scratch since she despised mixes almost as much as I abhorred the passengers who boarded my train at Majestic Meadows, the stop before the airport. Sweaty, smelly and often drunk, their doomed expressions were identical to the people I remembered from Intensive Care.

Every evening after Hope picked me up she massaged my temples as soon as we got home. One of the hazards of my job was headaches triggered by anxiety. After a stressful day, before dinner, she did everything in her power to make that pain go away. During these sessions I learned about knowledge, skills and a thoroughness I never dreamed she had.

No chess groupie here!

She was a licensed aroma therapist.

If my headache was severe, she rubbed chamomile oil into my temples. It had a calming affect and dispelled pain quicker than most other remedies.

If my headache was caused by emotional tension she preferred the scent of lavender. It acts on the limbic brain to encourage relaxation while releasing neck and shoulder muscles that are tight.

If my headache stemmed from staring at a computer screen too long she leaned toward peppermint oil. Its brisk, refreshing scent wakes up important olfactory nerve centers, increases mental clarity and banishes pain in the blink of an eye.

If my feet were sore and calloused from standing all day Hope would make me take a long, hot shower which softened the calloused skin. After extracting what she could with a towel she used a pumice stone to gently remove the rest till my soles were smooth. Afterwards she spread coconut oil over both feet, heels and in between my toes, preventing future callouses from developing.

If we were out of coconut oil she used shortening.

When she was sure I felt better she'd take my hand and lead me to a dinner table set with fine china, the good silverware, a tablecloth she laundered after every meal, linen napkins and candles she'd light before serving - just like the fancy Parisian restaurants Vivienne coveted.

We were like a precision dance team. I led with needs and desires. She followed with solutions and action.

Each night before we went to bed she told me how lucky she was. In a world where there were few good men, she'd found the best of the best. Then she'd do things to me I never dreamed of, using many of the same oils and salves that relieved my pain. She insisted I tell her where they felt good and why. That way she could repeat the process flawlessly. When I finally got the courage to ask what she liked done to her she smiled and told me not to worry. A more appropriate question would be "What didn't she like if I was involved?"

Obviously, I'd never have to hide in my desk again.

If something good happened she wanted me to share it with her and her alone.

If something was bad she wanted me to cry on her shoulder.

There were many silences during these times, like when my father told me stories in the square I didn't understand.

Unlike those, none were awkward. We had no trouble communicating without words, like an old married couple who live in perfect harmony and know each other's every thought.

As on our honeymoon we always went to sleep holding each other, the folds of our bodies fitting perfectly like a puzzle.

Before we got out of bed each morning she'd repeat everything from the night before, both declarations of love and gymnastics.

I was used up before I had my first cup of coffee.

Little by little, day by day, she took over my life, unwilling to let me lift a finger because she didn't want anything to interfere with my love for her.

While this was extraordinary and more than I ever dreamed of, it was who she was more than what she did for me I admired most.

She had a complete lack of vanity.

Not once did I catch her looking at her reflection in a window pane or mirror. She was confident in her appearance and didn't feel the need to inspect it, amazing for someone so beautiful.

She had an intense civic consciousness.

She helped with charity drives. She did volunteer work at Florence Nightingale hospital, drawing up a proposal for a "women's wing." She was always available, as a matter of fact, if a woman was being taken advantage of and needed assistance, especially those she considered victims of misogyny.

God help her opponent.

Any means justified the end.

On the opposite side of the coin she started an all-woman barbershop quartet that sang Gregorian chants in four part harmony. She entered beauty contests and became something of a local celebrity, crowned Miss Photo Flash, Miss Fire

Prevention and Miss Magnesium Lamp, the first time anyone held all three titles simultaneously.

Even her handwriting was perfect.

Whereas mine was basically illegible and impossible to read with a magnifying glass, hers was book quality, every capital perfectly formed, every small letter the same size, circles and dots as symmetrical as her freckles.

If Hope ever guarded me while I was sleeping, I knew I'd be as safe as if it was Arthur himself.

* * *

For the first time in my life I looked forward to the new day. I leaped out of bed in the morning and enjoyed the train ride to work. Even the people who boarded at Majestic Meadows stopped bothering me. On the contrary, I felt real compassion and tried to lift their spirits.

I put in my hours with the same zeal the mechanic at the Chevron station did when he washed my windshield. And while I would never be described as gregarious, I began discussing

politics, bet on numerous athletic events and found myself socializing around the water cooler.

The universe opened its arms and embraced me in a way it never had before. It expected more from me and I, in turn, wanted more from it, needing to know as much about the things I'd taken for granted as the tasks I coveted.

Nature, for example.

Up till then I saw the flaws instead of its beauty. The ridiculous seasons. Bitter cold. Sweltering heat. Fall and its stupid leaves. Christ! Who cared about their brilliant colors? They needed to be raked for months on end. Even the flowers, which were pleasant to look at, could only be appreciated for a short period of time, like the young girls in the square. Considering what one had to give for a quick glimpse before they died, time was better spent on activities that allowed immediate gratification.

My father taught me that.

After living out of a suitcase half his life he was far more comfortable in hotels than puttering around a garden. He once described the major problem with nature for me, a belief I held till marriage.

"It doesn't have vending machines."

As soon as I stopped feeling that way I realized how wrong he was. Nature, like my wife, was the personification of innocence and beauty.

I started valuing the splendor of a landscape. When leaves changed color, it was like looking up at the ceiling of the Sistine Chapel in one of Vivienne's travel shows.

I discovered that objects, like leaves, did not always look the same. The weather. The time of year. Even the hour gave a unique appearance to each element, creating different perspectives.

I began to garden.

Though at first I was clumsy, often confused the weeds with the plants and pruned everything so far down they refused to bloom, I was a quick study. In no time I was enriching the soil, planting althea, hibiscus, petunias and roses - hybrids primarily. I grew tomatoes, squash,

cucumbers and red peppers.

I looked forward to cutting the lawn every Sunday because I cherished the smell of freshly-mowed grass.

I worshipped the scent of honeysuckle and night-blooming jasmine. It rid my mind of anything I considered petty and small. It also seemed suddenly familiar, as if there was an age-old bond between us as well.

If a bird flew overhead I watched the way its tiny wings bobbed up and down in the wind, riding it to its full advantage instead of fighting a groundless battle by flying straight into it.

I marveled at the sun light as it glistened, like diamonds, off early morning dew, creating a rainbow of colors more vivid than any painting in the Louvre.

I bought a lathe.

I erected a grape arbor.

I raised chickens and ate fresh eggs every morning.

Equally exciting, I could approach it all in the manner I was accustomed. I bought books. I read articles. I went to the library three times a week. If, by some slim chance, I couldn't find what I was searching for in print, I got online and cross-referenced thousands of helpful hints from people more knowledgeable than I.

Not a day went by, during our first year together, I didn't look out at the world with curiosity. I saw it all through new eyes as if I was reborn.

The miracle of life.

Revelatory.

Wondrous.

Fresh.

Beckoning.

I even stopped having nightmares, my dreams becoming comforting, guileless and pure.

I was truly blessed.

How many men have the good fortune to meet, let alone marry a woman who changes their life for the better? Very few. Believe me. And though my father wouldn't have understood, the thought of being with anyone else never crossed my mind.

Not only was there no future without my beloved, there was no past or present.

* * *

I found a folded, yellowed piece of paper in Vivienne's pocket the day she died. To the best of my knowledge she carried it with her wherever she went.

Beneath the words "You win" was the following:
"Sent sprawling into the world
with a fanfare
from space.
Arriving with little more than the promise
of something.
Not necessarily good.
Not bad.
A perfunctory world at best
where passion and love
come too soon
too late
or too often.
The victims of life demons
that force a pillow down
over the sounds of a child's laughter.
Sometimes these demons can be defeated
giving strength
and the promise
of freedom
to our body, mind and spirit.
See it.
Smell it.
Taste it.
Rejoice.
Because no one knows
when the demons will return.
They are clever and more relentless

than anyone can imagine.
They beckon me while I sleep
and haunt me while I'm awake.
They don't mind
Waiting
because they know I am flawed
and have only the illusion of freedom.
I would rather lie in pieces
than be whole.
I will never have the courage
to reclaim my life
from the demon who stole it.
Betrayal and trauma are stronger
than love.
Abuse is my soul mate.
I can survive
with the shame, anger and self-hatred.
You can not.
You will be dragged down
by your goodness
and I will become your demon.
I can't let that happen
to the only person
who ever protected me.
One of us must be free.
At least my heart will not burn.
Remember the heart."

The bottom of the page was brittle, jagged at the edges and
stained with strawberry ice cream.

* * *

It was still light when the 7:15 shuttle left the airport half an hour late. By the time we pulled into Lone Star Springs I had drunk way too many cocktails. But why not? Hope had called to say she had a special surprise for our anniversary and I knew what it was.

She was pregnant.

A son, God willing.

"There is no greater joy in a man's life."

My father said that even more than he called Vivienne a saint.

Looking out the window I scanned the immediate area. Flowers were blooming. People were smiling. I was lucky to live in such an idyllic setting although, for a fleeting moment, I thought I saw a coyote trot in and out of the shadows, a cat hanging from its mouth as if it had no bones.

The whistle blew as I stepped onto the platform. I saw Hope immediately, standing in front of the depot. She was holding a bouquet of my favorite flowers, a mixture of honey-suckle, night-blooming jasmine and roses from our garden. Lit from behind by a full moon, she was so beautiful she took my breath away even more than the first time I saw her at Vivienne's funeral.

Her makeup was perfect.

There wasn't a hair out of place.

Her heels were spiked and three inches high.

Her dress was the only thing under wraps, hidden beneath a rain coat that clung to her body as if it were part of her.

It didn't take a genius to figure out why she was the reigning Miss Magnesium Lamp.

The moment she saw me she rushed over, handed me the flowers and shoved her groin into mine so hard it was as if she was trying to push through to the other side.

"Happy Anniversary, Darling."

The aroma of her perfume and warmth of her breath on my cheek aroused me so much I almost forgot where I was.

When we reached the car she'd draped a banner across the windshield that read, appropriately, "Happy Anniversary." A silver bucket was in the back with a bottle of French champagne, a small tin of Caviar wedged into crushed ice.

"You drive," she said, easing into the passenger seat before I could answer.

I slid behind the wheel, started the engine and weaved through the parking lot. When I veered onto the main road she unbuttoned her coat revealing nothing underneath except bikini underpants, black stockings and a garter belt.

I could feel the heat of her body begin to rise.

Next thing I knew the fingers of her right hand disappeared between her legs. I heard the smack of wetness and I could smell her scent. The car reeked of it. Sliding forward she bent her knees, arched her back and wedged her feet against the dash. I was aware of sounds I never heard before. The fabric of her coat as it slid down onto the seat. The noise her shoes made when she kicked them off and landed on the carpet. The whisper of upholstery against nylon.

"Don't get into an accident, Darling."

Closing her eyes, biting her lower lip, her hips began rising to her hand. Within no time her hair became unkempt and sweat began running down her temples, dripping past her ears and settling in the base of her neck. As her breathing increased, as her chest heaved up and down, she began to sing.

"How do I describe
the morning after
when every morning is?
Even the simplest words
escape me
so I have to wonder

Is it me?
Or maybe it's that language
cannot accommodate what
cannot be portrayed.
If it's me, I cannot be afraid
to describe the scars
or try to sweep them
under the rug.
They need to be seen.
To be recognized.
To be dealt with.
Somehow, some way, I must tell
the world."

Although a sentimental favorite, it was an interesting choice for a half-naked woman masturbating at sixty miles per hour.

* * *

When we arrived home she threw her arms around my neck and kissed me the way she did the first day of our honeymoon.

"This will be a night you'll never forget."

The lights were off when we walked through the front door. Candles were already lit, shadows flickering on all four walls and the ceiling. I could see the dining room was prepared, as always, on a par with the finest restaurants. I also noticed a small mound of wax that had dripped onto the table. I pointed it out to Hope in a kind but firm tone, reminding her how fortunate we were that our celebration hadn't turned into a raging inferno.

"What a stupid thing to say, Hen-ry. You don't have a fucking clue what life is about."

Her voice was hard and cold, nothing like the tone I'd been accustomed to.

"Of course I do."

The look on her face made me feel even more awkward, as if all her innocence had fled.

"God, you're tiresome."

She turned and disappeared into the den. The moment she left I regretted my words. A special occasion like a first anniversary took precedence over basic safety precautions, even if they were called for and you'd practiced them all your life. At the same time I wondered if it was wise to

drink alcohol in her condition.

Music drifted in from the other room.

"The endless shrill

of anticipation.

Taunting and unrelenting.

My ears

reject the sound

of long heavy strides,

arms swinging while he walks

as if they were suspended

and prohibited

from touching his own body."

It was another one of Peggy's poems, turned into driving, bass laden rock and roll. Vivienne played it often and it was a favorite.

When Hope reappeared her mood was as different as the outfit she'd changed into. Positively radiant, she now wore white pants, a white blouse, white shoes and her hair was pulled back and fastened with a white scarf.

Walking toward me she stopped in the center of the room, checked her watch and gazed out the front window like a cat who'd seen a bird.

"I was only kidding about the candles," I said, sensing I was skating on thin ice.

"You wouldn't know how to kid if your life depended on it, Hen-ry."

"I don't understand why you say that."

"I know, Hen-ry. Believe me."

Her disgusted tone and the way she kept saying my name, emphasizing each syllable, began to annoy me.

"I was kidding," I repeated.

"I don't give a shit about candles, Hen-ry."

Grabbing the champagne off the table she filled my glass.

"I care how men treat women."

"I still don't know what you're talking about."

"I know that too, Hen-ry."

Her brow knotted with anger as she crossed to the far side of the room and retrieved a gift-wrapped package.

"Open it."

"I'll get yours" I said, and started to leave.

"Now!"

She was growing more tense and ill tempered so I carefully tore through the wrapping. Inside the box was an album filled with photos of her over the years, much like the ones I showed her of Vivienne on our third date.

It was interesting to see her so young. The beauty. The confidence. The poise. The woman she would become was on display when most girls were awkward and praying for maturity to make them special.

At the same time, I was amazed her looks could change so radically, as if she'd mutated into a different being every few years. I couldn't help wondering what it must have been like to be the center of attention her entire life.

My next observation wasn't nearly as positive.

Hope's hair was the color of fire in every photo, her natural pigment.

The freckles. I should have known.

I was overcome by a wave of nausea and felt as if my chest was going to cave in. Hope, in turn, stepped back and began dancing seductively.

"Sinewy legs
brutally pried apart.
Smelling of sickness
not sleep.
Always embarrassed.
Always ashamed.
Always wondering
what I did
to cause this."

Undulating every which way, she moved toward me with a determination I hadn't seen before.

"If I'm responsible
So be it.
I'll pay the price.
But if it wasn't my doing,
why did fate choose me
when so many others,
unprincipled people
who spit
in the face of decency
and embrace corruption
like a newborn,
live rewarding lives
without the slightest hardship?"

She straddled my legs, squeezing tight with both thighs.

"Why me?"

She kissed me again and, when she pulled away, her light touch was gone forever.

My lip was bleeding.

"I look forward to your leaving for work every morning and I dread you coming home at night."

I laughed nervously, although there was no appropriate response, and I began to feel the familiar tentacles tighten around my Adam's apple.

"Do you know what I do after I drop you off, Hen-ry?"

I felt like a kid being instructed by his teacher the first day of school.

"I pick up as many men as I can. Sometimes one. Sometimes three. I bring them back to the house and fuck them."

She gestured toward the sofa.

"Right over there."

She was the one who was kidding. Nothing could change this drastically in such a short period of time. I kept quiet, careful to avoid anything that might upset her or work against me like the candles, although I couldn't stop calculating, allowing for weekends, weather, sickness and holidays.

"I know you're counting, Hen-ry."

While I have always prided myself on having a sense of restraint and even temperament, patience was impossible under these circumstances. I closed my eyes and took a series of

deep breaths to try and calm down. When I opened them Hope was lighting a cigarette.

"There were all types, Hen-ry. Men. Boys. Married. Single. Short. Tall. Fat and skinny. Black and yellow. Even a few cripples. They had only two things in common. I didn't know or care about any of them."

"I don't believe you," I said. "I don't know why you're doing this, but I don't believe a word you're saying."

"It's not difficult, Hen-ry. I'm here to teach you a lesson you should have learned years ago."

"I still don't know what you're talking about."

"You must take responsibility for your thoughts and deeds."

She looked at her watch again.

"Am I going too fast for you Hen-ry?

"No. It's not that. I...uh..."

"While I was fucking those men, Hen-ry, I had the best orgasms I've ever had. Not like with you where I had to pretend."

Another glance.

"The only thing worse than when you ogle me, Hen-ry, is when you touch me."

I started to say something but she wouldn't let me get a word in.

"You know why my orgasms were so good, Hen-ry? Because I always thought about this moment while I was coming."

Her lips curled into a sneer.

"I hope it hurts."

"It doesn't," I said without hesitation.

"You'll never be a good liar, Hen-ry. You have to have an imagination."

Turning, she walked toward the door. I watched her carefully before blurting out words the way I did in the needlepoint chair the night my father died.

"I thought you had no future without me!"

She didn't answer till she reached an extremely durable looking valise I'd never seen before, partially hidden beneath my father's jacket. Stubbing out her cigarette on the wall she picked it up and shrugged.

"Stop thinking."

She left without a backwards glance.

Rushing outside, I watched her casually shift the suitcase

from one hand to the other as she moved toward a taxi that had pulled up to the curb, her hips swaying in a forced, choppy motion. I was positively ill as you might imagine, by her words and actions. Most of all, I was sickened by her matter-of-factness.

"There must have been something good," I screamed.

Her head was bent forward a little but she straightened it up before turning to face me with a faraway look in her eyes.

"The silences."

It was the last thing she said before stepping into the cab and slipping out of my life as easily as she removed her stockings on the way back from the station.

For the first time I realized her nose was a little crooked and not aligned with her mouth. One eye was smaller than the other and her right shoulder was significantly lower than her left, as if she was about to topple over.

It was as if a switch had been thrown and drained all the beauty out of her.

"Stop the world, I want to get off!"

It's odd what races through your mind at a time like this. As I watched the taxi move slowly west, sliding through the darkness till it was little more than a Chesire's grin, I remembered an old Gahan Wilson cartoon in one of my father's Playboys. A car comes to a fork in this long

winding road. A detour diverts traffic to the right. In the distance you can see a dragon gobbling up cars as they try to make their way back to the main highway.

Though I'd obviously been out there many times before and reveled in the darkness, this time I was scared.

There was absolute silence.

No moon.

No stars.

No wind.

Not the ruffle of a thought.

I began hyperventilating when Arthur trotted up.

"Leave me alone," I said.

He barked and started for the house.

"Bad dog."

It was the only time I'd called him anything but his human name.

"Go home!"

He ran off. I turned. Before I reached the front door Arthur reappeared with a stick in his mouth. Dropping it at my feet he crouched down and waited for me to throw it, but my rage was stronger than my gratitude. Stronger than my love. Stronger than anything I'd ever experienced.

I kicked him in the ribs, knocking him down.

I wish I could say it wasn't a malicious act, that I only wanted to scare him off, teaching him caution and respect for situations beyond his making, like Vivienne's preemies. I wish I could say that, but I knew the moment I released my foot it was intended to hurt.

As Arthur stared up at me, confused, I watched the rise and fall of his chest, the way Vivienne must have watched me the day she brought me home from the hospital.

He didn't try to escape.

He didn't whine.

"Stop being a wimp" I screamed.

I kicked him again, almost losing my balance.

"Rip my fucking throat out."

Harder.

That's what you're bred for."

Using every facial gesture at his disposal Arthur tried to ask why I was acting so...human. What had he done to deserve such a response? Crawling over on his belly he placed his nose on my shoes and cocked his head slightly.

"You have the balls of a lap dog!"

His ears pointed forward then back.

"Go the fuck home!"

Stomach low to the ground he slinked away. The moment he was gone I breathed a sigh of relief, turned toward the house and stepped in dog shit, right foot first.

* * *

During Ethan's fourth session at the prison hospital, Doctor Coonan suggested the following tips to combat anger; most of which he found on the internet in books by "Belligerent Experts."

1. Breathe deeply. Not only will it help you relax, it will allow you to gain control and stop you from doing something stupid you'll regret.

2. Remove yourself from the situation that's making you crazy, even if it's only for a couple of seconds. If that's not possible, count to ten. If you're on the verge of losing it completely, keep counting till you calm down.

3. Drink more water. People are more easily annoyed when they're dehydrated.

4. Repeat a reinforcing thought. "Everything's going to be okay," "Slow down" and "Life is good" will work wonders.

5. Think about a happier timer; a vacation you'll never forget.

6. Smile. Sing "You Are My Sunshine." It will lessen the anger you or someone else is feeling.

7. Become Buddha. Replace your aggressive emotions with

compassion for everyone. "If we don't look after each other, who will look after us?"

8. Be positive. Expecting the worst makes relaxation impossible and fuels anger.

9. Speak softly. There's a biblical proverb that says: "A soft answer turns away wrath." Simple as that.

10. Look for humor. Even in the most horrific situations, laughing tricks the nervous system into feeling happy, releasing endorphins that decrease stress-related hormones. Whatever you do, however, don't laugh at the other person. There's a good chance this will have a negative effect.

11. Stretch. When you feel like your anger is reaching critical mass, stretch your body out. Roll your neck and shoulders. Reach for the sky.

Ethan disagreed.

He insisted those tips, while nice in theory, wouldn't work in a real-life combat situation and were a complete waste of time.

Doctor Coonan said nothing. He didn't blink or move a muscle. Having read through Ethan's file many times, he not only knew the nature of his crime, he knew Ethan was trained in all facets of unconventional warfare. No subterfuge was off limits. This included pervasive surveillance, propaganda, censorship, warrantless searches, detainment without charge, the suspension of habeas corpus and concealing human rights abuses from journalists. If necessary, it also included paramilitary activity and acts of terrorism. He even knew how to gauge the psychological climate of a country during covert operations, as he did in El Salvador, to determine whether it would wind up anti-American.

Although he'd read a half dozen articles about Doctor Coonan's "Belligerence Theories" in the prison library, Ethan, on the other hand, knew nothing about the man trying to help him.

He had no way of knowing he grew up in Hell's Kitchen, was the boy he described who was beaten by his father and, at sixteen, the New York Golden Gloves featherweight champion.

He did not know the good doctor was once a member of The Westies, a Manhattan gang, and had been instrumental in the murder of a man from Iowa, driving a yellow Mercury Cougar

convertible with red leather upholstery and eight track cassette player, who had the misfortune of taking a wrong turn and stopped to ask for directions.

He had no idea Doctor Coonan was a marine and awarded a Silver Star, Purple Heart and Congressional Medal Of Honor.

Nor did he know anything about his activity as an anti-war protester after that or his years in the seminary.

He also did not know Doctor Coonan's right eye was beginning to twitch, his throat close and his broad shoulders shake imperceptibly, the way they did when the Mercury convertible accidentally strayed onto his turf.

* * *

I slept badly, waking at 2:00 A.M. exhausted, nauseous and alone in bed for the first time in over a year. At first I had no memory of my anniversary and thought I was coming down with the flu.

Then I remembered.

I felt the same way I did after one of my nightmares, unsure if I was safe in my room or trapped in the backyard being yelled at by deer heads. It took almost fifteen minutes before I summoned the courage to lift my head off the pillow.

"Forgive me, Arthur."

It was my first thought and I said it out loud.

"I didn't mean it."

I was out of control, the one thing I feared more than anything else.

Early morning quiet made matters worse, a far cry from the peacefulness I experienced watching Hope sleep or running a comb through her hair, things that never failed to delight.

It made me realize there were two types of silences just like there were two types of dark:

1. Those that comforted you.

2. Those that felt like the earth had stopped spinning and it was the end of the world.

Hope's closet and chest of drawers were wide open. She'd taken everything except the items we'd purchased together. A snow globe. T-shirts with our photos. Silhouettes from the County Fair - strewn haphazardly around the room as if scattered by an unexpected gust of indifference.

They were all that was left.

The precision, harmony and laughter were gone and it sent a chill down my spine to think that she, that anyone, could be so calculating.

It reminded me of Vivienne's travel shows. I watched an episode about a small town in the Atlas mountains. Young Moroccan girls would come up to male tourists, expose their breasts and ask if they wanted to suck on them. To the best of the narrator's knowledge, no one had ever refused. Unfortunately, they woke up the next day with a horrible hangover, robbed of everything. Drugged nipples!

Obviously, there's a steep price to pay for enjoying life to its fullest all over the world.

The only thing Hope didn't take was her scent. Perfume. Shampoo. Even the smell of her breath still sweetened the room and made me think of fields of bluebonnets during my imaginary birth.

"God help me. God help me. God help me."

I blurted out the words over and over. This surprised me almost as much as Hope's betrayals because Christianity was more myth than doctrine for me then.

Like Zeus or the Alamo.

Instead of receiving the aid I requested, a surge of pain shot through me, spreading quickly from my spine to the rest of my body. I had trouble breathing. My vision blurred. My muscles cramped. My hands shook like an old man. It was the closest I'd come to cancer. Child birth perhaps. Even my equilibrium went haywire, like the first time I stepped off a roller coaster and the ground felt like it was tilted.

I got so dizzy I had to grab hold of the bed frame. I wasn't afraid of falling. Not really. I could just feel my soul, whatever it was that held me together, trying to escape.

Like Peggy must have felt when she sat down in the middle of the street.

Like my father before the car accident, racing toward the heavens.

If I could have flipped a switch and never been born I would have done it without a second thought.

In the ensuing weeks I woke up every morning at 2:00, automatically, as if paying homage to the night Hope left. While annoying, it amazed me I could maintain that type of consistency. I started wearing a watch to bed to see if the pattern continued. It did and I became hypnotized by the second hand as it swept toward the twelve, as if counting down the final moments of a championship game. This only increased my frustration, unfortunately. As I lay there, I couldn't decide if I was waking because of my pain or to verify the time.

I was still used up before my first cup of coffee.

I stopped washing my clothes. I didn't iron or mend. Small maintenance jobs went undone. Dishes stacked up as if they were part of the sink. Greasy fingerprints led from the faucet to the refrigerator, the refrigerator to the counter, the counter to the cabinets, spreading from room to room as if I needed them to find my way back - like Hansel. Ivy began growing through cracks in the walls, twining around anything within its grasp. Windows got so dirty I couldn't look out and see the nature I'd come to rely on. Not that it mattered. The garden had grown so thick and unruly it was impossible to walk through it.

I found myself staying under the covers each morning as long as possible, placing a pillow over my head to filter out whatever light and memories managed to creep into the room.

Occasionally, if only for the briefest second, I woke up feeling the relief that comes with the stoppage of pain, convinced I had the mental and physical strength to put things right.

An orderly life had held my life together before Hope. There was no reason to think it wouldn't do so again.

What better enemy of the abnormal than the normal? I went over the ten key ingredients to a successful business meeting. I recited the first page of "Roberts Rules Of Order." I listed the requirements for an Air Traffic Controller as well as the major errors that led to suspension and dismissal. In deference to Vivienne I conjugated the past, present and future tense of the verb agacer, using the je, il, elle and vous forms. I even included my father's twelve positions of female subjugation.

Nothing worked.

Debilitating thoughts flashed before my eyes like the slide show about Martin of Tours. No beginnings, middles or ends.

Just pieces. My talks in the square. Strawberry ice cream. Hope picking me up at the station wearing a low cut blouse, not realizing it was because she didn't have time to change. Messing up my father's hair. The naked secretary bouncing on her bed. Butterscotch shakes. I thought of my real mother too, lying on the road before she died, staring

down at me with the expression one makes when they first smell a skunk.

My love affair with order had left me as abruptly as Hope walked out the door. If I was going to survive I had to ignore the percentages, admit that life was random, no longer predictable and didn't progress in the way I thought. A. didn't always lead to B. Sometimes it was F. Sometimes it wasn't even a God-damned letter.

It was the end of an era.

"Hope."

I blurted the word out angrily.

"Hope."

This time I wasn't asking for help. I was trying to minimize her power over me and distance myself. If I said her name over and over as fast as I could, by the hundredth time maybe it would sound as silly as the girls talking about Saint Jude and she'd become more of a joke than the flesh and blood woman who'd plotted against me.

* * *

I began receiving Hope's mail a few days after she left, advertisements and promotional material mostly, but bills told the story of her feminist-conscious travels across the U.S.; each shelter for battered women visited a brutal reminder of her less than charitable behavior toward me.

I knew how Julie felt every time she went to the mailbox.

There was also a receipt from The Luggage Barn in Majestic Meadows. It was attached to a lifetime warranty from Tumi along with a cardboard photo of its light, stylish and practical Alpha 28 inch Travel bag. It was charged to the Visa account I opened for her in my name, in case of emergency, and forgot about.

On the back of the receipt, in Hope's handwriting, was one of the dark secrets I told her on our honeymoon.

"I'VE NEVER TRUSTED ANY WOMAN, ESPECIALLY ONES WITH RED HAIR."

Next to it was a smiley face with long, scarlet curls.

Disgusted, I threw it across the room, landing in a corner beside a copy of Vivienne's second book, yellowed and frayed around the edges like Peggy's suicide note. Hope had forgotten it in her haste. The third page was dog-eared.

Opening to it, I was staring at the last half of Vivienne's introduction, a section she never divulged while pacing late at night. It was highlighted in yellow.

"Neither Catherine nor Margaret felt it necessary for Joan to die in order to liberate France. That was a decision by the Archangel Michael who was in charge. Joan being burnt at the stake as a martyr, to his male way of thinking, was the only way to motivate the French. He even arranged for a white dove to fly overhead as she begged for a Crucifix and forgave those who sentenced her while she burned to death.

Dramatic, yes. Necessary, hardly.

For hundreds of years Catherine and Margaret continued to think about what Joan might have accomplished if she'd lived. She could have reminded the world that a woman's sensibilities were not only life-affirming, but reinforced the importance of self-examination; as opposed to men who were destructive and focused on political and military might.

She might have also taught women to express those same

sensibilities, their inner strength, through their bodies which contained the miracle God created us for. We are, after all, the only source of life on earth and, therefore, must be respected - one of the few things that require men to behave properly.

I agree with Catherine and Margaret. Women need to emphasize their strengths not their weaknesses, although sometimes they appear to be identical. I also believe that Joan's voices came from a higher power, a God she loved and followed with all her heart who showed her how to deal with men who waged war for hundreds of years.

Now, all He has to do is show me.

I conducted an experiment with my stepson, Henry, a wonderful boy but with no life experience except for what his father taught him - offensive at best. I asked him to evaluate two written speeches, almost identical in content. One, I said, was written by a man. The other, by a woman.

He rated the exact same thoughts higher if he thought they were coming from a male.

Why?

He considered the woman pushy and a bitch. Centuries change. Women's struggles have not.

We are still the river to man's sea.

I believe God chose Peggy to empower me so I would have the strength to go to war, like Joan, to teach boys like my stepson that misogyny is destructive to men as well as women.

Unlike his father, he must learn that relationships are about quality, not quantity.

I've spent my life being supportive and patient, but it's time for this old dog to learn new tricks. I might even enjoy being pushy. And if being a bitch is what it takes to rid the world of injustice and abuse against women, I'm more than happy to go that extra mile and encourage you to do the
same.

We will be the biggest ones you've ever seen, with a capital B."

Air stopped circulating. Light became opaque and thick, like before a tornado. There was no sound because none could describe my feelings of betrayal.

Except maybe one.

"God damn. God damn. God fuckity fuck fuck shit piss damn!"

It would have been more merciful if I'd gotten up in the middle of the night and found Vivienne towering over me, hands balled into fists, her blood stained knuckles scraped to the bone.

* * *

Over the next few months my daily commute felt like it took forever and I started hating my job, especially the people who now happily approached me with their politics, betting pools and despicable social interaction.

Unlike the courageous Bactrian camels Vivienne admired, I became more and more introverted. I spoke with no one, came home and went directly to bed. Like Peggy, I started touching things. Like my father, I started worrying about my next breath. When I went out I made sure I had I.D. in case I had a heart attack, was found unconscious and they needed to cart my body off to the

morgue. Then again, I rarely left the house. Every street, every corner, every store reminded me of Hope. I stopped listening to the radio as well.

The country music I despised with its ludicrous "Yippie-yi-yo-ki-yays" and sloppy sentimentality now made me tremble.

Adding to my discomfort, I was constantly passing homeless people wearing my father's clothing.

A shirt here.

Pants there.

Shoes no longer with a military shine.

A month went by before I woke up feeling like my old self, but by the time I showered, dressed, brewed a pot of coffee, walked out the door and drove to the station, there wasn't a sense or bodily function that hadn't risen up and laughed in my face.

On this particular Monday, the idea of walking into work and seeing all those smiling faces seemed too much like the notes I received from Hope. When the train stopped I stumbled off, barely reaching an empty bench behind the depot.

In dreaded Majestic Meadows.

Of all places to fall apart.

I felt like I was going to pass out so I leaned forward and put my head between my legs, hoping blood would reach some brain cells. It took about thirty seconds before I felt strong enough to raise my head again, get my bearings and take a quick look around.

A Downs Syndrome child confined to a wheelchair was breathing through a portable respirator. A homeless man was seated next to a dog whose ribs were exposed and looked scrawnier than he did. A couple of teenagers standing beside the train schedule started pushing and shoving each other till it escalated into a fight.

It wasn't like scuffles I'd seen on TV.

Even though the boys were friends, they fought as if their lives depended on it. The way Vivienne and I watched lions protect their cubs.

I assumed the larger kid would win easily, but the smaller boy was more compact and had what they commonly referred to as "killer instinct" on the travel shows. Stronger and faster he got his full weight behind every punch and threw four to the larger kids one. He appeared clumsy as a result, put up little resistance, wore down quickly and was beaten into submission within a couple of minutes.

Instead of being the end of the fight, much to my horror, it was only the beginning. The smaller boy started kicking his friend while he was down, knocking out teeth, bloodying both ears and tearing cartilage. He kicked him again and again. The way I'd done to Arthur.

That he was relentless and, apparently, unable to stop, tapped into my worst fears. Not just loss of control. My feelings about music too. Like I once said, it's odd what goes through your mind during times of crisis. As I watched the fallen boy's skin ripped apart, welts appearing on contact, all I could think about were quotes from jazz musicians who were never afraid.

"You must own it to play it."

"Once you discover that you can, then you must."

"Just allow yourself to go along and you'll find yourself carried away."

I don't know why exactly, maybe because the larger kid wasn't displaying any signs of life, but the beating finally stopped. And the victor turned toward me.

Aware that I'd been watching from the outset he glared as if challenging me to intervene. Although I was far more inter-ested in fighting my own demons, something passed between us at that moment. A camaraderie if you will. A ruthless respect for cause and effect and I couldn't keep quiet.

As surprised as Peggy was by the words she spoke with her dying breath, I was even more shocked by mine.

"Kill him," I said. "For Christ's sake, just do it."

Convinced I posed no threat he turned and stomped down hard on the top of his friend's head. You could hear the impact clear across the platform, like the crack of a bat when someone hits a home run or beats a non-union driver to death.

It's mind-boggling when you realize that chance, like zealots, can completely alter the course of your life. As the kid disappeared inside the depot I rose, stepped over the boy's mangled body and moved toward track #2. Although it was little more than a fleeting thought, as I scanned the

schedule for arrivals and departures, it was the first time I realized my problems could be solved if Hope ceased to exist.

"Once you discover that you can, then you must."

No imagination my eye!

During my first break at work I walked over to the international terminal and bought a new journal. At lunch I divided the days into regimented segments. On the ride back from the airport I started appraising my progress, allowing me to anticipate, prioritize and not get bogged down with anything trivial.

By the time I got home my equilibrium was perfectly sound and the bedroom had a bitter smell, like something I'd put in the back of the refrigerator, forgot about and could no longer identify.

* * *

I found this online.

Thirty-one million crimes were reported in the United States last year, about one per second. Out of those, 389,100 females were victimized by an intimate partner as opposed to a stranger. Out of those, 6,945 were murdered, roughly twenty each day.

The majority of women killed were ex wives. Married women came in second. Common-law wives had the next highest percentage with girlfriends and ex-girlfriends tied for last, but certainly not least. Sixty-nine percent involved abandonment.

While women are less likely than men to be victims of violent crimes, women are five to eight times more likely than men to be victimized by their intimate partner.

Domestic violence is the largest single cause of injury to women in the U.S., more than auto accidents, muggings and cancer combined.

Every twelve to fifteen seconds a woman is battered by her mate in the United States. This includes all social, economic classes, races and religious groups.

Just for the record, I do not condone violent behavior toward anyone, especially women. I consider it a cowardly thing to do. A man who hits a woman, under any circumstances, should be incarcerated. At the same time, there is obviously a common thread at work here that cannot be ignored.

I may be a lot of things. An aberration is not one of them.

* * *

As long as I'm on the subject, murder is one of those rare acts that cannot be defined by details alone. Even the legal definition involves variables.

"An unlawful killing of another human being with "malice aforethought."

I found that in the library.

The problem is, what constitutes malice? Some say it's as simple as "intent to kill." It can also be implied when a death occurs by "extreme recklessness to human life" or "during a serious crime." Then again, what if the motive for killing is more fair play than murder?

What if the person deserves to die like you know who? By law, justified killings are not considered homicides. Most times they're not even criminal offenses.

Acting in self-defense is generally accepted as legal justification for killing another person.

Killing of enemy combatants in accordance with lawful orders in war is also considered a necessary evil for the good of mankind.

Therefore, murdering a vengeful, duplicitous wife is both self-defense and for the good of mankind.

* * *

Things began to improve, one Friday afternoon, when Mrs. Fairweather came to the house.

"Every time I saw a Toyota I wanted to throw up."

These were the first words she spoke when I opened the front door, before taking my arm and dragging me into the sunlight.

She'd heard about Hope leaving and wanted me to know how much she empathized. A few years ago her husband was run down by a Japanese driver from Majestic Meadows. Although

she knew it was important to spend time alone, that experiencing grief was one of the best ways to appreciate living, she also knew she'd go crazy if she sat around feeling depressed. So, she turned to the one thing she knew would give her a healthy perspective on loss.

Tennis.

Ushering me toward her car she insisted on showing me something that would give my life a new and healthy perspective as well.

I couldn't wipe the smile off my face.

"I'd be crazy to pass up a chance to sleep with a woman who wanted to sleep with me."

My father really should have had a street named after him.

Ten minutes later I was sitting on a love seat in Mrs. Fairweather's den, staring at dozens of tennis trophies while I waited for her to come back from the bedroom with my life-changing surprise.

Possibilities were endless.

Would sex be safe and conventional or wild and illicit? Would we be gentle and go to sleep holding each other or would there be oils and salves and battery-driven devices the size of a wildebeest? Either way, Mrs. Fairweather would have an orgasm. Orgasms. I'd see to that. No faking. Not on my watch.

That's when it happened.

WHAM!

I felt like a small child who'd been separated from his parents in a strange city.

What if I was going down on her and I heard gagging. Even if she was wearing high heels, fishnet stockings and a girl scout uniform it would be impossible for me to stay aroused while someone named Spot threw up my Fruit Of The Looms.

Worse, what if I came prematurely like the night I lost my virginity, on my eighteenth birthday, to the waitress with breasts the size of volleyballs?

Mrs. Fairweather would come back into the room. She'd saunter over to the couch. She'd shake my hand. A simple greeting for her. For me, a complete sexual experience and I'd need a cigarette.

WHAM!

Fear changed to sorrow.

Maybe because the idea of living life to its fullest was new to me, the thought of being with another woman other than Hope, even after everything that happened, made me feel like I was cheating.

"Christmas present. Christmas present. Christmas present."

I began rocking back and forth, trying to focus on the lessons my father taught me. Instead of calming down I started worrying about my balls. For an instant I even wished aliens had sucked them out with their damned juice straws during one of their invasions. The problem would have been resolved years ago.

By the time Mrs. Fairweather appeared in the hallway, dressed in the same tennis outfit as when she left, my back ached from sitting, my hands were shaking and I was perspiring so profusely, the right side of my shirt was two shades lighter than the left.

She was holding two equal lengths of nautical rope and a piece of paper, which she handed me, that listed forty different types of knots.

"Name one" she said proudly.

I didn't know what to say.

"Your choice."

"Two half-hitches."

"The interlacing of ropes around an object by making two half knots, one after another."

With minimal effort she tied the ropes into the knot she'd described.

"Another."

I scanned the page.

"Reef knot."

"Interlacing of ropes made of two half-knots inverse to each other."

During the next half hour, Mrs. Fairweather made a Full Windsor, a Half Windsor, a Halyard, a Bowline, a Sheet, a Figure Eight, an Overhand and every other knot I called out. She explained that she learned all of them while taking sailing lessons, something she'd wanted to do since she was a teenager but never had time for while she was married. She'd also started playing the piano and signed up for a pottery class in the fall. Not that there was anything positive about her husband's death. There wasn't. It did allow her to do things, however, she couldn't have done if they'd been together.

The joy of learning gave her a new appreciation for living.

She took me for a long drive after that, into Dallas, and pointed out different types of houses, styles of architecture and plant life I wouldn't ordinarily see in Lone Star Springs. She recommended some old movies that would put a smile on my face. Ones with Cary Grant, Jimmy Stewart and Marilyn Monroe. She urged me to read a few self-help books that sounded cliche but held kernels of truth that would guide me through the rough spots. Though it was essential to keep busy, I also had to remember it was equally important to speak with someone, an empathetic person like herself, whenever I felt bad. Hopefully, in the future, if I ran into someone who needed assistance, I would remember what she'd done for me and happily provide it. That person, as a result, would feel compelled to do the same. The person after that. And so on.

Empathy was the key to everything.

Whatever she told me was said with enormous optimism and affection. No regrets about things that hadn't gone her way or lived up to expectations. As a result, I found it impossible to lie and wound up telling her things I usually kept to myself. I didn't have to explain or make excuses

because she listened carefully, absorbed everything I said and didn't offer advice about the way things should have been done.

The more I spoke the more I could be myself, be it witty, outrageous or profound, as deep as I was capable of at any rate. That I was willing to purge like that surprised me more than anything else. I was never big on taking emotional risks and it was easier than I'd imagined.

It was like we were old friends who hadn't seen each other for years, met by chance and picked up where we'd left off.

I was ashamed.

How could I have thought Mrs. Fairweather was interested in me sexually? She wasn't anything like the women my father described. She was a kind, decent person whose only motive was reaching out to someone who'd experienced a terrible loss like herself.

"Thank you," I said, glancing up from a menu filled with photos of every meal the restaurant had to offer. "I wish I could tell you how much I appreciate this."

"You are," she said, signaling our waiter.

She wanted to take me to other types of restaurants too. Indian. Mexican. Chinese. Thai. It was good for me to expand my tastes because, one day, I would be in other cities, other countries hopefully, and would know how to take care of myself and where to go.

A future man of the world.

As the waiter approached she hunched forward, close enough so I could smell peppermint on her breath, and moved her water glass from between us.

"Have anything you want."

A big smile crossed my lips as I studied a glossy picture of a 72 ounce Porterhouse that was free if you finished it in forty-five minutes or less, unaware that the last person who'd success-fully accomplished that had a heart attack and died on his way home.

"There's just one thing" she said, looking me up and down as if I were a column of numbers, her nipples suddenly erect.

"Don't order anything with garlic or onions."

* * *

Later that night, after I'd returned home and was preparing for bed, I found myself staring at my reflection in the mirror. Although I usually avoided vanity of any kind, I thought of my father's face, hoping to catch a glimpse of the talented, sensitive boy I learned about at his funeral.

Something must have rubbed off!

No matter how hard I looked, however, all I could see was how much I didn't have and never would. There were no signs of the God-given good looks, charm or confidence that allows one to accomplish anything they set their mind to.

Nothing that would make me feel special.

Regardless of what happened with Mrs. Fairweather, I was ordinary. Disheartened, I started to leave but managed one last look.

That's when I saw it.

My widow's peak.

Like Vivienne when she returned from Paris, my mind became filled with profound insight. Rushing downstairs I vaulted over the needlepoint chair and didn't stop till I reached the front door. Snatching my father's jacket off its rack I slid both arms into the sleeves. It was at least a size too large but I didn't care. It made me feel good and powerful and ready to conquer the world.

The sky was clear, the air cool as I walked outside and picked up the evening paper. Sliding my finger down the front page it took barely a second to find what I was searching for.

The section advertising Cadillacs.

*　*　*

The 1957 Eldorado Brougham, my father's meticulously maintained first impression, was considered the car of the future at the time and is still regarded as the pinnacle of American design and luxury, the best the automotive industry had to offer.

The name Eldorado was chosen to celebrate Cadillac's golden anniversary. There are several stories attributed to this, but my favorite involves the Spanish word meaning "Golden One." The name had first been used by the chief of a South American Indian tribe. His followers would sprinkle his body with gold dust on ceremonial occasions and he would cleanse himself by diving into a lake.

Another version says they named the car after the Eldorado country club in Palm Springs where GM executives spent clandestine weekends with girlfriends instead of their wives.

This was my father's favorite.

Features were endless.

America's first completely pillarless four-door body, rear doors were designed to open opposite the front doors to allow for comfortable access when entering and exiting. Forged aluminum wheels. Brushed stainless steel roof. Wide oval whitewall tires. Quad headlights that dimmed whenever another vehicle approached. A 325 horsepower engine that started and restarted automatically. Hydra-matic transmission. Power steering. Power brakes. Power windows. Tinted glass. Polarized sun visors which darkened when tilted. Air conditioning. AM signal seeking radio with front and rear speakers and self rising antenna. Quadruple horns. Electric drum dial clock. Doors that locked when the transmission was in "Drive." Individual front and rear heating systems with under seat blowers. Six way power seats with two position memory settings. Air ride suspension that kept the car level regardless of the road conditions or the load being carried inside the vehicle. Cigarette lighters, two front, two rear. Front and rear fold down arm rests, the back containing a pencil, note pad, mirror and Arpege perfume atomizer. A bar. A fold out glove box tray that included tissue dispenser, a case for cigarettes in matching interior leather, lipstick, powder puff, comb, six steel magnetized Demitasse cups and, last but not least, forty-four choices of trim combinations.

It cost a little over $13,000, expensive under any circumstances when you consider it was more than a Rolls-Royce Silver Cloud of the same year.

My father swore it was worth any price because, when I was a baby and couldn't sleep, he'd carry me out to the car, strap me in and drive through the neighborhood till my eyes shut, the Caddie's ultra smooth ride preventing road hazards from interfering with my comfort. When I awoke the next morning I was in my crib, rested and warm.

"Sanity-saving rides" is what Vivienne called them.

The car was also a comfort to the many women in my father's life and a lot more luxurious than any motel he would have taken them to. They were willing to screw him right then and there, whether straddling him while he drove or parked along the side of the road.

In both cases, suspension and memory settings surpassed their intended functions.

Although I couldn't find a red car like my Dad's, I found one in azure blue and was able to make the down payment with the silver dollars that had materialized behind my ears over fifteen magical years.

Jack was right about illusion.

Girls who'd ignored me in the past smiled when I approached in my shiny new automobile. I looked good, they held me in higher esteem and I had a chance to score with every one of them. I knew it the moment they wiggled into the passenger seat, skirts dancing up their thighs as the doors locked automatically behind them.

My spirits were high. The community was safe. Life was better than I ever imagined.

Except for one thing.

I didn't swim in the pond any more. I didn't bound through tall grass or jump over fallen trees.

Although I often saw him circling the house at night, watching for intruders from a distance, Arthur never came back. If anybody knew about the world it was him, not Elvis.

* * *

Word must have gotten out about me and Mrs. Fairweather because all the Lone Star wives started showing up at my door. Instead of bringing food as was customary, like after my father died, they were offering something far more appetizing.

Themselves.

Vivienne was happiest when she woke up thinking about God. He stayed with her, no matter what she did or where she was, throughout the day. She went to sleep praying to Him and He inspired her dreams. I finally knew how she felt.

I began waking up with thoughts that stayed with me for twenty-four hours, although my happiness was inspired by a much lower power.

When I opened my eyes in the morning, swung a wobbly leg onto the cold floor and lumbered toward the bathroom, I thought about Mrs. Lewis' nipples. As I drove to the station and saw the magnolias beginning to bloom, I thought about Mrs. Harvey's completely shaved bush. While I rode the train to work, I thought of the world class pornography collection Mrs. Clifford downloaded onto her MacBook Pro.

Amateurs, anal, Asians, big butts, big tits, bisexuals, blondes, blowjobs, brunettes, coeds, compilations, couples, creampies, cumshots, cunnilingus, dildos/toys, ebony, Europeans, facials, fantasies, fetish, fingering, gays, Germans, gonzo, group sex, hairy, handjobs, Hentai, instructional, interracial, interviews, kissing, Latinas, lesbians, although this was unsettling, masturbation, mature women, MILFs, panties, pantyhose, public sex, rimming, shaved, shemales, solo girls, solo males, squirting, straight sex, swallowing, teens, threesomes, vintage, voyeurs and webcams.

The only thing missing were pink marble lions on either side of her computer.

The sun reminded me of pussy.

The trees reminded me of pussy.

Hamburgers. Pasta. Paper clips. Peanut butter and jelly.

My father didn't lie to me again, not per se, but he was guilty of crimes of omission.

He never warned me about obsession.

Do you have any idea how many words there are for pussy?

Ace Of Spades. Alcove. Ax Wound. Bacon Strip. Beaver. Bat Cave. Bazoo. Beef Curtains. Bloody Mary. Bearded Clam. Baby Pooper. Black Bess. Black Hole. Belly Dingle. Bluebeards Closet. Botany Bay. Box. Bush. Burial Ground. Camel Toe. Cock Alley. Cock Pocket. Cookie. Chicken's Tongue. Crawl Space. Corner Cupboard. Cape Horn. Cherry Pie. Cabbage Patch. Child Cutter. Cave Of Harmony. Clit. Cooze. Cuckoo's Nest. Dark Abyss. Deli Meat. Dead End Street. Dripping Delta. Divine Monosyllable. Dog's Mouth. Dirty South. Door Of Life. Eye That Weeps. Fur Burger. Fur Pie. Factotum. Female Crucible. Flapdoodle. Frumunda Squid. Fort Rabbit. Front Porch. Fruit Cup. Goodies. Gusher. Gallimaufrey. Gi Gi. Gnarley Hatchet Gasp And Grunt. Grove Of Eglantine. Gracy Maker. Gib tenuck. Glory Hole. Groceries. Grotto. Ham Wallet. Hoo Haa. Hershey's Kiss. Hooch. Hog Eye. Home Sweet Home. Honey Pot. Hey nonny nonny. Hymen Altar. Half Moon Bay. Itching Jenny. Jaws Of Hell. Kooter.

Knick Knack. Kebab. Love Glove. Lady Jane. Lobster Pot. Lavender Lick Hole. Lower Lips. Love Canal. Love Muscle. Maidenhead. Morris Minor. Mrs. Drips. Main Street. Muff. Moose. Mine Of Pleasure. Man Trap. Man Hole. Meat Curtains. Mouse Trap. Nick-in-the-notch. Nonesuch. Nookie. Oat Bin. Oyster Catcher. Pandora's Box. Pink Parts. Pink Taco. Pink Wings. Pink Sock. Parking Garage. Parsley Patch. Perfumed Mouse. Poontang. Rat Trap. Rob-the-Ruffian. Sushi. Smurf Lips. Sloppy Joe. Second Mouth. Slit. Stream Town. Sperm Dumpster. Snatch. Skin the pizzle. The Little Man In The Boat. Third Eye. Tool Shed. The Business Channel. V-Jay. Vag. Vaheena. Vertical Smiles. Vertical Vacuum. Wet Kitty. Wound. Whim Wham. White Tiger's Cavern. Whisker Biscuit. Yoni. Yum Yum and my personal favorite: CUNT!

When I went to sleep at night and dreamed, in lurid detail, about my sexual escapades with each and every Lone Star woman, I even started licking the corners of my lips.

* * *

Monday, Wednesday and Friday nights I started going to The Red Lion Inn. Unlike work, I looked forward to socializing and made friends easily, people whose own lives were staid and boring the way mine used to be. They didn't know my father except by reputation, were elated to meet his offspring and inspired by my insights.

I commented on every girl who walked by, both looks and availability, grading them from one to ten depending on a combination of legs, ass, chest, skin and attitude, cheekiness being a priority. If I was inadvertently in their way I would rise, step aside and gallantly gesture for them

to pass.

"Beauty before age," was what I always said.

While my new friends and I watched them walk away, as their hips swished back and forth, I analyzed every sway, championing a flowing, pendulum type of motion.

My primary message to them never wavered and they grinned in appreciation every time they thought about it, whether at work or while giving their wives a quick five minute screw before watching prime time reality shows.

"Sex with the right woman was the greatest pleasure a man could experience. More important, sex with the wrong woman was just as good."

I extolled the benefit of using all five senses when making love to a woman, why it didn't matter what they did with their lives and the importance of fishnet stockings. I warned them about the pitfalls of sexual gratification, religion and education and explained why Cadillacs were a Venus Fly Trap for pussy.

I became the man they could never hope to equal, but I was also the man responsible for lifting their spirits three nights a week.

Occasionally, one of Jack's old buddies wandered in and overheard my stories. Rather than give me away, as I feared, they too were elated. While the spirit of my father's conquests would stay with them forever, specifics had long been forgotten. As far as they were concerned, I was a chip

off the old block. Listening to my stories not only enabled them to relive their fondest memories, it reinforced the belief their youth had not be misspent.

I finally understood why my father hung out at bars with men like this. Compared to them he was a God and they treated him accordingly, hanging on every word as if waiting for a punch line. It was different with family.

You didn't have to do anything special for them to revere you. You were larger than life because of your position, be it father, mother, daughter or son. Friends hung on every word because of what you accomplished, things they wished they could do like fishing, riding a bicycle and attracting girls who could swallow an entire salami.

For the first time people were envious of me. I loved it, couldn't get enough and never dreamed of giving it up.

Until one Friday night.

A Slavic-looking, middle-aged blonde with big hair and long, red fingernails was seated near the end of the bar. She'd been gawking and listening to my stories since I arrived. When the waitress announced last call she casually got down off her stool, walked over and slapped me hard along my jaw line.

"Too bad I didn't fuck your mother. I could've had the whole family."

Pleased with herself, she sauntered toward the exit, something vaguely familiar as I watched her leave with a pendulum type of motion.

Undaunted, I turned back toward my friends and, before they could speak, happily explained why girls were like Christmas presents, Elvis-fucking-Presley's philosophy and the story about my dog, Arthur, who threw up a super model's thong while I was going down on her.

If you have a choice between the truth and becoming a legend, always choose the legend.

* * *

The travel channel is a lot like the Airlines. They tell you things like this:

The Bactrian camels of Mongolia have five potential uses. Milk. Meat. Wool. Working capacity as a riding or pack animal and a source of fuel.

The milk yield amounts to between one thousand and fifteen hundred liters per year, the maximum reached in the third month of lactation. The total can only be estimated because the calf consumes a substantial part of the milk which is rich in fat and has a higher caloric content than cows' milk.

Bactrian camel meat has coarser fibers than beef but is comparable in terms of quality. It has a sweet taste because of its high glycogen content and the color is raspberry red to dark brown.

Bactrian camels have a long, desirable winter fleece. Length and width of fibers differ depending on the part of the body but the wool is particularly fine and dense around the mane, elbow joints, ribs and shoulders.

In the desert the camel still plays an important role as a riding animal, although it has lost its dominant status since the Second World War. It's remarkably well adapted to extreme climate where temperatures can fluctuate as much as 90° C during the course of the year.

Dried camel dung is one of the few sources of energy available to camel owners in the central Asian desert. Every year about nine hundred and fifty kilograms of dung are collected per adult animal and made into compact balls.

The travel channel never tells you things like this:

In Mongolia it's illegal for a man to have sex with the same camel his father had sex with. This is not an unwritten law. It's on the books and severely punished. While this is wrong on so many levels, the act far more than the repercussions, after what happened in the bar I became concerned with the familial shame I might be responsible for with women who knew my father.

If I was in their homes while they were in the kitchen preparing a meal, in the bathroom or changing to go to a party, I snuck around and searched behind every closed door looking for stacks of pots, pans, vacuums and sets of outdated encyclopedias.

* * *

Ethan's fifth Anger Management class was cancelled due to illness. Doctor Coonan had come down with a bad case of the flu, something that surprised him since he'd only been sick once in his life, the night before he shipped off to Vietnam. He also couldn't understand why, when his wife came to bed the night before class, he turned his back, the thought of her touching him suddenly repulsive.

* * *

Legend, like education, religion and career, wasn't all it was cracked up to be. The more I thought about the women I slept with, the more I realized I'd been lied to again.

My father never listened when they confessed their inner-most secrets. He couldn't have because, if he let in the tragedy around him, like at the hospital in Paris, it was far more than a relatively painless exchange.

Mrs. Damiani, for example, was being stalked by her ex husband in spite of a restraining order prohibiting him from coming within a hundred yards. During ten years of marriage he'd beaten her up at least once a month, justifying it because "A man had the right to do anything he wanted to a woman if she refused to give him sex."

Mrs. Kozlowski spent most of her high school years home-less, moving from one flop house to the next. Somehow, she managed to graduate with honors, but had to work as a stripper in Houston to pay her college tuition. She was wild and unpre-dictable till she met an Iranian man who convinced her to change her wicked ways. She stopped drinking. She stopped doing drugs. She even found a respectable job in a cleaners owned by a nice Lebanese family. Two days after she moved in with her saviour, he accused her of dressing like a whore, hit her, drove to a McDonald's and blew himself up.

Mrs. Holloway traveled to India at a time when her problems were insurmountable. After four months she had a vision. She should take all the things that were haunting her on the inside and tattoo them on the outside. That way, she would be able to look each one straight in the eye.

It took three painful years, her face, neck and a small patch on her upper right arm the only skin untouched.

In no particular order:

Spot-on portraits of Princess Diana at her wedding. An unflattering image of Prince Charles looking up the skirt of Camilla Parker Bowles as she hung from a gallows. The faces of at least two-dozen unidentifiable men. A clown taking a bite out of a vintage Ken doll. Crop circles. A wreath of dead roses. Russell Stover candy. A John Deere tractor. The different phases of the moon and a cloud with three bolts of lightning coming down and shattering the heart of a giant

squid wrapped around an erect penis.

Mrs. Burton's daughter, Layla, had three abortions by the time she was fourteen, relating to them more as birth control than medical procedures. She was also addicted to pain killers.

The previous month Mrs. Burton woke up from a sound sleep to find two policemen standing at the foot of her bed. When she sat up it nearly scared them to death, both officers instinctively drawing their weapons. In a drugged out stupor, Layla had called 911 and said her mother was dead. Worse, she was pregnant again.

Mrs. Harvey had been abducted by aliens.

Mrs. Lewis tried to kill herself when Pluto, the dominant planet in her horoscope, was downgraded to an asteroid.

Mrs. Gentry couldn't say no to a man.

Mrs. Clifford used to be one.

I also realized that women didn't turn on my dad because of their vulnerability. They rebelled because, when they did come face to face with their true selves, they knew men weren't the solution to the problems. Living well was and, in a world where everyone wanted a piece of them, it was more important to find a way to stay whole - something close to impossible.

I doubt my father would have approved but, as they confessed one tragedy after another, I found myself pretending to be asleep, sneaking looks at my watch or saying I had to race home and take care of my sick Pekingese, ending the evening before it was time.

If none of those worked, I looked for an escape route.

* * *

I finally understood how Vivienne felt the day she dedicated herself to her mother and others like her.

I started waking up at 2:00 A.M., exhausted and nauseous for the first time since Hope walked out the door. "God help them. God help them. God help them." I blurted out the words over and over. As usual, the aid I requested was not forthcoming.

Surges of pain shot through me till I had to grab hold of the bed. When I finally calmed down I retrieved Vivienne's medical books, leafed through the pages and looked for psychological treatments to combat anxiety, co-dependance, adults abused as children, adult children of alcoholics, divorce, eating disorders, drug addiction, stress, depression and sex reassignment surgery.

This too was easier said than done since there were far more solutions than problems.

Art therapy. Aversion therapy. Biofeedback. Cognitive. Dream analysis. Eye Movement Desensitization Reprocessing.

Freudian. Gestalt. Jungian. Rational Emotive therapy. Transactional Analysis.

To name but a few.

Once again I found myself staying under the covers each morning as long as possible, placing a pillow over my head to filter out the horrors that had begun to consume me. When I could no longer procrastinate, I swung a wobbly leg onto the cold floor, lumbered toward the bathroom and thought about Mrs. Lewis's Bulimia. As I drove to the station and saw the magnolias I thought about Mrs. Harvey's acrophobia. While I rode the train to work, as people boarded at Majestic Meadows, I thought of Mrs. Clifford's hoarding.

Do you have any idea how many words there are for suffering?

Afflicted. Agonized. Distressed. Hapless. Hurt. Miserable. Tortured. Tormented. Woeful. Wretched.

The only positive slant to this tragic situation, and I doubt you could actually classify it as such, was the fact that there weren't nearly as many synonyms for suffering as there were for pussy.

* * *

Two potentially troublesome envelopes arrived in the mail. I didn't look at them right away. I didn't have the energy. When I finally gained strength, I ripped open the first and found a calendar from the sponsors of the Miss Magnesium pageant. Hope was featured, along with some of the other contestants, in seductive swimwear.

The second was from a travel agency. The enclosed receipt had another one of my darkest

secrets scrawled on the back.

"I'VE NEVER FELT LOVED UNCONDITIONALLY."

The smiley face beside it was larger than usual. The receipt was for $594 which included a round trip air fare from California to New York and four nights at the local YWCA.

Hope's plane stopped in Dallas Fort Worth airport at 11:59 A.M. during my shift, the morning of February 14th.

VALENTINE'S DAY!

As on the night I kicked Arthur, my rage was stronger than anything I'd ever experienced.

Even though it was premature, I went on line and checked to see if a pilot had been assigned her flight. To my delight there was the same pilot who'd failed three check-rides and been suspected of fatigue.

God did work in mysterious ways.

* * *

Airspace is divided into what we call controlled and uncontrolled sections. Controlled is that part of the sky where traffic is so heavy, strict aircraft supervision is necessary to avoid collisions. Uncontrolled airspace is, quite simply, the rest. This is where most light aircraft and some smaller regional airlines operate, although they often use controlled airspace during take-off and landing. Collision avoidance in uncontrolled airspace relies largely on the wits of the pilot and on agreed ways of separating traffic, such as flying at different altitudes. Procedures

for uncontrolled airspace, just for the record, have been controversial as long as I can remember.

I also control the ground.

Large planes may look graceful in the sky, but on the tarmac they're awkward and unwieldy and need to be directed carefully. I rely on modern technology to monitor and manage an aircraft's position at any given time and my workstation, with four computer screens, reflects that.

MAIN SCREEN - A map of the sector shows the location of all aircraft in controlled airspace as reported by one of several data sources: radar data, flight data and automatic dependent surveillance.

WEATHER RADAR DISPLAY - Shows fronts moving in and out across the country as well as forecasts.

VOICE COMMUNICATIONS CONTROL PANEL - A touch-sensitive screen allows me to choose the radio frequency I need to talk to pilots and ground staff with, or an intercom for speaking with other controllers.

AUXILIARY FLIGHT DATA DISPLAY - I can call up a wide range of information to relay to pilots.

There is also a network of VHF radios so I can keep in touch by voice with pilots, although text messages are becoming more common.

Despite all these technological safeguards, the system is not foolproof and, under extreme circumstances, can be a recipe for catastrophe.

What that meant was simple.

Hope was toast.

For the first time in my life I would know what it felt like to wake up, get dressed, eat breakfast, go to work and kill someone.

* * *

She wasn't unattractive. Short hair a little jagged in front because she cut it herself. Good weight. Enormous blue eyes. Like Peggy, she had the look of someone who wouldn't last long, although she showed no pity and wore her self-destruction like a badge of honor - proud she hadn't learned a single one of life's lessons.

Reaching into her purse she removed a pack of Marlboros and lit one up.

"Do you think that's wise?" I said, keeping my eyes on the road.

"Why? It'll hurt the fucking baby?"

She took an enormous inhale before running her fingers along the edge of the dashboard.

"Do you like oral sex?"

Losing control momentarily, I swerved toward the shoulder, missing a telephone pole by less than a foot.

"I'll blow you if you let me drive home."

When we walked into the clinic I was shocked. It was filled with girls who didn't look old enough to be out of grade school. Some were accompanied by boyfriends who appeared even younger, their voices years away from lower octaves. Some were accompanied by a parent, usually a mother. Some were there with girlfriends, chewing gum and gossiping as if this was one of Vivienne's church socials.

"Diane's all freaked out about this" she said as we signed in.

"Your mom's worried about you."

"Then why isn't she here?"

I didn't know what to say.

"She's afraid someone will see her. That's why."

"I'm sure that's not the reason."

"I ought to have the damned thing just to spite her."

"Layla Burton."

A man behind the counter gestured in her direction and Layla jumped up.

"Do you want me to come in with you?"

"Fuck, no. What are you, crazy?"

With that she turned and approached the man.

"You can spare me the bullshit lecture."

As she followed him into the hallway, a young girl seated to my left reached out and gently brushed the back of my hand.

"Your daughter will be fine. Don't worry."

"She's not my daughter."

"Oh."

"She's not my girlfriend, if that's what you're thinking."

"Oh."

"Her mom couldn't make it."

"Oh," she repeated. This one seemed more sympathetic, although her voice was frail and frightened. "I've got two girls already," she said. "Five and nine. My boyfriend put a shotgun to his head last week when he found out I was knocked up."

Her eyes began to flood.

"I love kids, but what man's gonna want a woman with three?"

"I'm sure it won't make a difference."

She seemed surprised.

"You think?"

I nodded.

Removing a pencil and scrap of paper from her purse she scribbled something down. "That's my mobile."

She placed the paper in my hand, giving it a little squeeze. She was still caressing it ten minutes later when Layla reappeared around the far corner holding a brown paper bag.

As we walked toward the exit she smiled.

"Picking up a girl in an abortion clinic. Jesus, dude. I underestimated you."

I froze.

Camera crews and hundreds of people were milling in front of the entrance, now cordoned off with yellow police tape. Most held signs depicting fetuses in various stages of development or destruction, although some were there to protest

Proposition 16, a bill supporting gays in the military. Others advocated sterilization of politicians who voted for health care. A handful wanted subversive Communist literature, Vivienne's "With A Capital B" included, removed from public schools. There were even a half dozen mini-skirted young women demonstrating the new Hula Hoop, having confused the clinic with the children's wing at the Presbyterian hospital around the corner. It was the 35th anniversary of Roe versus Wade.

As we elbowed our way through angry protestors, ignored by police assigned to crowd control, I had an epiphany. If I was ever going to get a good night's sleep, I had to stop sleeping with Lone Star women. It was better if we just talked, banding together to use all the expertise at our

disposal to solve the problems that were destroying us.

The way Vivienne originally planned to do with my dad.

We would face the world united. Committed. Vulnerable. As one.

"I'll drive," said Layla, snatching the keys out of my hand as I tripped over the power feed that led to a half dozen news cameras.

It's the last thing I remember before one of the Hula Hoop girls picked up a rock and threw it at my head.

* * *

It never occurred to me that, when a man refused to have sex with a woman, she would seek reprisals. A cross was burned into my front lawn. Five times I was hung in effigy. Buckshot was fired through kitchen windows.

One morning I found the sharpened edge of a three inch heel smashed through my right headlight, although I have no idea how somebody broke into a locked garage.

Everyone except Mrs. Fairweather stopped returning my

calls and threatened to file a complaint if I came within a hundred yards.

Even Mrs. Gentry, for the first time in her life, said "no."

This led to two more realizations.

1. Somewhere, my father was shaking his head, wondering why I never listened when he told me his innermost secrets.

2. Excluding Mrs. Fairweather, all women, regardless of age, size, shape or color, were immoral pieces of shit.

* * *

It was the first clear day, after two weeks of rain, when Mrs. Fairweather strolled onto center court and tightened the laces on her tennis shoes. As she began a vigorous sequence of calisthenics, she assured me this was exactly what I needed.

I couldn't help thinking, once again, how different she was from the women my father warned me about. Not only didn't she mind being vulnerable, she felt it was necessary. For her, it was a much needed release. For me, it was important to know a woman's strengths as well as her weaknesses, no matter how bleak, if I was to grow into an empathetic human being.

"I'll serve," she shouted, positioning herself at the base line, the sun at her back.

I nodded in agreement.

"Remember," I said, "This is all new for me."

I didn't see the ball cross the net.

"That," she said proudly, "was the serve that won the Jiffy Lube fast serve contest benefitting the homeless."

"I've only played a couple of times," I reminded her.

Her second serve knocked the racket out of my hands.

"Thirty-love."

The next two were aces, curving power shots that bounced over my head.

"Bend your knees," she said before tossing me the balls.

My first serve rose about six feet into the air and fell harmlessly into the net. My second floated over it like something from a child's bubble pipe. Coming in fast, utilizing all the strength of her legs and upper body, she smashed a forehand, the ball whizzing past me before I could raise my racket. She won the first set in nine minutes.

"Change sides."

"This can't be fun for you," I said.

"I'm fine. Come on. Second set."

The first four games were like the rest. She slammed one unreturnable shot after another and forced me to run till I could hardly breathe. She was serving for the fifth game when I hit a backhand, quite by accident, that struck the top of the net, dribbled over and died before she could reach it.

"Nice shot," she said, turning away and muttering something under her breath.

She hit the next ball wide, as she did the one after that. I won my first game.

"Beginner's luck," she said, and I could see she was grinding her teeth as she prepared to receive my serve. For some unknown reason, I started playing better, making clean, crisp shots that caused her to make one unforced error after another, smashing the ball harmlessly into the net or over the fence.

"I feel better," I said.

Disgusted, she shook her head and her muttering grew louder.

She was ahead 4-2 when her shots began to click again. She took the next game with ease and her smile came back.

"Time for that education."

I never got my racket on the ball again. Never hit another

one over the net. Set point came quickly and she ended it with an ace down the center of the serving box that struck the line, whistled past me and kept on going.

"Third set."

* * *

Mrs. Fairweather had invited two of her oldest friends to join us for dinner the night after our match.

They liked me the moment we met.

Part of it was due to my even-tempered manner. They weren't threatened. Part was due to my new-found confidence. Mostly, it was the way I related to them. I listened to every word, never cut them short and gave them their due. When I did speak I had the ability to make small talk or

bypass it completely. Whatever I said, while not necessarily the truth, was their truth, so it was irrefutable.

My dad would have been proud.

When dinner was over and her friends gone, I could barely keep my eyes open. Blame it on the three helpings of roast beef and seven sets we played in 100 degree heat.

I dozed off.

When I awoke my wrists and ankles were bound to Mrs. Fairweather's bed. The knot around my wrists was a Bowline. The one around my ankles was a Full Windsor.

I recognized them both from her demonstration.

"Hopefully, I won't have to tie a hangman's knot," she said with the same smile she had on the court during her comeback.

Mrs. Fairweather went on to explain that life wasn't worth living unless you were willing to experiment.

What that meant was simple.

Role playing.

She wanted us to pretend to be somebody else. Other than

my father, I couldn't think of anyone I'd choose and he was out of the question. Mrs. Fairweather, on the other hand, knew exactly who she wanted to be.

Pam Shriver.

Throughout the eighties she was ranked among the world's top ten in women's singles, she explained, peaking at number three. Since she didn't have the natural ability or strength of players like Chris Evert or Martina Navratilova she always tried harder.

When I told her I still didn't have a clue who I wanted to be, Mrs. Fairweather slapped my butt so hard she left an imprint of her palm. It was punishment, now that I think back on it, for winning those two games. It continued for at least another hour and, without a doubt, she proved to be as resourceful as Pam Shriver herself.

* * *

"You are not alive unless you know you are living." This was written on the wall in Modigliani's studio and it, like his art, represented everything Mrs. Fairweather held

dear.

"The most talented artist of the 20th century."

She called and told me the moment she read about his traveling exhibit coming to Dallas

"The Maid." "Jeanne Hebuterne with Straw Hat." "Portrait of Chalm Soutine." "Jacques Lipchitz And Wife." "Brunette." Those and dozens more were on display for the first time in the United States and everyone except Mrs. Fairweather was there to enjoy them.

She was an hour late.

I must have called six or seven times but she didn't answer.

I assumed it was because she was on her way, but she still hadn't arrived thirty minutes later.

Frustrated, I went outside to wait but it was 107 degrees and my throat was dry after a couple of minutes. Seeing a life-saving, and still appreciated vending machine in front of a motel, I crossed the street and inserted the necessary coins. As I waited for a Coke to drop I heard sounds coming from inside the room on my right. Noise increased quickly and all hell broke loose. A dull thud.

Laughter. Loud, lingering moans. Overturned furniture.

Nothing was left undone like my honeymoon night.

I was about to leave when the door opened. Bouquet of flowers in hand, Mrs. Davidow tugged at the hem of her skirt as she exited and moved toward the parking lot, hips swaying in a pendulum motion.

"Mrs. Davidow."

I said her name to myself before repeating it out loud.

I don't think she heard me because she sped away the moment she slid behind the wheel of her car. When I turned around I got an even bigger surprise. My father's boss stepped out of the same room. Since I was considerably older than the last time we'd met he didn't recognize me. He, on the other hand, was unmistakable. There wasn't a hair out of place, his clothes were wrinkle free and his shoes had a military shine.

Gesturing after Mrs. Davidow he smiled immodestly, exposing a mouthful of gold.

"She's one of a kind" he said before winking at me the way my father used to.

"Every Friday afternoon, like clockwork, for the past fifteen years. She can't get enough. The woman is a saint."

Once again my equilibrium went haywire.

I started to list and felt like I was going to leave my body. Without a bed to hold onto, there was only one choice available. As my dad's old boss watched with bewilderment, I sat down in the middle of the street.

Twenty minutes later I was knocking on Mrs. Fairweather's door. When she finally answered her face was puffy from crying and she looked ill, a condition I recognized immediately. Instead of asking what was wrong or where she'd been, I made nervous small talk, discussing the weather and how I'd rented a movie I promised to see. When I ran out of subjects I reached out and squeezed her shoulder, but she winced and twisted away, clearly uninterested in anything I had to say.

"It must be awful walking around with so much anger, Henry."

"What?"

She remained silent, watching me reproachfully as she leaned against the door frame.

"For your sake I hope it's because you're so young. I can't imagine anyone, as an adult, intentionally doing the hurtful things you've done."

"I have no idea what you're talking about, Mrs. Fairweather."

"Then it might be due to age. Good for you."

The irritability was still in her voice.

"I thought we'd reached a mutual understanding, an appreciation for what we could do for one another. But after the stunt you pulled the other night, after watching you sabotage our relationship so blatantly, I had to ask myself, who is this person who shows no gratitude? He certainly isn't the extraordinary young man I thought he was. And if he's not, do I give him the benefit of the doubt? Is it worth hanging around till he becomes exceptional? Is it inevitable or just wishful thinking?"

"I don't know what I've done," I said.

"There's no limit to your arrogance, is there?" She exhaled a long sigh of disgust. "You didn't help me wash the dishes."

"But, I was exhausted. I told you."

"It's no excuse."

"You didn't ask."

"I shouldn't have to."

She took a step forward and I could see the anger creep its way up from the corners of her mouth till it wrinkled her brow like her blouse, which looked like she'd slept in it.

"I've known people all my life who expected me to tell them when I needed something before they'd do it. They weren't real friends. Real friends know when you're physically and psychologically drained. Real friends know when you need a break from everyday chores so you can chill out and regain your center. Real friends just show up and do whatever is necessary."

She took a step backwards this time.

"You have absolutely no empathy."

Then she slammed the door in my face, the way our neighbors used to when Vivienne just showed up with a torte or pudding at arm's length.

* * *

Another thing my father forgot to tell me in the square was this:

The problem with getting sexually involved with someone is that, when they leave, you're empty. Like being wealthy during a depression and watching yourself get poorer every day.

Riches to rags.

It's how I felt the night of my first anniversary. It's how I felt as I made my way toward Travis Street, the one place I knew I'd be welcomed.

I knocked twice.

Receiving no response I pulled opened the screen door, stuck my head inside and looked to see if anyone was home.

Mrs. Scott was in the living room when I found her. Dressed in a tattered nightgown and terry cloth robe she was seated on the edge of her sofa and sobbing. As best she could, she told me the following:

She'd been awakened by a high-pitched whine the night before, a little after midnight. When she got up to see what was wrong she saw Arthur, standing in silhouette in front of the window, his stomach bloated to the size of a barrel.

She took him outside immediately but, after a short walk, realized it was far more than a faulty bladder. Three minutes later they were headed toward the emergency vets in Majestic Meadows.

Arthur loved the car.

He always sat in the passenger seat, leaned out his window and relished the wind in his face and the blur of trees as they sped by. On this night, he wedged his full weight into her shoulder, like a teenager at a drive in.

Arthur had a habit of never looking her in the eyes when he was sick or in pain. She couldn't explain why, but it didn't seem to matter till then.

Sitting straight up he placed his right front paw on her right shoulder, his left on her left. As she pushed the accelerator to the floor he nuzzled his head into the nape of her neck and squeezed with both paws. Like a hug. When the car picked up speed Arthur moved away and stared at her till she had to look back. The moment their eyes met he barked once, jumped into the rear seat and died, his body rising up as if hoisted by a magician's invisible wire.

The vet initially thought old age was to blame, Arthur outliving most of his breed. Because of the bloat, however, he thought it might have been a tangled stomach, something common in large dogs and horses. After a thorough examination, he changed both diagnoses. Arthur's heart was

swollen to three times its normal size, causing the rest of his body to flood and short circuit.

Mrs. Scott said Arthur had been acting strangely. He went out one night, to see me she assumed, but came back distraught and never seemed to recover. Unlike Vivienne's preemies, Arthur knew what hit him.

What they should have built into his genetics was self protection. Some sort of canine Kung Fu against humans who never learn about unconditional love or, God willing, empathy.

He could have saved himself.

I wanted to console Mrs. Scott, to provide some relief, but the best I could do was offer to get her something to drink.

Opening her refrigerator I found a container of cold water and filled the largest glass I could find. I then disappeared into the pantry, searching for chips and dip or whatever was available.

I was surrounded on three sides, from floor to ceiling, by shelves filled with canned goods and other staples. Campbells soup. Lipton's tea. Cocoa. Sacks of potatoes. Giant tins of tuna. Ketchup. Vinegar. Spices. Preserves. Tubes of Cheese Whiz...and something that almost made my heart stop - multiple sets of pots and pans, encyclopedias, vacuum cleaners and boxes of unopened office supplies.

The moment I stepped outside to go home I looked up at the heavens and screamed.

"You fuck! You stupid, dumb ass, fuck! How could you do this?!"

He'd destroyed an animal who'd done nothing but bring joy to the world. The Prick just didn't give a shit.

Thirty minutes later I trudged into my own entrance-hall,

switched on the lights and found a letter slipped under the door.

It was another bill, this one for a Chanel sweat suit costing five thousand dollars.

A note on the back announced my fear of premature ejaculation in bold, black letters.

The house suddenly reeked of the same decay it did after Vivienne left for Paris.

My initial thought was to slit my wrists, but I didn't have Peggy's resolve. Besides, blood made me queasy. Especially my own. A gun shot through the mouth was out of the question. I wouldn't have the nerve to pull the trigger. If I did I'd probably miss. Plus, I knew it would hurt, if only for an instant, more than anything I could possibly imagine.

Electrocution. Hanging. Asphyxiation. Pills. Drowning. Conventional wisdom said nothing was appropriate.

Crossing to the needlepoint chair I fluffed the cushion several times before collapsing, leaning back and waiting for insight. Instead, I felt a sharp, jabbing pain in my right thigh. Standing up I discovered Vivienne's French cook book wedged underneath the pillow.

As with most landmarks, a seemingly innocuous event winds up being anything but.

I knew what I had to do.

I would eat myself to death.

The same food that provided refuge and brought me untold pleasure would put an end to an existence that had become dark and malignant.

Unfortunately, Poulet Basquaise was a far cry from Kraft macaroni and cheese.

I began staying up late reading and familiarizing myself with terms and procedures. I woke up three hours before work to knead dough and prepare sauces, wild mushroom, pesto and balsamic glazed shallots especially. I made stock, quickly favoring brown veal and duck to vegetable and chicken. By the time I left for the train everything was blended and reduced.

The moment I arrived home I would filet fish, braise whatever needed braising and make sure fat was plentiful and never trimmed off meat of any kind.

Chickens were plucked.

Hams cured.

Fresh herbs chopped and vegetables brought to room temperature.

I always made enough for leftovers because they drove my coworkers crazy, their envious noses twitching in the air over the best France had to offer.

Blanquette D'Agneau au Vin Blanc.

Saute de Veau aux Carottes la Boutarde.

Baeckeofe Caveau D'Eguisheim.

I'd come a long way from "Hostess Sunday."

This was a religion Vivienne would have devoted herself to and never forsaken. Its God wasn't an angry fuckhead and wouldn't dream of betraying her.

Its God was creamed spinach, browned slightly on top. The only mandate, whenever you knelt before it, was to smile and say a little prayer of thanks.

* * *

As everyone arrived and took their places in the circle, Ethan stepped forward. He'd given a great deal of thought to the things Doctor Coonan had discussed concerning the possible effects of passive aggression, and he wanted everyone to know that he never, not once in all his years,

got seriously ill or had trouble getting it up. As the other men whistled and applauded, Doctor Coonan practiced deep breathing from the diaphragm. When that didn't work, he drank two quarts of water. When that didn't work, he told himself to relax and smiled. Everything was going to be okay. When that didn't work, he thought of a cross-country trip he took with his family to the Grand Canyon. When that didn't work, he pretended to be Ghandi, suppressing all bad thoughts. When that didn't work, he told himself these sessions were going extremely well and everyone gathered was benefitting tremendously. When that didn't work, he told Ethan, in a soft, caring voice, to sit down and they would begin the day's session. When that didn't work, he made a joke about his own sexual prowess, hoping to be half the man Ethan was. When that didn't work, he rolled his neck and shoulders and reached for the ceiling, stretching his arms as far as they would go. When that didn't work, he picked up the empty chair on his right and crushed Ethan's skull with a single blow, killing him instantly.

* * *

Like Vivienne, it didn't take long for me to go from normal to stout to paunchy.

One seventy-five. Two hundred. Two fifteen.

I awoke each morning drenched in sweat, so it was only a matter of time before my heart, like my father, his father, Vivienne and now Arthur, betrayed me.

Jack's jacket grew snug after six months. At first I left it hanging on its rack near the door, its shapeless form standing guard over me the way I once protected Vivienne. As time passed, as it failed to defend me as surely as my own efforts had fallen short, it too wound up at Good Will.

It was a Friday, if I remember correctly, the middle of June. I was exhausted after a long, stressful day of near misses. I didn't have the strength to cook. I barely had the energy to breathe, increased bulk making the shortest distance seem like a marathon.

My priorities were still intact, thankfully, so I left my briefcase on the kitchen table, turned and trudged back outside.

Twenty minutes later I parked in front of Blue Beards Cupboard, a local restaurant known for the size of its portions more than the quality of its food. Its marquee was missing a few red, white and blue bulbs, but there was no mistaking the message.

"AL U CAN ET ROST BEF WENSDAY.

Twenty-four ounces of prime rib cooked to order and carved at your table. It came with a twice baked potato, dripping butter, piled high with bacon bits, grated American cheese, chives and a dollop of sour cream, although I added more from a bin at the salad bar.

It wasn't the best France had to offer, but it would clog at least a dozen arteries.

I was tearing apart a loaf of warm bread when I noticed her, partially hidden behind the specials' menu. She was devouring the largest strawberry sundae I'd ever seen, hunched over her food like an animal that just escaped from a zoo.

Two hundred pounds if she was an ounce, her clothes clung as if they'd been stapled to her skin.

Sickened by the thought that a woman, that anyone, could have so little self control, I had to look away.

By the time I turned around, she was gone.

The following week I saw her again, seated at the same table, gulping down another sundae. When I got up to go to the salad bar our eyes met and she nodded.

All I could think about was the lions gorging on the wildebeest, the poor animal's eyes rolling back further into its head with each bite taken.

I turned away again.

A week later, I couldn't take my eyes off her, transfixed as she returned from the soft ice cream dispenser with a bowl overflowing with vanilla-chocolate swirls.

Watching her eat, the way she guided the spoon to her lips with her chubby little fingers, closing both eyes before swallowing, I realized we had a bond stronger than anyone I'd ever known.

It wasn't sickening in the slightest.

I was ready to walk over and introduce myself, the way Jack would, but my social skills suddenly abandoned me, reverting back to my teenage years; on a par with Vivienne's spontaneity. It would be easier to play quarterback for the Dallas Cowboys on Thanksgiving than approach this woman and strike up a conversation. Even if I did, what would I talk about? It would be one long, boring monologue about my broken marriage or flight control till she excused herself to go take care of her sick Pekingese.

I didn't care.

I stood straight up and charged across the room, my heart pulsing like it never had before. By the time I reached her table all my fingers and toes had gone numb, like Mike the night of my real birth. I started to introduce myself when I noticed a small dollop of ice cream trickling

down her chin. Before it reached her collar and stained, I removed my handkerchief, leaned forward and dabbed it away. Unlike some women who might have been offended by my actions,

she found it ingratiating and smiled, although she wouldn't look at me directly.

Her name was Audrey and she seemed vulnerable and a little lost, the way I used to feel when my father described his philandering.

Once again Vivienne's wisdom sprang to mind.

"God had a reason for everything."

I still don't know if His greasy fingerprints were on this meeting, but after so many heart-felt catastrophes, I figured the law of averages was on my side. Besides, food has a way of turning complete strangers into old friends.

We ordered every dessert on the menu. These I remember.

BROWNIE OBSESSION - A warm brownie covered in Ghirardelli chocolate fudge, vanilla ice cream, caramel sauce and pecans.

VANILLA BEAN CHEESECAKE - Made with Mexican vanilla and layered with white chocolate mousse, it was baked in a vanilla cracker crust and served with fresh strawberry compote.

CHOCOLATE PEANUT BUTTER PIE - Peanut butter graham cracker crust filled with layers of chocolate ganache and fluffy peanut butter mousse topped with whipped cream and a

Reese's Peanut Butter Cup.

BANANA SPLIT - Three scoops of ice cream, marble butterscotch, burgundy cherry and coffee truffle swirl, with hot fudge, marshmallows and melted toffee.

Somewhere between the warm bread pudding with rum sauce and the key lime pie, Audrey leaned forward, slipped off her shoes and stared into my eyes the way Vivienne did the day she told me about love.

She'd recently gone through unbearable heartbreak and decided to eat herself to death, more expedient methods ruled out because of her aversion to blood.

She moved in the next day.

She brought surprisingly few belongings but said it didn't matter since neither one of us was going to be around very long.

Sex wasn't an issue for a change.

Both of us valued decreased longevity more than enhanced

libidos. That said, we ate with the excitement of new lovers, each gram of fat a seduction unspoiled by the desire for intimacy, trust or a yearning to enrich our lives with a tiny, screaming, incontinent blob of flesh that followed us around while we fed, clothed and entertained it till it was old enough to steal money from us for drugs.

* * *

If we did go to bed together, it was because the dining room table wasn't large enough.

We'd toss the pillows onto the floor, pull back the covers and lay out a meal the size of a Volkswagen bus. Every few weeks we rotated the mattress because it began to sag, afraid that stuffing would ooze out like the custard filled tarts we devoured on top of it.

We ate on the lawn.

We ate sitting at the kitchen counter.

On tables.

Straddling chairs.

Even in the linen closet next to the front door.

We ate entire jars of preserves while we were on the toilet.

We finished off fruitcakes while we bathed.

We ate while we drove.

We ate while we shopped.

We ate in the gas station and, by the time the attendant checked our oil and water, we'd consumed two pounds of marble fudge.

Because we couldn't eat twenty-four hours a day we ate in shifts to maximize our intake - like rest time in kindergarten. We slept four hours then woke up to eat. We went back to sleep for two hours then got up again.

At first Audrey was similar to the other Lone Star women

who rejected the food at my father's funeral. She was more comfortable with chicken fried steak and cheese burgers than anything ending in "aux." Gradually, and I say it with great pride to this day, her palette changed. Dreams of cornie dogs, chili fries and Tapioca were replaced by roast duck, risotto and flan.

I also taught her proper etiquette.

Nothing was more frustrating than spending painstaking time and energy cooking one delicacy after another and watching her cram it into her mouth like a coyote eating a cat.

On the plus side, unlike other Lone Star women I'd befriended, Audrey's appetite never waned.

We wrote our weight on the inside of the bathroom door near the scale, the same way Vivienne measured my growth over the years. We recorded any changes when we got up in the morning and before we went to bed at night, coveting the smallest increase the way most Lone Star families celebrated grandchildren.

Before I went to work I prepared lunch and snacks for Audrey so she could get through the day. Sandwiches mainly. As many as I had time for. Some were filled with julienned prosciutto, wedges of Saint Nectaire and sliced figs. Some contained sun-dried tomatoes, chunks of goat cheese and slab bacon. On Fridays I made crab cakes on country bread with red pepper sauce.

I hid surprises throughout the house before we left for the station, like an Easter Egg hunt. Butterscotch scones with strawberry jam, lemon curd and clotted cream. Walnut tortes. Individual sour cream coffee cakes and toffee eclairs.

During our ride I'd surprise Audrey with a box of assorted candies I bought at The Chocolate House, a new addition to the international terminal that specialized in high-end sweets. After she dropped me off she'd eat half on her way home, depositing the remaining fifty percent in her purse beside the occasional duck breast, to be eaten on the return trip.

We drove with the windows shut so the aroma couldn't escape.

I tried not to think about food while I was at work. I tried to focus on incoming and outgoing planes, as I always had, but it was impossible.

A death wish makes you hungry.

Sometimes I blanked out completely, sitting there thinking about Clafoutis aux Poires or Creme Brulee. Although no warning sirens went off, I'm sure planes flew perilously close to one another.

Personal calls weren't permitted during working hours. Since we had up to six planes on our screen at one time, uninterrupted attention was necessary. I had to wait till a break, every three hours, or lunch to speak with Audrey about upcoming meals.

I'd bring Xerox copies of recipes I'd chosen so I could guide her through basic preparations, something that would save precious time when I returned.

"Cut the sorrel very fine and place in a pan with three sticks of butter."

"Dip frogs legs in milk seasoned with salt and pepper and pass through flour."

"Arrange the salad stalks in a deep dish in concentric circles using different varieties to simulate petals."

"Remove top from orange and thin slice skin from bottom."

If ingredients were lacking, I'd tell her where to shop and what to look for, tips I'd learned watching Vivienne over the years

Clams - Hit the shells together. If they sound like rocks, the inhabitants are living and eatable.

Fish - Eyes should be shining and tongue damp. The skin should be slippery, not sticky.

Lamb - Must have a delicate, pink color. Lamb that's red is inferior in quality.

Lettuce Firm and crisp. If it's been soaked in water to revive it the inside will be doughy.

Tomatoes - If freshly picked, the scent can be detected a yard away.

If a recipe proved too complicated, I happily substituted a simpler dish.

More often than not, Audrey ate everything I'd prepared before I got home. When this happened she grew irritable and called me at work.

Thankfully, Mister Davidow was more than an employer. He was a kind and empathetic mentor. Knowing full well how devoted I was to him and the job, he allowed me to leave my post to speak with her. I tried to be reassuring.

It was only a matter of hours before we'd be gorging on mousse au chocolat or tarte citron. We'd gleefully pass out in the middle of a sentence, as we did most nights, from the sugar rush.

Sometimes this calmed her down.

Sometimes it didn't.

If not, I stayed on the phone as long as necessary, keeping a watchful eye out for Mister Davidow. If I saw him coming I'd hang up, hide till he passed and call Audrey back. If he saw me I'd make an excuse like I got a cramp and had to walk it off or my driver's license fell out of my wallet and I was looking for it.

I don't think he believed me but, as with the Lone Star women, there was really no reason not to.

* * *

By the time Audrey met me at the train station she was trembling with anticipation, throwing her arms around my neck the moment I stepped onto the platform. Unlike Hope there was nothing sexual in her actions. It was merely gratitude for the meal we were about to consume.

On the drive home she'd describe, in great detail, her afternoon, making sure everything was in place so nothing would slow me down once the oven was lit. As we pulled into the driveway my heart was beating the way it did on my honeymoon and I sprinted toward the kitchen.

It wasn't uncommon to find my car door wide open when I left for the train in the morning.

We too became a precision dance team.

This time I led with entrees and desserts. Audrey followed with salads and hors d'oeuvres.

It was only a few months before she began craving foods she never thought possible.

Oysters.

Tripe.

Squid.

Tongue.

"Things you don't think you'll like always turn out to be the things you like best."

The transformation was as surprising to her as it was rewarding for me, although I should have realized something was wrong after she told me that.

Since Audrey was now an integral part of my suicide, it was important she didn't lose enthusiasm. Instead of sleeping during our first late-night shift, I stayed awake combing through cook books and magazines, looking for new recipes to please her.

Vivienne would have been proud.

We gained thirty pounds in two months, our stomachs

expanding proportionately to their increased capacity, all duly noted and recorded near the bathroom door.

We went shopping together for new wardrobes since nothing fit any more, settling on solid-colored, matching kaftans. This was particularly rewarding because, for the first time since Vivienne stopped choosing my clothes, I didn't have to worry about conflicting colors. The nightmares that had returned were replaced by dreams of lobster bisque and home-made gelato.

If we accidentally ran into a neighbor on our way to lunch or dinner they waved and smiled, mistaking a full belly for the glow of Lone Star love.

Everything was going according to plan till one day, while I was preparing a flourless chocolate torte, Audrey started examining my fingers the way my father analyzed girls in the square.

"You have beautiful hands," she said. "They're wasted on your dumb fuck job. You should be home cooking for me."

If I'd been better at friendships, I might have seen it coming, but I was a lot like my father in that regard.

Acquaintances were many, friends few and far between.

I explained how food costs had spiraled since that fateful Roast Beef Wednesday. If I didn't have a job we wouldn't be able to eat in the style we'd become accustomed. We'd lose the weight we'd gained and be back to square one. She said she understood and seemed fine till I stepped out of the shower the next morning.

She cried all the way to the station.

There were lots of things I could tolerate in those days. Some bad. Some worse. A woman's tears wasn't one of them.

I took two of the thirty vacation weeks due me to try and sort things out. Mister Davidow wasn't thrilled but, like I said, he was an understanding soul. He found another controller to take my place within an hour.

My heart leaped.

Fourteen days with nothing to do but eat.

* * *

At sunrise we drove to the farmers' market in Majestic Meadows and bought ingredients for the day's meals. More than that and quality would have suffered, freshness being the one thing Vivienne insisted upon besides etiquette.

Rabbit quickly became Audrey's choice of meat.

"Lapin aux Olive Vertes" pumped waves of cardio- blocking bliss through her veins, its scent teasing our neighbors the way leftovers taunted my coworkers. Plus, it was one of those dishes you could put on the stove and all but forget about.

She liked to begin with La Tartine Chaude au Bleu des Causses Et Jambon Cru and finish with a pallet cooling Riz au Lait.

"Lapin a la Moutarde was second best. This one had a history to boot, one of the all time favorite Bistro dishes because of its delicate combination of assertive flavors. It also took no time to prepare. Audrey preferred when I served it with noodles in sweet butter.

Both main courses were heavily laced with garlic Audrey separated after we returned from the market. Desserts ranged from fresh pineapple flan to a Swiss Chard Torte.

We used as much salt as possible because it promoted water retention.

The more we ate the more we craved.

I added a touch of Italy to every meal and it proved to be a stroke of genius on a par with Lone Star marketing.

Smoked Salmon ravioli with lime-dill butter sauce.

Pasta rounds with spinach-ricotta mousse.

Angel hair with goat cheese, broccoli and toasted pine nuts.

Potato gnocchi with Creme fraiche.

Every spoonful was saturated in heavy cream and butter, never margarine, which is only one molecule away from plastic.

After dinner, as Audrey prepared for the first of our nightly naps, I came into her room, sat on the edge of the bed and read to her.

No degradation or torture of mythical saints here.

Not by a long shot.

"The day before you plan to serve the dish, combine the tomatoes, onion, garlic, fennel, olive oil, licorice-flavored aperitif, saffron, herbs and seasoning in a nonreactive Dutch oven. Stir to blend."

"When the fats are hot but not smoking, season the chicken liberally, add to skillet and brown on one side until the skin turns an even, golden brown."

Tantalizing snippets of menus we'd discussed during the day made her weak in the knees.

I prepared more desserts while she slept. If it was something I hadn't baked before, if it turned out less than stellar, I walked down the road, knocked on a neighbor's door and offered it at arms length. They were shocked initially. They'd assumed their pastry invasion had ended the day Vivienne did. When they smelled what I'd cooked, however, they reached out, grabbed whatever I was holding and mumbled under their breaths.

"Just like your God-damned mother!" Then they slammed the door in my face.

Serving platters were left outside the following morning. They were never washed or accompanied by a thank you note but were always scraped clean.

Unlike my "God-damned mother" I looked forward to their weight gain, rise in blood pressure and subsequent medic alert bracelets.

We gained another ten pounds, writing it down on the wall as if we were signing The Declaration Of Independence.

I was a robust two-seventy.

Audrey tipped the scales at two-thirty-five.

The closer we came to our impending goal, the more I tried to show my appreciation.

I began setting the table with fine china, the good silverware, linen napkins and a tablecloth I laundered after every meal. I lit candles before serving.

If we were out of food Audrey desired I'd drop whatever I was doing, drive to the market and rush back.

"Whatever you want, my new best friend."

We lingered for hours over every meal, the echo of forks and knives scraping against plates the only music necessary.

Since her shoulders and neck were often tense and stiff afterwards, I began massaging them with some of the oils Hope left behind, using the knowledge I'd acquired to release discomfort caused by indigestion.

If her feet ached from standing too long on the hard kitchen floor, I rubbed them with the pumice stone.

On the third day of my vacation I started noticing some of the more blatant differences between Audrey and Hope.

Hope had freckles. Audrey had none - thank God. Hope's hair was dyed. Audrey's was natural. Hope was tall, slender and perfectly proportioned. Audrey was short, fleshy and big boned. Hope's eyes were perceptive and blue like turquoise. Audrey's were unobservant and brown like chocolate pudding. Hope had long graceful fingers like a pianist. Audrey's were pudgy and stubby like pigs' feet. Speaking of feet, Hope's were slim and dainty. Audrey wore the same size shoe I did, although her foot was wider and her instep higher.

Hope picked at her food.

Audrey ate like a man, devouring everything set in front of her.

I found the last distinction particularly appealing.

On the fifth day I drove to Dallas and bought her a J.A. Henckels twin gourmet eighteen piece block set with instructional knife skills video.

On the seventh day, while Audrey was peeling and coring pears for fruit tarts, I said I had to run to the store to buy fresh bread and would be back within the hour.

It was the first and only lie I told her.

I drove to Costco in Majestic Meadows.

I wanted to surprise her with something I knew would assuage her anxieties when I returned to work.

Later that night, prior to our evening nap, I came into her room, sat on the edge of the bed and began to read as she modestly adjusted covers around any skin that accidentally revealed itself. This time I read from a pamphlet that came with her present, listing the features of a glass door, reach-in refrigerator that would allow her to see all our food when she felt insecure.

I'd read a spec, study her face for a reaction then move on, words rolling off the tip of my tongue.

"The world's #1 manufacturer, Amana.

Highest rated of all models for temperature control and energy efficiency as well as the all important temperature performance.

Forty inches wide. Thirty inches deep.

Two swing doors with triple-pane thermal glass that were also self-closing and sealed themselves.

Durable non-peel or chip laminated white vinyl exterior.

Eight adjustable, white vinyl shelves.

Thirty-five cubic foot capacity.

White vinyl coated aluminum interior.

Stainless steel floor.

Foamed-in-place polyurethane high density cell insulation - CFC free.

Fluorescent interior lights.

Energy efficient self-contained refrigeration system.

Bottom mount compressor for easy access to service.

Environmentally friendly R134A refrigerant.

Illuminated sign panel.

115/60/1, 1/2 HP, 9.2 Amps.

Weight - 650 pounds.

Unit completely pre-wired at factory and ready for connection."

I started to leave when I was finished but she sat straight up, knocked the pamphlet out of my hands and pulled me on top of her, like one of the beached whales from my childhood. I wasn't sure this was the best idea for either one of us, but I was powerless to stop it. The softness and

bountifulness of her skin was too much to resist.

She licked my fingers.

My toes.

The inside of my thighs.

She made love the way she ate and her cries excited me in a way I'd never known before. The last thing I remember, as she forced my mouth down hard onto her breasts, was that her areolas were the same color as the Belgian truffles from The Chocolate House.

Two hours later I lay beside her while she slept, a little unhinged by the experience. I heard what sounded like coyotes, the way they "yip" after a kill. I heard the sounds of the Great Green Bush cricket, a short ratcheting noise repeated quickly to attract females and warn rivals to keep

their distance.

I wanted to get up quietly, collect my clothes and tip-toe

out of the room, as one does when he doesn't want to disturb a loved one. When I was in the hall, I'd ease into a jog. By the time I reached the front door I'd be moving full speed, although I knew, deep down inside, my legs didn't have the strength to outrun an image that had attached itself to my brain like a leach, its three serrated jaws destined to make small wounds for the rest of my life.

"Sex with Audrey was a four flusher."

* * *

"General Ethan Parks, 72, Korean War veteran and Dallas resident, died on December 4th in Huntsville, Texas of a brain contusion from injuries sustained during a work-related accident. Ethan was born in Alabama on June 8, 1932, and moved to Houston where he joined the army and began his lifelong military career. Somehow, Ethan found time to be an active member of the Houston Volunteer Fire Department and received many awards and citations for his community service. He was also an avid swimmer and, as a member of the U.S. Army Diving Team, traveled the world extensively, competing in championship meets throughout the United States as well as El Salvador, Venezuela, Chad, Sarajevo, Columbia and North Korea. Those who knew him best remember his ability to make friends wherever he went during this time. It was his devotion to his family and his faith in God, however, for which he was most admired. He is survived by his wife of 35 years, Aileen, and their three children: Tony, Wendell and Rickey C, all from the Houston area. Family will receive friends from 7 - 9 P.M. in the Mid-Houston Funeral Home and a Christian Burial will be held Saturday at 11:30 A.M. at the Houston Methodist Church where he'd been an active member. In lieu of flowers, donations may be sent to the Christian Halfway House for abused children.

The Houston Fire Department will honor General Parks by taking him on his final ride in their antique fire truck, carrying him from the funeral home to the service.

At the end of the notice was a controversial quote Ethan was famous for.

"I'll respect anyone who has the balls to get in my face, but if you mess with my family you deserve what you get."

Laying the newspaper down flat on her kitchen table, Julie began carefully cutting along the edges of Ethan's obituary, given page one headlines in the Lone Star Chronicle because of Peggy's association with my family.

* * *

The refrigerator was delivered the next morning. I could see by the look in Audrey's eyes, the sudden shift of her voice to a higher register, that she was energized by its presence.

I almost said "Good girl, that's my girl," but stopped when I realized it was how I spoke with Arthur when he brought me a stick. Instead of lapsing back into regrets and shame, I made club sandwiches with fresh Atlantic tuna, guacamole, blue cheese and a dash of chutney.

Audrey's peace of mind lasted one day.

After dropping me off at the station she stood in our kitchen, staring at the food under its environmentally friendly fluorescent lights that made it look just like on TV and in print ads. She listened to the low, steady hum of horsepower and couldn't believe I wasn't there, by her side,

when she needed me most.

She called three times before I arrived for work.

At first she just wanted me to read a few recipes. I was

happy to oblige in a whisper that was barely audible to anyone but her. When I was done she begged me to come home and cook. I told her it was impossible. I had responsibilities.

"I have responsibilities!"

She mimicked me in a high pitched voice and accused me of being selfish, screaming so loud my coworkers heard her on the other side of the room.

Mister Davidow included.

A saint in his own right, he told me to get my personal life in order and promised to cover for me while I was gone.

I hailed one of a dozen taxis parked in front of the terminal. It was twice as fast as the train but cost five times as much, especially since it had to wait while I ran inside the house and cooked.

By the time I returned to work I'd spent half a day's pay.

There was a benefit to this that I shouldn't ignore. After a month of rushed, impromptu lunches, our waist lines ballooned. The wall next to the scale told the story. I approached three hundred. Audrey was twenty pounds behind, her skin stretched so tight she looked like a sausage.

The weeks passed and we stopped dining out. Audrey preferred the selection of food we had at home and its easy accessibility. I preferred being in a place where people didn't rubberneck as if we were a fatal accident along the side of the road.

One night while I was combing through my books and magazines I inadvertently glanced at the clock. It was two in the morning. I couldn't help smiling, knowing how far I'd come. Placing my reading material on the night stand I tip-toed to Audrey's room, cracked open the door and peeked inside.

Sound asleep, curled like a child, it was as if I were seeing her for the very first time.

Underneath those mounds of flesh was everything Hope

pretended to be. Down to earth. Caring. Kind hearted. Humble.

Once again I longed for the words that would allow me to express my feelings the way my father could, but I wasn't able to think of anything till I walked over to the window and looked up at the stars.

Audrey awoke a few hours later and I was waiting for her in the dining room, prepared meticulously as always. Sliding her chair away from the table, I helped her sit before excusing myself and disappearing inside the kitchen.

The appetizer was a spicy consomme, something I felt would replenish her energy after a sound sleep. Happily, her sluggishness vanished within minutes. The main course consisted of Tendrons de Veau with what Audrey called "Tarte Henry," a potato, onion and tomato gratin. This was followed by a fresh spinach salad with sauteed gizzards. When it was time for dessert I gave an elegant, sweeping gesture toward the back yard and told her we'd enjoy it more if we ate in a cooler place.

The Big Dipper hung suspended over the trees as I escorted Audrey through the trellised archway that led to the garden. Once again I helped her sit, this time at a picnic table surrounded by few trees, although inundated with night-blooming Jasmine.

It smelled like an enchanted world.

In the center of the table were four candles and a cut-glass bowl filled with clear, still water garnished with orange blossoms from surrounding trellises. Leaning forward, I blew out the candles and gestured toward the bowl, the Big Dipper in all its incandescent glory reflected in the water.

"My new best friend," I said, lifting a silver serving spoon, "it is my pleasure to serve you a slice of the heavens I used to fly through when I was a kid."

She remained silent for a few seconds before becoming impatient, wondering when we were going to have our real dessert. I asked if she was happy and the question made her uncomfortable.

"Compared to six months ago when we first met," I persisted, "are you more content?"

She thought about it for a moment.

"I guess."

"Well then, if we're this compatible in death, just think of the possibilities living has to offer."

Stunned, her eyes became flat and dull.

"Whether we like it or not," I continued, "we've fallen in love. It doesn't matter that it's with food. Most couples don't have that much in common after twenty years of marriage. If anything, it holds our love to a higher standard because it's about something pure and provides

sustenance to the entire world."

"I don't know what you want from me," she said.

"Time. I want you to start eating healthy, balanced meals, get in shape and live."

She took a step backwards.

"I want us to spend the rest of our lives together more than I want a torte."

For an instant I thought I saw a sense of resignation come over her, a calm like when you arrive at your destination after a long, turbulent flight.

I was wrong.

Lifting the bowl high over her head, Audrey smashed it against a rock.

"I don't know you."

"I don't know you either," I said.

"Stop copying me! You think I'm stupid? You think I don't know a verbal contract is binding? I can sue your ass."

"Why don't we have another glass of wine?" I suggested.

"You're just trying to get me drunk so I'll consent to something I don't want to. Well, that ain't gonna happen. I may not know you, but I sure as fuck know myself."

She stormed back inside, went into her room and refused to come out till I honored our original agreement.

Three days later Audrey was still brooding and locked away. I had movers pick up the glass door refrigerator and replace it with a more conservative top-freezer model like the one I grew up with. Even with its smaller size it still provided plenty of storage. The biggest disadvantage to its

design was also its biggest advantage. You had to bend to reach your most commonly used foods. It wasn't high impact aerobics, but it was a start.

When Audrey finally emerged I was at work. She called, screamed, and I could hear her smashing things from one end of the house to the other.

She wanted to see her food.

It continued like this for two weeks. Mister Davidow was at his wits end till one Friday afternoon.

The calls stopped.

Audrey was waiting on the platform when I stepped off the train that night. She'd thought about what I'd said and realized I was right. Love of food was a bond that few people were lucky enough to share. She apologized for her behavior.

As with Arthur we became inseparable, a real, contented Lone Star couple, and lived the life Vivienne longed for when she met my father.

While I worked hard to restore Mr. Davidow's faith in me, Audrey restored my faith in her.

She started cutting the lawn every Sunday because she cherished the smell of freshly-mowed grass.

She worshipped the scent of honeysuckle and night-blooming Jasmine. It rid her mind of anything she considered petty and small.

If a bird flew overhead she watched the way its tiny wings bobbed up and down in the wind.

She marveled at the sunlight as it glistened, like diamonds, off early morning dew.

She reconditioned my lathe and fixed my grape arbor.

The only thing I couldn't understand was why, over the ensuing months, my weight plummeted and Audrey's continued to balloon.

* * *

I was only buying organic foods. No red meat, bread or fattening sauces.

Few starches.

Lots of vegetables.

Low sodium cheese and nothing with sugar.

The larger she got, the less self-conscious she became. I'd come home and find her prancing around naked in front of the full length mirror in my bedroom, bumping and grinding and singing to herself like a little girl. I was embarrassed at first, but she did it so frequently I got used to it.

With Hope, nudity wasn't something I was totally comfortable with. I appreciated it, God only knows, but there was part of me that felt like I was invading her privacy.

With Audrey it seemed like her natural state.

While she slept I returned to my library of books and magazines. I searched for foods that were approved by the American Heart Association and increased metabolism. Since there was nothing Audrey didn't crave, the transition wasn't like going to rehab where you're suddenly deprived of

everything you hold dear. Moderation, on the other hand,

was a relentless assault, like learning how to walk again after a serious accident. You hoped to regain the use of your legs and move the way you once did without having to think one two, one two, or if it was time to put your right foot in front of your left.

I stopped preparing meals before I went to work. Normal sized breakfasts. Normal sized lunch. No snacks in between. I stopped calling with instructions. I still phoned during breaks, but only to remind her how much I missed her, the way all Lone Star husbands did.

Her behavior, in turn, became stranger by the day.

One night, after I cut my toe on a piece of broken glass, she smiled, leaned against the kitchen cabinets and said: "Well, put it up on the table and I'll suck on it, honey. God knows it's not the worst thing I've had in my mouth."

She started calling me "Sweetie" and "Babe" and talking graphically during our conversations. She was naked. She was lying on the bed touching herself. I had the biggest cock she'd ever seen and got soaking wet just thinking about it.

I tried not to dwell on what she said after I hung up, but it was far more difficult than trying to ignore a casserole or roasted eggplant terrine.

My sense of purpose and strategy were replaced by an erection so stiff and painful I thought my eyes would pop out of my head.

I started working through lunch without calling home and could see from the look on Mister Davidow's face that he appreciated my sacrifice.

On this particular day he walked up to my station several times and said he needed to speak with me when my shift was over. Since he'd never done that before I assumed I was going to be fired.

I'd disappointed him like everyone else who ever mattered to me. That much was certain.

When I walked toward his office it felt like I was on my way to the gallows. Mister Davidow asked me to close the door as I entered. I did, bracing myself for the bad news. Instead, he shook my hand and congratulated me on putting my affairs in order. He'd known many men over the years, personally and professionally, who'd lost sight of their priorities and never recovered.

He then told me something I didn't anticipate. He was being pressured to retire as a result of the many complaints he'd filed on behalf of passenger safety. He expected it years ago, truth be told. He'd been around fragile egos during the war. The military, especially pilots, were known for them. He was naive to think that would change because they belonged to people overseeing the flights instead of sitting in the cockpit. The whistle-blower laws didn't protect him but, due to his longevity, he was being offered a way out before the shit hit the fan and everything was taken away.

It wasn't really all that bad, he explained. There were two types of controllers, those who didn't care and treated it as a nine-to-five job and those who cared and had a passion for it, the way he felt when he first learned to fly. The excitement was no longer there so he was ready to retire. Though he sounded convincing, I knew a lie when I heard one, even if it was more to himself than anyone else. He recommended me to replace him.

I sat there dumbfounded as he told me how I was the only person who took the job as seriously as he. I was the only one he could trust. I was the person he knew I'd become when we first met.

At that moment I passed from childhood into manhood and

it was difficult not to shout with the joy that began to swell inside me. For the first time I felt larger than life. Finally, I too was beyond reproach.

I ran over to the international terminal as soon as work was over and bought a bottle of champagne.

My train rolled into Lone Star station an hour later and I literally jumped onto the platform. I couldn't wait to share my news, to bask in my accomplishments, but Audrey was nowhere to be found.

I was surprised to see every light on, as if Audrey was giving a party, when my cab pulled in front of the house, but the moment I walked through the door I knew something was wrong.

"Hello?"

Hearing a noise in the kitchen I went in, found the faucet running and put water on for herbal tea.

"Hello?"

At first I heard nothing but the murmur of crickets jostling leaves outside the window. As the sound rose and fell with the wind, I heard another noise, one I couldn't identify but knew was bad.

My face was flushed and my heart pounding as I moved quietly down the long hall leading to the bedroom, afraid what I was about to discover. When I pushed the door open it felt like someone punched me in the stomach.

"How could you do this to me?!"

Sprawled on our sagging mattress, Audrey looked away when our eyes met, as all guilty parties do, but continued gorging herself from the dozen platters of food laid out in front of her.

La Tartine Chaude au Bleu des Causses.

Tranche de Gigot la Boutarde.

Smoked Salmon ravioli with lime-dill butter sauce.

Pasta rounds with spinach-ricotta mousse.

Angel hair with goat cheese, broccoli and toasted pine nuts.

Potato gnocchi with Creme fresh.

Riz au Lait.

Fresh pineapple flan and Swiss chard torte.

Every spoonful was saturated in heavy cream and butter, every bite exactly as I'd taught her to prepare it.

"Don't touch the flan," was all she said, her voice strained as she continued focusing on the food.

I stood there in shock and watched her swallow without chewing. When my pulse returned to normal I held up the champagne and explained what had happened.

"I thought we'd celebrate."

Taking the bottle, Audrey untwisted the cork with her stubby fingers and giggled as liquid flowed over her hand onto the carpet in long, bubbling spurts.

"Let's take a walk," I suggested, trying to stay calm and keep my voice down.

"I can't," she said.

"Why not?"

Lowering the bottle, her expression chilled.

"I have responsibilities."

* * *

Thirty minutes later we were driving through a deserted, wasted looking area the antithesis of everything Lone Star Springs stood for.

No grass.

No hills.

No water.

Streets were littered with garbage.

There were more pawn shops than banks. Abandoned

warehouses outnumbered trees and the homeless huddled in alleyways, puffing other smokers' discards.

We were stopped at a light when a brand new Mercedes cabriolet pulled alongside. The moment Audrey saw it her face lit up as if she'd won the lottery.

"When I'm rich and famous," she said, "that's the car I'm gonna drive. I'm never gonna put the top up, not even if it rains, so everyone can see me."

The light turned green and the Mercedes pulled away with a spray of gravel, Audrey watching it fade as a mother watches her only child leave for their first day of pre-school. Only then did she confide in me the way she did the night we met.

The reason for her heartbreak was a lot different than I'd imagined.

She explained how she'd been fired from BBW's, a strip club catering to men with a fetish for obese women. The owner, after numerous complaints from clients, reluctantly let her go because she wasn't fat enough.

After I served her the Big Dipper, after I convinced her life was worth living, she realized she'd been given a second chance. If she could just keep eating, if she gained forty more pounds, she could get her job back. She was too young to settle down anyway, especially in a boring place like Lone Star Springs. She didn't want to look back when she was twenty-five and realize she'd sacrificed her dreams of becoming a star, the life she was meant to have, when it was within her grasp.

"Twenty-five?" I asked.

She nodded.

"How old are you?"

"Old enough to have beautiful things," she said with pride.

Up till that point, old and beautiful were not words I thought of in the same sentence.

"Nineteen," she finally confessed. "The same age as my mom when she was already divorced twice."

We drove in silence the next couple of blocks before she told me to turn left in front of a Circuit City that had closed due to bankruptcy. She instructed me to turn again when we reached the BBW parking lot, pulling beside a limo whose driver was smoking a joint in front of the tattoo parlor next door to an arcade.

Painted bright orange, the club was constructed entirely of cement and had no windows. Now that I think about it, it did have one thing in common with Lone Star Springs. Their marketing was impeccable.

"Best Breasts in the mid-west."

"Why did we come here?" I asked

"This is where the money is."

Audrey hugged the broad-shouldered bouncer outside the entrance before leading me down a hallway flanked with posters of naked girls, weighing upwards of four hundred pounds, in what I considered unnatural, possibly inhuman positions, their private parts covered with jagged, construction paper circles.

No clocks, like Vegas.

The place was packed, although Audrey said it was a slow night due to thunderstorm warnings.

On stage in the main room two girls wearing five inch heels and nothing else seemed to be performing an elaborate tribal dance, gyrating to music pounding with bass. Their every move was watched by tall, fearsome, steely-eyed cowboys who still had Napoleonic complexes and the same expression Audrey did when she was hungry.

As we worked our way toward a table in the front I started to say "excuse me" but stopped myself when I realized it would start a fight.

Push my way through. That was the manly thing to do and would be respected.

These men were different from the ones I grew up with in Lone Star Springs. These were blue collar workers who were strong from toiling hard for a living, not battling rowing machines in their Great Rooms. Men who'd made their share of mistakes along the way, never learned a damned thing and didn't give a shit. Men who clung to violence the way Vivienne clung to God, their rage so close to the surface, anything could happen and there wasn't a thing I could do to

stop it if it did. These were also men who recognized Audrey and shouted her name enthusiastically.

"Bliss."

The only benefit to these men, as far as I could see, was that none of them would proselytize about morals and religion the way they did in Lone Star Springs.

But...they could never prepare pasta rounds with spinach-ricotta mousse!

Egged on by applause Audrey flipped her hair back, jumped on stage and began dancing with the other two girls; bumping and grinding the way she did in front of my full length mirror, awkwardly removing one item of clothing after another.

Making matters worse, I knew the song.

"The endless shrill
of anticipation.
Taunting and unrelenting.
My ears
reject the sound
of long heavy strides,
arms swinging while he walks
as if they were suspended
and prohibited

from touching his own body."

"Stop," I yelled, but she had already turned toward someone else. Even if she'd been staring directly into my eyes, it was almost impossible to hear what I was saying.

"Let's go home!"

I felt as if I was disappearing, becoming smaller and smaller with each pounding bass note.

"I'm happy," she shouted, more interested in the beat of the music than anything I had to say.

"I'll get the refrigerator back."

Climbing onto the stage I gripped her wrist.

"Let's go home."

"I don't have to listen to your shit any more."

Someone grabbed me from behind at that point and started dragging me toward the exit. The bouncer. He was even stronger than he looked and I didn't have the strength to resist, not that I would since his bulging arms were obviously capable of inflicting great harm.

Once outside he threw me onto the pavement and I skidded a good three feet, face down, like a rock being skimmed on the pond.

"Nobody touches my girls!"

I thought that was the end of it but he moved forward quickly, two steps at a time, and kicked me in the ribs.

"If you come back, I'll break every bone in your ugly fucking body. Got it, dude?"

It didn't take a mental giant.

"Look at me when I'm talking!"

My nose was bleeding and the right side of my cheek was scraped to the bone. Still, as I turned to face him, that was the least of it. The worst part was when I noticed my blood, my hard earned DNA, smeared up and down the sleeve of a jacket that once protected me.

* * *

During my drive home I started feeling queasy the way I did the night Hope left. My legs ached. My breathing was labored. My hands shook.

I wondered if this was how Peggy felt when she walked naked through the hotel lobby. If it was, I understood. A complete breakdown was a lot simpler than I imagined, little more than not having a bed to hold on to when your life spun out of control.

It would have been easy for me to blame God at this point. He'd made a mess of Vivienne's life. Peggy's. And let's not forget His sacrificial Son. There was no reason to think I'd slip through the cracks, but even God couldn't be held responsible for the brain of a nineteen-year-old, something my father drummed into me on numerous occasions.

"The only thing you can count on with a young girl is enthusiasm."

One and one person alone was responsible for my predicament and there was nothing divine about it.

Hope.

If she hadn't come into my life none of this would have happened.

"HOPE HOPE HOPE HOPE HOPE HOPE HOPE HOPE HOPE HOPE

HOPE HOPE HOPE HOPE HOPE HOPE HOPE HOPE HOPE HOPE HOPE HOPE

HOPE HOPE HOPE HOPE HOPE HOPE HOPE HOPE HOPE HOPE HOPE HOPE

HOPE HOPE HOPE HOPE HOPE HOPE HOPE HOPE HOPE HOPE HOPE HOPE

HOPE HOPE HOPE HOPE HOPE HOPE HOPE HOPE HOPE HOPE HOPE HOPE

HOPE HOPE HOPE HOPE HOPE HOPE HOPE
HOPE HOPE HOPE HOPE HOPE
HOPE HOPE HOPE HOPE HOPE HOPE HOPE
HOPE HOPE HOPE HOPE HOPE
HOPE HOPE HOPE HOPE HOPE HOPE HOPE
HOPE HOPE HOPE HOPE HOPE
HOPE HOPE HOPE HOPE HOPE HOPE HOPE
HOPE HOPE HOPE HOPE HOPE
HOPE HOPE HOPE HOPE HOPE HOPE HOPE
HOPE HOPE HOPE HOPE HOPE
HOPE HOPE HOPE HOPE HOPE HOPE HOPE
HOPE HOPE HOPE HOPE HOPE
HOPE HOPE HOPE HOPE HOPE HOPE HOPE
HOPE HOPE HOPE HOPE HOPE
HOPE HOPE HOPE HOPE HOPE HOPE HOPE
HOPE HOPE HOPE HOPE HOPE
HOPE HOPE HOPE HOPE HOPE HOPE HOPE
HOPE HOPE HOPE HOPE HOPE
HOPE HOPE HOPE HOPE HOPE HOPE HOPE
HOPE HOPE HOPE HOPE HOPE
HOPE HOPE HOPE HOPE HOPE HOPE HOPE
HOPE HOPE HOPE HOPE HOPE
HOPE HOPE HOPE HOPE HOPE HOPE HOPE
HOPE HOPE HOPE HOPE HOPE
HOPE HOPE HOPE HOPE HOPE HOPE HOPE
HOPE HOPE HOPE HOPE HOPE
HOPE HOPE HOPE HOPE HOPE HOPE HOPE
HOPE HOPE HOPE HOPE HOPE
HOPE HOPE HOPE HOPE HOPE HOPE HOPE
HOPE HOPE HOPE HOPE HOPE

HOPE HOPE HOPE HOPE HOPE HOPE HOPE
HOPE HOPE HOPE HOPE HOPE

HOPE HOPE HOPE HOPE HOPE HOPE HOPE
HOPE HOPE HOPE HOPE HOPE

HOPE HOPE HOPE HOPE HOPE HOPE HOPE
HOPE HOPE HOPE HOPE HOPE

HOPE HOPE HOPE HOPE HOPE HOPE HOPE
HOPE HOPE HOPE HOPE HOPE

HOPE HOPE HOPE HOPE HOPE HOPE HOPE
HOPE HOPE HOPE HOPE HOPE

HOPE HOPE HOPE HOPE HOPE HOPE HOPE
HOPE HOPE HOPE HOPE HOPE

HOPE HOPE HOPE HOPE HOPE HOPE HOPE
HOPE HOPE HOPE HOPE HOPE

HOPE HOPE HOPE HOPE HOPE HOPE HOPE
HOPE HOPE HOPE HOPE HOPE

HOPE HOPE HOPE HOPE HOPE HOPE HOPE
HOPE HOPE HOPE HOPE HOPE

HOPE HOPE HOPE HOPE HOPE HOPE HOPE
HOPE HOPE HOPE HOPE HOPE

HOPE HOPE HOPE HOPE HOPE HOPE HOPE
HOPE HOPE HOPE HOPE HOPE

HOPE HOPE HOPE HOPE HOPE HOPE HOPE
HOPE HOPE HOPE HOPE HOPE

HOPE HOPE HOPE HOPE HOPE HOPE HOPE
HOPE HOPE HOPE HOPE HOPE

HOPE HOPE HOPE HOPE HOPE HOPE HOPE
HOPE HOPE HOPE HOPE HOPE

HOPE HOPE HOPE HOPE HOPE HOPE HOPE
HOPE HOPE HOPE HOPE HOPE

HOPE HOPE HOPE HOPE HOPE HOPE HOPE
HOPE HOPE HOPE HOPE HOPE
HOPE HOPE HOPE HOPE HOPE HOPE HOPE
HOPE HOPE HOPE HOPE HOPE
HOPE HOPE HOPE HOPE HOPE HOPE HOPE
HOPE HOPE HOPE HOPE HOPE!"

As I shouted her name over and over, a hare the size of a small terrier darted onto the road. Yanking the steering wheel hard to my left, I swerved across the median, careened into a field, and tried to hit it.

* * *

Although the grass appeared solid, it was all mud underneath, at least three inches deep, and I got stuck. I tried rocking the car back and forth but that didn't work. I put branches under the wheels but that didn't work either. They were too small. So, I looked around for a piece of wood

large enough to give me traction.

The buds on the trees hadn't opened yet so the view, even at this hour, was clear and I could see forever. It reminded me of better times and I got a sudden urge to do something I'd been sorely missing.

I ran as fast as I could.

I bounded through tall grass and jumped over fallen trees. I leaped into the air. I pretended to catch a stick in my mouth and hunt jaguars. I was aware of every sight and sound.

Except for one rotted stump covered with toadstools.

I lost my footing and was airborne. Although both hands broke my fall I hit the ground hard, tearing my right pants leg at the knee and twisting my ankle. As I lay there cursing my clumsiness, I heard a sound I didn't recognize. Looking inside the stump I discovered two kittens, a few weeks old at most, huddled together for warmth and hiding from a world that could do them harm. One was all white like Hope the day she left. The other was a brown tabby, markings identical to Arthur's. Even its eyes had the same yellowish tint. Lifting them gently, I put one in each jacket pocket before resuming my search for wood.

I went online as soon as I got home and looked up the best way to care for animals that had been abandoned.

The first few months of a cat's life, I discovered, were the most important in terms of growth and development. Since the mother was missing, I'd have to act fast if the kittens were going to survive.

I found some old towels that were heavy enough to keep them warm, absorbent and free from threads they could get tangled in. I kitten-proofed the house, closing cabinets, closets and shutting toilet seat lids. I drove to the new Pet Smart in Majestic Meadows and bought baby bottles, a giant tin of milk replacement rich in protein, a mechanical litter box that cleaned itself and a scratching post so they had something to claw other than furniture.

I maintained an around-the-clock vigil, checking and rechecking their covers, making sure they were breathing properly.

I studied veterinarian journals and text books about fleas and parasites.

I caressed them gently, rubbing their backs, stroking their tiny chests, dragging my fingers over every appendage and muscle, massaging them deeply till they meowed and cooed.

In no time they were climbing, grooming and wrestling with each other, although it was amazing how quickly they became territorial and protective of their own space. The little tabby, a male, was more affectionate than his sister who was loving but did it on her own terms. She liked me close but didn't need to lie all over me. He, on the other hand, followed me from room to room, happy to wait if I closed the door behind me. The moment I sat down he was hurtling through the air, landing on my lap or chest, staring up at me and purring like my dad's Cadillac.

He also slept with me.

He snuggled as close as possible while his sister preferred the floor. I, of course, was as pleased with their company as they were with mine.

I buried my nose in their fur.

I rubbed them behind the ears.

I pawed their stomachs, the way they did to me, as if I wanted to be fed.

We chased after ping pong balls and wooden spools of yarn.

We watched travel shows, even though I knew they were more interested in the flicker of light and movement than content.

We made mad dashes around the house.

I read them Doctor Seuss, all about his own remarkable cat - their favorite.

Unlike Hope and Audrey, their eyes were a radiant yellow.

Unlike Hope and Audrey, they didn't pick at their food or inhale like a vacuum, preferring to eat small portions several times a day.

Unlike Hope and Audrey, they could leap from a great height, do a somersault and land on their feet.

I found this last distinction particularly appealing.

At the end of the third week I drove to Dallas and bought them each a cat nip mouse that said "I love you" when you squeezed the belly, although I kept a watchful eye out for the smallest signs of addiction. I wasn't lonely any more.

For the first time in as long as I could remember, I experienced the luxury of love without pain. Not only that, my companions kept the rodent population in check.

It didn't get more meaningful than that.

The only drawback was when I left for work. I felt as if part of me was missing, like I'd awakened without an arm or a leg. When I returned home I always found them sitting on the sofa in front of the window, waiting for me to appear and fascinated with the life I'd saved them from. I sympathized, but had no intention of letting them run free.

Bad things happened outside.

* * *

It had been raining all day, nonstop, when I came home from work with a fifty-pound bag of litter. As I climbed the stairs to store it in the attic, I had no idea the fire retardant roof had begun to shift and dissolve, causing leaks that dripped down walls, damaging plaster and floors. When I opened the attic door, keepsakes and cardboard boxes were bobbing up and down in three inches of water. Vivienne's wedding dress, stained and yellowed, floated by as if it were a teenager lounging in a motel pool.

Mementoes from my childhood followed suit.

Flannel Pajamas with guitar-playing cowboys.

A floppy brown and yellow teddy bear, its left eye hanging by a thread.

A blue button that said "Congratulations, It's A Boy."

I scooped them all up as best I could and carried them downstairs for a closer inspection before deciding what could be salvaged. When I was finished, while I waited for the plumber to arrive, I made one final check to make sure I hadn't missed anything.

That's when I saw it.

Hidden in a corner was one more box, weathered but dry. I didn't look inside till I got into the kitchen and was stunned by its contents.

On top was my father's twelfth grade report card. All A's except for an A plus in art. It was attached to a ventriloquist's dummy, Jerry Mahoney if I'm not mistaken. Underneath were two letters, one opened, one sealed, and a rolled up piece of canvas held together with a rubber band.

I placed the dummy and the letters on the kitchen table before slipping off the rubber band and unfolding the canvas.

It was a drawing my father made when he was sixteen, judging by the date at the bottom, of what he imagined he'd look like as an old man - an amazing accomplishment considering his age.

His face was in shadow and partially hidden by a hat that seemed to be part of him, a thin red stripe across the center. It was pulled down to his eyes, but it couldn't hide deep circles underneath, the size of silver dollars.

The imaginary years had taken their toll.

My father's pain, sadness and struggle were all on display.

There was a lot more than suffering, however.

I could still see the boy, the real catch, the one everyone liked because he could take the awkwardness out of any situation.

I could also see the things my father held dear.

Imagination.

Passion.

Whimsy.

I don't think Dwight ever saw this drawing. If he had he couldn't possibly have said the things he did. He wouldn't have been disappointed either because, in my aged father's face was everything Dwight cherished as well.

Common sense.

Dedication

A complete lack of pretentiousness and exaggeration.

At first I thought it was his way of dealing with his own mortality - never expecting to live past thirty-three.

For awhile I thought it his way of cheating fate. If he could envision himself living to a ripe old age, maybe he actually would. Eventually, I settled on a more plausible theory.

Jack couldn't stand the ugly way his body and mind would deteriorate during his twilight years.

The frailty.

The atrophy.

Unlike other facets of life, positive thinking or acceptance wouldn't help or mean a damned thing, not when he couldn't be repaired or restored.

All give. No take.

Not a young boy's or a salesman's best scenario.

I spread the drawing out gently on the table, weighting down the ends with salt and pepper shakers before removing the opened letter from its envelope.

D-TANNING COMPANY, INCORPORATED

Tanners and Processing Plant

15 Porcupine Court, Waxahachie, Texas

"Dear Jack,

I should be hard at work trying to complete orders for the fall season. Instead, I find it necessary to sit down and write this. If it were something being said for the first time, I'd consider it an effort well spent. But, it's something you've heard before and, obviously, hasn't made a dent in your stubborn and oddly resistant armor.

You're fourteen. Fourteen is a very young boy. But, you're mature, physically and mentally, so your mother and I treat you as if you were older. We take you places and do things we believe you're capable of handling. You prove that you are, except in one area.

Sex.

I remember mom going downstairs one night and finding you and some girl in an embrace. It wasn't pleasant for her to see two youngsters behaving this way, believe me.

To you, it's a symbol of manhood. To us, it's the act of a child trying to prove he's a man.

Times change. Standards change. Morality doesn't.

I must say, again, how disappointed I am. I was sure I could count on you to be of assistance to your mother while I was working so hard. Instead, you've given her cause for alarm. That's not fair. You see, I'm the dearest thing in the world to her. It's reciprocal, of course, so it's very hard when we're apart. She knows, thank God, that it's necessary and is willing to make the sacrifice.

For your sake, for mine too, I hope you're mature enough one day to be and act just like her.

I'll leave you with something my father told me when I was your age.

There's an old story about a man who was hit by an automobile. In terrible pain, he refused to go to a hospital. Later, they discovered why. He didn't wash his feet that day and was ashamed that the people who found him might see the filth. The analogy I make is, you never can tell when you'll be placed in a position where you might have to reveal what's under your clothing. Don't be caught with filth, even in your pockets. People would relate it to your mind and it's tough to live down.

Dad"

This was written two weeks before Jack's fifteenth birthday

because his mother found an unopened box of condoms in his pant's pocket.

It was also one month before she drove to Majestic Meadows for takeout and never returned, running off to Italy with Alberto, a waiter she met while ordering a large cheese pizza.

While she waited, Alberto showed her a letter from his good friend, Ilona Staller, also known as Cicciolina; a former porn star who had the lead role in "Zombie Strippers," was elected to the Italian Parliament and offered to have sex with Saddam Hussein for the release of all foreign hostages.

Star struck, Jack's Mom fucked Alberto in his delivery truck, parked outside the restaurant. It might have been nothing more than a momentary indiscretion, but police were called when neighbors, hearing screams, suspected foul play.

From that day on, Dwight never uttered her name again.

The unopened letter was addressed to me. It was from my father, something I recognized immediately by the handwriting.

"Dearest Henry,

I've been trying to get up the courage to talk with you over the past few weeks but, for one reason or another, haven't been able to. Though you insist you're perfectly fine, there's something in your voice I recognize, a heavyheartedness that's reared its ugly head in my own life.

Years ago, a waitress I knew described me after our first date. She used a German word I can't recall. I do remember its meaning, however. "The weight of the world."

She said I walked around looking as if it was on my shoulders.

I had different reasons for feeling that way. Sometimes it was because of a girl. Sometimes it was because I felt as if I'd wasted my life. Sometimes it was caused by trying hard to accomplish something and failing. Sometimes it was because I got scared and failed to try.

More often than not, it was because of my father.

I still feel that weight occasionally, which is why I don't want it for you, especially because of something I've done.

I don't know if this will help, but being around you has made me realize a few things I wish I knew years ago. Anything is possible. If you try hard and fail, try again. No big deal. Nobody likes being knocked down, but it's part of life. The trick is what you do when you get back on your feet.

At the same time, being happy has little to do with success, girls or even fathers. It's how you feel when you wake up in the morning and stare the world in the eye. It's how you feel when you go to bed at night and shut those same eyes.

If you can greet the day and leave it knowing you've done your best, you can start the next one with a smile.

I realize I screw up at times and have done things that caused you pain, but please know this. I think you're terrific. A great kid. A great person. A kind soul.

All I want for you is to wake up with more smiles than not.

I love you very much.

Dad

Starting at the top I read it again slowly, as if it was Peggy's most cherished book.

One way or another, I was determined to wake up with a smile every day for the rest of my life.

* * *

There was nothing all that different about the woman who walked into the hardware store that Wednesday afternoon. From a distance she was perfectly dressed and coiffured like every other Lone Star housewife. She moved carefully down one isle after another, taking her time as she examined rows of power tools, ceiling fans and pipe fittings. Whenever salesmen started her way she politely waved them off before they could offer assistance, preferring to look on her own.

As she walked toward the back of the store, however, those same salesmen noticed a difference. There was a rip along the seam of her dress. The red polish on her nails was chipped and uneven. The soles of her shoes were worn and her right heel had split down the center, traces of glue bubbling over where the crack was forced together.

Although they had no way of knowing, overdue telephone and electric bills were wedged into her back pockets next to Christmas catalogues and a carefully folded copy of General Ethan Parks obituary.

As she approached the gadget department she grabbed a small cookie tin off one of the shelves and shoved it into her purse. When she reached the post office she smiled at the clerk who was talking to a trainee, a girl I knew from school, both women chatting away so intensely they failed to notice her.

"Christmas is supposed to be a time that brings people together, don't you agree?"

"Of course," said the clerk, turning to face the now smiling woman.

"Even people who despise each other should put their differences aside, find a way to mend their fences and get along."

"Absolutely," said the clerk as the woman shoved her body against the counter.

"Better to look for the humanity in someone, even if they don't normally demonstrate it."

"Amen," said the clerk.

"A person should also respect anyone who has the balls to

get in their face, but if they mess with their family they deserve what they get."

"Ma'am?"

The trainee, mostly because of nerves, started giggling. As she covered her mouth with one hand, trying to stifle the laugh, the smiling woman reached into her purse, pushed aside

the cookie tin, withdrew a .22 caliber pistol and shot her in the throat. Before the clerk could move the smiling woman shot her too. As the bullet smashed through her skull and entered the occipital lobe, the clerk vaguely remembered a photograph in her boyfriend's wallet of this same woman surrounded by four young children, three boys and a girl. The smiling woman fired two more times, watching each slug enter the body that had stolen her husband and ruined her

life.

By the time the third cartridge exited the back of the clerk's head, severing her brain stem, the photograph was officially gone.

Reaching back inside her purse, Julie removed a coke bottle filled with unleaded gasoline. As women in patent leather boots ran screaming out of the store she emptied its contents over her head and set herself on fire.

The flames spread with astonishing speed, burst through the gadget department and roared upward. Within five minutes chunks of the ceiling began to fall, like shooting stars, scattering sparks in all directions as Julie's skin turned black and crisp and began to bubble. Within ten minutes windows glowed and exploded. By the time firemen arrived the blaze had spread to the Chevron station and my father's old place of business, leaving nothing but the stench of paint, rubber, overheated metal and the charred remains of cabinets that once proclaimed Jack's triumphs. Each was enclosed by a great ring of fire and soot, columns of smoke billowing so high they were visible in Majestic Meadows.

* * *

It grew more and more difficult to start the day with a smile.

One month after half of Lone Star proper burned down, the federal government ruled there weren't enough people in the community to warrant a new Post Office.

Mail was rerouted to Majestic Meadows which had three branches. If Lone Star residents wanted their letters and packages, they had to make the trek to one of those.

As with Captain Kangaroo, a town meeting was called and a letter drafted in protest. As with Captain Kangaroo, it appeared to fall on deaf ears till the council received a reply from the Postmaster General himself. It reinforced the government's position but left the door open, like God was famous for, if Lone Star's population rose to a minimum level.

Until they came up with a plan to accomplish that, Lone Star residents begrudgingly made the drive.

And a funny thing happened.

While they were in Majestic Meadows they began shopping there, enjoying the variety of choices found at numerous malls, especially one with an ice skating rink. Wal-Mart and the newly designed 7-11, which they'd resoundingly shunned, were their favorites, thriving since stocking a new product from southern France - flavored Camembert sold in individual boxes of chocolate, vanilla and strawberry or combined, in a larger container, as Neapolitan.

After they shopped, depending on the hour, they stopped for something to eat. If it was late, if alcohol was involved, rather than risk the long drive home they stayed at one of a dozen Majestic motels, each offering complimentary continental breakfast,

The hustle and bustle of modern convenience, much to their astonishment, wasn't nearly as debilitating as they'd imagined.

Except to Bee's cafe.

For the first time since she opened, Bee had to throw pies away at closing. They were never as good the day after they were baked and she refused to serve an inferior product, unlike restaurants in Majestic Meadows. Six months later she went out of business and moved to Miami Beach where she suffocated on a five point, self-drilling screw that had somehow become wedged into the crust of a key lime pie she bought at a local bakery named "Mom's." This more than anything else rejuvenated my neighbors, reminding them they not only needed to find a way to increase Lone Star's population, but had to replace Bee's which, now that it was gone, was sorely missed. Great debate ensued and the council eventually came up with a plan to solve both problems.

They would bring in a 7-11.

Lone Star Springs, in all its nineteenth century grandeur, was ready to enter the new millennium.

The opening was to take place in early spring. All that fall I waited anxiously while watching the structure take shape, serenaded by the sounds of workmen's hammers, saws and drills. There were doubters, of course, who still believed the store would become Lone Star's Waterloo, but most were optimistic, like the doctors in Paris.

It opened a week ahead of schedule and was an overnight success. Other companies, as a result, decided to build nearby. This pleased the council who approved every permit submitted because the more expansion, the closer they were to achieving their resident quota.

Within six months construction began on a Super Wal-Mart. Banana Republic. Timberland and Liz Claiborne. Outlet stores followed.

Bulldozers tore up picturesque roads and razed forests to install pipes for new electricity, water and sewage.

A designated Lone Star exit between U. S. Highway 287 Business and U. S. Highway 287 Bypass was also added, requiring supports, walls and fences which prevented deer from feeding, let alone walking down the street. This forced many of them to relocate along with foxes, rabbits, possum and the occasional pheasant. Because their territory was shrinking and food supply dwindling, coyotes began hunting outside their natural habitat.

I walked into my garden one morning to collect eggs for breakfast and found the scattered, half-eaten bodies of my chickens, chunks of flesh missing as if they were pieces of a puzzle that hadn't been completed.

Since this was the first recorded coyote attack in the history of Lone Star Springs everyone, including myself, assumed it was an abnormality.

I was wrong.

A security guard patrolling Eddie Bauer was bitten when he accidentally disturbed a coyote rummaging through bags of illegally dumped household trash.

A jogger was nipped on the thigh.

A father and son were attacked in the park while unpacking their car for a family picnic.

And much worse.

Heather McAndrew's two dogs, Amethyst, a five-year-old Maltese, and Cinnamon, an eight-year-old Jack Russel/Shih Tzu mix, were playing in the back yard while she prepared dinner. Hearing a commotion, Heather stopped chopping Habanero peppers and went outside to investigate. The moment she walked through the door she found herself facing two coyotes,

each with a beloved pet in their jaws. Instinctively, she picked up a deck chair she'd bought at "Terrific Teak" and began swinging it at them. She managed to free Amethyst when she slammed it into one of the coyote's necks, but the other one dragged Cinnamon into the bushes before she could save her.

Amethyst had to be euthanized the following morning because she had over thirty puncture wounds and abrasions on her upper body and head.

Authorities suspected the same coyotes of an earlier attack on an elderly couple walking around the community's nature trail. They were also suspected of entering the lunch area at Lone Star Elementary school and attacking a fourth-grade child from behind, biting his backpack. The teacher threw water bottles and rocks at the coyotes who turned and fled, nipping at other students as they made their escape.

Donald Trevor was playing Frisbee with his five-year-old daughter, Jenny, when he heard his phone inside the house. Under normal circumstances he would have let it ring, but someone had forged his name on six checks and cashed them at six different stores in Majestic Meadows. His account was nearly a thousand dollars overdrawn. Since it might be the bank calling he rushed inside.

As he lifted the receiver and said "hello," Jenny was knocked to the ground by a forty-pound female coyote. She tried to defend herself but the animal was too large and too strong, ripping at her face and neck with its teeth.

Having convinced the bank manager his identity had been stolen, Donald returned in time to see the coyote dragging his daughter, by the head, across the street. Horrified, he ran after them, although the coyote refused to drop Jenny till neighbors came out to see what was wrong.

Donald drove as fast as he could to Florence Nightingale's emergency room, running every light. Doctors did everything they could to save the little girl's life but her injuries were insurmountable.

Children stopped walking to school after that.

It was all on the news, which residents now watched, along with the rest of the world's trials and tribulations; reports laden with gang rapes, suicide bombers, Amber alerts and people who killed each other over a pair of sneakers.

It forced the good people of Lone Star to admit they'd been living in blissful ignorance and there was more suffering in the world than they'd imagined.

Shotgun sales quintupled.

The hill my father and I once sled down became crammed with lopsided looking houses on quarter-acre plots that were built with inferior materials, fake brick and fake stone. Not surprisingly, they were inferior and looked like they were built with fake brick and fake stone. This came to pass because, in Lone Star's haste to qualify for a post office, permits were approved when contractors emphasized quantity over quality; like my father. The committee even agreed to extend the community's boundaries onto an ancient, uncharted flood plain, unable to find ten good residents, what would have constituted a simple majority, to vote against it.

Walking paths became littered with Neapolitan cheese wrappers. Wooded groves became lovers' lanes for same sex liaisons. Once lush lawns showed patches of weeds and rust appeared on the American flags attached to every mail box. Sprinklers went on and off without reason and, if you drove down Davy Crockett Lane with your window open, you could smell sewage from backed-up septic tanks or garbage that had been discarded in the lakes, ponds and water supply in spite of "No Dumping" signs.

Home prices plummeted, allowing a lower class of people to move into the neighborhood. You had trouble understanding them when they spoke English, if they spoke it at all. They drove old Volkswagens and Japanese cars which, more often than not, wound up gutted on their front lawns with the rest of their belongings when they hit rock bottom and were evicted by the Majestic Meadows banks that financed their mortgages.

Occasionally a three alarm fire spared them this indignity, which may or may not have been caused by faulty wiring.

After forsaking their homes, these same people started showing up at stop signs holding bottles filled with a blue, soapy liquid they squirted on your windshield till you couldn't see. No matter how many times you told them not to wash it off and go away they ignored you and got belligerent if you refused to pay for their effort.

They were also spotted at several fireworks stands that sprung up behind the outlets and the dog track that opened on the outskirts of town. This was a stone's throw from the stock car track being built on the scale of Bristol Motor Speedway, a popular half-mile course in Tennessee used for Winston Cup events.

Copper pipes were stolen daily from the construction site.

Graffiti covered the seats of swings and other vacant spaces in the park, including fruit trees that already had hearts and obscenities carved in their bark and were infested with bugs the undesirables brought with them when they moved into the neighborhood.

Traffic casualties increased, averaging somewhere between ten and twenty every six months, slightly higher than the number of teenagers who turned the gas on and stuck their heads in ovens because of increased Cyber-bullying.

Women went to bed at night and dreamt of younger men, waking up with a smile because they knew that was the best the world had to offer. They didn't miss their husbands while they were at work and barely greeted them when they came home, if they were there. Men avoided their wives just as much. New outfits. Perfectly styled hair. Hot meals. They stopped noticing because their wives, unless they were having an affair, stopped caring, became sloppy and let themselves go.

Children didn't remember birthdays, never wrote thank you notes and developed yellow teeth from smoking cigarettes and crack. They locked themselves in their bathrooms because they were bulimic, played games like "Seek And Destroy," fought, fucked and drank till they passed out in their own feces. One out of three girls had piercings. Two out of four were pregnant when they graduated high school, about the same time their parents' divorce was finalized.

Paxil was the antidepressant of choice even though it was linked to many suicides and other violent crimes.

Pat Robertson, the good pastor, was discovered to have a billion dollars and lived on top of a mountain in Virginia in a mansion with its own private airstrip.

On Saint Patrick's Day two of the welcome wagon girls were arrested for solicitation in front of The Pleasure Palace, a sex shop that sold erotic aids named "The Giant Claw" and metal-studded underpants displayed proudly in their window like my father's drawings.

As police hustled the girls into their van, a man on the other side of the parking lot, with a tattoo teardrop on his cheek, placed three crisply folded playing cards on a table with collapsible metal legs. He shuffled them in intersecting circles, calling out to people who walked by offering fifty to a hundred dollars to anyone who could find the queen of hearts.

This meant only one thing, something even my father couldn't have accounted for.

Lone Star Springs had looked the devil himself in the eyes and made a grave mistake. 7-11, not Captain Kangaroo, was the Anti-Christ.

* * *

Another town meeting was called after Jennifer Trevor's tragic death. Minutes from the previous meeting were dispensed with, as was discussion of the rapidly approaching Frontier Days. Benefit that raised money for "Cleaning With Good Reason," a non-profit organization offering free, professional housecleaning to Lone Star housewives who could not afford maid service.

Something had to be done about the coyotes at once, only nobody seemed to know exactly what since there wasn't a lot of information available.

Mitch Jonas raised his hand. He'd called his nephew, who was a big shot at the Agriculture Department, and described everything that had transpired. His nephew told him coyotes were probably the smartest wild animal alive. Catching them was near impossible because they were cunning and wary of anything unusual in their habitat. In spite of their recent aggressive behavior and fearlessness around humans, they would have to be hunted from a distance. Although the Agricultural Department had some success in the past using feet and neck traps as well as bait containing poison gas, aerial gunning was their preferred and most effective means of extermination. Unfortunately, government agencies were not allowed to provide manpower, assistance and especially helicopters for a community too small to have its own post office - although he would do everything in his power to circumvent that policy.

Donald Trevor stepped forward. They didn't need the Agricultural Department to fight

their battles. They could hunt the coyotes just like any other animal. Considering the information Mitch received from his nephew, Donald thought the best gun for them to use was the Savage model 24F, an over/under, break-open rifle with the top barrel in a caliber ranging from .220 to .30-30. The bottom barrel could be 16, 20, or 12 gauge. If the coyotes came in close, like in the school yard, teachers would have a shotgun to hit 'em with. If they turned and ran, like at Heather McAndrew's, they could reach out and get 'em with the rifle top barrel. The problem was, nobody except Donald owned one. Even if they did, a couple wouldn't suffice. We needed dozens if we were going to be as effective as the Agricultural Department's aerial shooting

and that created another problem. A purchase of that size would deplete the entire Frontier Days' budget. Of course, what choice did we have? A dirty house was shameful, but if we didn't buy guns our children could suffer the same fate as Donald's beloved Jenny.

An immediate vote was called for.

All those in favor were about to raise their hands when Bobby Gilchrest stepped forward. He had a problem with the 24 F. He'd shot one a few months before and it didn't come close to living up to its publicity. The ejector mechanism barely pushed back a spent shell which would make it

difficult to remove an empty casing in the heat of a coyote battle.

Donald disagreed.

The fact that the Savage came with a synthetic, camouflaged stock more than offset any so-called design flaw. It would kill coyotes better than most. He guaranteed it.

That assurance was worthless, Bobby went on, because the synthetic stock in the newer models only came in silver and, therefore, was not glare free. They were better off using a .223 caliber 12 gauge that had a black stock. Not only wouldn't they have to purchase expensive reloading equipment, since it used 3" magnum shells it could double as a turkey gun during the Thanksgiving holidays.

Donald started to sweat, looking as if he'd just stepped out of the shower. His eyes burned. His face turned bright red and he began to sob. Bobby felt bad. You could see it as he walked over, put a consoling arm around Don's trembling shoulders and patted him lightly on the arm.

"I know you're upset, Donnie, and nobody in this room can blame you. But, that still don't change the fact we need to use the best equipment available and, let's face it, the Savage just ain't savage enough."

Donald lifted his head enough to look Bobby in his sorrowful eyes.

"Shut up."

He hit him flush on the jaw with a hard, chopping right.

"Just...shut up."

As Bobby fell he hit him again. When he was on the ground Donald leaped on top of him and shattered his twice broken nose with an elbow, his right cheek bone too, blood spurting onto his forearm.

When Vivienne first left for Paris, I realized how she felt after performing many of the same chores. I appreciated her daily routine and sacrifices.

Now, I also understood how she felt while she was cooped up in the waiting room at the hospital.

"WHAT THE FUCK AM I DOING HERE?! WHY IS

THIS HAPPENING TO ME?! SOMEBODY HELP! I'M SCARED TO FUCKING DEATH?!" HELP! HELP! GET ME OUT!"

I didn't leave.

Instead, I raised my hand and waved it frantically back and forth, trying to get everyone's attention.

I read an article in The New York Times about a man, Ken Hartman, who hunted coyotes with greyhounds, a practice that went back to President Theodore Roosevelt himself near Oklahoma City in the early 1900's. Although greyhounds were generally thought to be tranquil, docile animals, it said they were also very effective hunters. If you didn't let them hunt you were denying what they were born to do. While Mr. Hartman had enormous respect for coyotes because of their intelligence, he felt that greyhounds were not only smarter, but the coolest dogs he'd ever seen. If they could cook he'd marry one.

Allison Bradley raised her hand as Bobby sat up, somewhat disoriented, and rubbed his nose.

"Even if that were true," she said, "wouldn't we run into the same problem as the guns? Where would we find enough?"

I suggested we contact the owner of the new dog track. Greyhounds, when too old or broken down to race, were discarded like trash. Vivienne and I had seen that on the travel channel too, an episode about New Jersey, which upset us for weeks. Instead of destroying them, maybe he would donate them to the community. The committee, in turn, could contact the coyote hunter and hire him as a trainer.

Everyone, especially Allison who believed that animals and people were put on this earth to do what they were bred for, was duly impressed.

"Fair is fair," she said before crossing to a water fountain that still said "Coloreds."

They put me in charge. The next day I contacted Mister

Rossi, the dog track owner who, after some discussion, agreed to let us have the dogs for ten dollars apiece. I found the coyote hunter's

phone number on the internet, called him and explained what had gone on. He volunteered his services without hesitation, free of charge. He would travel to Lone Star Springs, a good two-day

drive, and train the greyhounds to chase and kill for sport.

* * *

When I opened the door, Allison Bradley was standing there with a bottle of Texas champagne and a C harmonica.

"I did it," was all she said.

Walking past me she sat down on the sofa, put her legs up and smiled.

Allison had a yellow nape parrot, Roy, named after her dearly departed husband. She bought him from a breeder when he was just a month old, too young to feed himself. Every day she had to prepare a special formula and bottle-feed him by hand. Like an infant. When he was old enough to eat solid food, Allison taught him how to crack seed. Roy, as a result, thought she was his mother.

She clipped his wings, a common and acceptable practice for indoor birds to make sure they don't fly into walls or windows and injure themselves.

She taught him numerous songs, jokes, passages from best-sellers and anything else she happened to think of.

Her favorite Roy story, she went on to explain, involved a carpenter she hired to build a redwood deck in her back yard.

He swore it would take seven weeks at most.

He was still there seven months later.

It got to the point where she asked him, politely, to call if he wasn't going to show up. She understood his business. She knew he had other jobs. She just wanted to know if he was coming or not since she planned her day around it.

He agreed.

A week went by and everything was fine till one day he didn't arrive till six P.M. When she asked him why he didn't call his response was as simple as it was annoying.

"I'm here, ain't I?"

She had to go into the kitchen to try and calm herself down.

When she was gone the carpenter walked over to Roy's cage and waved.

"Hello, little birdie," he said.

Using his beak to maneuver from the rear to the front of the cage, Roy stuck his head through the bars and told the man to fuck himself.

In Allison's voice.

She loved Roy more than any other pet she'd ever had after that. Both husbands too. She desperately wanted to show her appreciation but couldn't come up with anything appropriate till she heard Mister Hartman talk about birth rights.

She stopped clipping Roy's wings.

When she took him out of his cage that morning, she opened the front door and set him free.

Popping the champagne cork, she took a healthy swig before passing me the bottle.

"I never would have done it without you."

I took a swig as she moved closer.

"I want to show my appreciation."

Lifting her harmonica she played "Peg Of My Heart," made famous by The Harmonicats in 1947.

When she finished the cats bounded into the room, jumped onto the couch and snuggled beside me.

"Oh my."

She was duly impressed.

"Do they ever leave little presents for you at the door?"

I didn't know what she meant.

"Like mice or birds. When I had cats they used to do that all the time. It's their way of showing affection. Have you ever seen a cat eat a mouse. They actually growl like a wild animal. My last cat brought one to me and ate it on my shoes, leaving the head and the feet. Disgusting but amazing."

"They've never done that," I said.

"Don't worry. They will."

"I don't let my cats out."

She looked puzzled.

"What do you mean?"

"They're indoor cats."

"You don't let them out at all?"

"I don't want anything bad to happen to them."

Sliding her C harmonica into her pocket, she rose and rushed toward the door.

When she was gone I walked upstairs, crossed to my desk, removed the top and climbed inside.

* * *

As Ken Hartman arrived at the barn to collect his dogs for Monday's hunt, about fifty people were gathered in front of the entrance, none familiar, including a television camera crew. Having gotten wind of Lone Star's coyote problem, the Humane Society was there to protest the sadistic treatment of coyotes as well as greyhounds.

It was all on the six o'clock news.

During a ten minute interview Ken told an ABC correspondent that what took place in Lone Star Springs was not an isolated incident. It was happening all across the country.

Ranchers and farmers were at their wits end because coyotes routinely killed their livestock. Now that it had escalated to Maltese and children, eliminating them was a necessity. Using greyhounds was the most natural, cleanest way imaginable.

Sue Burnham, the Humane Society spokesman who lived in Lone Star Springs, vigorously disagreed.

Coyotes helped control the rodent population and were an important part of the ecosystem. Even if you took the tragedy into account, a horrible loss for everyone concerned, this was as far away from natural as possible because coyotes being killed by dogs was considered the same as dog fighting; the reason hunting coyotes with greyhounds was banned in most states except Texas and Oklahoma.

Ken repeated his belief that greyhounds were born to hunt, but that didn't hold water either. Since electric shock collars were required to train them not to kill anything but coyotes, their natural instincts were still being infringed upon.

He brought everyone inside the barn to show how all his dogs were collar free but it didn't matter. There was one and only one reason for this, Ms. Burnham explained. Over the years several of Ken's animals had broken their necks when their collars snagged on rocks or fences. They might not be wearing collars now, but it was a necessary part of their training. Without them it was impossible to control their killer instincts. It was just a matter of time before the greyhounds became as big a problem as the coyotes.

She had graphic photographs to back up these claims, remains of domestic animals greyhounds had attacked, though she wouldn't say how the pictures were obtained or attribute ownership. Additional photos showed the aftermath of a hunt. Several greyhounds had crippling leg wounds. Others were bitten repeatedly in the face and neck. One photo showed a dozen dead coyotes piled up in the back of the Ken's pickup, their bodies ripped apart, nerves and guts exposed. Some even showed greyhounds gnawing on coyote carcasses, cleaning their teeth on the bones.

They had a video.

There was Ken, loading all his dogs into specially made pens on the back of his pickup. He drove to the outskirts of Lone Star Springs and used binoculars to search for prey. When he saw them he drove closer, got out and yelled "Yee-haw" at the top of his lungs before releasing the dogs. They raced about a 1/2 mile before disappearing into a cluster of trees. Though it was difficult to see because of the distance, if you looked hard enough you could make out the dogs fighting a pack of coyotes, biting their legs and necks.

They had an audio.

"Every time I turn them loose I never know how many are gonna come back. Sometimes they run off in a ditch and break their necks. Sometimes a shoulder. Sometimes a hip. One time I lost four dogs when they ran over a God-damned cliff. It's upsetting. I mean, they're family. But, it's the risk you take when you chase coyotes."

The fact that he kept a blood-clotting agent and bandages in his truck made no difference.

Undaunted, he returned to the barn every morning at sunrise, rounded up his dogs and went to work trying to rid the community of the horror that encased us. Every day the Humane Society was waiting and protesting, as Lone Star residents did years before with the abortion doctor. After a couple of weeks multiple lawsuits were filed, including a restraining order preventing Ken from hunting till the dispute was resolved in court. With no workable alternative he packed up his crates and drove back to Duluth, Minnesota, the hometown he'd lived in since the day he was born.

Before he left he shouted "Yeehaw" and set his dogs free.

* * *

The elderly woman was breathing as if, with each breath, she inhaled something sharp, like the sword swallower from Romania Jack and I saw at the circus. She just didn't understand why she couldn't find the Queen of hearts when so many before her had, receiving a crisp, fifty dollar bill for their effort.

"Luck is on your side, lady. Come on. Five will get you fifty. Ten, a hundred."

Reaching into her purse the old woman removed a ten.

"Ten for a hundred," she said and handed the man her money.

He showed her the red queen before mixing up the cards, rotating them slower than the previous six times. When he stopped the old woman knew she would win. Victory was hers and she could taste it. Pointing to the card on the far right she had trouble restraining herself.

"Pay me."

She held out her hand as the man turned over the three of clubs.

"You must be lucky at love, lady."

He shuffled the cards without showing the other two.

"You cheated," said the old woman.

"Listen, lady..."

"I've spent sixty dollars."

"What do you want me to do, give it back?"

"Yes."

He looked at her with disbelief.

"You fucking with me?"

"I'll call the police," she said and he could hear the bitterness in her voice.

Turning imperceptibly, the man with the tear drop tattoo nodded to another man in the crowd, larger than the bouncer at

BBW's, who started tapping his foot before clenching and unclenching his massive fists. Grabbing the old woman's arm, he pushed her down and tried to steal her coat.

"Let go," he said.

"No."

"I'll bust you up."

"Not the fox."

The man's right arm shot out in a blur and grabbed her around the throat, squeezing till she thought her windpipe would burst.

"Give me the fucking coat."

"Never," she gasped.

Reaching into his back pocket, he removed what looked like a shiny black fountain pen with a raised silver button near the end. His finger slid down toward the button and a flash of steel exploded out the side of the handle. He stabbed her in the heart three times and nobody interfered as she fell to the ground.

Raising her head with her last ounce of strength, the minister's wife watched in horror as her beloved coat, slung over the man's right arm, vanished into an assortment of drugged-out teenagers and gang members with badly drawn prison tattoos that said "Death Before Decency."

"Fuck, shit, piss," were the last words she spoke.

It was all people talked about.

Lone Star residents couldn't believe the minister's wife met such an untimely end. She, like her dearly-departed husband, was a pillar of the community. She was adored by everyone who knew her and was a righteous woman to a fault, her life an inexhaustible fight against lust and greed, an amazing feat in today's morally bankrupt society.

Sadly, this too contradicted one of my father's sacred tenets and I had to make sure I learned its lesson.

"Even with contact lenses, you can still be blind-sided."

* * *

I was getting ready to leave for the station when I heard music outside my kitchen window, the now familiar "Peg Of My Heart," although it had been transposed using an augmented 4th. Pulling back the curtains I caught a glimpse of Allison as she tramped across the front lawn. Harmonica in one hand she had a picket sign in the other, held straight in front of her like those majorettes during halftime shows at Dallas Cowboys games.

When she saw me she stopped playing, slid the harmonica into her coat pocket and replaced it with a bullhorn.

"FREE THE CATS!"

It was the same message that was printed, in stern black letters, on both sides of her sign. Stepping outside I spoke from the doorway.

"What are you doing?"

"You're destroying the lives of two animals who should be free and living the life they were born for!"

"They're fine," I said.

"You don't know that."

One of our neighbors, an elderly woman Vivienne used to see in church, slowed her car and leaned out the window.

"What's going on?"

Allison pointed an accusing finger in my direction.

"He's destroying two poor animals."

"I am not," I said, raising my voice just a little.

"They need to run and play and hunt the way they were intended to."

"They need to live," I said as the woman put on her hazard lights and stepped out of the car.

"You should be ashamed of yourself."

"Cunt."

I turned and went back inside, slamming the door behind me.

As I walked into the kitchen a loud rumble of thunder shook the walls. By the time I looked outside the sky was hidden by thick black clouds, the wind was bending trees till they looked like they would snap and Allison was running for shelter.

The next morning I was pouring myself a cup of coffee when I heard the music again, followed by the shuffle of foot-steps. There were a handful of protestors this time, Allison's cause celebre joined by some of the bitter, overweight neighbors Vivienne and I had fed over the years.

"FREE THE CATS," shouted Allison and the other women did their best imitation of a Greek chorus.

Drawing the curtains I decided to ignore them.

I finished my coffee.

I made sure my hair was in place.

My suit wrinkle free.

I had exactly fifteen minutes to get to the station when I backed my car out of the garage. Allison ran over and gestured for me to lower my window. It was barely halfway down when she sneered and spat in my face.

In twenty-four hours her protest gained momentum, a dozen women on my lawn, now including some I'd slept with, holding signs in front of them and marching back and forth. In the lead, Allison was more determined than ever.

They were still there when I returned from work.

Five days later there were thirty, Mrs. Holloway second in line behind Allison. As she passed the kitchen window I caught a glimpse of her right arm. The empty spot was empty no more. Underneath the box of Russell Stover candy, to the right of Prince Charles looking up Camilla Parker Bowles' dress, was an unflattering tattoo of me.

"FREE THE CATS!"

By the end of the week I received a letter drafted by the Lone Star Committee demanding the cats release. I was drawing negative attention to the community at a time they were negotiating with Nike to open a factory with over a thousand employees.

I refused.

There were fifty protestors lined up on the lawn by 7:00 A.M. on Monday, many from surrounding neighborhoods who had no idea what the protest was about.

I was enjoying my fourth cup of coffee when a rock crashed through the window, shards of glass barely missing my eyes. A note was attached.

"Extremism in defense of liberty is no vice."

Underneath was a photo of a dismembered fetus.

The elderly grandmother, having seen me on the news with Layla in front of the clinic, assumed I had something to do with the abortion doctor she'd been instrumental in driving out years before. Unable to cope with a community once again under siege, especially after the coyotes, she decided to destroy my resolve along with my window.

It worked again.

Like my predecessor I ate, dressed and vowed never to return. It didn't make sense to live in a house that was no longer a comfort.

Not that it mattered.

It was February 14th, Valentine's day, and I wasn't coming back anyway.

I walked out the front door, one beloved cat under each arm, and released them into a world everyone except I believed they deserved.

As they pranced and leaped across the lawn they'd been observing most of their young lives, the women cheered. They were too busy celebrating to give me a second thought so I made my way toward the garage. As I waited for the automatic door to rise I heard what sounded like someone

walking up behind me. I turned in time to see two grey-hounds, running full speed, scoop up both cats by the scruff of their necks, blood spurting everywhere, and continue on toward the woods.

Though I was horrified by this unexpected turn of events, another loss of a loved one, I couldn't help thinking of the sordid satisfaction my father must have felt when he discovered his own father had cancer.

The women stopped celebrating and let out a collective cry, like Vivienne in her bedroom when she first returned from Paris.

It was followed by the sound of rotors.

A camouflaged army helicopter appeared over a rise, like some mythical beast, the words "Agricultural Department" stenciled on either side. It was impossible to see the pilot through darkened windows but a man leaning out the door, strapped in for safety, was a household name; Donald Trevor, peering down the rifle top barrel of a Savage 24F. As the heli-copter swooped down over the world's fastest dogs, already moving close to sixty miles per hour, as Donald's

finger tightened around the trigger, his blood curdling cry of "Yeehaw" echoed throughout the entire neighborhood.

* * *

The Red Lion Inn was closed when I jumped the curb and turned into their parking lot, coming to a full stop facing the entrance. I hid the keys under the driver's side floor mat. I taped a note on the dashboard with detailed instructions for proper maintenance and the benefits of elevating the car to cult status.

As I stepped out, clouds parted and a single beam of light shone down onto the Caddy's grill, like the fake day I was born. Even more amazing, the most beautiful bird I'd ever seen, some sort of parrot with vibrant yellows and blues on its stomach and wings, fluttered down and perched where the previous year's hood ornament would have been if it hadn't been eliminated for a more streamlined design. It was an omen. I knew it as surely as I knew how to breathe and I was filled with optimism for the first time since my tragic anniversary.

Maybe life wasn't so bad after all.

Maybe there were better things to come.

Maybe God was looking down, finally paying attention, and this was His way of telling me what to do or, more important, what not to do.

"Hello, little bird," I said with affection.

"Eat shit and die," it replied, the resemblance to Allison's voice as uncanny and precise as Mrs. Fairweather's backhand.

* * *

I'd been at work less than an hour when the Cessna Citation Excel on my screen reached takeoff speed and began its ascent. As I gave the first officer instructions, I started to feel the dreaded umbilical tighten around my throat and the ensuing waves of vertigo. Although I felt like fleeing, finding a beloved desk to crawl into, there was no way I could hide or even slip away, not with Mister Davidow nearby and all hell about to break loose.

Leaning back in my chair I began breathing slowly through my mouth but it did no good. The dizziness would not subside. Panicked, I shut my eyes as tight as I could.

You won't believe what happened next. It must have been

so ingrained, buried so deep inside me, as if I was some archeological dig, I was caught completely off guard.

Dropping to both knees like a humble penitent, I prayed. Not to God. He was still a heartless prick like my ex, lacking compassion and justice. Besides, He'd had His chances.

"O most holy apostle, St. Jude. People honor and invoke you universally as the patron of desperate causes. Well, I'm here to tell you, this is your lucky day. My life's been filled with more desperation than anybody you'll ever know. So, please show me some compassion. Don't let my plans be for nothing. For once in my life, let justice be served."

Slowly but surely my equilibrium returned to normal and my fears were replaced by an overwhelming calm, like when I sat in the needlepoint chair.

Next thing I knew I was flying. Head thrown back. Arms extended. High above the fields I loved with joyful children, cobblestone streets, red roofs and winding roads. High above my coworkers and their despicable socializing. High above my father's infidelities. High above Vivienne's emotional, linguistic and non-fiction abandonment. High above Hope and Audrey's betrayals. The Big Dipper was brighter than I'd ever seen it before.

Somewhere in the distance I heard people shouting but I wasn't coming back, not even when Mister Davidow screamed that the Cessna was headed straight for a 767 that was making its descent, the same type of plane, ironically, as flight 516.

It would be the pilot's fault. Mister Davidow would see to that. I'd made sure he had all the details at his fingertips and no foul play would be suspected; my present to him for the kindness he'd shown me over the years. This was an opportunity to secure the airways he loved and keep his job.

As I drifted further and further away I noticed the face of one of the children in the field beneath me. If I hadn't known better I would have sworn it was me when I was his age. The resemblance was uncanny and I was filled with remorse for never having a boy of my own; someone I would have taught how to fish, taken to ball games and drank butterscotch milk shakes with. I would have even showed him how to ride a two wheeler, knowing full well, if I had something to hide, I did so at my own peril.

If I had a son I would have watched over him, given him refuge and protected him from all the harm life can inflict before he's squashed.

I would have been more than just a normal father too. I would have been his mother, his friend and teacher. He, in turn, would be my music, my literature and art - the things my father wanted but was afraid to pursue. I'd savor the miracle of family the second time around. He'd be the person I wished I'd become.

When it was time to sit down in the square for a heart to heart, I knew exactly what I'd say. I wouldn't use funny anecdotes to steer him down the straight and narrow. He'd see right through that. My son would be a lot smarter than I was at his age. I'd tell him the truth.

"Enjoy every day because, with each subsequent one, you'll change. It probably won't be anything drastic. In fact, you won't even notice. A change will be taking place, however, and nothing that came before will be the same."

Like after my father died.

"As a result, you can't be afraid to live with uncertainty. You may not know what's around the corner but nobody else does either. Whether it's good or bad is irrelevant. If you look, you just might catch sight of something you wouldn't have ordinarily seen. And when your time is up, if you can look back and glimpse just one extraordinary moment, your life would have been worthwhile."

Contrary to what you might expect, I'd also respect my father's teachings.

"There's a reason the world revolves around sex," I'd say. "It's fantastic. If anyone tells you differently, they're lying. The thing is, sex will always be there. When the timing is right, it will happen. I tell you this for a simple reason. As soon as you begin obsessing about sex, and you will the moment you start having it, you can kiss your childhood goodbye. Your priorities will change. So, my advice is to wait. Stay a kid as long as you can, with a child's heart and mind, and enjoy all the things kids enjoy. Look forward to summer vacations. Laugh. No. Giggle. Don't keep your nose to the grindstone. Don't care about goals and for God's sake, don't prioritize. It will destroy your spirit and all you'll remember, when it's time to look back, is the pain."

"How long should I wait?"

He'll ask me that because, being my son, he'll need details. Details are still clues. Clues eliminate supposition.

I'll look him squarely in the eyes, the way my father did with me, and tell him "the longer the better."

"How long is that?"

Again, no matter what I say the boy will have exacting questions that demand specific answers.

"If it were me," I'd say, leaning closer so he knows just how serious I am about breaking the chain,.."If I had it to do all over,..."

Closer still, so he can see how much I miss my own child's heart and mind.

"I'd wait till I was dying...and even then."

"Henry."

Life doesn't start when you first make love to a woman. It ends. You stop looking for anything else.

"Henry!"

If I had a son he'd be heroic, never afraid. He'd get up every morning confident in his abilities. He'd make a name for himself, fearlessly rising to every occasion. He'd be gloriously in love, married and faithful to the same great woman. He'd have hundreds, no, thousands of magical moments to look back on when it was time.

And he'd always part his hair on the right.

"Henry!"

For an instant I thought it was Vivienne calling me, speaking in her tone that warned me not to go any further or there'd be consequences.

"Henry!"

It was Mister Davidow, repeating my name over and over.

I couldn't help but smile.

"Henry!"

If I had a son he would miss me when I died.

"What the hell's wrong with you?"

There'd be no smirk on his face or the slightest joy.

"Please, Henry!"

God, would I be missed.

* * *

Dallas, Texas, February 14th - Rescue workers struggled for five hours against heavy winds and rain to reach the sole survivor of a plane crash that claimed four hundred lives.

Cold, wet weather prevented an immediate evacuation and the injured woman had to be treated, initially, in a makeshift shelter.

When it was safe, Dallas Civil Protection Director Steve Harris told the AP the thirty-one-year-old was carried by stretcher to a spot where a helicopter could land. She was then airlifted to Florence Nightingale Memorial hospital where she was in stable condition with hypothermia,

contusions and muscle injuries.

"Ms. Maisey doesn't remember much about the crash," said Dr. Donald Mousseau, head of the medical team treating her. "She lost consciousness and only remembers the plane falling into a cloud."

Doctor Mousseau expects Ms. Maisey to remain hospitalized for up to a month.

A preliminary investigation showed that a private jet, a Cessna Excel, struck the much larger 767 and disintegrated, sending debris and bodies plummeting to the ground. The 767 split in two, the front half spiraling down toward Lake Ray Hubbard, the rear destroying a restaurant, The Red Lion Inn, near the heart of downtown.

"There were people falling out of the sky like it was snowing," eyewitnesses told KCBS-TV.

"It's incredible that anyone could survive that impact," said a spokesman for United Airlines. Then he smiled for the first time since the tragedy took place.

"It's a miracle."

Aviation authorities said the exact cause of the crash was not yet known, but pilot error was suspected after speaking with the head of Air Traffic Control at DFW Airport.

Ms. Maisey's only words when she was found were "Henry saved me." It took a week till she was strong enough to elaborate.

"The one thing I remember before the accident was that I had this overwhelming sense of anxiety. It was like somebody grabbed me by the back of the neck and told me to brace myself. At the same time I knew it would be okay. Someone was praying for me and I would be saved. Then everything went black. When I woke up the only person I wanted to talk to was my ex-husband, Henry. I called him at work but his supervisor told me he'd lapsed into some sort of trance right before the crash, was praying out loud and crying so hard he thought he'd burst an artery. Only then did I realize it was Henry who saved me. There was no other explanation. After everything I put him through, the fact that he would have a kind word for me, let alone pray for my survival, is a miracle. I'm ashamed of myself and will make it up to him the moment I'm released from the hospital. No matter what happens, no matter how long it takes, I will never leave his side."

Hope read this to me from the Dallas Morning News. It didn't matter that I couldn't respond. She seemed to know I heard and understood every word, just like Claude with Peggy. When she was finished she placed the paper on the floor, reached into her purse and withdrew a relatively new copy of Vivienne's second book.

Life didn't make sense.

My father was right.

The people I wanted to live, died. The one person I wanted dead, lived.

As Hope flipped through the pages, I could see she'd dog-eared a portion near the end.

"I know it's cliche, but there's a reason cliches exist and are passed down through generations. When you're born, you're crying and everyone around you is smiling. From then on anything goes. While you're out there trying to survive, hopefully, you learn that living well isn't about money or power. It certainly isn't about harming yourself or others. It's not even about food, although it should never be taken for granted. Life is about tenderness, discovering what touches you the most and moves you down deep.

Most important, we must learn that whatever obstacles we encounter along the way can be overcome with a single word.

Forgiveness. Forgive yourself. Forgive your family. Forgive the people who have done you wrong. Do that and, when your time is up, you'll be the one who's smiling and everyone else will be crying."

I suddenly felt bad about the four hundred lives lost. It was a tragedy, but sometimes people had to die in order for others to live. Like war. In this case tens of thousands would be spared because the airways were safe. It was for the greater good and I hoped they would be remembered for that. Collectively if not as individuals.

The nurse entered and announced that visiting hours were over as Hope reached the end of her passage. Shutting the book gently, as if she'd pressed a flower between the pages, she kissed me gently.

"I do pray I die first, darling. If you did I really couldn't face another day."

She promised to return the following morning. Eight sharp. You could set your clock by her arrival. She hated to leave, as always, but the weather forecast was grim. A storm front was moving into the area with hundred-mile-an-hour winds and predictions of rain for twenty days and twenty nights, possibly longer. She needed to get back to my house and make sure all the windows were shut.

As I watched her walk into the hall I caught a glimpse of myself in a mirror next to the door, the yards of plastic tubing and electrodes that helped monitor my heart rate and sampled my blood. I wondered if the nurse would come back, pat my back and massage me till I giggled and cooed. The thought almost made me laugh till I caught a glimpse of thick red hair underneath her cap.

My eyes began to flutter.

Next thing I knew I was flying again.

Unlike previous flights this was a short one, depositing me

on the road leading to my front door instead of the French countryside. As always I turned right at the porch and entered our back yard. The moment I opened the gate I froze. My teacher. The principal. Jack's friends. The girls who made my skin crawl. None of them were there, possibly because the prophecy had been fulfilled. Instead, there was only one person seated on an orange crate.

My father.

Not a hair was out of place.

His clothes were wrinkle free.

Some habits, obviously, die a lot harder than we do.

"It's amazing how blind we can be, son."

It started just like one of his stories when he returned home after a long trip and I was thrilled.

"The love you so desperately craved from your mother, Vivienne and every woman since, Hope gave you. Sure, it was bullshit, but it was an incredibly unselfish act of bullshit. Your mother put her values ahead of you. Vivienne. Audrey too. Hope never did. She despised you from the beginning. So, now that she's back, that love is real and it's a testimony to your specialness. You should thank her for it not hate her. As a matter of fact, you should consider yourself lucky. It's so rare to be loved these days. Who gives a shit if it started out false? Big fucking deal. It doesn't matter in the long run."

Rising slowly, he placed his arm around my shoulders and drew me close.

"I hope you've been paying attention to the way she walks."

He ruffled my hair.

"Just like a pendulum."

I opened my eyes.

To my amazement, my father was still there, sitting on the edge of the bed. I assumed the drugs being pumped into my veins had invited him but, as I noticed the bouquet of flowers in the vase next to the TV, he seemed too real.

Grasping my hand, his speech slowed down the way it did when he imitated his father. This time, however, his tone softened to fit the smile that had gradually taken over his face.

"I remember the day you were born," he said, both eyes glazing.

"The horned owl can see farther than every other bird on our planet. A gray whale can swim longer than any fish or mammal. An arctic tern has been known to fly thousands of miles during migration, all the way from the north to the south pole where Chilly Willy lives."

He was on a roll like all good salesmen. If they have a captive audience they're the same as I was when he took me to the state fair. They never want to leave.

"Now, imagine fields of bluebonnets, dancing back and forth in a cool, gentle breeze, stretching beyond all of those."

I loved my father more than ever before at that moment, more than I had imagined or wished for, and I began inhaling deeply, trying desperately to preserve the story of my birth in my entire body, knowing full well its memory alone wasn't reliable.

When he finished Jack reached behind his back. Retrieving a gift-wrapped present, meticulously decorated with ribbons and pictures of cowboys, he held it out at arms length.

"What's that?" I asked.

"Tomorrow's your birthday, son."

His smile began to fade.

"Thirty-three. You didn't forget?"

"No," I said, but I had.

"Open it."

Still the obedient son, I tore into the paper.

"I think you'll like it."

I don't know why exactly, but the closer I got to what was inside the more I began to see the truth as Vivienne defined it.

Things with no shades of gray.

My fear of losing control had little to do with hurting someone. It was the deep, insurmountable sorrow lurking behind the anger that scared me. If I let go, if I got past the rage, I'd come face to face with a sadness I could not fathom. That's what I was really afraid of and the reason why Peggy, who was all sorrow, made me so uncomfortable.

Revelations kept coming.

Certain people entered my life for a reason. They came and went from the day I was born to provide me with lessons on how to live. That's all I could ask for, being lucky enough to meet people who had the ability to create situations that helped me evolve. Some made me better. Some made me worse. Some humanized me. My father was one of those persons. Lillian. Vivienne. Audrey. Hope. Even Mrs. Fairweather. If it weren't for them I could never see myself for who I was or what I'd become.

"I know you'll like it," Jack repeated, pointing at the box and winking again.

I stopped unwrapping.

"Something wrong, son?"

I didn't care what was inside. It was a gift. That was enough. Even if it wasn't, I couldn't possibly concentrate on anything else except the larger revelations that started flashing before my eyes.

All the answers to all the questions to all the mysteries in the world from the beginning of time.

Stonehenge.

Extraterrestrials.

Anti matter.

Consciousness.

Even a way to prevent premature ejaculation.

It was the Readers Digest version, sure, but what the hell.

As predicted, it was my crowning achievement. Finally letting go. Giving up control. Improvising. Risking. Flying free as a bird over the Big Dipper where feet were never dirty.

If I could have a photograph of the one moment I wanted to remember for the rest of my life, perfect in every way, this would be it.

It only made sense that I would share it with my father. I had so much to thank him for. Now more than ever I wished I possessed his powers of speech but I didn't. That hadn't changed. Whatever I wanted to say would be awkward at best. So, I said nothing. Instead, as my lips turned up into a smile of total repose, I reached out to touch his face.

"Wait a minute."

Revelations stopped as abruptly as they began.

"Didn't you mess up my hair?"

"But, dad..."

He turned away, dismissive and, apparently, indifferent. As I tried to get his attention, to explain, he faced me again, poked me in the ribs and smiled.

"It's only hair, Henry."

Reaching behind my ear, he produced a shiny silver dollar. He then apologized for his extended absence. To some, death was a damned good excuse but, to him, it didn't matter. Wherever he was, regardless of what was going on, he should be there if I needed him.

"There are only two sure things in this world," he continued.

"Fathers and sons."

His smile broadened.

"I said that. If anybody knows about the world, it's me."

I began to feel the blood rush in my ears and my heart pound faster than I could ever remember.

"Did I ever tell you the best way to know if a girl likes you, Henry?"

I shook my head, although I was concentrating on breathing evenly.

"When they're close, see if they blush."

I started feeling nauseous.

"You have to be careful, though, because there are two types. Good and bad."

I felt a small prick in the nape of my neck, like the pop of a flashbulb or someone breaking a balloon.

"One, they feel sorry for you. This is bad."

Everything slowed down.

"Two, their blood boils, they're excited and can't wait to do all the things their parents warned them about."

With my last ounce of strength I reached out and touched my dad's face, outlining every inch.

"This is good."

I was immortal again.

Finally, God smiled.

POSTSCRIPT

Dearest Morgan,

The twenty plus years since you uttered "Whales swim naked" have been interesting to say the least; somewhere between "Christina's World" and "The Garden Of Earthly Delights." During this time I've experienced every emotion a father can feel on his son's behalf. Euphoria. Disappointment. Anxiety. Fear. I've cradled you in my arms and held you till I cried. I've snuck into your room while you were sleeping and tried to make you disappear, like a magician's assistant.

I wouldn't change a day of it.

I hope you know that.

Not one, single moment.

There were times, I must admit, I felt overwhelmed; a heavyheartedness that seemed like the weight of the world was on my shoulders.

Not any more.

You have provided me with lessons on how to live. I now feel like anything is possible. If I try and fail, I'll try again. No big deal. I don't like being knocked down but it's part of life. The trick is what you do when you get back on your feet.

God knows I've said this to you dozens of times, but I'm a glutton for punishment and it's still worth repeating.

Being happy has little to do with girls or success. It's how you feel when you wake up in the morning and stare the world in the eye. It's how you felt when you went to bed the night before and shut those same eyes. If you can greet the day and leave it knowing you've done your best, you can start the next one with a smile.

All I want is for you to wake up with more smiles than not.

You have your entire life ahead of you, son. I assume all will go well but, if there are days when you feel the weight of the world on your shoulders, remember two things:

1. As far as I'm concerned, you already are a hero, fearless and capable of rising to every occasion.

2. Every sunrise is a second chance.

I will always be there for you and, if necessary, would step in front of a speeding truck to protect you. I wouldn't hesitate for a second although, to be perfectly honest, I really, really hope it never comes to that.

I love you,

Dad

AUTHOR'S BIO

Over the years Eric Gethers has written and rewritten scripts for every major studio and some of Hollywood's biggest stars. During that time friends and associates encouraged him to write a novel but he never had the time or the confidence. Since moving to France, thankfully, he found both. This is the book and he hopes you enjoy reading it as much as he enjoyed finishing it.

OTHER TITLES BY RUNNING WILD

Past Titles

Running Wild Stories Anthology, Volume 1
Running Wild Anthology of Novellas, Volume 1
Jersey Diner by Lisa Diane Kastner
The Kidnapped by Dwight L. Wilson
Running Wild Stories Anthology, Volume 2
Running Wild Novella Anthology, Volume 2, Part 1
Running Wild Novella Anthology, Volume 2, Part 2
Running Wild Stories Anthology, Volume 3
Running Wild's Best of 2017, AWP Special Edition
Running Wild's Best of 2018
Build Your Music Career From Scratch, Second Edition by Andrae Alexander
Writers Resist: Anthology 2018 with featured editors Sara Marchant and Kit-Bacon Gressitt
Frontal Matter: Glue Gone Wild by Suzanne Samples
Mickey: The Giveaway Boy by Robert M. Shafer
Dark Corners by Reuben "Tihi" Hayslett
The Resistors by Dwight L. Wilson

Open My Eyes by Tommy Hahn
Legendary by Amelia Kibbie
Christine, Released by E. Burke
Running Wild Stories Anthology, Volume 4
Tough Love at Mystic Bay by Elizabeth Sowden
The Faith Machine by Tone Milazzo
The Newly Tattooed's Guide to Aftercare by Aliza Dube
American Cycle by Larry Beckett
Magpie's Return by Curtis Smith
Gaijin by Sarah Z. Sleeper
Recon: The Trilogy + 1 by Ben White
Sodom & Gomorrah on a Saturday Night by Christa Miller

Upcoming Titles
Running Wild Novella Anthology, Volume 4
Antlers of Bone by Taylor Sowden
Blue Woman/Burning Woman by Lale Davidson
The Re-remembered by Dwight L. Wilson
Something Is Better than Nothing by Alicia Barksdale
Take Me With You By Vanessa Carlisle
Mickey: Surviving Salvation by Robert Shafer
Running Wild Anthology of Stories, Volume 5 by Various
Running Wild Novella Anthology, Volume 5 by Various

Running Wild Press publishes stories that cross genres with great stories and writing. Our team consists of:
Lisa Diane Kastner, Founder and Executive Editor
Barbara Lockwood, Editor
Cecile Sarruf, Editor
Peter A. Wright, Editor
Rebecca Dimyan, Editor
Benjamin White, Editor
Andrew DiPrinzio, Editor
Lisa Montagne, Director of Education & Marketing

Learn more about us and our stories at www.runningwild-press.com

Loved this story and want more? Follow us at www.running-wildpress.com, www.facebook/runningwildpress, on Twitter @lisadkastner @RunWildBooks